CW00763591

THRILL SWITCH

TIM HAWKEN

Seahawk
Press

Copyright © 2022

All rights reserved.

ISBN: 978-0-6455791-0-9

Cover art
by Stefan Koidl

People think it's impossible to kill someone for real in VR. They simply lack imagination.

If you can give someone a seizure by flashing a strobe in their eyes, consider what you can do by hijacking their entire sensory system.

Light. Dark. Light. Dark. Light. Dark.

On. Off. On. Off. On. Off.

Flip the Switch. Reap the consequences.

- Excerpt from the Hyperrealist's Manifesto

1

Rama woke from his nightmare to an even worse reality. His hand was cuffed to a dirty hotel bed. A steady drip, drip, drip from the roof landed on the pillow next to him.

Where was he?

Had his politics finally caught up with him?

Had she?

Rama struggled to sit up. He noticed three hunting knives laid out neatly on the bedside table. They weren't his. His heart froze. He checked himself for injuries. There were no cuts on his body. No blood on the sheets. Not yet. Rama thought about yelling for help but didn't. The owner of the blades might arrive instead, as cold and sharp as those implements of pain.

Rama rattled the handcuff around his wrist as quietly as he could. No use. Held tight. He twisted to look at the bedhead he was tethered to. Old. Metal. The frame was joined to the base in a rusted corner. Pushing his weight back, Rama tested the strength of it. The joint groaned and cracked a touch.

A noise in the hall. Rama's eyes darted to the door. He held his breath. One count. Two. Three. Silence.

Quietly, carefully, Rama leaned back onto the bedhead again. It separated further. Rama rocked back and forth, pulling at the bedhead with his spare hand, eyes trained on the door. He strained with everything he could. No use. He was weak. Skinny. Out of shape. He wished he'd used his muscles more. Had done the workouts recommended for people like him.

Rama pushed back and forth on the headboard with his shoulder, trying to gain leverage.

Another noise outside. Scraping?

Rama stopped his rocking. Waited. The door remained mercifully closed. Rama eased the end of his cuff down the bedhead, onto the cracked joint. He pulled again, hard. The metal around his wrist dug into his skin. Pain lanced up his arm. The thought of those knives digging instead kept Rama trying, desperate, tug after tug. The bracelet of the cuff started to pull through the joint. The metal was now slick with blood that seeped from his wrist.

More scraping in the hall. Rama could feel himself getting frantic, his breath coming in gasps. Sweat joined the drips from the roof.

Still, he pulled.

Almost there.

Rama wiggled the cuffs.

Wrenched.

He pulled free to a groan of metal. Bang! The headboard snapped back into place. The noise sent a jolt through Rama. He scrambled up from the bed and snatched one of the knives from the dresser, holding it in front of him. The blade point shook, as unsteady as Rama's heartbeat.

No other movement.

Rama crept toward the door and looked through the peephole. Outside seemed deserted. Then something made him pause.

It couldn't be.

The carpet. Red with yellow swirls.

He was in his own apartment building.

Rama opened the door, creeping out, knife first. He looked left, right. The hallway was empty.

Where had that scraping come from?

No marks on the carpet. No scratches along the walls.

Not waiting for an answer, Rama half walked, half ran toward the lift at the end of the hall. Each door he passed felt like a trap ready to be sprung. His captor could be hiding behind any one of them, watching, waiting.

Rama got to the lift and punched the button again and again.

Down. Down. Down.

The doors slid open. No one inside. The lift's light flickered off and on. Rama didn't care. He stepped in and hit close.

Close. Close. Close.

A scraping out in the hall. Footsteps coming. Rama lifted his knife, ready for the worst.

The door shut, cutting off the sound. The lift began to move downward. The dread in Rama's gut lifted. He dared to hope. Allowed himself to breathe.

The light above strobed.

Darkness. Light. Darkness. Light.

The lift stopped mid-floor.

'No!' Rama gasped.

He pushed the ground-floor button again. All went black.

That scraping again. Metal on the door outside. Impossible between floors. Terrifying.

Scrrrrrratch. Scrrrrrratch. Scrrrrrratch.

The light flicked on.

A blade poked through the gap in the doors. Sharp. Deadly.

Rama pushed his body against the back of the lift. The knife stabbed in and out, trying to catch him. It slid up to the top. Down again.

The light went off.

Darkness.

Then on—light glinting against the metal of the blade.

'Help!' Rama banged on the side of the lift. He pushed the emergency alarm. Grabbed the phone. No dial tone. Dead. He let it drop, tears welling.

The blade scraped and stabbed at the empty air in front of Rama.

Darkness.

Rama pushed into a corner.

Another noise. Breathing. Not Rama's. He felt hot air on his face. Smelled rotten meat.

He tried to move away but a hand grabbed his throat. The light came on. No one there.

The invisible hand squeezed Rama's windpipe. Lifted him off the ground.

Rama choked, knowing this wasn't real. Not a nightmare either. Something in between.

He gasped for air. His feet kicked.

A pixelated face digitized in front of Rama. Horrid. Half man, half spider. Its pincers dripped venom, moving as the thing spoke.

'Where is it?'

Rama clutched at the hands around his throat, trying to tell himself this wasn't real, that he could breathe if he tried hard enough.

'You're... working, for her,' Rama managed to say.

'Maybe I *am* her,' the spider replied.

'I don't have it!'

'Time will tell,' the spider said. 'Tick, tock.'

The spider rammed a blade into Rama's gut. Again and again and again.

Rama screamed in pain.

The spider smiled in delight, then bit down on Rama's face. Blood sprayed.

The light flicked off again.

Darkness.

2

I almost did a fist pump when my first murder case came in. Then I remembered it was because someone had died. Rather than look like a total douche-canoe, I smoothed my suit out, grabbed a notepad, and took a self-drive to the crime scene.

Las Vegas streets whipped by. I headed to the Old Strip, its former glitz now a faint glimmer in the center of the city. Over the decades, all the casinos had turned into mass jack-in centers—cheap accommodation for those who spent most of their lives in the virtual world, the Holos. Vegas was no longer the gambling capital of America. Now, we were the virtual hub of the planet. Our secure electrical grid powered servers instead of neon lights. Our towering high-rises were the perfect place to fit the city's skyrocketing population. Thanks to relaxed laws protecting virtual rape, murder fantasies, and worse as 'freedom of speech', people from all over the world flocked here to live out their darkest desires with impunity. It was still Sin City, just in a different way. Give me your poor and your huddled masses, Lady Liberty once said. What she'd really meant was give me your paying customers to plug into our system. That might all change with the new legal proposals coming but, for now, it was full steam ahead into damnation. Not that I took part. The Holos was a sewer. You wouldn't catch me dead inside. Not since that first trip so many years ago.

I self-consciously fiddled with my tie. I needed to look pristine. Together. A reflection of how I should feel inside. I checked my hair in the derm screen of my wrist-comm. Red bangs snipped as straight as a cutthroat's razor. Good. At least that part of me looked sharp.

The whole way to the Strip I thought *why me? Why this case now?* I'd been banging my head in the missing persons unit for a year and hadn't been granted a transfer to homicide, even with a Ph.D. on serial killers. *The* serial killer. Maybe my lack of progress was because I was a woman, or because they thought I was too young. More likely it was my unfortunate habit of making off-color jokes at inappropriate times.

Knock knock.
Who's there?
Not Billy, he's missing.

Not funny, apparently.

The car stopped at the building address I'd been given. This place used to be called Treasure Island. Now it was called the Bolodair Apartments. The elevator ride up to the crime scene was nauseating. Old casino lifts had a habit of jerking upward before smoothing out. The worn carpet along the hallway wasn't much better. It reminded me of vomit swirls and blood. Or pineapple on top of pizza. Just as disgusting. Since most of the residents of this place spent all their time in digital, the common areas were never upgraded. As long as the connections were fast and equipment state-of-the-art, no one cared about the rest.

A streak of yellow tape at the end of the hall indicated where to go. Standing outside the unit was Gibson, homicide department lead. A bollard of a man. His thick neck and bald head made him look like a giant thumb with a face. Gibson turned to see me. I gave him a thumbs up, figuring it might look like a tiny mirror and keep him happy. It didn't.

'Byron?' he grunted as I approached.

I was a full head taller than him but there were no illusions about who held the most power.

'Ada is fine, Deputy Chief Gibson,' I said. 'Have the scan team been through?'

'Yes. That's why I called you.'

Without another word, he dipped under the tape blocking the door. I followed but stopped when confronted with the scene. A VR immersion rig sat in the corner with a limp body strapped into it. The corpse's back was to us, so I couldn't see the helmet or head. Its fingers were covered in blood. The plasma dripped into a puddle that spread along the floor. A Holos unit was stacked onto the back wall along with feeding tubes and a store of liquid nutrients. On the far side of the room, black writing was scrawled on the wall. The script was too small to read from this distance.

'Trauma includes abrasions on the fingertips and a burst eyeball,' Gibson said. 'No DNA or fingerprints, other than the victim's.'

'Right. So no eye-popping evidence?' I asked.

Gibson just stared at me.

'Any security footage of someone leaving or entering the room recently?' I hoped vainly.

'Plenty of footage of empty halls,' Gibson said. 'The only person that came near this room was a cleaner who found the body this morning.'

My mouth went dry.

'Cause of death is from a massive loss of blood?'

Gibson nodded.

'Through the eyes?' I managed to ask.

'Through the eyes. Time of death was around midnight last night,' Gibson confirmed.

This couldn't be right. My gut clenched. I saw now why I was called here. *The* serial killer. But that wasn't possible.

'You think this might be linked to the Specter Slaughter?' I asked, point-blank.

'You did your thesis on it,' Gibson said. 'You tell me.'

'Did the scan team note anything else?' I asked, grasping for evidence to the contrary.

'The victim's blood contains mildly elevated traces of potassium.'

'Maybe he had a banana addiction?' I offered, trying to lighten the darkness I was feeling.

Gibson leveled a cold gaze at me.

'Bananas?'

'You know, high in potassium?'

'Is that a professional opinion?'

'Perhaps an unprofessional one,' I said.

'Then give me some actual insight, if you have any.'

I swallowed my creeping dread, looking at the scene again. I didn't want to say it yet, lest it became real. I straightened my tie again. It was dark crimson, like my hair. At least I wouldn't have to worry about bloodstains.

'May I?' I indicated the body.

Gibson stepped aside to let me through. I tentatively walked up, took the corpse's wrist, and checked the hands. The fingertips were lacerated like Gibson had said, fingernails all broken backward. I considered the helmet. Scratch marks studded the edges where the victim had clawed his own immersion rig trying to get out. There was something strange about the marks that I couldn't quite put my finger on. They weren't exactly what I expected. Pushing that information to the back of my mind, I twisted the body in its rig. The Holos resolution screen had already been pulled up. The corpse's blood-caked face stared at me, his black eyes bugged out. One of them had ruptured into a gory mess.

I stepped back at the sight. My mind swam. I tried to drag my thoughts to the surface. How could I prove this wasn't possible without stating the obvious? They'd know the obvious already; wouldn't have called me if it were that simple. I glanced at the helmet again.

'Isn't it standard procedure for a scan team to return anything they moved back to the original position?' I asked.

'Yes. So?' Gibson shifted.

'So why didn't they put the victim's display shield back in place?'

Gibson looked over at the body and frowned. He clicked the comm-screen attached to his wrist and scrolled through some information.

'Says here it was already open.'

'That's odd,' I clicked my tongue, thinking. 'If it's supposed to be a Specter slaying, this guy shouldn't have been able to turn off his Holos simulation at all.'

Gibson simply stared, waiting for the punch line. He seemed to be growing impatient. Was he going to say it?

'Could Jazlin Switch have done this?' he asked.

And there it was, the Devil's name. Hearing it aloud oddly calmed me because I knew this couldn't be her work.

'She's been in digital confinement for the last seven years. Still is.'

'But no one has spoken to her in there for five years,' he countered. 'Not since her last three interviewers committed suicide.'

'She's still there,' I said. 'We can see her avatar on the virtual feed.'

I didn't say that I looked at it every single day, just to reassure myself.

'And she's done nothing but sit and meditate in there,' Gibson said. 'She won't respond to audio prompts. For all we know, the footage is on some kind of loop and she's found a way to jack out of virtual into the real world.'

Hairs stood up on the back of my neck. If that had really happened there'd be more than one body found this morning. Her first slaughter had clocked into the hundreds in a day. I could hear the screams. Feel the shock of people dropping all around me. The terror of dashing to escape my first trip to the virtual world, hoping my dad made it out too. The Holos. The horror. There had been more killings the day after that and again the day after, until they caught her. Almost a thousand people had been murdered in the end.

I squeezed my eyes shut, then opened them again to steady myself in reality. Actual reality.

'No one can unsync their mind from digital confinement,' I said, sounding calmer than I felt. 'Not even Jazlin Switch. If someone found where she's plugged in and tried to pull her out manually, she'd die. And good riddance too.'

'I want you to go in and interview her. Make sure.'

I actually laughed. That wasn't going to happen. No way, no way, no way. Gibson and I locked gazes—a stare off I had no interest in winning.

I looked over to the body again.

'It could be a copycat,' I ventured. 'Perhaps someone broke in here and killed this guy, making it look like a Specter Slaughter.'

'Really?' Gibson raised an eyebrow. 'No footage. No DNA. No nothing.'

'But no one has been able to do what she did— kill people inside the virtual world so they die here. Not even close. Filton Fukami confirmed his Holos developers refactored the code that made it possible. How has that changed?'

Gibson stood silent, letting the question hang in the air.

I walked over to look at the writing on the far wall. Neat, block letters read:

IT'S MORE ABOUT MONEY THAN POWER.

Above that was a scrawl in different handwriting.

Free the body and the spirit will soar.

I shuddered. That was something Switch had written in her Hyperrealist's Manifesto. A blank set of fingerprints signed off the scrawl at the end. It was the mark of a movement Switch had belonged to that prized anonymity as the way to freedom from government and corporate manipulation. It was as if someone was trying hard to connect this to the Specter Slaughters. Really hard. But if this was supposed to have been a Specter killing, the victim must have written it. This was getting more confusing by the minute. I didn't like it.

It's more about money than power was new, too. Something different. I used my wrist-comm to take a photo of it.

'That looks like a motive perhaps,' I mused. 'Do we know who the victim is?'

'No,' Gibson said. 'Zero DNA match in the national system. Probably an anonymous jack-in. Indian descent. Male. Twenty-seven.'

'What about the lease of the unit?'

'Paid for in SureCoin under the name John Smith. Untraceable.'

I thought for a moment, gathering all the relevant information to recap aloud.

'So,' I said, 'we have something that looks like a Specter slaying, but it's a one-off. There's also the potassium in the blood, the open display helmet, and a possible motive beyond mere psychopathy. Those things all point away from Switch. I don't think we need to interview her.'

'I do,' Gibson pressed.

'Then you do it,' I snapped.

Gibson's face turned as red as a Vegas sunset.

'You're the expert,' he said through gritted teeth. 'It's why I called you in. I thought you'd jump at the chance. You're more qualified than anyone to do it. I've started the clearance process with the military unit who's holding her. Took a lot of string pulling.'

'I don't go into virtual,' I said, crossing my arms.

'You what?' Gibson scoffed. 'Not even unsynced? You're not one of those Luddites are you?'

I paused. *The screams. My father's body dead in my arms.*

'No. I just prefer the stability of the real world,' I said.

'You must be the only one.' Gibson shook his head.

'Look,' I said, still wanting to make my mark here. 'Let me work the clues of the scene first. Switch isn't going anywhere. Hasn't gone anywhere. I'm sure of it. I'll find something. I promise.'

Gibson mused, rubbing the top of his thumb-like head.

'I'll give you 24 hours,' he said. 'It will take that long to finalize digital confinement access with the military anyway. If you find nothing promising, you interview her. It doesn't have to be long—just enough to confirm she's safely locked in digital confinement. Right?'

I dipped my head in a reluctant nod.

'Good. I'll leave you to it then.' He turned to leave before pausing. 'And don't say anything about the murder to anyone outside the unit. If this gets into the media we'll have a panic. Right?'

'Right.' I nodded, my own mini-panic rising.

I had a day to find a real lead or march into electro-prison to face the woman who killed my dad.

3

Filton Fukami strode onto a giant stage in the virtual world. A deafening roar went up from the crowd of millions gathered, come to see the creator of the Holos. These people had voted him in as a senator of Nevada—their official place of residence, even if they never went outside.

Fukami's avatar was the perfect picture of how he looked in real life—the quintessential Japanese businessman. Fit. Suited. Groomed black hair with hints of grey on the sides. The stadium around him was like a colossal Coliseum. Ancient-looking pillars contrasted with cutting-edge, Tru-Res screens. On the top tier of the stadium were glass skyboxes fitted out as full luxury apartments. The elite's way to view history.

A shimmering screen unfurled behind Fukami, showing lush green fields. He held up his hands for silence. The crowd gave immediate respect, the roar dropping to a hum.

'The Holos is our world of promise,' he said. 'We must fight to keep it free!'

Cheers erupted again. Cyberpunks, military nuts, fantasy freaks and more, all watched in supplication. Every faction clapped with their hands in the air.

'The Holos has been the only place where we can express ourselves as we truly are,' Fukami continued. 'The only place we can fulfill our deepest, darkest desires without harm or fear. It used to be we could say, write or print what we liked in this country. That same freedom of speech should extend to digital visions too. Fantasies of the mind that feel truly real. That stimulate our souls.'

The screen behind Fukami flashed with writhing naked bodies, then a gun battle with zombies, then back to the clean, clear fields of grass.

'But our paradise is under threat!' Fukami shouted.

The cheers turned to boos.

Fukami's background changed to an image of polluted skies. Of trash mounds, heaped and rotting.

'Before the Holos,' he said, 'our scrambling for material wealth was raping the planet. Pandemics were commonplace.'

Footage of crowded hospitals and piles of dead lit up around the space. All then flashed back to green fields.

'Now we can have everything we desire. All the prestige and physical possessions we want, without using resources and polluting the land. All of our physical needs and fantasies fulfilled without the risk of getting infected.'

Images of people driving luxury cars roared to life through the air above the crowd. Then models sipping cocktails. The good life as a light show. All went black again. Bright images of the world's capital cities strobed on the big background screen. Clean streets of New York City. Flawless skies above Beijing. Orderly traffic in New Delhi. People lounging on lawns in front of the Eiffel Tower in Paris.

'Since the Holos started, our carbon emissions have dropped globally,' Filton went on. 'All electricity is produced sustainably from solar. The climate has stabilized. People are enjoying themselves in both the virtual and the real on unprecedented levels.'

He stopped. His avatar grew. It towered above everyone, projected lifelike as a hundred-foot giant in the front of the stage.

'And it's all because of freedom,' he boomed.

The applause from the crowd was ear splitting. People screamed themselves hoarse, stomping their feet. Fukami raised his arms for silence.

'These new laws Senator Rommel has proposed will take that away,' he said gravely.

Silence. Not a peep.

'Your freedom will be gone. We will go back to the poverty and pollution of the past. To the disease and famine and suffering. Do we want that? Or do we want a free Holos?'

The reaction was instantaneous.

'FREEDOM. FREEDOM. FREEDOM.'

Fukami let it go on for a full five minutes. He stood with hands clasped in front of him, nodding sagely. His projection then shrank back down. Fukami glowed with pure light on stage. The crowd hushed again.

'Let Senator Rommel know how you feel. We will not stand for her tyranny, for draconian laws in the digital world. Blog. Vlog. Flit. Feed. Scream it from the rooftops. She is a public servant just like me. She needs to serve your will. Let that will be known. Squash her policy proposal before it gets put on the open market. Show her it won't be successful. Tell her you'll not invest in a dark future. Let her know the Holos will not be shackled. Anonymity. Freedom. Fulfillment.'

The three words lit up behind him in neon. A slogan anyone could remember. The crowd took up the call.

'ANONYMITY. FREEDOM. FULFILMENT.'

'Now go!' Fukami said. 'Create action. Show you'll protect your home by any means necessary!'

People streamed out of the public square, jazzed up, ready to do his bidding. It felt like an incitement to riot, even though he hadn't used the words.

I sat back from the hologram screen, taking out my earphones. The police station buzzed with movement around me. Coffee slurped, donuts chomped—the sound of cases being cracked. I tried to filter it all out and concentrate. That Fukami speech was utter drivel. It was the eighth result of millions that had come up when I'd searched for 'Money, Power, Holos.' There was no way it related to the case. Fukami might have once worked with Jazlin Switch on coding and connecting the Holos, but that was ancient history. He'd disavowed anything to do with her when she went full psycho. She'd almost destroyed what he'd worked so hard to create.

An endless scroll of unread articles sat beneath the speech footage. That avenue was starting to feel hopeless.

I rearranged my things, shifting my keypad to be parallel with the edges of the bench. Dead center. My earphones went in their case, lid securely closed. The case went in its dedicated slot. Order. Now that I could concentrate again, I swung around to another screen, which showed security footage of empty hallways in the Bolodair Apartments. A cleaner appeared on the day of the body discovery. He meandered from room to room in the hall, doing his thing inside each one, then exiting again, until he came to room 842.

He opened the door, paused for a few moments in shock, then ran back down the hall. The cleaner had reported the murder right away and made a statement with the scan team. Nothing unusual. No one unusual. Nothing he didn't see every day... except for the dead body.

'Go back 24 hours and play again on four-times speed,' I said to the screen wearily.

The footage kept rolling. I grunted in frustration. Five years ago I would have just clicked a mouse or banged the side of the monitor if that didn't work. These new hologram screens were a nightmare.

'Go back 24 hours and play again four-times speed,' I said slowly and loudly, as if talking to an idiot.

Still nothing. I wanted to hurl something at the screen, but it would just pass right through.

'Need a caffeine injection?' a voice said behind me.

I turned to see Cline, our digital analyst. More hair than man, he had an unkempt afro, bushy beard, and eyebrows you could hang a hat on. He held out an extra-large cappuccino. I took it gratefully.

'Cline, if you waxed your fun nuggets, you'd be marriage material,' I said, taking a glorious sip. 'Can you fix this stupid thing? I want to rewatch the footage again, but faster.'

Cline nodded knowingly. My I.T. support savior. He never got frustrated with me, just fixed things and moved on.

'Q, back 24 hours. Quad speed, please.' The footage immediately jumped back and ran. 'You have to say 'Q' first, remember?' He smiled.

Q. Siri. Alexa. It was hard enough remembering people's names, let alone computer systems.

'Do I have to say please too?' I asked grumpily.

'Well, manners never hurt.' He shrugged. 'You find anything?'

'Not yet,' I admitted. 'Waiting for a doc's report on the potassium in the blood. I've read that it could mean kidney failure, but we both know that's not what killed him.' I indicated the hallway on the screen. 'You sure this footage hasn't been tampered with?'

He nodded.

'I ran it through the AI. No scrubbing found *at all*. It passed all the deep-fake detection programs news media need to run before being allowed to publish anything too. You could stamp it with a blockchain watermark and call it legitimate in any jurisdiction on earth. More to the point, there were no suspects pinpointed. Not in a whole month of footage.'

'I don't get it though,' I said. 'Most security systems like this run on motion detection. There shouldn't be footage of empty hallways. It's too random. There has to be some kind of manipulation here.'

'Maybe they've got rats?' Cline shrugged his shoulders. 'You know what those places are like. Did you get anything on the keyword search from the writing on the wall?'

'Money, power, Holos. Are you kidding?' I said. 'I may as well have typed in 'free music, porn, cat photos'. It's even worse with Senator Rommel's Holosian bill hitting the policy market yesterday. Every man and his vlog are covering it.'

'I hear its only paying $2 already,' Cline said. 'I got it at $3.50. If it gets down to a dollar five for a whole day and becomes law, I'll make a handy profit.'

'You bet on it?' I asked, surprised.

'Didn't you?' he asked. 'I thought you'd be all over more law and order in the Holos.'

'I don't bet on policy,' I said. 'We should vote on them, like the old days.'

'You're kidding, aren't you?' Cline asked, getting worked up. 'It's bad enough we still vote on what goes into the National Welfare Index. Old-school democracy is dead. Futarchy is the future.'

'Whoever named that system needs an old-school bullet in the head,' I said, looking back at the screen. 'Now, how am I going to sort through this junkyard of articles?'

'Have you tried narrowing the search by adding anything like 'Indian Man?' or something?' he asked.

'I should have done that already,' I said, chastising myself.

The pressure of interviewing Jazlin Switch had me rattled. I was about to put fingers to keys, when a new result appeared at the top of the scroll. Its bold headline thundered out from the screen like a throat punch.

My breath faltered. Cline saw it too.

'Shit,' he said.

I almost did one in my pants. This wasn't good.

CHRISTOS RAMA SLAIN IN SPECTER STYLE KILLING.

An image of the crime scene from the apartments sat beneath, True-News watermarked to prove authenticity.

'Mother...'

'...Fucker!' the shout came from Gibson's office.

His door swung open a mere second later, smacking into the wall behind. Everyone in the place turned his way.

'You two,' he said, leveling a finger toward Cline and me. 'Briefing room. Now.'

4

Lilith's self-drive crept through traffic toward Coliseum 2.0. It seemed like half the population of the Holos were heading to one event—Senator Rommel's first virtual rally. Thousands of soapbox preachers stood on raised sidewalk platforms, yelling their three-word slogans at the masses streaming by. Some held signs reading #KillHerBill, a hash tag Lilith had created and now partly regretted.

Lilith could tell by people's avatars who was there to support Rommel and who was there to protest. The Free expressed their individuality in wild ways: Mohawks, body mods, clip-on augmentations. The Luds looked like they did in the real world—regular people with regular hopes and dreams. Lilith could respect that. There was a lot to be said for normal hopes, fair opportunity, nurtured families, and safety. That kind of life hadn't been possible for Lilith, but she did envy it. Lilith looked around at the crowd again. This wouldn't be like Fukami's fanfests in virtual—it would be polarized chaos. The unrest already bubbled on the street. A group of ragtag paramilitary grunts were hassling two well-dressed women doing their best to stay calm. A giant boy soldier in fluorescent camo slapped one of the women on her ass. The woman flinched away, but another one of the goons slapped her on the ass again from the other side. It was tame behavior for the Holos, but things could easily escalate. Fear and confusion already gripped the women. The scene made Lilith's blood boil.

'Q, stop car,' she ordered her self-drive.

The all tinted-glass vehicle instantly obeyed, to honks of anger behind. Lilith stepped out casually, glad she was still wearing her business avatar from earlier today—an elderly Englishman dressed in a three-piece suit. It grated her that this was still the best look to demand respect during contract negotiations, but if there was anything Lilith knew, it was how appearances created mood and mood set the foundation for all interactions. Her normal avatar, the one she called her true self, wasn't practical right now anyway. The appearance of Holos celebrity Lilith Lace would cause a flat-out riot in a crowd this charged. Another horn honked. Lilith waved her apologies then tapped the top of her self-drive twice. A steel casing materialized from the vehicle and formed a ramp up and around that other cars could drive over. The Politisphere of the Holos was coded to prohibit flying cars for safety reasons, but that didn't mean traffic should get too backed up. The small disruption had done enough to cause the paramilitary crowd to look her way, taking their attention from their would-be victims. Lilith turned their way theatrically.

'Trisha! There you are, Trisha!' she boomed in her modified, English accent toward the women who had been in trouble. 'Do you need a lift?'

The woman Lilith had addressed as Trisha looked utterly confused at the use of a name that clearly wasn't her own. Her friend, a diminutive brunette, caught on immediately though. She grabbed 'Trisha' by the arm and led her toward the car.

Lilith smiled a friendly grin, nodding curtly at the women's harassers, who lost interest almost immediately. 'Trisha' and her companion came within a few feet but held their ground, still tentative.

'Hello, ladies,' Lilith said, 'Why don't you take this car where you need to go. It'll be safer and easier.'

The small brunette frowned. 'Are you sure? That's awfully kind of you.'

'Seems like you deserve some kindness after those brutes laid hands on you,' Lilith said in her most appeasing voice. 'It's the least I can do. Not everyone in the Holos is so rude, I assure you.'

With that, Lilith tapped the door of her self-drive and it opened. At that moment, a car buzzed over the top of the self-drive's ramp. The motion made the women step back. Lilith could tell they were still on edge. They must be full-time real worlders, only here to support Rommel.

'It works like a regular self-drive,' Lilith said. 'Just tell it where you want to go and it will drop you at the door. It's programmed to go to my virtual garage afterward when not in use.'

'What about you?' 'Trisha' said.

'I'll walk,' Lilith replied, 'I'm almost where I need to be anyway. Good day.'

With that, Lilith promptly turned and started to walk away with the crowd. The women would feel safer without her avatar standing over them.

'Thank you!' The words followed behind her.

Lilith glanced back and waved again, seeing the women enter the car. It detracted its ramp and started crawling through the traffic again. The sight made the knot in Lilith's chest ease a little. They were safe, for now. Lilith knew only too well the fear of being a target. She'd been one for years where she grew up, in a poor neighborhood of a rough city. People took what they wanted in that life if they were strong. She was physically petite, so the apex predators took all they wanted from Lilith. She could feel their hands groping her even now. The cold of steel pressed against her throat and the disgusting whispers in her ear that if she moved the wrong way she'd never move again. She wouldn't wish that life on anyone. And yet, perversely, it had made her what she was. From that original terror she'd built a strong will block by block. She had reclaimed her power by recreating her attacks in the bedroom, but with her in control. At first she was disgusted with herself, thinking she was sick in the head. But she'd learned that whatever she needed to do to feel whole, to feel pleasure again, was healthy—as long as it didn't hurt anyone else. That epiphany had led her into the Holos to recreate and create more depraved acts. To mix them in with her love of music. To perform. In this playground, she always had control. She radiated that power to others who enjoyed watching. At first, Lilith was niche; a novelty. But the combination of two viral phenomena, sex and K-Pop, had spawned the X-Pop genre. Many tried to imitate, but she was the original, one of the biggest stars the virtual world enjoyed. She'd earned her fortune and regained her sanity in the process. She'd also campaigned tirelessly against domestic and sexual abuse in the real world. Pushed for those burdened with dark desires to only unleash their evil in the Holos. But now those lines were blurred for Lilith. She didn't know if she was helping the problem or making it worse. Did X-Pop give people ideas? Whip them into spirals of escalating fantasy? Make them want more? Make them want the real experience? Crimes in the real world seemed to be declining but virtual sex without consent in the Holos was skyrocketing. That's what the media were calling it: virtual sex without consent. She called it what it was: rape. It was why she was willing to hear out what Senator Rommel had to say. These new laws for the Holos might protect victims, but still allow actual fantasy to help satiate and rehabilitate those who needed it. There were, however, some points that made Lilith's gut churn. Having Mercury instead of SureCoin as the official Holosian cryptocurrency was the main one. It meant less anonymity for her and for others wanting to do as they pleased without feeling like social outcasts. To not be judged for desires that weren't entirely in their control. Anonymity also protected them against becoming targets of those wanting to harass the same person over and over and over, mobbing them no matter what avatar they took on.

Lilith snapped out of her reverie. She'd made it to the resident's entry of Coliseum 2.0. Stepping up to the door, she pushed her hand onto the security disk. It read her unique biometric rhythms through her avatar—a failsafe only those who had permission to access the Skybox Apartments could pass. The door opened and she stepped into the lift, using her hand again to select her floor.

Upstairs, Lilith swept into her apartment. It was one of many she owned in the Holos, but the key place where she felt safe. The wide windows looked over the inside of the Coliseum, which rapidly filled with people below. Lilith went straight to her wardrobe and opened up to find her specially-made selection of avatars. She had spares of them at all of her homes. Another one of her business avatars was on the rack. There was also the charity face she dressed in at giving events—a chaste-looking matron in a modest-cut dress. Then there was her. The real her: Lilith Lace. Black hair cut into a short bob, slim yet sensual Korean body dressed in tight, all-black leather, and Stiletto heels that ended in knife points. Sex and power in a five foot five package. Of course, she was all of her avatars really: the businessperson, the altruist, and the BDSM musician goddess. She could easily reconcile all three sitting in her true self, but others couldn't. The real world had trouble with complexity. It was easier to break down appearances and play directly to the audience she was speaking to.

Lilith slid her consciousness out of her business avatar and into her true self. She breathed a sigh of relief. Even dressed in the leather and heels, it was how Lilith felt most comfortable, most in control. She walked across the lounge and over to the windows. The sea of people roiled below—a cauldron ready to boil over. Lilith tapped her wrist and her Feed screen flared to life. She typed out a quick post: LET'S HEAR WHAT ROMMEL HAS TO SAY. STAY CALM. SHOW RESPECT.

A few moments later, the lights in the stadium dimmed. A single spotlight lit the stage. The figure of Sheila Rommel walked out. A mix of jeers and cheers rumbled through the place. A large backing screen flickered to life, showing Rommel at a wooden lectern, dressed in her tweed power skirt and jacket, hair short and pinned up neatly. There was no pomp. No lightshow or Fukami flare. Lilith recognized that this was a statement all in itself. Rommel was projecting that the focus should be on the issues. That this would be truth without spin. Whether that was actually the case remained to be seen.

Rommel cleared her throat and the crowd's noise dropped enough for her to be heard clearly. Her face on the big screen showed calm determination.

'Fellow citizens,' Rommel said. 'Americans, Holosians, friends in other parts of the world. This is a critical moment in history. A moment where we can choose to live in order or chaos. For too long, evil has been able to run unchecked in this virtual heartland of opportunity. You come here to play and work and enjoy your lives, yet now all you do is look over your shoulders in fear of violence. We've turned our backs on this threat for too long. We need to face it head on. To look that darkness in the eye and say 'no more'. We deserve better than this. We *are* better than this.'

Rommel paused to let her words sink in, before continuing. 'Folks, ask yourself right now: am I truly happy? Do I feel safe here? Would I be willing to bring my children into the Holos without worry?'

The last few shouts of protests fell silent at Rommel's words. It wasn't a question anyone could easily say yes to. Rommel pressed on.

'We know that when a country brings in laws to protect their citizens against digital crime, quality of life goes up. America is the very last country to follow this logic. Our state of Las Vegas the slowest of all.'

Jeers of WE LEAD! and FREEDOM! went up from the crowd.

'Yes, Freedom,' Rommel nodded, pointing at one of the protesters. 'That's the reason you've been given by those who run this place to avoid any laws. Those like Senator Fukami, who stands to profit from leaving criminal behavior unchecked. Those people are elites who can afford personal security and digital fortresses inside this metaverse. They *buy* their freedom. But again, ask yourself, are *you* really free? Are you free to exist without the terror of being attacked? Are you free of bullies? Free of thieves? Free to call for justice? Do these criminals respect you and your personal freedoms? I say no. You are not free! You live in a prison of fear while *they* go free!'

Now Rommel's supporters cheered. The noise was an upwelling of song. Some protesters still tried to have their voices heard, but the tide had well and truly swung in Rommel's favor.

'I say enough!' Rommel slapped her hand onto her lectern. 'It's time we show these lowlifes what real freedom is. What real justice is. That common people deserve common decency too. It's time to put laws in place. We need a way to track these enemies and shut them down. This is what my new bill will do. Give you real freedom again. It's time we took back our lives! It's time we had justice for all!'

Clear white words stood out on Rommel's background screen: JUSTICE FOR ALL.

The spotlight went dark. The noise was raucous. Lilith looked down to see what was happening. The main lights of the Coliseum went on. Rommel was gone from stage. Both sides of the aisle were now turned to each other, yelling, screaming, waving hologram-generated neon signs. They held back on actual violence though. Even the Fukami diehards knew that to attack anyone now would prove Rommel's point for her. They had to keep the peace.

Lilith folded her arms, thinking. Rommel hadn't engaged with the Mercury issue properly. She hadn't talked about how the unique cryptocurrency could trace its users to a verified real-world identity. Lilith shouldn't be surprised. No politician dealt in nuance anymore. No marketer willingly pointed out the weak points of their product. Lilith stared out the window absently, trying to think about how she might be able to help bring these laws in without resulting in people's anonymity being sacrificed. She'd have to send Rommel yet another message about her concerns and how they could be addressed. Commit her celebrity to promoting a middle ground for the campaign, if they could agree on it.

Then a reflection in the window caught Lilith's attention.

Someone was behind her.

Lilith spun. A half man, half spider hung in the shadows. It stepped out, taking slow, deliberate steps toward Lilith.

'Who are you?' Lilith gasped, backing up against the glass.

No one could get in here. *No-one.* How was this even possible? Lilith searched around for weapons, something to defend herself with. She'd let her guard down completely. There was nothing. The creature was almost within reaching distance to her now. She was cornered.

'What do you want?' Lilith asked, pulse rising. 'Who the fuck are you?

'I am your fears become real,' it growled, then lunged at Lilith's throat.

Lilith couldn't even scream. The grip of the beast cut off all air and all sense of hope.

5

A reporter's face filled the briefing room screen. She was Chinese, with three different colored eyes. If this wasn't her Holosian avatar, the real world was getting too weird for my tastes. Our True-Resolution display made it feel like the reporter was larger than life in the room. Titles below her talking head announced her name as Yu Ying.

'This morning,' Ying said. 'Las Vegas Police discovered a crime scene that bears similar hallmarks to the Specter Slaughter, where Holos pioneer Jazlin Switch killed hundreds of people via virtual link seven years ago. A phrase written on the wall of the apartment ties the victim to Christos Rama's real world identity.'

'Pull a file on this Rama person!' Gibson barked at Cline, who nodded.

Ying's report continued. Virtual footage showed Rama dressed in a Christian priest's cassock, dyed saffron like Buddhist robes. He was giving some kind of sermon. Ying's voiceover drawled on over the scene.

'Rama, who has been publicly supporting the new Holosian Crime bill via his evangelist Feed channel, has long been campaigning to bring morality to the virtual world. His catch cry 'it's more about money than power,' calls out those who benefit from keeping the Holos free of government interference, saying they're hiding behind the idea of freedom for monetary gain.'

Rama's sermon kicked into volume. He was animated behind his pulpit, passion dripping from every syllable.

'We need real laws to stop the filth of virtual rape, pedophilia, murder, and violence running rampant in the Holos,' Rama preached. 'We need a transparent currency that allows governments to trace those who benefit from pimping immorality for their gain. That's why I support Senator Sheila Rommel's move for this new policy.'

'Find out the full details of that policy too, Cline.' I said. 'What are people most polarized about?'

Cline typed like his fingers were on fire, swiping documents into files for us to digest later. His wild eyebrows caught sweat dripping down his forehead. The large screen in front of us flicked back to Yu Ying, who seemed to stare right at me with all three eyes.

'Considering Jazlin Switch was a passionate supporter for absolute freedom in the virtual world, there is concern she might be involved directly with the murder,' Ying said. 'Is the Specter Slayer loose? Or has someone else finally been able to replicate her method of killing after all this time? I'll bring you more news as it comes to hand. This is Yu Ying with a Feed Original Investigation.'

The screen went dark. Gibson slapped the table, making me jump.

'Detective my ass,' he said, glaring my way. 'Cline, find out how those images got leaked to the press. I kept this team small for a reason and I know I'm not the fucking rat.'

Cline stood and scurried from the room. Gibson wheeled toward me. His thumb face looked like it had been hit with a hammer.

'Jack-in station, one hour,' he said. 'You're interviewing Jazlin Switch now whether you like it or not. Clearance just came through.'

He left without another word. I sat there staring at the dark screen. It reflected how I felt at my core. Black. My thoughts tumbled into that hole, back to my seventeenth birthday when my dad bought me a trip into the Holos. Fully synced avatars. Top line gear. Harnesses that would allow us to jump, fall, fly. True-Res helmets that projected the Holos as a perfect representation, with olfactory vents that simulated taste and smell too. Virtual reality without the V, as the slogan went.

I'd resisted the lure of the Holos up until then, afraid of the dark side of human nature on display there. My mother had described it as a brain sewer, where all the sludge of our minds mixed together. She refused to go in. As a gym teacher, she demanded all her classes were in a physical space. She even mistrusted virtual classrooms linked only to the National Education Network, saying I should never trust what I couldn't touch and see with my real body. Anything else was too easily manipulated for someone else's gain. I should have listened, but I was seventeen. I wanted to experience the worlds. Both of them. Dad was more liberal. He agreed there was some darkness in the Holos but thought it was eclipsed by light —the creative side of what we could imagine. The art. The ideas. The experiences. They were the fantastic creation of the human mind. He said we should be willing to draw inspiration from everywhere. That fantasies were there to be enjoyed, not to be taken too seriously. Now that I was becoming a woman, I had to see and decide for myself.

The day started innocently, soaring through the clouds, wandering ancient civilizations, letting the music of generations flow over me. It was wonderful. Dad showed me everything he loved. The bright side of the Holos, he called it. The true side. He wore an avatar that looked just like his smiling self. He encouraged me to do the same, saying if I wasn't comfortable with who I was in the real world, I wouldn't find peace in the virtual one. Still, he let me try on outfits of outrageous designs, rolling his eyes good-naturedly at my choices. He then helped me pick out something that reflected the sweet girl I was at that point. It was right then that a tall, warrior-looking brute walked past and said only true sluts dressed like librarians. I wanted to cry with the shock. Dad simply put his hand on my shoulder and smiled.

'Don't worry about what other people think of you,' he said, 'Take the world as a joke and you'll always be smiling. Take the work you do seriously and you'll always be successful.'

It sounded wise, so I smiled. He was successful after all. Liked. Happy. His skill at refitting vintage cars drew people into his showroom from all over the country. His easy charm had people buying them too, despite the premium pricing. 'If you can afford the insurance to manually drive it yourself, you can afford the car as well,' was his favorite line, delivered with a grin.

I shook off the brute's comment and refocused on the moment. Dad worked such long hours, it was wonderful to have one-on-one time with him.

'What's next?' I asked Dad.

His eyes sparkled with excitement.

'I hear there's a new showcase happening from one of the Holos's brightest minds,' he said. 'Something that will knock us flat.'

We went arm-in-arm to the public square where all the biggest events were held. All kinds of people were gathered—beings that defied description. People experimented freely with how they could look now that they weren't burdened by biology. It was like performance art.

Just after we got there, the stage burst with light. A person walked onto the platform. A woman of impossible grace. She had an assurance that only came with true power. Everyone watched Jazlin Switch. She waved her hands theatrically and screens swept around the space, boxing everyone in. People started looking a little uncomfortable but no one objected.

My mind had wiped exactly what happened next. The details of it. There was a sense of pressure. Of neon glare from all around that penetrated the skin. There was screaming. Bodies spasming. People running. I ran with them, yelling for dad. Only screams responded. Through the chaos, a voice came to me. A face appeared. It was Switch. Her cat-like eyes bored right into me.

'You're an innocent one,' she said. 'Only the darkest will die this day.'

And all went black.

I knew Switch was a liar as soon as I woke, because my dad didn't wake up too. He shuddered as I held him, covered in blood that wouldn't stop coming. It streamed from under his helmet that I couldn't get off. When two technicians came to help, Dad was still breathing. Still alive, just. They took him away then, said they'd do all they could. But 'all they could' wasn't good enough, just like my pitiful attempts. He died and I hadn't even been there. For some reason that was the worst of it. That I hadn't held him until his last breath.

For years, that woman's face haunted me at night, spoke to me when my mother wouldn't. That face almost drove me insane before it drove me to study. To understand. To bring order to the chaos of that day. To figure out why she'd killed my father. To see how I could make sure it never happened to anyone else again.

Closure didn't come, but an accelerated Ph.D. fuelled by my obsession did. There was also police training and escape to Las Vegas, away from my mother's silence. A new place to take my work seriously but treat the world as a joke. That face. That face. No joke there.

And now, I had to face it. Her. In virtual reality without the V.

6

I shook like a shitting dog. The jack-in room was sterile and white, like the morgue they took dad to. I forced myself to breathe. This technically wasn't going into the Holos, it was digital confinement, carefully controlled. I'd be in an unsynced avatar that wasn't hooked into my body rhythms and brain waves. Safer. Harm free. Not quite as real.

And yet, she'd be there: Jazlin Switch, the only person to ever truly kill people in virtual. Someone who somehow convinced her last three interviewers to suicide in the months after they spoke with her. We'd since left her in her electronic cage to rot.

Switch was jacked in somewhere at a secret location, stuck in her mind, kept alive by nutrients the most committed virtual-worlders stockpiled to last entire lifetimes. She was beyond committed. She was a zealot.

Gibson checked the monitors, already watching Switch in her prison on the virtual feed. Two female, military technicians double-checked the equipment. They confirmed clearance through their firewall. One of the technicians, who had a head like a ferret with a perm, handed me a specially-designed immersion helmet.

'You'll go through three separate firewalls,' she explained, 'each of which is a different color. Green. Orange. Red. As you go, you'll be exposed to stronger and stronger deep-brain stimulation that holds people's minds inside. The helmet filters out most of the actual sensation. If something goes wrong, which it won't, we can simply pull off the helmet and you're free. A 24-hour migraine will be the worst of it since nothing is synced. If you manually unjacked with a normal rig in a synced avatar, it's a grand mal seizure followed by brain death.'

'Same reason I don't go to rave parties.' I smiled weakly, taking the helmet.

Gibson stood and turned to me. If I hadn't known better, I'd have thought he even looked a little sympathetic. He put his hand on my shoulder and looked in my eyes.

'All we need to know is that she's still safely locked away. Anything extra is a bonus.'

I nodded once, clenching my teeth to keep my lips from trembling.

'You'll be fine,' Gibson continued. 'We'll be here, watching. We'll pull you out at any hint of trouble.'

Ferret-head helped me strap on the helmet while the other tech turned some dials.

I put on some haptic gloves to simulate a sense of touch and gave a thumbs up. My visor snapped shut. It was pure darkness for a second, then my vision opened up.

I was now in a green room. I looked my body up and down, studying my hands that weren't my hands. They looked plastic. No use in getting too deep into the illusion, I guessed.

'Walk toward the orange wall,' a voice said in my ear. 'Go straight through, wait in the next room for us to stabilize everything, and then move through into the next.'

I did as I was told, approaching the far orange wall. Reaching my hand out to touch it, I felt a brief resistance before it turned to a thick liquid. The membrane let me pass through. It felt like I was walking through a waterfall of jelly. Sounds rushed in: squeaks and hisses. Tastes followed: sour lemons, bitter craft beer, sweet honey. Smells were next: awful pungent wafts that made me gag, frying fat, excrement. I felt disoriented. Nauseated. There was a buzz around my head. I stumbled. Steadied. I was now in the orange room.

Slowly, surely, everything settled back down.

'Okay, all looks stable. Move to the next room,' the technician said again.

This time, I marched toward the red wall. Barely stopping, I pushed through. The same feeling. The same assault of sensory overload but with more touch: stings, tickles, tingles. Visions flooded past my retina into my skull, and then disappeared like dreams upon waking. I emerged into the red room. I swayed on my feet but kept upright. I could do this.

After a few moments, I felt normal except for a low buzz at the back of my brain.

This had better not give me a tumor, I thought.

'You're clear,' the technician told me. 'Go through the white wall and you'll be in Switch's cell.'

I stopped. Steeled myself. I could do this. I knew everything about Switch on record. I had the advantage. All I needed to do was check she was there in digital body and actual mind. I might even learn something valuable. Valuable enough to risk my sanity? What choice did I have?

'The white wall,' Gibson's voice prompted. 'Just in front of you, Detective Byron.'

I moved forward, one foot in front of the other. Silently, I pushed into the room, emerging into a ten-by-ten space. On the far wall was a bookshelf with a handful of fat tomes. Philosophy. Psychology. Coding. Metaphysics. A single piece of art hung on the left wall: The Garden of Earthly Delights by Hieronymus Bosch. A Spartan bed sat below it.

In the center of the room was Jazlin Switch.

She wore a plain, black singlet and pants. Her face was exactly as I remembered it. Smooth Egyptian skin, high cheekbones, a pointed chin you could have cut diamonds with. Her entire avatar was covered in spider web tattoos. They spindled along her arms, up her neck and across her chest. Each strand glinted like steel. Two spiders sat on her collarbones, both with seven legs instead of eight. At the center of every web was an eye, closed like the ones on her face.

I took this all in silently, standing perfectly still.

Then the eyes in the webs opened. Stared at me. The eyes on her face stayed closed, her expression serene.

'You've had a murder then?' she said in a voice like silk. 'This new killer isn't I. They are a mere mirror, where I am the radiant reality.'

My heart ground to a halt. *How could she know someone had died? She was totally cut off from the world. No external media. No contact with people. Nothing.*

I forced myself to speak.

'Are you confirming that you didn't commit any new murders in the past month?'

Now her real eyes did snap open. Yellow like a cat's, those eyes I'd seen before. A smile graced Switch's lips. Lazy. Predatory.

'And how exactly would I execute that?' she said, weighing me up.

I'd expected her to recognize me somehow. To read my soul inside a different avatar. She didn't. Couldn't. That was a start at least. She wasn't an actual demon, just a simulation of one. And, I had confirmed she was really here and interacting.

'Okay. Excellent. That's all I need.' I said, turning to go.

But the wall behind me was solid. No give.

'Your own needs are not the same as your overseer's,' Jazlin said from a hair's-breadth behind me.

I jumped back, smacking into the wall. How had she gotten across the room that fast without me knowing? Stuff this. She stood barely a foot from me now, her hands casually by her side. I resisted the urge to lash out. *Punch her, kick her, bite her,* my mind screamed. It was hard to separate my fear of her from my hatred.

'Your avatar is awful,' she said. 'Surely they can assign a much better design.'

Her lilted style of talking was throwing me off. That and how close she was. I bunched my fists, digging my nails into my palms.

'Whoever designed yours overdid it a bit, didn't they, fuckface?' I snapped. *You just can't help yourself, can you Ada?* I knew full well she'd coded and created the avatar herself.

Switch simply shrugged. 'So, who expired?' she asked.

'How do you know there's been a murder?' I shot back.

'Only one?' She blinked. 'How unsatisfying.'

I could feel her breath on my skin—she was that close. Or could I? Did avatars breathe? Hers would. 'Matching reality is the only way to then go beyond it' was one of her often quoted lines from the Hyperrealist's Manifesto.

Switch must have taken my confusion for stoic silence. A strong woman waiting for an answer. She continued.

'Why else would you come?' she said simply. 'No one has visited in years.'

'Maybe I want to know how you killed your last three interviewers.'

'Oh, excellent,' she smiled. 'I didn't expect the last one to follow through. Should I demonstrate on you then?'

I shook my head. A crackle sounded in my ear.

'You're now clear to leave whenever you like,' Gibson said.

Instead, I stood firm. I could do this. I wanted to stand up to her. Prove to myself it could be done. I took a steadying breath. 'No,' I said both to Gibson and Switch.

Switch inclined her head, taking a single step back, giving me space like she wanted me to stay. She held my eyes with hers. I stared back, clenching my jaw, but then lost my nerve and looked away toward the painting on the wall.

Switch followed my line of sight. 'You're familiar with Hieronymus Bosch?'

'My mother said this painting was a warning of what happens when we lose our morality,' I said before I could stop myself.

Switch looked at me again and smiled. The reaction didn't reach her eyes, but it was still meant to show her appreciation.

'That's one way to decode it,' she said. 'But I don't see it that way.'

She indicated the first of the three panes in the painting, which showed Adam and Eve in a lush field among the animals. 'The initial image is obviously Eden. Pure. Perfect.' Switch then moved onto the larger middle image that showed a more crowded garden, full of people mid-orgy. 'Most think Bosch shows judgment in these succeeding scenes of sin. Fucking. Feasts. But they're having unbridled fun. He even called it The Garden of Earthly Delights, not The Fall of Man.'

'Then what about the third image?' I said, pointing at the darkest of the three panes. 'There's judgment in Hell.'

'No,' she shook her head. 'The only men truly suffering there are those with their ears stoppered.' She pointed out the figures. 'They're not hearing the message they should be receiving.' Switch stepped forward and rested her fingers on the painting. 'See this smiling Tree Man with a plethora of personalities inside him? One of them sits atop a toad—a design of the devil. I take that to mean he has grown to overcome his darker nature. The Tree Man's roots also stand in two boats, skating over the dark waters toward the edge of the pane, which would cycle again into the Garden of Eden. This isn't a fable about maintaining morality—it's prophesy that if we move through our dark sides, we return to paradise.'

I wanted to scream that she was insane. That she was seeing things that weren't there. But the images she pointed at did now take on a new light with her explanation. I blinked, trying to steady myself. She was getting in my head. I didn't want this. I looked away from the painting, down at my plastic hands—a reminder that none of this was truly real.

'Tell me about the murder,' Switch continued, folding her own hands in front of her. 'It becomes so boring in here.'

I hesitated. Considered. It might help prove beyond doubt that she didn't do it if we spoke some more. They'd be running lie detector software all over her avatar and voice rhythms.

'Someone was found dead in an apartment rigged for long-term immersions,' I said, not wanting to give too much away.

'One of the casinos they converted when virtual vice forced Las Vegas to its knees?'

My eyes narrowed. *How could she know that?*

'They have more reliable power for those who call the Holos home,' she explained.

This *was* good. Was she telling me she might be in one of those buildings too? I needed to keep her talking.

'The victim was registered under a false name,' I said. 'Lease paid with SureCoin so totally untraceable. However, we're reasonably certain he was the Holosian evangelist Christos Rama.'

'Haven't heard of him.' Switch shrugged. 'Is he handsome?'

I thought about the burst eyeball in Rama's head. The bleeding fingertips. 'Maybe. If he scrubbed up a bit,' I offered, wanting to keep her engaged.

Every eye on Switch's body took a long blink. 'And why do you deduce it's him if there's no other evidence?' she asked.

Her tone reminded me of how a lawyer asks questions when they already know the answer. It made me not want to give it to her, but I needed something more to go on. 'There was a message on the wall of the apartment. It's more about money than power. It's something he liked to say.'

'Anything extra?' Switch said, clasping her hands.

I had the uncanny sense she knew, but how could she? I was letting her get to me. 'Above it was written, 'Set The Body Free and The Spirit Will Soar.''

A smile flickered on her lips at that. 'Maybe that's the message you should be receiving. Wonderfully wise words indeed.'

She would say that, the narcissist. They were her words. She'd lectured on them endlessly.

'He won't be the only body that is freed of its spirit,' Switch said, interrupting my thoughts. 'More dead will follow.'

Prickles swept up the back of my spine. 'How do you know?'

'Why simulate a serial killer if you're only erasing one person?' she said matter-of-factly. 'Also, this Rama was missing for seven days in the Holos before he died.'

'He was what?' I asked, confused.

'Missing,' she repeated. 'For a week. Please check that. It will confirm no one has replicated my most seductive secret.'

'Why seven days?' I asked, my mind racing. There was something there, hovering just beyond my recollection. A reason why that might make sense. I couldn't pin it down.

'I can't give up all my tricks,' Switch smirked, interrupting my thoughts. 'Where'd the earthly delight be in that?' She stepped forward again, within reaching distance.

I backed up a touch.

'Of course, if you furnished me with a few articles to follow. Displayed more details, I could help further. It would be exquisite to exercise my mind beyond contemplating what's already inside it.'

Another crackle in my ear.

'Time to come out,' Gibson's voice said. 'We have enough.'

'I'll see what I can do,' I said to Switch. 'Thank you for your time.'

I turned to go. Switch's hand shot out like a viper. She grabbed my wrist. Stepped up. Pushed her avatar next to mine. Every nerve of my body vibrated with energy. I struggled. No use. She held me fast.

I tried to calm myself. Tell myself I wasn't synced with my avatar. If I concentrated, I should be able to separate myself from this body. Move my real-world arm and pull through Switch's grasp like a ghost. I closed my eyes. Tried again. Nothing.

I felt her lips against my ear, making my eyes shoot open again.

'It's amazing what you can accomplish with the will of mind alone,' she said. 'Even when it's chained by ignorance.'

Switch closed her eyes then and stopped her breathing. She clawed her nails into my skin. I gasped with the pain, trying to scramble away. She held me like a vice.

'I can almost touch silence if I try,' she said. 'If it weren't for that screaming deep down.'

She was crazy. I struggled again, telling myself this wasn't real.

'Let go of me, fuck muppet,' I blurted.

She looked intrigued by my choice of words, then blinked again.

'If your spirit was stronger you'd be able to break free and soar too,' Switch said in my ear. 'But it's not. You need me to help you.'

She let my arm go and swept away. I stumbled backward. She was in the middle of the room again, sitting, legs crossed, eyes closed.

'Missing seven days,' Switch repeated. 'When you find out I'm correct, come back to ask more questions. It's so fun to play policewoman.'

I turned and ran back through the firewall. Shouting in my ears just barely made me stop before I dashed from one room to the next. I had to decompress, gain equilibrium.

But how could you find balance when all sense of control had just been torn away from you?

7

I gasped up from virtual, fumbling to get my helmet off. The white of the room was an anchor to reality. Gibson stood by my side, hand on my arm. I pulled away. I didn't want anyone to touch me right then, possibly not ever again. I could still feel Switch's fingers in my flesh. No, not my flesh, my avatar's. Still, I could feel it, the lasting impression.

The technicians stood away from me, watching, wary, making sure that I wouldn't collapse. I'm glad they didn't touch me. A supportive hand would feel like it was dragging me to hell.

'So, it's not Switch,' Gibson said glibly, trying to pull me back to the present. 'Excellent work.'

I stood for a moment, gathering my wits. I took off my haptic gloves, shakily folding each finger in neatly. I stacked them on top of each other and held them firm.

'Really great work,' Gibson said.

The praise helped. It had been good work. Painful work often was. The extra information Switch had given could prove useful. Was she jacked in at one of those old casinos like where the murder took place? There was also something extra there, nagging at the back of my mind.

Seven days.

I put my gloves aside and made my way to a chair at the back of the room. I sat, letting my mind work as my body recovered. That face. Her face. Her power to get inside my skin. She'd spoken about that power during her trial. How only she knew how to deeply affect the physical through the mental, but would never give up her secret. It was too open to abuse she said, as if she hadn't abused it in the most horrible way herself. She had explained her motives in her manifesto. Jazlin had seen how total freedom effected people in the Holos. As a psychologist, it made her curious that our shadows inside just got darker if we let them. We didn't settle and correct, we just kept escalating to greater depravity. Then Switch had an epiphany. It wasn't the freedom that was the issue.

Freedom was an undiluted good to her. It was the lack of consequences that was the problem. Without real consequences, the thrill of the game was diminished. To continue getting a rush, people had to seek out new, more radical desires in virtual. If she brought back greater consequences to people's actions, the thrill would return and equilibrium with it. And what greater consequence than death? The master consequence.

Switch announced her spectacular invention with her initial show of power. Then she melted into the shadows, appearing at people's shoulders when they experimented with being shot, shooting others, pushing the limits of their own shadows. More and more turned up dead. An epidemic. She'd gotten away with it for seven days before she found there were consequences for being a fucking psycho. *Seven days*. Was that it? No, that was a coincidence. It didn't feel right. There was something else. Something I couldn't quite grasp. All I needed to do was keep thinking.

'I think she likes you,' Gibson interrupted my contemplation. 'If you solve this, the powers might let you reopen her case, see if you can trace her to her jack-in spot somehow.'

It was tempting. To make my mark as a detective like that. To finally bring Jazlin Switch, the Specter Slayer, to proper justice. Yet the thought of confronting that creature again threw me off balance. The world was safe while she was in digital prison anyway. As long as her mind was caged, I didn't need to catch her real body. I just wanted to make sure no one did what she did ever again. I wanted to understand her actions better. Make sense of my dad's death somehow. I didn't think that understanding was possible anymore, not now that I'd seen the depth of her delusion first hand. But I could stop her copycat. I checked my pulse. It was slowly returning to normal, even though the fingers on my wrist still trembled.

'We won't catch her by speaking with her,' I said. 'If there was hope that way, we'd have done it by now.'

'There's always a chance,' Gibson said.

'Let's just concentrate on this case,' I said, wanting to steer away from Switch. 'She said Rama was missing for seven days before he was found dead. Can we confirm that?'

'I already checked with Cline while you were in there,' he said. 'Rama was reported missing almost exactly a week before he was killed.'

A thrill ran through me that quickly turned to a shiver. Switch was right. She'd said that meant this was a physical murder. But how could she know? How did that confirm it?

'What if someone can do what Switch did but it takes them longer?' I thought aloud. But that didn't fit. She'd said it would confirm that people still couldn't replicate her methods. 'Or what if Rama knew someone was after him and he went underground on purpose? Who reported him missing?'

'Sheila Rommel,' Gibson said. 'He was a supporter of hers. Apparently he missed a campaign meeting and she got worried.'

This *was* something.

'Senator Rommel? So it could be politically motivated?' I said, working to fit the clues together. 'Someone trying to silence critics of the bill?'

'Makes sense,' Gibson said. 'But why seven days missing?'

A pinging on Gibson's wrist drew our attention.

'Cline,' he said, looking down. 'Hopefully, he's got some more info.'

Gibson clicked accept and held up his comm so we could both see. Cline's afro filled the whole screen. He looked concerned.

'Cline, we've just had a break through,' I said. 'We've ruled out Switch. There's also a strong suggestion these weren't Specter slayings.'

I now felt energized. It's amazing how one small success can make you forget about all the negative in a heartbeat.

'All thanks to Ada,' Gibson confirmed.

First name terms now, I noted.

'Oh,' Cline said, not reacting like I hoped he would. He looked like he was going to be sick.

'What is it?' I asked.

'You had better come back to the station,' he said. 'Someone just claimed responsibility for the murder of Rama. They said they're going to kill more people.'

The crowd sat on the edge of their seats, watching Lilith on stage. She was chained to a chair. Blood dripped from her gagged mouth. She wanted to scream. To tell these filthy cretins that this wasn't part of the act. How long had she been here before they arrived? It felt like days. Would they believe her if she begged them for help? Probably not. She'd run this twist to her own show before, but that was all pure fantasy. Theatre. Acted. Virtual in every way. Didn't they understand that?

Lilith struggled again. Zero movement. The frustration of it made her want to cry. As if she'd give the crowd the satisfaction of seeing her tears.

It felt like there was something crawling beneath her skin. The Spider had injected her with something, and it was worming around her, spiking worse with every jolt of panic she felt. Lilith wrenched against the chains around her wrists. They dug into her skin, but she didn't care about the physical pain—it was the frustration and fear that hurt her. That sense of powerlessness took her back to her darkest days, the times when she'd been a victim with no way out. It paralyzed her.

Then applause.

Lilith whipped her head to the side to see the Spider wheeling a little girl onto stage. The beast who'd kidnapped her leered with multiple eyes. The girl was dressed in leather, her black hair cut in a bob. She was a mirror of Lilith, but younger. Much younger.

No.

Lilith screamed against her gag. She could take the punishment on herself, but an innocent? That wasn't fair, was never part of what she'd stood for.

The burning and churning under her skin got worse again, flaring white hot. It only added to Lilith's sense of terror.

The Spider stopped in front of Lilith, letting his eyes linger on the little girl. Lilith screamed against the cloth in her mouth. The Spider reached out and ripped Lilith's gag down.

'Stop this!' she rasped. 'You can't.' She looked into the crowd, pleading. 'This isn't an act! Call the police! Call someone!'

They cheered. Actually cheered.

Tears almost came then, but Lilith swallowed them down. The worming sensation beneath her skin intensified.

The Spider glanced at something on his wrist. A screen display.

'Goooood,' he said, watching Lilith again. 'It's started. I'll find you soon.'

The strange comment made Lilith feel even more disoriented.

'What do you want?' she scowled at The Spider, anger churning over her fear.

'I want you to suffer,' he said softly, bringing his face right up to hers. 'To die for trying to bring laws to my playground.'

'I don't want laws,' she spat. 'I want protection for victims. For innocents.' Her eyes flashed toward the little girl who was whimpering.

The Spider clicked his fingers and a synth drumbeat started from above. A catchy keyboard riff kicked in. The crowd started to clap.

'I saw your letter to the senator,' The Spider said in her face. 'You asked for laws. For oppression.'

Lilith struggled again, lost for words, her thoughts only for the girl. Surely this Spider wouldn't. But she knew he would. She knew the depth of depravity some people in the Holos would sink to just for kicks.

The pop music got louder, building the crowd's anticipation. Whatever virus or parasite was inside of her, it fed on her rising dread. While it squirmed and writhed with satisfaction, people started whistling, calling for the show to start.

'She's the daughter of one of your fans, you know,' The Spider said over the music, pulling out a knife. 'He's in the audience. He wanted to see you play together.'

'Stop!' Lilith begged, her voice hoarse now. 'Please stop.'

The Spider paused, holding the knife to the girl's throat. Tears spilled down her young, terrified face.

'Only you can make it stop,' the Spider said to Lilith. 'Tell me where you are in the real world and this goes fast. I'll find you anyway, you know. You can feel it inside you, can't you? The tracer? Tick tock.'

The Spider brought his knife up. Lilith's screams mixed with the sounds of her most popular song, an upbeat tune about love and sacrifice.

I sat in the briefing room at HQ. A shadowed figure stood paused on-screen in front of us, half hidden in the murky background. The only detail visible was a mouth with fanged teeth.

Gibson crossed his arms and nodded for Cline to hit play. The figure stepped into view. A troll's face. Green skin. Boils. Grotesque. He smiled directly at the camera.

'I have killed an enemy of the Holos,' the troll said.

Then the screen split. Now we were looking at two faces. The troll and a goth vampire with incisors tipped with blood. Both avatars spoke as one.

'Our virtual world must remain free from the tyranny of government,' they said. 'We must be allowed to satisfy our shadow side if we want to see the light. The more real this is, the more we will emerge from the darkness we have harnessed throughout history. Matching reality is the only way to then go beyond it.'

My ears pricked up at that last familiar sentence. I was about to speak up when the number of faces grew again. Four avatars now. Two beautiful women to offset the ugly others. Then eight faces. Then sixteen, all appearing in quick succession, each saying the words of the broadcast.

'This is why I have delivered death to the virtual world. So our lives here have consequences, just like the real. We now know what we do in the Holos truly matters.' The screen continued to split into more speakers. 'It's beyond a game', they all said. 'It's hyperlife. Ultimate freedom. Ultimate thrill. Ultimate meaning. Christos Rama was a threat to this way of life, so needed erasing. I will delete anyone else who stands in the way of our right to an untouched playground. You are next, Senator Rommel. You too…'

By now there were hundreds of thumbnail videos, all speaking the words in a single, dark chorus. Each said 'Senator Rommel' in a collective growl. Then more names were rattled off, but every face listed different people. The whole thing turned into a mess of chaotic noise.

'Pause!' Gibson barked. 'Lights!'

The briefing room snapped into bright relief. It felt like we'd just emerged from the end of a horror film. Really, it was just beginning. There would be more than one body. *Why copycat a serial killer otherwise?* That's what Switch had said.

'What do you have on those people in the clip?' Gibson asked Cline.

The hirsute analyst clicked a few buttons on his wrist-comm. 'The first avatar is a well-known Holosian troll called Bleesh. He started the broadcast on a public chat board in The Feed. We have no IP linking him to a real-world location or identity. He's famous for spewing hatred and death threats wherever he can. The next are other trolls who piled on. Some are just full virtual freedom advocates. People around the web are already saying these are false claims of responsibility. It's hard to know.'

'Do you have a list of all the people they threatened at the end?' I asked.

'I'm having the AIs parse everything out now.'

'Good,' I said, feeling a growing sense of urgency.

This wasn't about solving one murder any more—it was about stopping future ones. Gone was my sense of imbalance after meeting Switch. I was on the hunt now. It wasn't her doing this, but it was someone just as dangerous. Hopefully, someone easier to catch.

'Cross reference all of those names with people who have been reported missing in the Holos in the past two weeks,' I said. 'We obviously know who Senator Rommel is and she's not missing. She held a big rally in virtual a day or two ago. It's worth alerting her security teams to make sure they tighten protocols, just in case they haven't done it already.'

Senator Rommel was no stranger to death threats and controversy. I was sure she would have this in hand. She'd originally become a public face as Lieutenant Rommel, commanding ground forces during the Unification Wars between North and South Korea. At first there was intense resistance from the public to that war, but the success of the campaign, without resorting to nuclear attack, made Rommel a rising star of US politics when she returned.

She'd first resettled in her home in Salt Lake City, but soon moved over the border to spread her influence in the more powerful state of Nevada. Her first move was to revive dormant laws enabling the death penalty both as a deterrent and punishment for murder in the state. It was something people resisted initially. Since then though, real-world murder had plummeted. Her critics attributed the statistics to most of the population shifting into virtual. Her supporters though, loved her. She was about law, order, safety and family values; something I could get behind as a cop. Now she was trying to extend the always-increasing safety we enjoyed in the real world to the Holos. Rommel wanted to put laws in place there. Obviously, looking at that screen, there were plenty who didn't want that to happen. But there were just as many who did. Just as many who believed in her vision. The market price of her current policy proved that. This murder could be a threat to its success. The threat to her life was more pressing in my mind though.

'Okay,' Cline said, 'First step, I'm going to see if I can match the speech patterns of the broadcast to anyone on public record. There's billions of hours of just about everyone in the world speaking now. It's bound to turn up something.'

'Don't bother,' I said.

Now it was Gibson's turn to spark up. 'Why the hell not?' he asked. 'That sounds like good detective work.'

'Because apart from a few minor tailored pieces, it's all lifted from The Hyperrealist's Manifesto by Jazlin Switch,' I said. 'And we've just ruled her out.'

Determination gripped me. We could do this. But we'd gone from barely any clues to too many leads. Questions started rattling through my brain. *Who did that first avatar belong to in real life? Was he working alone, or with the other trolls who jumped in to take credit too? Was this Bleesh troll just taking credit for kicks? Did he have any links to Rama? Was anyone else missing now as well? And, why the link to seven days with Switch?*

Just then, someone else burst into the room. Sheriff Rosa Maria Mendez. She looked like a Latina doll—if that doll was used for evil hexes. Five foot nothing, dark eye shadow, a jawline as strong as her titanium will. Someone who, despite coming from nothing, had clawed to the top of the Las Vegas police department. Fierce. Arrogant. What everyone else called a total bitch. My absolute hero.

She leveled her gaze at me, then Cline, then Gibson.

'Who is running this joke of an investigation,' she asked, 'and where is their resignation?'

My heart stopped, actually froze in my chest. Gibson looked directly at me. I could sense him about to throw me under the self-drive bus to save himself, but the Sheriff bulldozed on.

'I've just had Senator Rommel on the phone, demanding we track down who's threatened her and who's killed Rama. The policy markets are in chaos. People are starting to log out of the Holos afraid that it's the Specter Slaughter all over again. This city doesn't have the infrastructure to handle an influx of people actually leaving their homes. It's crowded enough as it is. Tell me something good. Where are we at?'

All three of us stood silent. You could have heard dust mites fart in the carpet through the stillness.

'Gibson!' Mendez snapped, jolting everyone back to life. 'How on earth were the media ahead of us on this? The bloodsucking media! And what about these people claiming responsibility? People are saying one of them is Jazlin Switch in disguise.'

'If I may…' Cline started to speak.

'You may not,' Mendez said, holding up her palm to stop him talking.

'Someone leaked the details of the crime scene,' Gibson said, regaining his composure.

'They were on the station's open server so it could have been anyone,' Cline added quickly. 'I've since created a secure file that only this team has access to.'

'We also ruled out Jazlin Switch as a suspect,' Gibson barreled on. 'Interviewing her produced a new lead too.'

It was Sheriff Mendez's turn to pause.

'Who interviewed Switch?' she asked Gibson. 'I know you didn't have the huevos.'

My hero.

'I interviewed her,' I said, stepping up. 'Switch denies any involvement. She can't have done it from digital confinement regardless. She also provided a clue I think confirms this wasn't a Specter slaying. We just need to confirm the details.'

Mendez sized me up.

'Ada Byron, right? Aren't you normally Missing Persons?'

The fact Mendez knew my name made me stop. What had I done to get on her radar? Something good, or…?

'I pulled her into this one,' Gibson said, moving back into responsibility mode. 'She did her thesis on Jazlin Switch.'

'You're a Holos expert?' she asked, her look turning even more positive.

'A Specter Slaughter expert,' I corrected reluctantly, not wanting to spoil the moment.

'She doesn't go into the Holos,' Gibson added. The prick.

'Well, she does now,' Mendez nodded at me. 'If our victim lived his whole life virtually, you're going to have to investigate on the virtual ground.'

I was caught. A deer in the headlights of a small Latina Mack truck.

'I think that might be hasty,' I said slowly. 'We have other leads to follow first, starting with confirming why Christos Rama's avatar went missing in the Holos a week before his real body was found.'

'He went missing a week before?' Mendez asked. 'That's new.'

'It didn't clock on our radars at first because millions of avatars are reported missing in there every week,' Cline said. 'But Ada's interview with Switch prompted us to check.'

I could have kissed him, making me look good in front of the Sheriff like that. I made a mental note that I owed him at least two cappuccinos and fewer fun nugget jabs.

'Okay, so what's the significance of that?' Mendez asked.

I cleared my throat. 'Well,' I said slowly. 'We don't know. I suspect it might mean Rama was kidnapped in virtual. He was synced, so would have been unable to jack out if held the right way. His killer would have then been able to find where he was in the real world and murder him without any resistance. It could explain why the crime scene was clean of any struggle.'

'Okay,' Mendez said. 'I think you're right about it being a real-world murder, but we have no solid evidence yet, just a theory. How did they actually do it? Why is there no footage? Why is there no other DNA on the scene? Find some answers or someone'll get thrown to the media dogs—and it won't be me.'

She turned to leave. I was about to launch into a list of priorities with Gibson and Cline when the sheriff turned back.

'Speaking of media, Byron,' Mendez said, checking her watch, 'you're fronting a press conference with me tomorrow morning. Make sure you get a good night's rest. Wear make up.' She looked me up and down. 'And find tighter clothes.'

I cleared my throat, unsure what to say. I'd always made a point of dressing in my suit and tie at the station. I thought it was professional. People teased me that I was trying to look like a Fed. The red woman in black, they called me behind my back. They didn't understand I wanted respect for results, not winks for low-cut tops. Now Mendez was opposing that? As a woman, she should know better. Gibson smirked at my obvious discomfort.

Mendez's wrist-comm beeped. She looked down at the screen and let off a string of Spanish that sounded like the most wonderful curses possible.

'Puta madre, estoy rodeada de pendejos!'

She then blew out a breath and instantly clicked into professionalism. 'Gibson,' the sheriff sighed, looking back up to the department chief, 'make room for one more in your team. The FBI are sending someone to partner with us on this tomorrow as well.'

'Bullshit they are,' Gibson started.

Mendez silenced him with a glare.

'A senator's life has been threatened,' she said. 'Let's do this the easy way and cooperate or they might take over completely. Whoever they're sending is a Holos expert too. A real one.' Mendez looked at me then. 'He or she can show you how the virtual world really works. Now, get your house in order, prioritize your leads before heading home. And Byron? Shape up for media time bright and early. Amonos!'

10

It was almost midnight by the time I got home. I'd rewatched my interview with Jazlin Switch, went through the security footage again for glitches, and rewatched the Troll brigade claim responsibility for Rama's death. That Bleesh character seemed like he might be a lead if we could dig up more personal info about him. From what I'd seen so far, he was a total freedom zealot, so obsessed that his verbal boasting might spill into real-world action. Bleesh was also the first to claim responsibility before the pile on.

I wanted to visit Rama's apartment and check the security system manually if I could too. I had to move forward. To stay focused on the case. And yet, I was drawn back to Switch again. She haunted me. Something itched in the back of my brain about her. I went over her interviews with the three people who had committed suicide, to see if there was any crossover with mine. Had she somehow gotten in my head without me knowing it? It certainly felt like there were bugs under my skin. I needed to reassure myself that I wouldn't turn up dead tomorrow.

The interviews were nothing like mine, yet they were almost identical to each other. The investigators just asked the same questions as the last person. Perhaps hoping for better answers? In any case the results were the same: they'd killed themselves.

Because each discussion had been so similar, it was impossible to pinpoint how or why Switch had gotten to them. I contemplated watching them again to make sure, but then I'd heard my mother's nagging voice in the back of my head. *Watching that monster over and over won't bring your father back.* It wouldn't bring the interviewers back either. It wouldn't solve this new case. They had nothing to do with it. Still, it might give me closure. It might help me understand. It might help me sleep, knowing why instead of guessing why.

I sat down on my couch. The small unit around me was immaculately tidy. A photo of dad and me from the old days hung on the wall. Better days. The benches had been wiped clean after breakfast this morning. I'd put the toaster away so it didn't clog up the flow of the minimalist Scandinavian design. I didn't need to straighten up, but felt the compulsion to. Maybe I could straighten myself up. I went to the bathroom. Brushed my teeth. Combed my hair. Tidy rows of pill bottles filled the vanity cabinet. Proloft. The police psychiatrist had prescribed them when I started. She said they would help even my mood. Help me reconnect with regular emotions after suppressing them since my trauma. Help me sleep. I didn't take them anymore. Not because they didn't work, but because they worked too well. They stopped my nightmares. That was the only time I ever got to see my father. I couldn't abandon him like that. It would feel like giving up if I did. I'd rather feel crazy at times than feel truly alone. His memory was the only welcome companion I had.

I forced myself to stay still for a moment. Switch's voice intruded like it often did. My dark companion.

If your spirit was stronger you'd be able to break free and soar too. But it's not.

She sounded like mother there. Isabelle Byron never had confidence in my mind either. The day I'd been told I was accepted into the online Ph.D. program, I'd run home from high school, letting the long legs that she was so proud of carry me swiftly through the streets. I rushed through the front door. She was cooking dinner in the kitchen—mashed sweet potato, steamed corn, and steak. I showed her the acceptance letter on my phone. She just shook her head and said, 'You should worry about getting a proper job. A safe job. You didn't get your father's brains, you know. He's not here to help you now.'

Like I'd needed to be reminded of that.

Now, I looked at my shaking hands. A shimmer of light came off the silver ring on my thumb. It was Dad's wedding ring. Mom hated that I wore it, like she hated so much about me after he died. That event had broken her and she wasn't even there to see the horror of it. Isabelle had always been strict, but never mean. She was always moral, but never self-righteous, until she lost the one who'd made her smile. I rubbed my fingers over the ring. There was a deep scratch in the side of it that I'd never had repaired. I supposed dad's death had twisted me too.

I was tired, but there was no way I could sleep. I had to empty my head. I found my gym shoes and pulled them on. A hard run would help. I'd be able to lose myself in my body instead of my mind. I left my ear buds on the bench. Even those were too much right now. I'd had enough tech plugged into me today.

The cool night air of Las Vegas revived me. I ran down the streets, building up a good sweat, letting my fears seep from my skin along with it. I kept up a fast pace, concentrating solely on my movements. High-rise apartments passed by. I turned corners and went from shadow to streetlight to shadow again. I made my way toward the Strip, where I knew the neon signs would still be glowing at this hour. Even after the casinos converted to jack-in centers, they kept a lot of the signs up for posterity. The fake Eiffel Tower was still standing. The old Bellagio fountain was still running. Those landmarks formed a part of this city's personality—like The White House in DC, or the Empire State in New York. No one was casting that away so easily.

I felt the desert breeze blow against my skin. It didn't have the same warm kiss of reality as the sun, but it was still glorious. There was no air pollution now like the old days. I took comfort in the perfectly ordered streets, mostly empty now. I turned a corner onto the south end of the Strip, right where the Welcome To Las Vegas sign sat. It used to mark the start of the city. With the urban sprawl fanning further out, it was now miles inside the city's boundary. I had a four-mile run ahead of me to get up to the Stratosphere at the end of the Strip—another icon. I let the shudder of my footfalls reverberate through my body, losing myself in the physicality of it. I tried to re-center myself in the touch and smell of the material world. The thought jolted Switch back into my head. She'd spoken of material things to each of her last interviewers. Like so many of her rants, there was a core of logic to it, but it still reeked with something rotten. This rant was the worst of them. Her answer to the inevitable question—Why did you do it?

Next time you're outside, look around you. Sense how the stuff of the world presses in like a safety blanket and caresses you from all corners. The material world, made of things. When you step into the Holos, you step out of the material. That safety blanket is swept off and you come to a place made entirely of mind. Is it the spiritual world then? You can't truly touch it, but you can feel it. It's a place to ascend to something higher, material and spiritual both. When you enter, you emerge. When you come out, you're changed. You can't go back from that. If you try, you remember that you were just in a simulation—but it felt so real. Then what is it you feel now? Is the solid world just another simulation? The only way to find out is to jack out of the master simulation—to die and burst up from the darkness. It makes things exciting, not knowing what's on the other side. You want to know what substrate are we really running on? Who created our code? I believe that sense of excitement should belong in both worlds. It keeps us alive. It makes us question everything. Makes us see right from wrong instead of treating all of existence as an experiment. Death makes the immaterial world real. It makes us realize that the only way to know true spirit, is to jack out of all simulations. Free the body and the spirit will soar. I want us all to soar. Don't you want that too?

I shook my head clear of Switch's voice. Tried to anchor myself in the real world again—in the air, in the cement, in the lights, in the people. It was impossible. Then I realized there were people everywhere! I was close to the center of the Strip and, instead of being empty like normal, it was crowded. I checked my watch: 2 a.m. *Where did all these people come from?* I slowed, panting. More souls drifted out of apartment blocks onto the street. All of them, each and every one, had sallow skin and sunken eyes. Jack Ins. They were coming out into the night. Some walked onto the road, taking in the neon lights like it was the first time they'd seen them. No one really spoke. They just watched each other with uncertainty in their eyes. Anxiety gripped my chest. Had something else happened? Another murder?

There was an African woman near me: short, curvy, still dressed in her blue haptic body suit. Her face was more an ashen grey than black. A jack-in who never saw the sun. I took a tentative step closer to her, trying to calm my breathing.

'Excuse me,' I asked gently.

She flinched back, but then looked me up and down. Realizing I wasn't a threat, she regained herself.

'Can I help you?' she asked.

'What's going on? Why are there so many people out here?'

She looked around at the others and shrugged her shoulders. 'There's rumors that Switch is back. Chance Bradley, you know, the vlog caster? He said Switch can kill again. Safer to wait out here than take our chances in there.'

Who was this Chance Bradley character? Another Holos celebrity I was clueless about. I needed help on this case.

'But so many of you?' I asked, almost to myself.

The African woman peered around again and tilted her head. 'It's only a few of us. Most people inside think we're paranoid.'

Only a few of us? There must've been a few thousand people at least. Then it hit me. *Millions* of Jack-Ins lived here. *Tens of millions*, most in tiny, cramped units that barely had room for a Holos Stack. If they all jacked out, where would they go? This was just the nub of the ant's nest. Everything was relatively peaceful now, but if things got worse, my ordered streets would be overrun. Chaotic. If we didn't settle the masses, there would be a full-scale refugee crisis on our hands. They didn't have to cross oceans or climb border walls to get here either. All they had to do was walk out of their front doors.

I smiled a weak thanks at the woman and turned around. I looked back toward the shadows I'd run from. I needed to go home. I needed to get some rest.

The press conference tomorrow was suddenly more important than I had ever thought possible.

11

Scorpions were stinging the butterflies in my stomach. I stood behind a lectern on the stage as journalists filtered into our statement room. We were supposed to start an hour ago but everyone was running late. By dawn, tens of thousands of people had spilled out onto the Strip and other streets, blocking traffic, buying supplies and emptying out the stores of real food instead of nutrient tubes. There'd been an inexplicable run on toilet paper too. Toilet paper! Mendez didn't need to reaffirm the importance of generating calm from our statement. She did anyway. *This is your career. This is all of our careers.*

I tried to visualize being at the circus to calm my nerves. The circus part wasn't hard—these reporters already looked like carnival clowns below me. They stared up at the stage, mouths open, heads swiveling from side to side as people walked behind us, setting up mics and lights. I wanted to throw Ping-Pong balls in their mouths. At least half of the seats in the big top were empty still, definitely a relief. The sheriff coached me quietly from my left shoulder.

'Whatever you do, don't say we lack concrete evidence that this was a physical murder,' she reiterated. 'Just repeat that you've spoken with Jazlin Switch and confirmed she's in virtual confinement. If you're pressed for extra details, say that giving extra information would compromise the investigation.'

I smoothed out my suit jacket. I'd won the battle of wearing it instead of some scoop-neck thing. The compromise was some lipstick and makeup that helped my eyes look smoky instead of just tired. Some cops had been known to get 'filter' surgery before filling press roles so they looked more like the image they presented in their Feed profiles. I didn't have a Feed profile so at least that wasn't in my mind. Thank god the room wasn't full either.

'Are you sure you don't want to do this yourself?' I asked Mendez.

'Positive,' she said. 'Stats show that if we put a young, attractive detective on first, it boosts public confidence. I'll then come in for the hard questions and show experience has your back.'

'But I'm not that young,' I started to protest. 'And looks shouldn't matter.'

'You're a bit naive for someone in their mid twenties,' she said, handing me a pair of glasses with little ear buds attached to them.

'And these are supposed to make me look smart?' I scoffed.

They were going to make me look ridiculous.

'No,' she said. 'Just put them on.'

I did and gasped. They were augment glasses. The world around us now blended with virtual elements. Other reporters who had come in digitally now filled every empty seat in the room. Some stood around the edges too, hanging onto posts to get a better view. There was absolutely no room in the place. The reporters all looked perfectly real: no glow around them. No pixels or cartoons. I could even hear their chatter adding to the rest of the room's through the ear buds. The only way to tell the digital reporters apart from their flesh and blood colleagues was the fact they cast no shadows. That, and some of them had extra eyes, or were impossibly beautiful and buff. I wondered if these glasses had a setting where I could picture everyone in their underwear. For nerves. For nerves. Then a face caught my attention: it was Yu Ying, the tri-eyed reporter who'd broken the Christos Rama story. I wanted to jump off the stage and start interrogating her to find out where she'd gotten the photos. Instead, a spotlight shone down on the Sheriff and me. The chatter among the reporters stopped.

'Stick to the statement,' she murmured behind me. 'And for god's sake, no knock-knock jokes.'

Shit. She knew about that. *Was this punishment? Or her way of showing me she had faith in my work?* I straightened my tie. Fiddled with the printed statement in front of me. Made sure its pages were exactly the same distance from each side of the lectern. The sound of my long exhalation was picked up by the mic in front of me, signaling it was on.

Camera's flashed. Red lights on recording devices told me my face was being beamed all over the world. My name was probably sitting underneath my face on people's screens. I hoped they spelled it right. The sheriff nudged me in the back, alerting me to the fact that I actually had to say something.

'Thank you all for coming,' I said, reading the prepared statement in front of me. Did my voice really sound like that over speakers? God it was nasally. I had to push on.

'I can confirm reports that a body has been found in the Bolodair Apartments on the Las Vegas Strip and that it has been identified as the Holosian evangelist, Christos Rama.'

A low hum filled the room as reporters whispered to each other.

'However,' I continued, 'despite media speculation, this was not a Specter style killing. I have personally interviewed Jazlin Switch in digital confinement and can confidently say she has had zero contact with the outside world, has not participated in the crime, or revealed to anyone her still unreplicated methods.'

There were a few questions shouted from the room. I held up my hand and pressed on. Everyone fell silent again.

'Further, Switch has helped illuminate evidence that proves this was a physical murder, not a virtual one. We encourage all Holos users to feel safe in going about their lives as normal. I repeat: continuing to jack-in to the virtual world is as safe as ever. You are safe in the Holos. That said, there have been threats made to members of the public who have supported the new laws being proposed across both virtual and real worlds. If you're one of those people, we urge you to exercise caution in the physical world. Only log into the Holos using unsynced avatars, to ensure no real harm can possibly come to you there. Otherwise, go about your business as usual. Thank you.'

A clamor of voices accompanied microphones being shoved in my face. I caught the eye of a journalist who I knew from my own preferred news feed.

'Yes, Jeffery Jones.'

He primped up at being recognized, pulling his microphone back to ask his question. 'What evidence do you have to prove that these are physical murders?'

Thank you for being predictable, Mr. Jones.

'Unfortunately, discussing evidence may compromise the investigation. We want to stay a step ahead of this killer, so we won't be releasing our line of enquiry at this point. However, rest assured this is strong evidence and we believe it to be 100% accurate.'

Yu Ying stepped up and thrust her mic toward me.

'How do you expect people to feel safe in the Holos if you won't say what your evidence is?' she said in a polite but challenging tone.

'Yu Ying of The Feed, correct?' I asked.

She nodded but kept her mic pointed in my direction. At least she had a spine. I could respect that. I let my eyes linger on her in what I hoped was my best impression of a Sheriff Mendez death glare. It was time to turn the tables on her.

'We released crime-scene footage to you, thinking you would report on this responsibly and see the clear clues toward this being a physical murder,' I said coolly. 'However, it seems you either missed that through incompetence or twisted things to suit some sort of personal agenda.'

Loud murmurs boiled around the room. Reporters turned to look at Yu Ying accusingly; excitement gleaming behind their eyes at the new angle this story was taking. These vultures enjoyed nothing more than seeing one of their own picked apart when she'd gotten the jump on a story.

Ying's mouth dropped open. Her jaw worked and the sparkle went out of her third eye.

'As I said,' I continued, 'I have personally spoken with Jazlin Sw-'

'Are you going to release footage of that?' she cut in. 'Or are you simply expecting us to take your word for that too? We want evidence not hearsay.'

I stopped. Had she really just cut me off mid sentence? A police officer? I pursed my lips and smoothed out my suit again. I would not loose my cool. I would not. 'Knock, knock,' I said.

Yu Ying looked baffled for a second, then Sheriff Mendez swept in front of me.

'Thank you, Detective Byron,' she smiled down at Ying. 'Yu, if it makes you feel better, we will release relevant parts of the footage of the Switch interview. To all of you this time,' she added, eying the rest of the reporters in the room.

Thank you Mendez for backing me up. The sour look on Ying's face got more twisted. Mendez cleared her throat.

'Other questions?'

A cacophony of voices rose up from the crowd. Mendez pointed toward the back at a tall man with red hair.

He boomed out. 'With the threats to those speaking out in favor of the Holosian bill, do you think people should keep their political opinions private for now?'

'Absolutely not,' Mendez said. 'Not that you'd have much luck getting them to anyway,' she smiled. A few reporters chuckled.

'Freedom of speech remains a foundation of our country. We must uphold it always. Also, if this new policy is successful on the market, it will protect people against crimes and create real-world benefits.'

'Are you saying you support the bill?' Yu Ying asked loudly, seeing an opening again.

'I do not comment on politics,' Mendez said. 'But I think it's no surprise that I do support law and order everywhere. I agree with Detective Byron's statement that no one is at immediate risk of being murdered for real in the virtual world, but that doesn't mean there aren't other crimes that need to be guarded against. Go about your business as usual. We have our top detectives on the case and will be cooperating with the FB-'

'What?!' Ying blurted.

I wanted to jump down and slap her, but then realized she was no longer even looking at Mendez. Ying had her hand to her ear, apparently listening to something.

'I was right then,' she said, before catching herself.

She looked at those staring at her and suddenly winked out of existence. It took me a second to realize she'd just unplugged from the conference. It was probably just a way to save face. Mendez must have guessed the same thing because she smiled at the rest of the reporters.

'As I was saying,' she resumed, 'it's always a good idea to stay vigilant against other possible crimes, even if they aren't related to this case.'

Her statement helped the room refocus on the spotlight. Some people were still checking their wrist-comms, obviously scrolling to see if any news had broken that would explain Ying's exit. Most journalists, however, stayed in the moment.

Jeffery Jones stepped up again with his bouffant of perfect hair. I liked Jeffery.

'Do you think this murder, and the claim of responsibility by trolls, could have something to do with manipulating the Holos Crime bill's chance of going into effect?' he asked.

Mendez took the question in easy stride.

'It's certainly what the trolls would want,' she said. 'However, there's no proof yet those people are connected to the murder. We will follow that lead, but my sense is that it's simply another attempt by them to muddy the information markets for their own gain. Do not listen to them. Detective Byron's line of enquiry is leading us elsewhere.'

A collective gasp from journalists all through the room stopped Sheriff Mendez short. There was frantic whispering. Everyone was engrossed in their wrist-comms now, or pulling out tablets that buzzed and beeped. Digital reporters started winking out one by one. Some real ones left in a rush.

Jeffery Jones held firm. He thrust his microphone in the air again. 'Sheriff Mendez, what can you tell us about the new murder scene just discovered downtown that has all the marks of a Specter slaying?'

Mendez stood stock still. She looked to the side of the stage for help. A media aide from the police department rushed out and whispered in her ear.

'That is all for now,' Mendez said with authority into the microphone. 'We will comment further as the case unfolds.'

Mendez took me firmly by the arm and ushered me off stage. We were chased by the sound of questions still being yelled.

'There's been another one?' I asked.

'Exactly the same type of scene as the last,' she confirmed.

'Who?' was the first question that came to mind.

'We don't know yet,' the Sheriff replied. 'But we're goddamned going to find out.'

12

Whoever lived at the crime scene had more money than god. The plush carpets felt like warm grass. Masterpiece sculptures and paintings dotted the wide rooms. Unfortunately, there was a Jackson Pollock impression on the floor of the master bedroom—an abstract mess painted in blood. At the center was a young woman, Korean, slip of a dress on. Her True-Resolution helmet was still secured. Gore dripped from beneath the rim. Scratch marks were carved into the side from her black-lacquered fingernails.

I looked around the place with the Sheriff. There were security cameras everywhere outside, but not in. Journalists were swarming, trying to get the inside story. Only a couple had gotten here before the police kicked them out. A nutrient delivery person had called the scene in; the front door was sitting wide open when he passed. Media hackers had intercepted the call and got their scoop crews here first, just in case. They'd found the body and plastered it all over The Feed. Oddly, Yu Ying wasn't among those reporters. She hadn't posted anything on her Feed scroll either—I checked five times on the way over. Interviews with the delivery guy said he hadn't even stepped inside because he got the chills about it. According to external cameras, no one else had come in or out for days.

The scan team turned up a similar picture as before: no outside DNA, no finger prints, victim's identity unknown in the public database, no other residents to witness anything, elevated potassium in the blood. There was no writing on the walls this time though.

'This woman must have made her fortune in the Holos,' Sheriff Mendez noted, searching the room like an expert. 'Otherwise we'd know exactly who she is with a house like this.'

'So if she was fully anonymous, why all the security?' I countered. 'Isn't anonymity a shield by itself?'

'Only if you live simply,' the Sheriff said. 'This chica enjoyed her luxuries in and out of the Holos. That's a target all on its own.'

I pulled up my wrist-comm and punched in 'Missing Korean celebrity Holos'. A key result blazed out from the screen like fireworks.

'Look at this,' I said to Mendez, showing her my screen. 'The X-Pop star Lilith Lace went missing a few days ago in the Holos.'

A few more clicks took me to virtual footage of her act. Quite the show. Whips, chains, singing and sex—all to a catchy beat. 'She's got a beautiful voice,' I said admiringly.

The synchronization and lights on screen drew me in. It was almost hypnotic. I couldn't help but watch. 'Whoa, how does she do that upside-down with two guys?' I murmured.

The Sheriff cleared her throat. I flushed red and clicked off the video, considering the body again. This woman was shorter than her avatar looked, but that wasn't unusual.

I scrolled Lilith's Feed channel. Billions of subscribers. That would account for the money. Her last post was exactly three days ago. LET'S LISTEN TO WHAT ROMMEL HAS TO SAY. STAY CALM. SHOW RESPECT. That must have been just before the Senator's virtual rally. I scrolled further back into Lilith's feed. Normally, she'd post every hour or so. There'd been nothing about her feeling like she was in danger.

Some of her fans were saying on The Feed that they'd seen her last private act, which occurred after she stopped posting. It was live-cast in the Holos only. A one off. No recording available. There had been a half man, half spider with her on stage. Some were saying that it must have been him that got her. A man-spider? Thoughts of Jazlin Switch's spider tattoos made me shudder. The description didn't match our main troll suspect, Bleesh, who had claimed responsibility for Rama. Could that really just be a smoke screen? I'd still have to see if there was a connection among the rest of the avatars. Could we be working with more than one killer?

There was something else that didn't fit either. 'She's only been missing three days,' I said, 'That doesn't connect with Switch's specific direction of a week for the last body. What's changed there?'

The sheriff frowned.

'I don't know,' she said. 'Does her murder fit the political agenda of supporting the Holos Crime bill?'

'I think so,' I said. 'Her last Feed post said to listen to Rommel and show respect.'

I scrolled some more, frowning when I dug deeper. 'Hmm, listen to this… 'I agree legislation is needed to protect people from avatar sex crimes and violence, but Senator Rommel is out of her mind trying to mandate traceable Mercury as Holosian Currency. It will kill her bill.'

Lilith's fans had run with the slogan #killherbill, posting their support. They'd piled on that SureCoin was the only way to ensure personal freedom and anonymity online. Some pundits were saying the fact that Rommel had put a traceable form of cryptocurrency—which needed verified, in-person identity checks to have accounts issued—was one of the main reasons her policy hadn't slipped under the $2 barrier. Meanwhile, the price of the crypto coin Mercury had gone up anyway. Way up.

It's more about money than power, I thought. Maybe there was something more to Rama's saying in relation to this case.

'So this murder doesn't fit neatly into our theory at all,' Mendez said. 'Mierda.'

I crouched down next to the body. The corpse was as messy as our case. The scratches on her helmet made me pause again. This time I picked up why it didn't sit right. The marks were too uniform. Up and down, deep grooves along a couple of tracks. In the original cases they'd been wilder, like a caged animal was trying to rip it's own head off. I checked Lilith's hands for other marks. There was some bruising on the sides.

'Does this look to you like someone might have grabbed her hands and forced her to make those scratches?' I asked the sheriff.

She looked closely, pursed her lips, and pulled up her scan team report. 'Says here that bruising likely occurred as she tried to take the helmet off.'

The sheriff sounded as unsure as I was. It wasn't strong evidence, but it was another small piece of doubt on the pile. Lilith's visor was shut though, unlike Rama's. I struggled to find a way to flick the display up but couldn't find anything.

'Here,' Mendez said, bending down and clicking a tiny dot at the top of Lilith's helmet.

The display evaporated away. Expensive aeroliquid screen. Crazy. I'd never seen one in real life.

Lilith's true face beneath wasn't particularly pretty. Never had been, even before this. Now, it was worse. Her eye was ruptured like the last victim. Coincidence? Only a dozen or so people's eyes actually ruptured at all during the original Specter Slaughter. Maybe one in twenty. I filed the information away in the back of my mind for later consideration. We had to convince the media that this was done physically, not virtually. We had to keep those Jack-Ins confident enough to stay in their homes, or at least enter the virtual world unsynced. Gory details about eyes wouldn't help.

I studied the victim's face. She had scars on her cheeks. They weren't fresh though. They looked like old cigarette burns. I checked the rest of her body. There were scars on her arms too that looked like cut marks. A single, dark line also rested right across her throat.

'What do you make of these?' I asked Mendez, indicating the scars. 'Self harm maybe? Does that match with her online personality? A sexual thing?'

Mendez knelt down for a closer look. Her expert eye assessed the body. 'They don't match a typical pattern of self-harm or BDSM practices,' she said. 'No lover would willingly mark the face. People who self harm tend to only cut their arms, or inner thighs where they can hide it. Never the throat. It looks to me like she was tortured at some point. Poor thing.'

Her words were like a bolt of lightning. 'Tortured?!' I shot to my feet. 'Holy shit, that's it!' I said.

'What's it?' Mendez asked, standing as well.

I started pacing with excitement. This was why Switch had insisted Rama had been missing for seven days. 'Torture,' I explained, looking at Lilith. 'It's how someone would find an anonymous jack-in's real world location even if they held out against the pain!'

'I'm not sure I follow,' Mendez said.

'I'm not talking about her old scars', I said. 'I'm talking about a torture trace.' I almost laughed with how obvious it was. 'I'm an idiot. I should have seen this before. The military tried to use the technique on Switch. They tortured her avatar inside the Holos to see if they could follow those intense distress signals through the maze of code to where she was jacked in. Normal avatars have location disruptors to protect privacy, but the trace works on a unique program that gets inside the avatar and burrows back through the system.'

'Isn't that kind of interrogation illegal?' Mendez interrupted.

'Normally, but the military classed Switch as a terrorist so had it cleared. But it didn't work—she somehow overrode the pain signals. The military were forced to shelve the program after it was publicized, and simply held her in their digital confinement facility. Monsters *and* a laughing stock.'

'So how does this help us?'

'Don't you see?' I said, feeling flush. 'A torture trace takes around seven days to work. A full week to trace those signals of distress back to their owner, if they don't give up the information first. Just because it didn't work on Switch doesn't mean a killer couldn't use the technology on a normal person! If Rama's avatar went missing seven days in the Holos before he was found dead in the real world...'

'...then it proves he wasn't killed virtually but traced to his jack-in location and murdered physically in person,' Mendez finished for me.

'Exactly!' I said, holding my palm up. 'High fives for torture!'

Mendez's enthusiasm went dark. She glanced down at Lilith. I stopped too, lowering my hand.

'But not a week for this wretched soul,' Mendez said.

'Maybe she cracked early,' I said. 'Perhaps her killer got to her and she just wanted it to stop.'

We stood in silence, contemplating the body. I was torn between a rush of excitement at my breakthrough and showing proper respect for the victim. At least in her death, she had helped us. I resolved then that I'd use that help to catch her killer, no matter what. That's why I'd become a cop in the first place, wasn't it? To make sure no one else was killed in the Holos. No other lives shattered. It might not be a Specter slaying, but it was because of the Holos that she was dead.

Right at that moment, a man walked into the room. I stood up quickly, clocking his presence. Korean maybe. Dressed in jeans and a hoodie. A black mask shaded the bottom of his face.

I drew my taze gun from beneath my jacket. 'Stop right where you are,' I ordered.

13

The man in the hoodie looked at the taze gun I had pointed at his chest. He didn't seem too concerned. The Non-Lethality Act of 2029 banned proper firearms for police. That's when new Taser tech guaranteed rendering criminals unconscious with excellent accuracy; as much necessary force as you could want. There was still more than enough power in my hands to knock this guy on his ass cold. The threat of death would have been more effective though. I tried bringing a real gun to work on my first day and was told in no uncertain terms as I walked through the metal detector that it was my piece or my job. They'd said as much at training, but I still wanted to check. Reluctantly, I left my Colt at home after that.

I studied the intruder in front of me, or what I could see anyway. His mask obscured most of his face but the device wasn't a disguise, it was a germ filter, quite common these days with a certain type of person. The tinted steriglass edges framed his jawline, while the layered audio-slit in the middle allowed for easier speech. The top edge of the mask came to just above the tip of his nose. His eyes were young, with zero wrinkles around the edges. He was probably Korean but maybe Chinese? A teenager? Lilith's son maybe? I watched his hands for any quick movements. If he reached for anything, I'd torch him.

'You must be Detective Byron?' he said, his voice ever so slightly muffled through his mask. 'I was told you were mentally deficient.'

'Excuse me?' I said, keeping my weapon leveled at his chest.

He didn't even take a step back.

'It's okay, he's with us,' a gruff voice said.

A moment later Gibson strode in, his face dark. Cline was just behind, looking queasy. Still, I kept the taze gun up.

'This is Agent Min Joon,' Gibson told me. 'The FBI's Holos specialist.'

I looked Min Joon up and down again. A Fed in jeans and a hoodie? I was better dressed than him. So much for professionalism.

'Where'd they find you? Summer camp?' I said.

'Don't assume my age,' he said. 'Up until two months ago I was living almost 100% virtually. Less stress on the organs, resulting in a younger appearance for longer.'

'You're a jack-in?' I asked.

'Which makes you a jack-off?' he snorted. 'I can tell by the look of your skin you get too much UV light. What are you, forty?'

He was feisty, I'd give him that. If he kept this up I might actually grow to like him.

Sheriff Mendez stepped forward and extended her hand. 'Pleased to meet you, Agent Joon,' she said. 'We're looking forward to cooperating with you.'

Joon looked down at Mendez's hand and backed up a touch, wrinkling his nose. 'Has that been sanitized?' he asked.

Mendez pulled her hand back and rubbed it on her pants self-consciously. It wasn't like her to be cowed so easily.

'Okay, spankblanket,' I said, rising to the challenge of this new "specialist". 'We have no video footage of either scene, but we do have empty hallways outside the door of the first murder. No witnesses at either scene. No DNA other than the victims' but a strong sense that they're still physical murders. What are we missing?'

'That someone scrubbed the footage like they scrubbed DNA at the crime scenes?'

Good that he wasn't insisting this was a virtual crime at least.

'We've already confirmed that the footage wasn't scrubbed or photoshopped,' Cline said.

'Police AIs aren't worth the code they're written with,' Joon said. 'You need to get an analyst who knows what they're doing and look again.'

This kid certainly wasn't here to make friends. That was fine by me. Cline not so much. You could see him gritting his teeth through his beard.

'For the record, I trust Cline's judgment on that,' I said. 'He's the expert there.'

Cline nodded his head thankfully behind Agent Min Joon's back. Deep in my gut, I hoped Cline was right about the footage. Those empty hallways were still nagging me.

'I hear you're a Specter Slaughter expert,' Joon said. 'Where has that gotten us?'

'It got us confirmation that these aren't virtual murders,' Mendez said next to me. 'We believe the victims were torture traced to their locations before being killed in person. They have both gone missing in the Holos for a gap of time before turning up freshly dead.'

'A torture trace? But that's classified tech.' Min Joon said.

'Since when have criminals worried about using something that's illegal and hard to get your hands on?' I asked.

Joon nodded at that one. Fair enough.

Gibson and Cline both looked impressed, but pretended this wasn't all new information to them too. I felt a sense of pride that the team was taking my theory as fact. It was a welcome change from being second guessed all the time. If this kept up, I'd have to stop second guessing myself as well.

'Okay,' Joon said, looking down at the body. 'What else?'

'What do you think of the idea that this is Lilith Lace?' I asked, changing tack. 'And, what do you know about her?'

'Lilith?' he looked shocked for a moment but quickly recovered. 'She...'

He blinked his eyes rapidly. His pupils shuddered for a moment. Was he reading a file? I peered under his hood to see a glint of silver. A germophobe jack-in with a skull cap? He was fully wired for a zero-lag information interface. That was serious commitment. Even the inventors of that tech didn't have it fully embedded yet. The neural cap was a fine mesh of wires that bonded with your skin, then grew down through your skull into your brain like tree roots. You could connect with Wi-Fi and download information directly into your memory without the inconvenience of actually reading it. The mesh design allowed your hair to grow back through it, so, if you'd had it long enough, it could be covered without you looking like a cyborg. Min Joon's hair was still short. He either had just had it implanted, or decided to crop his hair to show off the tech. Probably the latter. He seemed like he had the ego for that kind of power flex.

'Lilith has been missing three days, so it could be her,' Joon said. 'She is in the top ten most influential entertainers in the Holos. Pro anonymity. Pro SureCoin. Anti bill in its current form. Pro victim rights and safety for domestic abuse and sex crimes.'

He looked at me like he'd just done something special.

'We know all that already,' I said. 'What's something you can't just look up on HoloPedia?'

Cline smirked in satisfaction behind Joon. Young buck zero, Ada Byron one.

'I've narrowed down a list of disappearances in the Holos for us to investigate,' Joon said. 'Your analyst Cline had a longer list, but I deleted anyone reported missing by lovers. More often than not, any sexual partner that goes missing has simply changed avatars to avoid the hassle of breaking up.'

'Okay,' I said. 'Thanks for the extra useless information. Is Lilith on your new list?' I asked.

He looked at the body. Nodded slowly.

'Then we don't need to go into virtual for that either, do we?' I said.

'Who else is on the list?'

He swiped his fingers along his forearm and a light display flickered up from his palm. Jesus, this little snot-poppet was like a digital Houdini. Bold names ran up the hologram screen. There were a lot of them. Still too many. More and more leads to spread our focus. I was about to say we should just concentrate on real-world clues when Joon cut in.

'I've ordered the names by those who were reported missing the longest. It's logical we should start there,' he said.

It did make sense, but I still didn't want to go into the Holos. He could go by himself and I could follow the leads here. Better for everyone.

'I've also pulled out a handful of missing persons who aren't necessarily pro law bill, but are definitely of interest,' Joon added.

That's when I saw it. 'Freeze frame,' I said.

Joon blinked forcibly and the scroll stopped. There was one name in the middle, stabbing outward like a bloody dagger. No, no, no, no, no. This couldn't be right. Joon knew it too. He'd put that name on the list after all.

'Why is Corpus on the list?' I asked. Corpus didn't have a second name. He didn't need one. He was *The* Corpus. Everyone knew who he was. 'How long has he been missing?'

Joon did his blinking act.

'Wait. The famous hacker?' Cline asked before Joon came up with an answer. 'The one who wiped the internet of everyone's personal data in The Great Reboot?'

'Yes,' I confirmed. 'He was also part of the group of developers who helped program the Holos into what it is today. That group included Jazlin Switch.'

'He's been missing two days,' Joon interjected, his eyes fluttering some more. 'Said he was going to turn up at a rally but didn't. He might normally be a bit of an enigma but he never missed an appointment he said he'd keep.'

'He's an advocate for freedom in the Holos, isn't he?' Cline said. 'Total anonymity?'

'Yes,' Joon and I said together. We locked eyes.

'And no,' I continued.

'What does that mean?' Cline said, waiting for the guillotine to fall. 'You're saying he doesn't fit our victim profile?'

'It's not that simple,' I continued. 'He's complicated. He advocates full anonymity yes, but he also supports very specific laws making avatar kidnapping and torture illegal.'

'How do you know all of this?' Mendez asked beside me. 'I thought you said you knew next to nothing about the Holos.'

I turned to her, dread creeping in. 'Yes, but as you know, I'm a Specter Slaughter expert.'

'So?' Gibson stepped in, perhaps feeling like he was missing on the action. 'Corpus wasn't involved in the killings was he?'

'No,' I said, gulping. 'But he was the first person Jazlin Switch said she'd kill if she ever made it out of digital confinement.'

Mendez's face darkened. 'That's not good.'

'That doesn't mean Switch has something to do with it,' I continued quickly. 'Corpus made his early law suggestions during Switch's trial. If someone is doing this to stop the new bill, they might think of him as being someone who started the debate. His ideas did kick off discussion about how to bring wider order to the virtual world. Switch loathed that influence, but more to the point, it put other powerful people offside too.'

'Like who?' Mendez asked.

'Like Filton Fukami,' I said.

'Senator Fukami?' Mendez said. 'The main opposition to *this* Holos Crime bill?'

'Yes,' I confirmed.

Mendez clenched and unclenched her fists. Gibson stepped in, all brusque business. 'We need to figure out where Corpus has gone then. How he was taken. Who his last contacts were.'

'That won't be easy,' I said. 'Corpus is known as prizing anonymity above all else.'

'Well,' Mendez said. 'Lucky you have experience with missing persons cases then. I think it's time you plugged in to investigate. Time to go virtual, Detective Byron.'

14

I stayed quiet the entire way back to the station. Normally, I'd be talking through the case. Instead, I wrestled with the lump of dread in my chest. I knew it was irrational. I knew that Switch was in digital confinement. That I would be safe from that monster in the Holos. I was sure this new killer was working physically. But how? And what had happened to Corpus? The fact he was involved set me more on edge. His ties to Switch were undeniable. That extra doubt was enough to debilitate me. I needed air. I needed space to think. I needed to go for a run.

I tried to excuse myself as soon as we got to HQ, but Mendez pulled me into a briefing with our press team. She wanted to send out a snap release to the media, detailing that the new victim was Lilith Lace and confirming that we now had strong evidence from both scenes suggesting they were physical murders. After some wrangling, I signed off on a quote from 'case detective Ada Byron' and said I was going for lunch.

'One hour, not a minute longer,' Mendez said. 'I want you into the Holos with Agent Joon as soon as you can. Strike while the trail's spicy.'

What trail? I thought, keeping my opinion to myself. We were already two days behind at least and I knew absolutely nothing about Corpus's usual haunts. Hopefully the FBI toddler had something hidden up his diaper.

I went to my locker, changed out of my suit into some running gear, and left without another word. Instead of food, I ate up the road. There was no way I could stomach anything else. I headed on autopilot to my regular route along the Strip but this time from North to South. I curved down Alta Drive, past the Primo Mall, and through the Arts District. I could see The Strat not far off.

My head was a rattle of thoughts. One image dominated all of them: Switch. Her hollow smile. Her shark eyes. Her silken voice that felt like it could persuade anyone to do anything. I could hear her answers to those interviewers about why she'd slaughtered so many. About what it meant to engage fully with the Holos.

When you enter, you emerge. When you come out, you're changed. You can't go back from that. If you try, you remember that you were just in a simulation—but it felt so real. Then what is it you feel now? Is the solid world just another simulation? The only way to find out is to jack out of the master simulation—to die and burst up from the darkness.

I couldn't do it. I couldn't go into the Holos again. The screams from my first time still echoed deep in my soul. But what would I have left if I refused? Certainly not any respect. Maybe not my job. Gibson would sneer and say he knew I didn't have what it took to be a detective. Mendez would know I was a coward, not fit to be a cop. My path to being a lead investigator would be shattered. My ability to stop murderers like Switch from ripping families apart would be just another broken dream in the wind.

I stretched my legs out, going faster. My feet thumped down on the sidewalk. I let the beat of it drown out my thoughts. I forced my breaths to come deep and steady. My heart rate climbed. My sweat flowed and headspace cleared from the effort. With that physical clarity came the ability to refocus on the case. I shifted my mind toward solving that problem instead of my personal dilemmas. Corpus had to be the key. He was a live lead in all of this. Someone we could work to track down. A missing person. That I could do. Couldn't I? Missing persons was my comfort zone—if it was in the real world. This was different. Back to my personal dilemma. Perhaps I could rework the security footage and use that as a good excuse for Min Joon to go in solo. Did I trust him to find Corpus though? To share the leads and find clues that most might miss? I wasn't sure. I wanted to pick up my running pace even more but was forced to slow down. The Strip ahead was packed with people still. That refugee problem hadn't gone away with our press release then. If anything, it was getting worse.

Near where I stood now, rows of people hid in the shadows of the buildings, staying out of the desert sun. They all watched the derm screens over their wrists, keeping in their own bubbles. Further ahead, there was movement on the streets. People gathered in the middle of the road. Were they marching?

To the side of me I heard someone say 'turn it up, I want to hear.'

It was two young jack-ins, a girl and a boy, Caucasian, dirty blonde hair. They looked like brother and sister maybe. The girl grabbed the boy's arm, angling for a closer look at his wrist comm. I heard the snippet of a familiar voice: Bleesh. All I caught was 'Lilith begged for me to let her live.'

I went closer.

'Hey,' I said. 'Can I see that?'

The blonde boy looked at me with narrowed eyes, but then shrugged a 'why not?' and shuffled over so I could watch.

It was that same disgusting troll. This time he was alone though. No other crowd of contenders.

'I am Switch reborn,' he said. 'I unleashed my mighty power on Lilith and she died in virtual as I watched. The police say these are physical murders. As if I would risk getting so close to a diseased slut like Lilith. The Specter Slayer is back. This is what Switch's new avatar looks like. I have escaped. Be afraid. Be very afraid.'

'This is bullshit, Johnny,' the girl said to her brother. 'That dick weed is full of hot air. Turn on Chance Bradley.'

'He's a truth teller is what he is, Betty,' Johnny Blonde said. 'Why do you think I dragged you out here. We're in danger. Chance Bradley is a fake. He doesn't ever go on at the same time as Bleesh anyway. He knows it would crush his view stats.'

Johnny's sister grabbed his arm.

'Come awn! Swipe it over, I'm sure he'll be on.'

They struggled for a few moments before Betty managed to get her fingers on his arm. I stepped back to avoid being jostled, thinking maybe I should move on. Then a handsome, all-American quarterback came onto the screen. Was this Chance Bradley? He cleared his throat. The name appearing below him confirmed that it was the vlog caster I'd heard about from the other jack-in the night before.

'I'm deeply saddened and angered by the death of Lilith Lace,' he said. 'Shame on the hate-mongers saying she deserved it. Lilith was a beautiful mind with a vision for the future. She wanted safety and freedom of expression. But do you know what I want now? I want justice. Justice for all. Justice for Lilith Lace. If you're out on the streets, I hope you're as angry as me. I hope you're making your voice heard. Vote for Rommel's Holos Crime bill with your wallets. Scream justice for Lilith with your fists. It's time the police did something about these murders, before more of us die. Switch is back, that much is certain. We need to kill her and get justice for Lilith! Justice for all!'

A loud bang made all of us turn toward the Strip. There were more people out there now. It looked like they were arguing with each other. I had to go and see. I hit a sprint down the road. The crowd got thicker with each step, but I wove through them as best I could. The hub of activity was further up. A group of jack-ins struggled with something on the sidewalk. There was another bang that sounded like metal being kicked. Someone cheered and I realized they'd just ripped a public trashcan free of its frame. A tall male wearing all black raised it above his head and started running toward a building.

'Justice For Lilith! Justice For All!' he yelled.

He threw. The projectile slammed against the front windows of the building. I noticed it was the Bolodair apartments where Rama was killed.

The chant was picked up by some around me.

'Justice for Lilith! Justice for all!'

Others were rallying into other groups, pushing against those who started the chant.

'Anonymity!' one of them yelled.

'Freedom!' another chimed in.

'Fulfillment!' another half dozen finished.

That was Fukami's slogan, a rallying cry against Rommel's 'justice for all'. I could feel the unhealthy tension in the air. Someone knocked me from the side. The press of flesh and bodies closed in. It was stifling. I felt my anxiety rising. Pandemic protocols prohibited people gathering on the streets in groups of more than fifty. This was way more than that. Way more. And there was no sense of personal space. People started shouting at each other, growling for the others to step back. No one did. A fist flew and connected with a man's nose next to me. His blood sprayed and he crumpled to the sidewalk. I heard the shattering of glass from somewhere. More bangs and shouts as makeshift missiles were picked off the ground and hurled at the buildings. At least they weren't being aimed at people. Yet.

'Justice for Rama!' an Indian woman shrilled in my ear.

I grasped for my Taser gun. It was there, holstered under my arm where I always kept it. But what was I going to do? Zap someone with it? Then what? The mob would tear me apart. Not for the first time, I wished I was allowed to carry a proper gun. The noise alone from one shot of a Colt 1911 would be enough to scatter these people.

'Fuck justice!' someone shouted.

'Fuck you!' someone said.

'Justice For Lilith!' echoed up again between crashes. 'Kill Switch!'

Anger grew hot inside me. Kill Switch? If only it was that easy. We'd have executed her years ago if there was a way. Even if we did that now, it would just leave more questions. That troll wasn't Switch. I knew it. But who was it? And, were they really the killer? We had to find Corpus. If we did, we'd be able to solve this thing. Find Corpus. I knew what I had to do. It was that simple. I needed to get over my fear of the Holos. I needed to go through it. I needed to jack in.

But first, I needed to get out of this riot.

15

I clattered into the station, covered in sweat and flecks of blood. I'd managed to claw my way out of the crowd just as the riot police had shown up. They fired pacifying gas into the crowd. It didn't do much. The place was a frenzy of fear and loathing.

More cops streamed out of the front of the station now. It was all hands on deck. Mendez was in the foyer barking orders at people. Then she saw me.

'Byron,' she said. 'Wash up and suit up right now. Agent Joon has arranged all your jack-in gear.'

The comment threw me off. 'But…' I started.

'No buts,' she said. 'Unless you're going to tell me you found this murderer on your lunch break. Eyes on the prize. You need to get inside and get this cancer at its roots. I'll sort out the streets. I'm trusting you to do the rest.'

I looked down at myself. I was trembling. I had to go from this to the Holos? At least it couldn't be much worse. At least it was all fake, not like the real chaos out there. Switch was locked away. I couldn't be killed in VR. That's what I repeated over and over in my head anyway.

'Byron. You can do this,' Mendez said firmly but not unkindly.

Her vote of confidence was enough to get me moving. I could close my eyes all I wanted, but the virtual world was literally spilling out in my streets and breaking them apart. I couldn't ignore that. I hit the showers, put my clothes on, and went to find Agent Joon. Every instinct now thundered in me that if we found Corpus this whole thing would unravel.

Joon was in jack-in room six, waiting. We might not have jurisdiction in the Holos, but so many crimes touched both worlds that it was common for cops to go in and gather intelligence. Cops that weren't me anyway. Joon would be our team lead in the Holos. Having him as a companion was zero comfort though. As if an emo teenager could protect anyone if things went dark. He'd probably roll up in a corner and ask someone to bring his hug toy. Of course, I'd already be in that corner too, so at least he'd make me look like less of a wimp. Sometimes that's all you can ask for in a partner.

He stood in the room with the type of confidence only the really young can muster—cocksure and balls out. He threw me a flimsy suit. 'Put that on,' he ordered.

I didn't appreciate the tone, or what the suit implied. 'I'm not going in synced,' I said.

'I'm not expecting you to,' he answered. 'That full-body rig simply helps your stock avatar feel like something approaching real. It'll reinforce the experience of your optoacoustic neural stimulation rig without you needing to go total sync like me.'

'You're not syncing, are you?'

He screwed up his nose. 'Why wouldn't I? It's perfectly safe.'

'Tell that to the people who have been kidnapped inside their avatars and can't get out,' I said. 'Tell that to all the refugees out there on the street! Synced-in means locked in.'

'Only if you're stupid enough to be immersed somewhere with no outside help,' he said. 'We both know Switch isn't back. No one can do what she did. This killer has chosen wisely. Only anonymous jack-ins with few real-world contacts are in danger of being trapped like that. If I get taken, I simply activate a distress signal and a support team puts me into anesthetic sleep and pulls me out. It's not like digital confinement with the advanced deep brain simulation to stop that. No harm, no foul. We're in a police station. Half the people here are trained to do it.'

He said it so matter-of-factly it was like he'd been extracted before. He probably had. Being manually jacked out that way wasn't that uncommon apparently. You were supposed to tell friends when you were going in synced. *If* you had real-world friends. The Holos experience was so much sharper than unsynced virtual that not many went in the old way any more, precautions or not. Still, there was no way I was linking my body and mind rhythms with a digital avatar ever again. No. Fingerlicking. Chance.

'Why don't you have a suit?' I asked, trying to stall.

'I don't need one with this,' he tapped his skull cap. 'I'll feel everything in real time at hyperspeed. It's even better than the neuro helmets to generate sensory experience. But I need you to have at least a reasonable reaction time too if we're going to be partners.'

'I'm not going in synced,' I repeated.

'I'm not asking you to,' he said again, like he was talking to a simpleton. 'I'm just asking you to wear proper headgear and haptics. Stock police avatars don't have syncing functions anyway, so you don't even have the choice there. They're also tracked with coded homing beacons so you can't lose them inside. The police department are cheap like that. You're safe. Really. We're being watched.'

He pointed up at the 24/7 camera that was jacked into a public feed. It recorded everything that happened in the jack-in room, just no sound. Something about police transparency for use of public funds. I normally wouldn't like the intrusion. It did actually settle my nerves now.

'I'm fine with cheap avatars,' I said, handing back his fancy suit. 'I'm also happy to just go helmet and harness.'

'I'm not,' he said, passing it back. 'I need to know you can cover me in there as quickly as possible should anything happen. You're enough of a liability as it is without having solid synced reflexes. This is the compromise.'

I was about to throw the thing in his face when Gibson walked in.

'Ready?' he asked. 'Mendez sent me in to make sure, before I get out onto the Strip too.'

I gritted my teeth but nodded. Then I remembered something.

'I saw some footage of that troll, Bleesh, while I was outside,' I said. 'He was claiming responsibility for Lilith's murder—by himself this time.'

'He's lying, obviously,' Gibson said.

'I agree,' I said, 'But can you get Cline to look into it while we're inside? See if Lilith was on Bleesh's hit list of next victims in that first address? I want to scratch him off completely and be justified in doing it. Right?'

'Okay. Good call,' Gibson said gruffly.

I nodded, settled myself, then considered the suit in my hands. I glared at both Gibson and Joon. They stared back. I stared harder.

'What?' Joon asked. 'Put it on.'

'Turn around while I do then,' I pushed.

'Seriously?' he said. 'You're wearing underwear aren't you?'

Gibson jabbed Joon in the side and cleared his throat, prompting Joon to turn around. Gibson did the same, respectfully. Maybe he wasn't such a Neanderthal after all. I was indignant with Joon though. Of course I had underwear on. As if I'd change with the public feed camera on the wall if I didn't. It didn't matter if dozens of people were watching that. I could block them out. Two people right in front of me though. There was no way.

'You'd better be wearing something hygienic,' Joon said from over his shoulder. 'That's my personal back up suit.'

Refusing to let him get to me in front of Gibson, I peeled my clothes off and kitted up. The fabric of the bodysuit was cool to the touch. It slid on easily, then molded around my skin like it was made from gel. It wasn't tight, just perfectly form fitting. A second skin, which made me look like I had nothing on but a silver and black leotard. When I was done, Joon swung around. He looked me up and down appreciably. His eyes almost gave a wolf whistle. I crossed my arms over my chest. He laughed.

'Relax,' he said, 'you're not even close to my type. You are pretty fit for a grandma though.'

'Agent Joon,' Gibson cautioned.

'Sorry,' his eyes went to his feet.

It was good to know at least someone here commanded respect.

Joon grabbed some cables from the Holos stack on the wall. He plugged one into my helmet, then clicked some keys on an interface. I felt my suit hum all over and jumped.

'Calm your tits,' he said. 'I'm just getting the Wi-Fi link in order. We'll keep your helmet wired in as a failsafe, but we won't lose signal here anyway.'

He pulled up a display screen on the stack and flicked across a couple of avatars. 'Man or woman?' he asked.

I'd never even thought about it as an option. The decision had been made for me at birth. To have it asked now was unsettling. 'Woman,' I confirmed.

He selected an avatar from the screen, gave it red hair like mine, then dropped some black jeans and a white t-shirt onto the figure. I wanted to object, but that was what I normally wore off duty, so stayed silent. This little puckerball was profiling me. Despite me doing that to suspects all day everyday, it rankled having assumptions made about your personal choices, even something as simple as fashion.

'I almost forgot,' Gibson said to me as Joon started to link his own setup. 'The report you wanted just came back from the coroner.'

'The potassium?' I asked. This could be something.

'She said those levels are consistent with cell rupture,' Gibson explained. 'It could account for how the victims bled out, but there's no indication of any compounds in the blood or tissue that would set off a massive rupture event like that. It doesn't happen spontaneously.'

Another puzzle. This case was full of them, stacked on top of each other in 3D. At least it was a proper physical explanation, if not a complete one.

'That reminds me,' Joon said, finishing up his routine. 'Which folder is all the security footage from our crime scenes logged in? I want to run it by an expert I know. She's on the way to where we're going in the Holos.'

'Is she a verified police subcontractor?' Gibson asked. 'We can't risk any more media beat ups.'

'An FBI contractor,' Joon said straight faced, but maybe too quickly.

I narrowed my eyes at him but didn't say anything. I'd need to start trusting him if we were to support and protect each other in the Holos. The cliché of FBI and police battling over jurisdictions was a stupid one. I didn't want to be a cliché, I wanted to be an exception. A competent part of the squad. Calling Joon out in front of my unit lead didn't exactly promote team spirit. We could tease each other all we liked, but being a rat never passed muster.

'I'll grant you file access once you're jacked in,' Gibson said finally.

'Right,' I clapped once. 'I'm ready.'

'Are you?' Joon asked with a crooked smile. 'Are you really?'

With that, he hit a button on the wall and all went black.

16

I expected bright lights and fireworks. Instead, I stood in the same bland jack-in room I was supposed to have left. Joon must have messed it up. I turned to tell him so and stopped. Gibson was gone. So was Joon. In his place was an androgynous warrior. Neither clearly male or female, it was muscled like a prize sprinter—cheetah and human rolled into one. Metallic, rainbow tattoos swirled up each of its arms and the sides of its neck. I recognized traces of Joon's features in the face. Broad forehead, high cheekbones, prominent jawline, but he wasn't distinctly Korean or any ethnicity. Silver hair framed everything perfectly. My knowledge of who was driving the avatar formed the It into a Him. Strange how our minds do that, need to do it sometimes—put people in boxes so we can feel the calm of certainty instead of the chaos of maybes.

'Save your surprise,' Joon said. 'I'm a mere star in a galaxy of interest. We're about to enter The Arterial.'

I realized my mouth was hanging open, so closed it. 'Why this?' I said, indicating his avatar.

He looked down at himself and smiled. 'This is the real me, unburdened by meat baggage.'

'But it's not the real you, is it? It's who you'd like to be.'

His face turned dark, angry even. 'That's the big difference with the Holos,' he said. 'The real appeal. You get to make all of your choices here. You don't just have them thrust upon you by biology.'

'You can't escape biology. It's in us. Is us.'

'Have you been briefed on The Stockholm Effect?' Joon asked, changing the subject.

I nodded. 'Jazlin Switch coined the term and the tech,' I said. 'Her biggest curse on the Holos was inventing synced avatars.'

'That's right. I forget she brought things other than murder to our world,' Joon said.

'People think she somehow amplified the effect to do her killing,' I said. 'She was the first to realize that your mind can take your body hostage after being synced, hence Stockholm Effect. You're a willing participant in the abduction of your senses.'

'It's more than that,' Joon said. 'Even if you're not synced there's some effects. Some glitches if you're hurt or ripped from your avatar unwillingly.'

'I know,' I said.

'Yes, but do you really know?' he said, moving toward the door. 'Have you experienced it?'

I hadn't really. I wasn't actually hurt the one time I went in years ago. Physically at least. I pushed those thoughts back down. 'I'll pretend I know nothing then,' I said, trying to open myself up to learning.

'Shouldn't be too hard,' he said, and opened the door.

Neon light flooded the room. Noise hummed in just behind. I shakily stepped off the run disk at my feet. Was it moving in the real world? It had to be.

'Just trust the illusion,' Joon said. 'You'll be fine.'

He reached out a hand to steady me but I pushed it away, stepping alongside him. My body felt almost my own but not quite, like I was moving inside a code puppet. I could tell this was an illusion, albeit a very compelling one. I supposed that was the difference between being unsynced and synced. This felt fairly real, just not absolutely perfect. My movements were slightly uncoordinated, like the split-second lag between my movement outside and inside kept everything out of touch.

'Ready?' Joon asked.

Without waiting, I stepped beyond our room. The whirl of colors, sounds and smells hit me like a wall. It was totally different from what I remembered. The Holos had made years of upgrades since. It was like comparing a country town to Time Square. This place was a mix between the real and the dreamlike. On the sidewalk, a six-armed chef worked in a glass kitchen. He tossed vegetables, noodles and some other strange ingredients in a wok. The cuisine smelt like the ocean with an undertone of smoke and herbs. Vehicles of all kinds zipped along a main road. Odd characters streamed along the sidewalk. There was a man with a swirling black hole in the center of his face and tentacles for eyes. There was a seven-foot tall Amazon with heart-shaped grenades strapped across her chest. A group of babies the size of adults strutted past with the gait of runway models. Despite plenty of jack-ins being outside, there were many, many more in here. Their home. The current riot on the Strip would look like a pillow fight compared with what would happen if everyone here left.

Every single avatar on the street had some kind of flourish to their outfit—a splash of color, a metallic hue to tattoos, weapons worn out in the open, as much for ornamentation as for protection. Nothing was normal but it was all very real. Glass lifts dotted the sidewalk at perfect intervals, like shiny lozenges being spat into the air at regurgitator speed. Level after level stretched up, disappearing into a clear twilight sky strewn with hues of purple and orange. Joon stepped past me and started walking. I had no choice but to follow.

'It's not too far,' he said. 'I jacked us in as close as I could.'

'Couldn't you just beam us right there?' I asked.

'Right,' he said. 'I'll pretend you know nothing because you don't. Jack in and out locations are all on the ground floor of the Arterial,' Joon said, bringing my attention back to him. 'We can't just beam anywhere. It would ruin the illusion of reality. That all changed a good five years ago because too many people where just dropping into the place out of nowhere. It became untenable, so Fukami fixed it.'

I vaguely recalled that being headline news at the time but couldn't be sure. I looked around and saw that every building here was two-story. The first floor had rows and rows of jack-in stations—like catacomb holes in the walls. People streamed in and out of them non-stop. Above and between that, all kinds of shop fronts were jammed in without rhyme or reason.

Right then, a man with penises for arms stepped in front of me. Definitely not what I was expecting. He held an appendage up and ejaculated a light show into the air like some kind of fapcracker. Inside the strobe was an image of my avatar writhing and dancing among naked bodies, pure ecstasy on my face. Reality? Right.

'Want an experience you'll never forget? Level Two, Sub Floor Six. LoveDeath Nightclub.'

Before I could reply, Cock Arms went onto the next person. He was a moving ad, the Holosian equivalent of those pizza guys who stand on real street corners and twirl their signs.

A woman with rows of spikes up the bridge of her nose bumped me as she walked past. She hissed. I looked back and she flipped her middle finger up. The spikes worked right up her bald head in a Mohawk and down her naked spine.

'I assume you know how the Holos was built?' Joon asked bringing my attention back.

'Ah,' I racked my brain for the knowledge. 'Filton Fukami invented it by stacking all the other virtual reality platforms together.'

'Correct,' Joon said, pleased that I at least had some sense of history. 'That was the genius of Fukami, connecting all the existing virtual worlds of the metaverse into one Holos through this Arterial network. People could build their own places onto the open blockchain as part of the growing space. Low barrier of entry was key. More importantly, it meant people didn't have to change avatars between games or worlds. We could take our identity, and everything that came with that, anywhere we wanted. You could build a proper life and reputation and interact with others anywhere in the metaverse as a unified being. The more people who came in, the more social it became. Eventually it snowballed until it was the place to be. And this is *the* place in *the* place.'

Now that I thought about this as a connecting world, it started to make sense. The levels. The doorways. The walking billboards. The eclectic mix of shops. Gateways to fantasies and realities mixed into one. There was a certain logic to it, human made in every way.

A drumbeat caught my attention. Up the street, it looked like some kind of parade was coming our way. People carried signs at the front. They were chanting. Other people stopped and looked their way. Joon let off a low growl in his throat. A short Filipina woman next to us spat on the ground.

'They want to protest they should go to the Politisphere,' she said.

The group was closer now. I could read the signs, see their faces. They were religious folk by their dress—Hindu, Buddhist, Christian, Muslim, Jew, together, chanting.

'Sin is sin!' they said.

'Rape is rape. Murder is murder!' a priest with a megaphone shouted at their head. 'Bring morality and law to the Holos. Invest in Rommel's bill! Justice for all!'

I could sense people gathering behind me. They muttered to each other angrily. Apparently this wasn't the place to be making this kind of scene. Cock Arms from before stepped right up into the leading priest's face.

'Sin this!' he shouted and blasted a liquid lightshow all over him.

The protesters dropped their signs and pulled weapons. I was almost pushed off my feet as people behind us ran onto the street, ready to join the fight. Swords, guns, all sorts of lethal accessories emerged.

'Come on,' Joon said calmly like it was all nothing, 'this is our elevator.' He indicated glass doors opening right near us.

'But,' I started, watching the violent energy on the street—a ramped up version of the riot I'd just left outside. No one had drawn first blood yet, but the standoff was gathering tension.

'But nothing,' he said. 'There are no laws here. People enforce the norms they want as they see fit. We're on a case.'

'But it's anarchy,' I said.

'It's freedom,' he corrected, and ushered me into the elevator.

The doors closed off the noise outside just as a gun blast rang out. Our lift was packed with people, all looking impassively forward, not paying attention to what was happening outside or to each other. It was just like a regular lift in the real world, except it had multiple other doors right around its heptagonal shape.

'It's normally more peaceful on ground level,' Joon said, hitting a floor button that had a high-heeled shoe icon on it. 'The Holos Crime bill and the killings have made the whole place a tinderbox. Everyone's ready to flare up. Not that outside is any better right now.'

'Why don't they just stay in unsynced for safety if they're worried?' I said. 'Problem solved, in and out.'

'Yeah right,' Joon scoffed.

'What?' I asked.

'These people have built entire lives in here. It's their reality. You'd be asking them to pull back the curtain and have them feel like their lives are just imitations.'

'But they *are* just imitations,' I said.

Joon flexed his jaw. I could tell it was a visible effort for him not to shout at me.

'Life here is real if you make it so,' he said. 'If all your friends, all your possessions, all your experiences and all your memories are formed here, what else is there? Tell me, does this place feel real to you?'

I looked around. Rubbed my fingers on the lift wall.

'Not quite,' I said. 'It's close, but even putting aside all the weird people and architecture, I can tell it's fake. I don't feel... right.'

Joon nodded.

'That's because you're unsynced. Imagine feeling like that in the place you grew up, in your home, at work. You'd question everything about your life and who you are, every minute of the day. Reduce your sense of meaning.'

'But this place isn't real,' I repeated. 'It's all constructed.'

'In many ways that's the most real thing you can ever do,' Joon insisted, 'build your own life through your own choices. Create something where your identity isn't forced on you randomly. People would rather risk death here or go out into an uncertain world than have their entire existence shaken to its foundation like you're suggesting.'

He was sounding dangerously like Jazlin Switch. She said something similar in her Hyperrealist's Manifesto. That a life where you had true free will went beyond what we've ever been able to achieve before. Joon didn't parrot the words, but the sentiment was the same. She was insidious, that woman, seeping into everything she touched. I didn't blame Joon for that, but I was getting angry. I needed to settle. This wasn't the place to lose my shit. It was too public. I looked around instead, fixating on the glowing display on the lift wall. Joon noticed me staring at it. The buttons were in some wild grid. There was a pattern, I was sure, but I couldn't get it.

'Seven levels split into seven realms,' he explained. 'Then seven sub realms after that and so on.'

I must have looked confused, so he continued: 'We've just come from the jack-in level, which has ports to the real world and a few bars and shops for those who want to just come in and out quickly. Of course prices there are ridiculous too because real estate and rents are so expensive. Level two is sex. That's the core of Holos business still. Games where you try not to cum, fantasy lands where you level up in attraction to players, and free-for-all dens of dark desire.'

He indicated a row with various icons. 'Shooting, hunting and virtual murder is level three, with all its sub-realms that spin off deeper into the Holos.'

We paused on level three. Several of the inner doors opened and people streamed in and out. One guy was a zombie with half his head missing. He pushed a random button and stared ahead, drooling blood.

Joon continued without missing a beat. 'On level four there's Medieval World with dragons and all that shit, plus portals to the wider galaxy of space operas, and so on. Alternative universes, basically. We're heading to Mall and Media on five. The Politisphere is on six.'

'And seven?' I asked, indicating the top level.

'Heaven,' he said.

'Which one?' I asked, remembering all the different religious people in the protest.

'All of them,' Joon said. 'Plus all the Hells in different sub-stacks. Sickest part of the Holos if you ask me. I never go there.'

A new group of avatars flooded off the elevator at level four. More flooded on. A tall, bearded man watched me. He had black eyes and pointed teeth. He sneered at me.

'Narc,' he said.

'Excuse me?' I asked, angry.

'You don't belong here, cop,' he said and grabbed my shirt. 'Law has no place for the free.'

Before I could even react, Joon stepped in. His fingers pressed against the man's throat. They sharpened and glowed orange. I could see code swirling inside them. The man noticed too, holding his hands up. They shook with fear.

'Relax, lover,' Joon said softly to him. 'She's with me.'

The man stepped back without another word, his eyes dipping to the floor. An uneasy silence filled the space then the main lift doors jumped open.

'This is us,' Joon said happily as if nothing had happened. 'Time to go shopping.'

17

Corpus hung from the roof, his feet nailed directly to the rafters. Blood flowed down his bare legs. He knew it was virtual torture, but still, it was agony. He should have expected it would be every bit as bad as this. He'd programmed the very first synced avatars with Switch, but knowing exactly how they worked did nothing to combat the affects. He was as much a slave to the code as everyone else. Felt everything. Couldn't escape unless he went through a proper jack out process.

The Spider sharpened his knives. He made a show of it, as if they actually needed sharpening. He took out a blowtorch and started heating one of the blades up.

'You're not very original,' Corpus said through gritted teeth. 'You should think of more interesting methods.'

The Spider looked up. Tilted his head.

'Oh, I will,' he said. 'The drawback of there being nothing personal listed about you online is that I couldn't create your worst fears right away. The positive is, we'll get to discover them together.'

The Spider held up a knife and rammed it into Corpus's knee. White-hot pain lanced through his avatar into his real-world body—the Stockholm Effect synced and strong. Corpus gasped. Fought it off. Steadied his mind. Blinked. This wasn't doing flesh damage, but damn it hurt.

'I'll never tell you where I am,' Corpus hissed.

'You won't need to,' the Spider said. 'I have a trace for that. But I do need you to tell me where *it* is. Where have you hidden the file?'

So this Spider did know, had found out.

'Rama told me before he died,' the Spider said. 'He pleaded in the end. Told me he'd given it to you to break into and discover its secrets. Normally, I wouldn't attack an advocate of a free world like you, but you give me no choice.'

The Spider pulled out the knife slowly. Corpus felt every inch of it move over his muscles on the way out—the jagged edge sawing away. He flexed against the pain. Breathed.

'Even if you find the file, you won't unlock it,' Corpus gasped. 'I've made sure of that.'

A gurgle bubbled up from the Spider's mouth. A laugh?

'I don't want to open it,' the Spider said. 'I want to bury it. Right after I bury you.'

He stabbed the knife into Corpus's other knee. The hacker jolted. Spasmed with the impact. The pain was intense, and this was only the beginning.

I deserve this. Corpus thought. *I deserve this. I helped create this reality. I failed to keep my family safe.*

Maybe if he kept telling himself that over and over again, he might get through it. It might give some purpose to this suffering, instead of just pure, unadulterated pain.

18

Joon held his arms wide as he walked down the broad boulevard. Buildings towered around us. Familiar billboards sat on top. A blue bird. A big white F. A fluorescent camera. A little white ghost. Companies with decades of online heritage. Content storms circled over each of their headquarters with images and words and stories in the sky. Each info storm spiraled out toward one central building in the middle—The Feed, everyone's personally curated news scroll, aggregated from every other platform. There were also strips of designer stores running off the main road. Hundreds of them. And people. Thousands of them. I struggled to keep up, wanting to see everything, note everything, have everything explained. My curiosity was overwhelming the fear that lingered below the surface.

'How did that guy in the lift know I was a cop?' I asked.

'You're in a stock avatar,' Joon said without slowing down. 'Only newbs, anonymity extremists, and government use them. Your personal presence is too tough to be a newb I guess, even if you are one.'

'Well I'm certainly not an anonymity extremist,' I said. 'Those nut bars are crazy.'

Joon looked at me sideways.

'Why do you think that?' he asked, still walking.

'They're paranoid. The whole 'Great Reboot' was a sham. A way for criminals to cover their tracks. It's made our job so much harder finding the real bad guys. And don't even get me started on SureCoin. It's all a tax dodge.'

'Do you realize you sound like an extremist on the other end?' Joon said. 'Do you really think we should be able to look into anyone's private affairs and see what they're up to?'

'I don't have anything to hide,' I said. 'Do you?'

Joon shook his head in disbelief.

'It's not about having anything to hide. If people know your identity and your wants and needs they can manipulate you. Hackers fought for anonymity because big data on our private lives was a weapon for control.'

I snorted. 'So the Great Reboot was about making sure marketers can't sell you stuff you don't need?' I countered. 'Give me a break. Look at where we are.' I swept my arms to indicate all the fashion and advertising and media giants on display. 'The reboot did nothing to stop consumerism. It's part of human nature to want more stuff.'

Joon stopped walking, so I did too.

'You're totally missing the point,' he said. 'It's not about advertising. It's about manipulation of your actions. Look, if people know exactly who you are, they know exactly how you'll act. The closer they get to the truth of you, the closer they get to using what they know to totally control you. That's what being anonymous is about. Freedom.'

'Is that why you chose an avatar that isn't clearly man or woman, or any particular race? Because you don't want to be manipulated?' I said.

'Exactly,' Joon said, thinking I was getting it.

'That's horse shit,' I said. 'If you don't stand for something, you'll fall for anything.'

'Even if you stand for things with no real meaning to them?' Joon countered. 'Ridiculous.'

'You think I'm ridiculous for having pride in being a woman?' I asked. 'That being a woman has no meaning?'

'Not in itself,' he said point blank. 'Being a woman has no more or less value than being a man, just like being white doesn't have any more value or less value than being Korean, or black, or brown, or whatever. They're valueless. You shouldn't feel pride or shame at being one or the other. Why should I identify with any of that?'

'You identify with nothing?' I said. 'Then you are nothing.'

'Not at all,' he said. 'I identify with being honest, with being fair. I identify with being open. They have meaning. Those are *actual* values that should set the foundations for culture, not just physical traits. Being a 'jack-in' doesn't have value either. Freedom has value, maybe the most of all.'

'Freedom to kill and rape others virtually without any consequences?' I countered.

'No, not that,' Joon said. 'But that's why we have cultural norms. Why we need to help foster better ones in the Holos to create a better world here.'

'Well maybe justice has more value then,' I said. 'The law.'

'The law and justice aren't the same thing,' Joon said. 'As a cop, you should know that.'

I threw my hands up in the air in exasperation. This dundernubbin was playing word games now. 'Where are we going?' I asked, sick of arguing.

'To get our security footage analyzed by the best in the business,' he said flatly.

Before I could ask another question, someone down the road screamed. It was a tall woman with a masculine face. She pointed, yelling blue murder. Someone bolted through the crowd, away from her, towards us. A handbag was clutched in his hand. Handbag theft? Surely that didn't happen here. I moved to step forward but Joon stopped me.

'Don't give me that no laws shit,' I said. 'How about common decency?'

'It's fine,' he said.

The bag snatcher sprinted our way. He had an electrified baton in the other hand, waving it as he ran with disjointed movements. People stepped aside. His victim now gave chase. Joon swept me back so we were out of the way. Damn his avatar was strong. I tried to push forward again. Joon was going to do nothing! This wasn't right.

But just as the thief ran past, Joon held out an arm. He coat-hangered the guy right off his feet. The thief landed on his back with a thud. Virtual air wheezed out of his lungs. Joon planted a foot on his chest and put his fingers to the man's throat. They glowed again. The points. The swirling code inside.

'Drop the bag,' Joon said.

The man let it fall slack to the side. Then Joon stabbed his hand into the guy's chest. The avatar screamed. He glowed molten orange and oozed away, a puddle of goo on the pavement that evaporated into steam. Gone.

I stood, shocked. Others started clapping and cheering at the display. Justice done. The thief's victim arrived, panting. She scooped up the handbag and clutched it to her chest.

'Oh thank you, thank you, thank you,' she said, a towering giant of hairspray, fishnet stockings and bodybuilder brawn.

'Hold your valuables closer next time,' Joon said, and started walking again.

The crowd parted for us like the sea for Moses. Whispers followed at what Joon had just done. Avatar murder. How? Who was he?

'Hey!' I said, catching up. 'You just killed that guy! Weren't you just talking about better cultural norms?'

He barely turned his head. 'That's right. Stopping people from doing the wrong thing. That kind of scum has avatars to burn. Judging by his uncoordinated movements, he was unsynced too. It was nothing.'

'All for a virtual handbag?' I said.

'That wasn't just a handbag,' he said. 'Didn't you see the checkmark on the side?'

I had, it was purple. 'Yeah, so?'

'So that was an original Galatea,' he said. 'Uncopyable. One of a kind, verified by immutable blockchain code. It's worth more than most of the avatars on this strip.'

'You're kidding?' I said, looking back, thinking not for the first time that people are fingerlicking strange.

Then I noticed something on Joon's forearm, something I hadn't seen before. A silver check mark woven into his tattoo.

'Is your avatar one of a kind too then?' I said. 'A Galatea?' The name sounded absurd rolling off my tongue.

Joon laughed. 'Oh no, baby.' He flexed his arm and the code inside his checkmark shone. 'One of a kind, yes. But not a Galatea. A Sabi. She makes Galatea look like Digimart.'

Questions filled my head. Where did I start? With something my cop brain needed to know.

'And are those avatar adjustments you have legal?' I said, nodding toward his hand.

'You mean the Blanka Claws?' he said, giving them a flourish.

'Yes.'

'Well, they're not exactly *il*legal,' he said. 'Nothing is, remember? Still, that's Sabi's specialty. Bridging the borders between order and chaos. Finding that middle line to discover true beauty.'

'You sound like you know her,' I said.

'Know her?' he said. 'Who do you think we've come here to see?'

He stopped in front of a building. It looked like a nightclub. The facade was all black with blacked-out windows. A simple circle logo with a jagged line down the middle sat on top. Security guards stood at the front of a roped-off door. Photographers gathered, waiting, watching. Joon went straight to the front of the queue. People in line craned their necks to see. Faces twisted in anger at him pushing in. The security guard just nodded, pulled the rope back and stepped aside. Cameras clicked. People whispered. Joon took my hand and led me in. I didn't even pull away. Not until we got inside.

19

An art gallery. That's all it was. One bored looking receptionist sat behind a counter. This was what all those people were lining up to see?

Cyberpunk and dark fantasy artworks were on display on one wall, Renaissance classics on another. Japanese art and calligraphy took up the main back wall—stunning in its seeming simplicity. This was a nice place sure, but one worth struggling to be seen at?

The bored attendant caught Joon's eye. 'Sabi's in the studio,' was all she said.

She pressed a button and a panel between two paintings in the middle of the far wall slid open. Joon led me through.

Inside was a woman with her back to us. She was tall, lithe, fluid in her movements. She crouched over a lifeless avatar in progress, adding color here and adjusting lines there. Joon stood silently. The place smelled like crushed flowers and the sweet tang of ozone.

'Just a moment, Joon Baby,' Sabi said. 'The Muse has me.'

She swept her left hand along the lifelike creation before her. Fleshy tones came directly from her fingers onto the avatar. Her right hand followed, cleaning up any overshadow and molding parts into smoother shape. The form it took was a petite Pakistani woman with raven hair and light green eyes. When it looked like everything was perfect, Sabi took up a scalpel from the side and sliced an arcing cut down the middle, tearing into her masterpiece. I was shocked. Joon stood transfixed, watching but not reacting. Sabi picked up a tattoo gun and injected shimmering gold ink through the cut. It was like Joon's tattoos but rougher. When she was done, Sabi stood. 'It's beautiful now,' she said, then turned.

Sabi herself was beautiful. Strangely so. Her face was in perfect proportion. Her skin looked like it was made from ancient ceramic. Tiny hairline cracks splintered across her face, filled with spindly gold lines. A large gold vein split her features right down the center as if she'd been broken in two then repaired. Sabi positively beamed at the sight of Joon.

Then her gaze fell on me.

'Oh god, it's hideous!' she said, gagging. She shut her eyes and turned away from me, dry retching again. 'Joon. Why would you bring a Doe clone in here? Why?'

Joon shuffled uncertainly. Anger grew inside me. It wasn't like my avatar reflected my own personality, but having that kind of disgust leveled toward me was galling.

'Sorry, Sabi,' Joon said softly. 'I need a favor,'

Sabi opened one eye and looked at him, seeming in real physical pain. She shielded her field of vision toward me with her hand.

'Of course I'll make her a proper body,' Sabi managed. 'There's enough ugliness in the Holos as it is without that walking around.'

'I don't need a new avatar, thank you,' I said sternly. This had gone on long enough.

'What could be more important?' she gasped, still looking only at Joon.

'I need some footage analyzed,' he said evenly. 'To see if any artists or AIs have tampered with it, scrubbed anyone out.'

'Of course, of course,' she waved her hand like it was nothing. 'After you helped LeeLee it's the least I can do. He's back to his normal self now.'

'That's good to hear.'

'When are you going to join us in a tribody?' she asked, beginning to recover from her shock at seeing me. 'We'll blow the ink right off your sleeves. I promise.'

Joon looked at me sideways and blushed. I'd have to look into what a tribody was later. Something sick no doubt.

'Soon,' Joon said. 'Right now, we're on business.'

Sabi sighed and waved her hand in acceptance. 'Fine, send me the file', she said, 'but only if you do *me* a favor.'

'Anything,' Joon said quickly.

'Take a slip on your way out and cover that abomination you have with you. You can't be seen with it, Joon. I won't allow it.'

Sabi closed her eyes again and continued, 'I'd also like to be able to speak with her next time. Especially if she's your real-world girl.'

'Hey!' I said. 'I'm a woman not a girl, and I don't -'

Joon pinched his fingers together on his right hand and a beep sounded, cutting me off. An arc of blue zapped across the room into Sabi's head. A file transfer? Wow. I'd have to learn that trick.

Sabi turned her back and started studying the avatar she was working on again. The conversation was clearly over. Before I could say anything further, Joon ushered me out of the studio.

'Who was that bitch?' I said when we were back in the gallery. 'I don't care how artistic she is, she needs to learn some manners.'

'Manners?' he said. 'She just offered to give you an avatar slip worth two-million SureCoin for free.'

'What?!' That was more than my year's salary. 'There's no way we're taking it.'

'There's no way we're not,' Joon said. 'She'll be offended and won't help us.'

'Bullshit she wouldn't.'

'Trust me,' Joon soothed. 'I know her. And besides, it'll totally change your appearance. Better than looking like a cop, right? It's not a fully-coded avatar but it'll fit perfectly over the basic foundation you're in now. No one will know the difference but us.'

That made me pause. It wasn't actually a bad idea. The fact that the guy back in the lift had picked me out as a cop so easily was definitely a concern if we wanted to get any intel under the radar. I'd have to pick out the cheapest, most low-key slip this Sabi woman had on offer though. I didn't want to be in her pocket, or draw any undue attention.

20

Everyone was looking at me. Or, rather, at my slip. The silver check mark right between the breasts was framed in a vee of shimmering material that clung to my body like liquid. There were splits up the sides of the thighs, showing off perfectly tanned skin beneath. Everything was free and loose. At least it didn't hinder my already lagged reflexes. I looked like a runway model though, not a cop. Joon had a big, smug smile on his face that I wanted to reverse spin-kick off. Instead, I stewed, keeping pace alongside him as he strode back down the mall boulevard.

'Oh my god, she's wearing a Sabi,' someone gasped as we walked past and into a new lift.

'Undercover my ass,' I said to Joon as the doors closed.

He smirked and pushed a button with an icon of The Whitehouse. I frowned, wondering where we were headed now.

'The Politisphere,' Joon explained at my look. 'Where everyone involved in politics is based. Senator Rommel has an office there, as does Senator Fukami. I mean, *he* has a residence on every level.'

There was awe in Joon's voice. Pure admiration. Another Fukami fanboy then.

'Aren't we investigating Corpus? Why go there?' I said, not wanting to get sidetracked on the subject of Filton Fukami.

I knew if we wanted to pursue him as a suspect, we'd have to have very credible evidence, not just hunches.

'It's not common knowledge, but Corpus has a small office in one of the back alleys.' Joon explained. 'Every hacker sees themself as a political activist deep down.'

'If it's not common knowledge, how do you know about it?' I asked.

'Because it's my job to know,' he said.

The doors of the elevator slid open and a handful of people stepped out with us. It looked like the whole place was fashioned from white marble—streets, buildings, even the signs. It had a regal feel to it.

Pompous. The majority of people wore suits and ties. In front of us was a wide semi-circle of politicians standing on soapboxes giving speeches to nobody, yelling over the people on either side of them. We pushed past, weaving through a crowd. An avatar of Abraham Lincoln dressed in hip-hop regalia stepped up and handed me a leaflet.

'Keep SureCoin our currency, yo' he said. 'Mercury will raise taxes, not crimp crime.'

He was muscled out of the way by an elegant woman in a power suit. Another leaflet was thrust in my hand.

'Invest in Rommel's Holos Crime bill,' she said. 'It's the only way to keep the metaverse safe now that Switch is back.'

I was about to tell her Switch was not back, when another activist stepped in, his own leaflet agenda in hand. I dropped the ones I had and pushed past, Joon right by my side. He paid zero attention to the activists.

'They're like hawkers,' he said. 'Offer no interest and they'll just move onto the next person who gives them eye contact.'

I did as he suggested, only looking forward. It was like magic. Some of them waved leaflets to get my attention, but if I held strong, they'd quickly give up.

Joon took a sharp left down a narrow alley. The shadows along one side gave it a darker feel. Clandestine. We walked for a few minutes then turned down another tighter alley weaving through a maze of streets.

'So what's your deal, Agent Joon?' I asked while we walked.

Joon looked at me sideways. 'What do you want? My biography?'

'You have something to hide?' I asked.

Joon blinked, assessed where we were going and turned another corner. After a few more moments' silence, he spoke. 'My family came to the USA to escape the Unification Wars between North and South Korea,' he said. 'There were twelve of us. We couldn't afford to live in real-world accommodations, so, like most refugees, we took the jack-in option the government offered us. Schooling, playtime, everything was online. I grew up knowing no different.

'We'd all come out of the Holos at night to sleep the "traditional way", as my grandfather called it. Those were some of the closest, most intimate experiences I had with my family—all huddled together in a cube between our harnesses and run disks, below our bunks on the wall. We shared ramen—our only rations other than what our nutrient tubes fed us inside.

'My closest sister, Kwan, hated that real-world time. She couldn't wait to escape back to the Holos. I enjoyed the simplicity—the warmth of my grandfather's hands when he passed us our bowls. Kwan and I would fight over what was real and what wasn't. She had a theory that those times together in our cube were just another simulation. Grandfather would laugh and say it's all the same. He said the synapses in our body have two options: off and on. Yes and no. All of our experiences arise from that complex sequence of yeses and nos, ones and zeros. All existence as we know it is something and nothing, two sides of the same coin. Computers are built on the same system. Binary. So, he said all experience, simulated or not, was just as valid.

'He warned not to give up on the outside though. That if we wanted full lives we had to understand both, just like the Yin and Yang. You can't have one without the other. You couldn't appreciate the freedom of the digital world if you hadn't tasted the constraints of the physical world. Their contrast creates something and gives context. True wonder is at the balance in the middle.

'Kwan thought that was philosophical mumbo jumbo. To her, life was what gave her the most pleasure. She spent less time coming out to eat with us. Would refuse. I didn't blame her. I would only come out once a week and sit for a full day in that tiny cube. I did it so I knew the walls that held us in could be escaped at the push of a button. My real world was inside, experiencing all the wonders our human imagination can create. I built a life more complex and fulfilling in the Holos than the simple one outside.

'Then, one week, I jacked out to have Ramen with grandfather. His hands weren't warm anymore. They were cold. He'd passed over to the other simulation, wherever that is. Kwan was so disconnected from our family and the world by then that it was just another annoyance to come out and say goodbye before they took his body away. Not me though. I woke up from my dream. I finally understood grandfather's words. That our small home gave the big world context. I thought maybe if I could come out and find true balance, half physical, half digital, that there might be deeper meaning to be found.

'The FBI needed jack-in experts who knew the digital world better than most. And so I'm here, seeing if one world can bring good to the other. My passion is helping to bring cyber culture to the physical. To see how it can inform the real world and better people's lives.' Joon swept his arm to indicate our surroundings. 'Maybe part of that is finding the right balance between freedom and justice here.'

I didn't know what to say so stayed silent.

Joon looked up. There were numbers above doorways—the only markings. Joon counted them as he walked, slowing. He stopped in front of a door with a 42 carved into the frame. 'And here we are.'

The door in front of us was slightly ajar, lock broken. The sight put me on edge. Joon was on alert too. He signaled to be quiet, slowly pushing the door open, his coded claws already out.

Inside, someone shuffled through the contents of a desk. A woman. She turned at our movement. Three eyes locked on us: two jade green and a violet one in the middle of her forehead. The reporter, Yu Ying.

'You,' I said. 'We'd like a word.'

No word. She ran straight through a doorway to the side. Papers flew into the air, trailing in her wake. Damn she was fast.

I gave chase. Joon was much faster. He pushed past and rattled down a wood-lined hallway after Ying. She disappeared through another door, slamming it behind her. Joon ploughed through it without stopping. Splinters exploded. I rushed through the space a few seconds after. My stupid avatar couldn't keep pace like Joon's synced version. He was already sprinting to the far corner of the room. He jumped. Ying was on a chair, trying to climb up through a hole in the roof. Joon grabbed her ankle before she could lift herself through. He pulled her down to the ground and she landed with a thump.

There was barely even a struggle. With light-whip speed, Joon twisted her arms behind her back. Held her. Ying squirmed, trying to break free. Joon was too strong. She twisted her neck back to see me approaching.

'Don't kill me,' she said, true fear in her eyes. 'I don't know where it is.'

'Don't know where what is?' I asked, finally catching up. 'We came here looking for Corpus.'

21

Ying sat, shaken. We dragged her back to the office space, explaining again and again we were the police. I had to take off my Sabi slip and show her my stock avatar, then give her a detailed account of our little confrontation at the press conference to convince her. As her realization dawned, she burst into relieved tears and slumped to the ground.

Files were scattered all around the room—paper, disks, memory buttons. Some were in uniform piles. Most were a mess. There had been some kind of struggle. A desk was smashed. A tall statue of a Buddha was snapped in half on the ground. A bookshelf had been broken, its contents half on the floor. I was about to start grilling Yu Ying when the front door swung slowly open. *Odd,* I thought, until I remembered the broken lock. I went back and propped it closed with one of the books that lay on the floor.

'I thought you were him,' Ying said, still rattled. 'Them.' She rested her head in her hands, staring at the ground.

'Who are *they?*' I asked. 'And what did you mean when you said you don't have *it?*'

'One question at a time,' Joon said calmly, crouching in front of the reporter.

I stood back and crossed my arms. Were we really doing a good cop bad cop shtick? I thought that shit went out in the 2020s.

'Who did you think we were?' Joon said.

Ying looked to me, then Joon again. 'I'm not a hundred percent sure,' she said. 'I think there's some kind of wider conspiracy to stop the Holos Crime bill passing. They're trying to muddy the information markets with manipulated media. That's why I'm here. There's supposed to be a file with the names of who's involved. The how and why.'

'How do you know this?' I asked.

'Christos Rama,' Ying said, staring into space now. 'He contacted me before he went missing. Told me he had something huge. He was getting

Corpus to hack the file first as proof. He wanted me as a third party to verify it was real and help spread it. Said it would change the very structure of the Holos once released.'

So that's how she'd gotten the scoop on us when it came to knowing who'd been killed at our crime scene. She'd already been dealing with Rama. It didn't explain the photos she'd gotten though. But, there were more important questions that needed answering.

'How did Rama get this file in the first place?' I pressed.

'He wouldn't say, just that he had it and that it was a conspiracy more about money…'

'…than power.' Joon finished.

A shuffling noise made me turn. No one was there. The door was still closed. Maybe there was a level above this one. It sounded like the noise came from the roof. *Or was I imagining it?* Damn this clunky avatar. Joon and Ying hadn't reacted. They were intent on the task at hand.

'When Rama was found dead,' Ying continued, 'I sent out the word that I wanted to speak privately with Corpus,' she looked around at the messy office. 'Then I got a tip off that he was missing.'

I pursed my lips, remembering the press release and her early exit. 'I thought you'd been tipped off about the Lilith Lace murder.'

'Lilith?' she asked, confused. 'No, I think that could be yet another distraction to throw people off the real story here,' she indicated the room. 'I've been trying to find anything that matches my theory or that looks like the file Rama described. I'm worried it was taken along with Corpus.'

'Your theory?' I asked, my ears pricking up.

She was gathering momentum now. A reporter on the hunt. No longer rattled, but focused.

'That's the weird thing,' she said. 'I think…'

BOOM!

A blast of orange light shot down from the ceiling. It struck Yu Ying in the neck. A web of cracks fanned out rapidly along her skin. Her eyes went wide. She tried to scream. Then her head exploded like shattered glass. A piece hit me, cutting through my skin. Pain lanced up my arm. Confused, I looked up to the source of the blast. Joon did too. There was a shadow moving along the ceiling. Barely a smudge. Then a glow.

'There!' I said.

'Move!' Joon yelled, diving out of the way and pushing me down just as another blast rained down from above.

It slammed into the bookcase, which burst into flames. The smudge dropped from the roof. In the smoke, it had a human shape. I scrambled for a weapon and realized I had nothing. Joon shot past me, his clawed hands up. The figure saw him and ran. It whipped open the door and disappeared onto the street. Joon was after it without pause. I glanced at

Yu Ying, who was in pieces on the floor. She was no use now—we'd have to track her down in the real world ASAP. I quickly took stock of the rest of the office. The fire on the bookshelf had died away, smoking. There was no threat of burning the place down and any evidence along with it.

I made my decision and ran out onto the street after Joon, already way behind. A flurry of movement caught my eye to the left. Joon's avatar disappeared around a corner down the lane. I gave chase, pumping my legs as fast as they'd go with their lag limitations. I ran down the alley and skidded around the corner again. Even stopping felt awkward. There. The back of Joon's foot just disappeared around another bend. They were headed back to the main strip.

I ran too, cutting through the way we'd come. That was the direct way. Maybe I could head them off, even with my handicap. I ran left and right, not catching sight of Joon or our attacker. I hoped I hadn't lost them.

When I burst onto the wide promenade of the Politisphere, it was chaos. People were scattered all over like leaves in a storm. Some were on the ground. Others swung cameras and wrist-comm screens in a single direction. I followed their sightline: Joon. He was sprinting. People ahead of him were being knocked out of the way by an invisible force—the figure. But Joon was gaining.

I ran harder. Joon jumped over bodies in his way. My path was clearer. I managed to narrow the gap a little.

Then the carnage of people toppling over ceased. There were moans on the ground from those who had already been knocked down. No new disturbances though. Joon paused. Scanned left and right. All was still. I caught up to him, panting. He touched his fingers to his temples and narrowed his eyes, then looked around again.

'The lift!' he said, pointing.

Its doors slid open a short distance from us. Joon ran toward it. People inside were shoved onto the street by something. Then a glowing orange formed within. A strobing of light.

The terror of the Specter Slaughter all those years ago pulsed before my eyes. The screams. The blood. My dad. Then back to now. Joon.

'No!' I yelled.

I pushed forward. The glowing got brighter. Joon realized, skidding to a stop. I managed to get within touching distance. BOOM. The blast arced toward us. I hit Joon from behind, pushing him down.

The light hit me directly in the chest. I was sent sprawling backward. The world went hot. Blinding. Agony swept through me. My cells were being pulled apart from the inside out, rupturing one by one.

I tried to scream. No sound. Just a world of pain. Then all went black.

22

Joon struggled off the ground. The stench of sizzling skin and code filled his nostrils. He looked back to Ada—a charred corpse, shattered into pieces. The violence of it rocked him.

He turned to the lift but it was already closed, gone, up or down he didn't know. That ghost would be hopeless to follow now.

Joon stumbled back to Ada. Checked her avatar. He'd never seen anything like it. People had been shot in front of him, stabbed, hung, drawn and quartered. He'd melted people's virtual bodies himself with the weapon Sabi built into his hands. But this? This was something else. His mind was a jumble. Did he rush back to unjack and check on Ada? Or go back to Corpus's office and stay on the case?

People were already crowding around, taking snaps and video of the scene. This was going to be everywhere. He needed to find answers and fast. Ada would be fine. She was unsynced. The Stockholm Effect wouldn't be strong enough to do any real damage, but she would be rattled. He clicked his comm link.

'Officer Ada Byron down in the Holos,' he said. 'Send a tech team to jack-in room 6 now. Check she's okay. I'm still on the case.'

He clicked off the comm, stood up and ran back towards Corpus's office. That file Yu Ying mentioned could be everything. It was something she said could change the Holos forever if released.

He had to get his hands on it, no matter what.

23

Ada's body lurched in her immersion gear. A trail of blood dribbled from her helmet. Her heart monitor on the wall flat lined. The long beep was replaced by alarms. Lights flashed. She convulsed, every muscle spasming.

Techs rushed into the room, running straight for the officer in trouble. They pulled the cables from her helmet to sever all connection to the Holos. Ada's body collapsed.

One of the bigger techs caught her, a dead weight in his arms.

24

Joon crunched into the wreckage of Corpus's office. Smoke wisped across the ceiling, choking up the air. Joon ignored it, knowing it was no threat.

Yu Ying's avatar had crumbled into tiny fragments. They were slowly decaying, like ash burning of its own accord. Joon wondered how she was holding up in the real world. Avatar death was especially rough if you were synced—physically and psychologically. If his own avatar were destroyed like that, Joon would feel like his whole world had been torn away. To him, it was just as real as his flesh and blood meat suit.

Pushing the thought aside, Joon surveyed the office. It was an absolute mess, but he had to find the file. If the Holos was under threat, Joon wanted a hand in helping protect it. It was his true home—he still felt alien and disconnected on the outside. But what was in the file? Ying had suggested it would be names of people involved in a conspiracy, yet she'd also said Rama hadn't explicitly told her what it was.

Where to look? The bookcase? The desk? In the walls? Joon considered. If this file was so important, it should have thick encryption protecting it. That meant bundles of intricate code. Rama had needed Corpus to hack it, so it would be especially complex. Joon tapped the side of his temple with his fingers. He ran through the different fields of vision Sabi had built into his avatar. There was a reason she was the best: no one else could do what she did, no one else knew how to change fields of vision yet. It wasn't like she advertised the option either. Joon had to ask if it could be done.

He clicked over to code mode. It was like wearing infrared goggles in the real world. The vision picked up 'heat' signatures created by intricate code bundles. Normally, that was just avatars. Synced ones especially shone with their framework that fully interacted with brain signals and haptic suits. Smells, sights, sounds, touch, taste—any stimulus could affect body rhythms subtly and feel totally real. Even the smoke fumes in the room were reacting with Joon's avatar now, sending signals back to his emersion rig that his lungs were burning. It took an enormous amount of coding to achieve reality with precision like that. He knew it wasn't truly real, wasn't actually happening. He'd trained his mind for years to be able to compartmentalize that when needed. Most people preferred to give into the illusion, but he wanted to master it. Even after all this time, the full embodiment sensations of a synced avatar were hard to override. Such was the power of the Holos and its perfect reality.

Now though, seeing the architecture of the Holos through Sabi's code, seeing it for what it was, Joon was able to detach easily. Ada's Sabi Slip was still folded on the floor intact. There were no other avatars present. That was good. Seeing that ghost in the lift and the surging of light coming from it had been terrifying. He'd been blinded. Paralyzed. If it hadn't been for Ada...

Nothing on the bookshelf looked out of the ordinary. There were plenty of code bundles but nothing with serious security. In the direction of the desk there were a few things of interest—some deeply encrypted files. Still, they weren't beyond Corpus's talents to hack in a few moments. He'd probably encrypted them himself.

Then Joon saw it: the snapped Buddha statue. One of its eyes shone, looking at Joon from the floor. He picked the statue up, pulling a small, golf ball-sized lump out of the head. Packets and packets of code were woven into it. Joon could see non-replication software. It was a one-off file that could never be copied, much like a Sabi avatar or slip. There were layers and layers of encryption too, so the whole wrap was too thick to see beyond. The thing even felt like a solid weight in his palm. This had to be it—the 'something' that might change the Holos forever.

Joon considered it carefully. There was no way he'd be able to crack this thing himself. No wonder someone had come to Corpus with it. He tucked the file safely in a storage gap beneath his avatar's skin. No one would get their hands on it now. Certainly not the police.

25

I sprayed vomit all over the medic. His reaction was the only silver lining to the situation. He looked like he wanted to be sick himself. He backed up and grimly flicked the muck off his sleeves. After a moment, he pulled out a needle and jabbed it into my arm. Calm rushed through my veins, working its way to my face in the form of a smile. I must have looked a sight—nose bleeding, spew dribbling down my chin, wearing a big dumb grin.

Cords dangled above me. My immersion helmet was tossed to the side. I was still in Joon's haptic suit. Every time I blinked, my dad's death flashed before my eyes. Then my own avatar death blasted into my vision. That ray of light had hit me and torn me apart. Every time I opened my eyes again, the world came into fuzzy focus. The sense of calm from whatever they'd injected me with filtered over me again. I swayed between sheer panic and doe-like serenity. The medics moved to cut the suit off me but I stopped them with an outstretched hand. I didn't care about the suit, but they weren't seeing me in my granny panties and bra. It was laundry day.

'You'll feel disoriented for a few hours at least,' the medic said, flashing a light in my eyes and checking God knows what. 'You'll be wiped out, mentally and physically, for at least a day. The Stockholm Effect is at its peak the first time around. Even if you aren't synced, it's pretty powerful. Considering such a dramatic avatar death, I'd like to put you under for the night.'

'Can't,' I said, putting on a brave front. 'I need to do my laundry.'

Gibson swept into the room. 'She okay?' he asked gruffly.

'Shaken but not stirred,' I said.

Gibson looked to the medic for a real answer.

'She'll be okay eventually,' he said. 'I think a night in the hospital is in order though. With enhanced rest she should be good to go by midday tomorrow.'

'Good. Do it,' he said.

'No, I'm fine,' I said, a big streak of drool dangling from my lip.

I forced my eyes wide. Must not close them. If I did, I would see my dad's death again. My own death. It would mean insanity. 'The case,' I managed. 'We need to stay on it.'

'I'll sedate you now if I have to,' the medic said.

I shut my mouth.

'What happened?' Gibson asked me.

'I got...' I trailed off, '...shot.'

'I saw that part. It's all over the news. You're already being hailed as a hero for saving Agent Min Joon.'

'Really?' My body got warmer again at the thought.

Bliss and disorientation mixed together. That medic had injected me with the good stuff.

Gibson snapped his fingers to get my attention. 'What happened before that?'

I tried to focus. Holding onto a thought was like catching a single snowflake in a blizzard. 'A ghost,' I said. 'A specter killed Yu Ying. She was looking for a file.'

Realizing he wasn't getting anywhere, Gibson went to the Holos stack on the wall. He stabbed two buttons. A crackling sound came into the room from some speakers. Heavy breathing.

'Joon here,' a voice said.

'Agent Joon, it's Gibson. How are you going in there?'

'I'm intact. How's Ada?'

'I'm a hero,' I said.

'You are. Thank you,' Joon's voice echoed around my head.

'Status report,' Gibson cut in.

'We were investigating a location that belongs to the hacker Corpus,' Joon said. 'We found the reporter Yu Ying there.'

'The one who scooped us in the Christos Rama ID?' Gibson asked.

'Yes.'

Joon ran through what happened. The existence of the file. A possible political conspiracy involving money. The mysterious figure that torched Ying's avatar and fled.

'After I lost the suspect, I doubled back to search the office,' Joon said. 'There's nothing here of value. No file. A dead end. I'm on my way to The Feed, where Ying works, to see if we can locate her in the real world. She has valuable information that might lead to a break in who's doing this. She might also be incapacitated after her avatar was killed. Even as a Holos veteran, the Stockholm Effects will be worse than Ada's because Ying was synced.'

'Good. Stay on it,' Gibson said, then paused, thinking. 'So we don't think it's one person anymore? It could be some kind of group?'

'I'm not sure,' Joon said. 'But that spook, whoever it was, has some avatar tech I haven't seen before. It's possible to ghost in the Holos, but code embedded in the system means there's still a narrow blue line around your silhouette. This person didn't have that—they were totally invisible. If they figured a work around it wouldn't have come cheap. They could be funded by someone. A professional hired to copycat Specter Killings and silence supporters of the Holos Crime bill. It's all conjecture right now.'

'Okay,' said Gibson, processing. 'I'll brief the sheriff and Cline. We've been making headway on the murder of Lilith Lace. It's definitely her. No tampering with the security footage has been found though. Cline's also developed a solid file on that troll, Bleesh, who claimed responsibility for the murders. Guess what the second name on his hit list was right after Senator Rommel?'

'Lilith?' Joon asked.

'Exactly,' Gibson nodded. 'We have the location of where Bleesh normally hangs out in the Holos every Friday night too. We'll be preparing for you to go inside and get some info. See if he has any connection with this ghost of yours.'

'Friday is still two days away,' Joon said. 'And we don't even know if Bleesh is actually involved or just taking credit for kicks.'

'The fact he threatened Lilith before she turned up dead is strong circumstantial evidence,' Gibson answered. 'Plus he claimed responsibility for it before anyone else. Him and that Chance Bradley joker are at each other on The Feed. Between them, they're calling for real world riots on both sides of the political aisle.'

I sat on the floor, listening, doing my best to hold onto the flow of the conversation. The medic put a monitor on my neck, looking at his wrist-comm for my vitals.

'Hold on,' Joon said. 'I'm at The Feed headquarters.'

The speaker above clocked the sound of a door opening, followed by the hum of conversation. My mind started to spin with the extra noise. The room started to spin with it.

'Hello,' Joon said to someone. 'I'm with the FBI.'

'More police?' a female voice said in response.

'More?' Joon asked.

'Someone representing the Vegas PD came by not long ago. I gave her Yu Ying's real world address. The officer said she could be in serious danger. Is she okay?'

'Gibson?' Joon said.

'We haven't had anyone in the Holos except for you on this,' he said urgently.

'Give me the address,' Joon snapped to the person he was speaking with in the Holos. 'Now.'

Right then I vomited again all over my already drenched haptic suit. Today wasn't turning out like I'd hoped.

26

Joon walked as quietly as he could into Ada's hospital room. He had no idea if someone as odd as her liked flowers, but he'd brought some anyway. It was the least he could do to say thanks for saving his avatar. His life. He adjusted his germ filter. God he hated hospitals. There could be bacteria on every surface for all he knew. Superbugs evolved to resist antiseptic and antibiotics. He preferred the certainty of the digital world in that respect. You couldn't catch physical viruses there, just memetic ones.

Joon noticed some flowers were already on the bedside table. The note was signed by Cline. He seemed to know Ada, and to like her. It made Joon feel like he was right in getting her flowers too.

Ada was asleep. Without that constant crease between her eyes like she was thinking too hard, she looked quite beautiful. Symmetrical. Natural. Her deep red hair spilled over her pillow like living blood. It reminded Joon of the scene he'd just come from: Yu Ying's unit. Ying was twisted in a heap on the floor, blood still dripping from under her display visor, pooling around her head. Deep scratches were scoured on the sides of her immersion helmet. There was no signed forced entry. Some of her belongings were smashed though and she had bruises up and down her arms. The scan team put it all down to Yu Ying's violent avatar death throes. Joon thought otherwise.

Ada's monitor beeped. She was moving into REM sleep. Her brain scans fluttered with activity. Joon went to the screen and swiped through her physical and mental reports. Things were mostly stable there, aside from the spikes that were flagged as disturbed dream states. Her body rhythms were back to a regular baseline after drug-induced rest. Looking over his shoulder, Joon pulled out a button drive and rested it on the screen. It downloaded the information with a tap of his finger. All done, he turned and took some close up pictures of Ada's face. Footsteps sounded in the hall and conversation followed. Joon calmly sat on a chair next to Ada's bed and waited—the picture of a worried partner.

Sheriff Mendez entered the room, followed closely by another woman that Joon recognized only too well: Senator Rommel. Lieutenant Rommel. The engineer of the war that had displaced Joon's family and so many others. That war had ripped Korea apart before unifying its two shattered halves together again. People only seemed to remember the unification part, thanks to military marketing's catchy name for the event. Joon remembered the other side though. He would always remember.

The stateswoman's face was severe. Her black hair pulled back in a bun showed a few hints of grey. Rommel's power suit was impeccably pressed like a uniform. Just looking at her, Joon knew she had a regimented life. A life of rules she wanted to impose on others. On the Holos. A life he found repugnant. What happened to spontaneity and creativity and the chance to be your own person?

'How's our hero doing?' Senator Rommel asked.

So that's why she'd come—to get the LV Police's latest Feed star on her side. Ada was a PR opportunity to push Rommel's political agenda. By saving Joon's avatar so heroically, Ada had spawned a raft of memes. People had photoshopped a cape and mask on her and remixed the footage to dramatic music.

'She's resting,' Joon said, indicating the monitor.

'We should wake her,' the sheriff said. 'The public are crying out for answers and she's our spokesperson. If we don't show her face soon, the unrest out there will flare up again.'

Joon watched Senator Rommel as the sheriff spoke. These murders certainly weren't doing Rommel's Holos Crime bill campaign any favors. With the police unable to crack the case yet, questions were being raised about how feasible adding a police force to the virtual world was. The bill's odds of success had blown out negatively as a result. Then there was the violence on the real streets. The low crime rates Rommel took so much credit for were also blowing out day by day. How much pressure was Rommel putting on the sheriff to succeed here?

'We've made progress on the case,' Joon said. 'The scene might not have any new clues but Yu Ying's estimated time of death was an hour *after* her avatar was torched in the Holos. That points again toward these being physical murders, not Spectre killings.'

'Does it?' Rommel raised an eyebrow. 'The words '*estimated* time of death' tell a story there. The media is in a frenzy now that one of their own has been killed. They're saying you're grasping and have no solid evidence.'

'That's not true,' Joon protested.

'The shining light is Ada here,' Rommel went on. 'She survived that spectacular blast, so people are starting to gain confidence they're not Specter killings. Still, she was unsynced. We need to find a way to calm things down. It might be worth interviewing Jazlin Switch again. I'm told during the last meeting she offered Detective Byron assistance.'

'In exchange for information about the real world and current events,' Joon said, wondering how the senator had gotten access to the case files. The sheriff had said 'no leaks.' Apparently that didn't apply to her higher ups. 'Do we really want that?' Joon asked.

'If it solves the case, the ends justify the means,' the senator said.

'We're not using the Devil to catch a demon,' Ada said from her bed.

Everyone's attention swung her way. Ada clocked the Senator's presence in the room and nodded with deference.

'How long have you been awake?' Joon asked.

'Long enough,' she said. 'So Yu Ying is dead. Any luck finding Corpus?'

Joon shook his head.

'What about the file?'

'What file?' Rommel asked.

Joon glanced at Sheriff Mendez, who nodded that it was okay to answer. At least the senator hadn't been given *all* the case info just yet.

'Before Ying was taken out in the Holos, she had a theory there was a file hidden at Corpus's office. One that could crack this case open. It was linked to some kind of conspiracy theory.'

'And did you find it?' Rommel asked eagerly.

'No,' Joon said, narrowing his eyes. 'Why?'

Rommel paused. She seemed to consider her options. 'This doesn't leave this room,' she eventually said. 'But I've previously heard intelligence that Corpus may have a secret file detailing how Jazlin Switch managed to carry out her murders.'

'No way,' Ada said. 'I've never heard of something like that, I'd know.'

'It was from a reliable source,' Rommel said.

'What source?' Joon asked.

Rommel didn't answer. Ada watched her closely. The senator was now deep in thought.

'That theory doesn't work with the info we have now,' Ada continued. 'The file we're talking about came from Rama for Corpus to hack.'

'But you found no such file?' Mendez asked Joon again.

'And no leads on finding Corpus,' he confirmed. 'But we're still looking. He's going to be the key.'

Ada sat up straighter in bed, her intense focus coming back. 'The person who killed Ying. Am I right in remembering they got her real world address from The Feed HQ before you?'

'Yes,' Joon confirmed. 'And The Feed had recorded footage of the exchange. Everything in their building is monitored.'

'So we have an avatar of them at least?' Ada asked hopefully.

Joon went silent. His eyes dropped to the floor.

'What?' Ada pressed.

'They were using an avatar exactly like your police-issued one.'

'What?!'

'It's not that unusual,' Joon said. 'That design is just a standard shell. Easily available, so easy to copy. Whoever it was would have changed into that avatar before going to The Feed's office. That's why reception thought the person was police.'

Ada fell still, thinking.

'So we have nothing on them then?' Rommel snapped. 'And you're still balking at the idea of interviewing Switch again to see if she might be able to give you more information?'

'Why would she help us find Corpus?' Joon snapped back. 'She's said publicly she wants him dead.'

Ada shifted uncomfortably in her bed. She shook her head, as if clearing it of a bad idea. Joon noticed.

'What is it?' he asked.

'Nothing,' Ada said after a pause, 'What about the troll, Bleesh? How's that lead going?'

Joon appraised Ada again. She was sluggish in her manner, but seemed as sharp as ever mentally, recalling the exchange at The Feed and now leaping to Bleesh. How she had these angles covered was beyond him.

'You already know he claimed responsibility for Lilith's death,' Joon said. 'He was also the only one who listed her right behind the Senator as a target in his initial speech.'

Senator Rommel's eyes flicked up at that, surprised. She was about to speak when Joon continued.

'We have no real-world ID on him, but we're going into the Holos tomorrow night to a virtual club he frequents. See if we can lock him down and get some info.'

Silence permeated the room. It felt like there were options to follow but no momentum to the case. Rommel wasn't happy. The sheriff wasn't happy. Joon could feel the pressure of making something happen. Perhaps it was a viable avenue to speak with Switch again. He was curious to meet her in person. A founder of the Holos. She was dangerous though; you didn't go down risky paths unless the reward was worth it.

'Okay,' Ada said, pulling the attention of the room back to her again. 'Let's recap what we know.' She held up her fingers and began ticking off items systematically as she went. 'This has to be politically motivated to keep laws out of the Holos. Christos Rama is dead. He supported Senator Rommel's bill fully. Anyone else supporting the bill, including Rommel herself, has been threatened. Corpus has been kidnapped, and while he didn't support the bill, he was the first real figure to suggest some laws in the Holos. One snag is that Lilith is dead and she didn't openly support the bill.'

'I wouldn't say that,' Rommel cut in.

'Why?' Joon and Ada asked together.

'I'd been speaking with her privately online about joining the campaign. She'd been writing emails to both Fukami and me, asking us to draft a new policy that suits both of us.'

'Why didn't you tell us this?' Joon asked.

'I'm telling you now,' Rommel said, annoyed. 'We were negotiating the finer points of her involvement. She wanted to keep the laws but also keep SureCoin as the currency.'

'Why?' Sheriff Mendez asked.

'Because it can't be traced and she believed it would help protect people's anonymity in the Holos. I explained the importance of a traceable currency like Mercury to help track down criminals.'

'And make charging tax easier,' Joon said.

The sheriff silenced him with a dark glance. Rommel folded her arms across her chest.

'We were making headway with Lilith,' Rommel said. 'She was coming around, but wanted more information. It felt like she might join our campaign.'

'Okay,' Ada said. 'So possibly two of your supporters have been killed. Then there's Yu Ying. She thought there was some kind of conspiracy that involved more people. People with money. Who would benefit most from keeping the Holos the way it is?'

Senator Rommel cleared her throat, then paused.

'What is it, Sheila?' Mendez pushed.

'It will sound like I'm being politically motivated,' she said. 'It will sound like another conspiracy.'

Joon narrowed his eyes at the words. He already knew where this was going.

'You think Filton Fukami is involved,' he said.

'Who has more money than him?' Rommel said. 'And, most of it is tied to the Holos. If there are law changes, or a change in currency, he'd stand to lose a lot. He's also publicly opposed to my bill.'

Joon couldn't believe she was saying this. The Senator was basically accusing her biggest political rival of murder.

'I can't be seen to accuse Fukami of anything,' Rommel continued as if reading Joon's thoughts. 'It's too transparent an attack. You shouldn't point any fingers either,' she continued. 'Unless you have absolute, undeniable proof.'

'The file,' Ada said. 'That would give us proof. We're back to finding Corpus again.'

Joon shifted. Everyone was still, thinking.

'Surely Fukami wouldn't do something like this,' Joon said. 'The Specter Slaughter almost destroyed the Holos. People logging out in droves because they're afraid aren't in his business interests either. There has to be something else.'

Ada watched Joon. She seemed to sense his reluctance to implicate Fukami. The man was every jack-in's hero.

'Let's keep Fukami in the back of our minds for now,' Ada said. 'He does have strong political motivation. Like Senator Rommel says, we'd want to have some clear evidence before we pursue him. Bleesh looks like a strong possibility, so let's dig into that and prepare to track him down tomorrow. Forget Switch. I'm still convinced she's not involved. Right?'

At that moment, Joon's wrist-comm beeped. An alert from Sabi. He pulled up the message quickly and scanned the text.

'Holy shit,' he said.

'What?' Mendez and Ada asked together.

He looked to all of them, barely believing his luck. 'We have footage of the killer,' he said.

27

I jumped up from my bed like an electrocuted frog. One of the monitors attached to me shrieked. I ripped a cord from my arm to silence it. Footage of the killer. This was huge! I rushed to Joon to see if I could get a look at his wrist comm. Senator Rommel and Sheriff Mendez also moved in.

'Is the footage from Sabi?' I asked, excited.

Joon stepped back at the sudden movement. He held up his hands, pushing his mask closer to his face. Mendez and Rommel stopped, but I didn't. I pushed his arms back down.

'Show me the footage or I'll lick your eyeballs,' I said.

Joon freed himself and I was forced to slow down. Mendez coughed into her hand and Joon jumped back. I suppressed a laugh despite myself. I needed to see that footage.

'Who's Sabi?' the Sheriff asked.

'An FBI contractor,' Joon explained cautiously, finally looking at his wrist again and reading the message. 'She says the original security feed from Rama's apartment was ghost scrubbed by military AI that most people don't have access to.'

'Then how does your contractor have access?' Rommel asked.

Joon ignored the question, clicked his wrist-comm again, and a hologram screen lit the room. It showed a man limping down the hallway on the same floor of Christos Rama's unit. He stopped at the door, looked around and pulled out a syringe. Then he entered. Fast forward and the person left not long after. His face turned up to the security camera and smiled. There was a full close-up as he tampered with the device. He must have hacked into the system via the camera and erased himself from all the footage. The killer had crystal blue eyes and a half white, half black goatee. His bald head had a big spider tattooed right over the top of his skull. He looked like methamphetamines in human form.

'This guy would stand out in any crowd in the real world,' Joon said. 'How on earth have we had no witnesses come forward?'

'More importantly, we should get this footage out there,' Mendez said. 'It proves beyond a doubt these are physical murders.'

My heart dropped into my stomach. My eyes were glued to the screen. 'I'm not sure that's a good idea,' I said.

Joon turned on me, surprised.

'Why? This will give the mob on the streets the confidence to plug back in. It could give us a lead on the killer's whereabouts. We have to release it.'

I looked to Rommel who I thought would join the pile on. However, she looked at me earnestly and said: 'Let's hear what Ada has to say first.'

I looked at the image again. I couldn't quite believe it. 'We have a bigger problem now.' I said.

'A bigger problem?' Joon asked, growing impatient.

'That tattoo,' I said hoarsely, pointing at the ink work over the man's skull. 'The spider only has seven legs. Jazlin Switch has the same design on her chest. Anyone who sees the footage and knows her history will release it. It will be all over The Feed. She could be involved after all.'

28

Corpus felt like a corpse. One that had been autopsied, buried, dug up and necrophiled. The smell in the room was horrid—grease and sweat and blood, overlaid with burnt hair and the sharp odor of piss. The Spider was gone for now. Off to hunt someone else maybe.

A code map was splayed out on the wall opposite from where Corpus was bound. Seeing it was part of his torture; the Spider wanted the hacker to watch each step the trace took along the web in finding his jack-in location. At least Corpus hadn't given that up yet. He'd buckled on other things though. Secrets he thought might keep him alive, or at least drag this out longer until he was found. He'd confirmed he had the file. That Rama had asked him to hack it, but that he hadn't unlocked it yet. He even told the Spider where he could find it. A screaming part in Corpus wanted it all to end. To quit. The survivalist deeper inside whispered over and over that if he just held out long enough, everything would work out. That this was his penance. That if he took the torture and survived, he would come out stronger than ever.

Automated insects roamed Corpus's avatar while their master was away. They bit, stung, poisoned. They crawled in his ears. His nose. Any orifice he didn't keep closed. Except his eyes. The Spider wanted him to watch, always. To see his own torment in True-Resolution.

It was worse when the Spider returned himself. He'd set to work with the pleasure of the sick and twisted. There was something in him that Corpus recognized. The Spider had the same zeal as Jazlin, just not the intelligence. This beast thought Corpus didn't see through that mask, but he did. He knew the truth. It gnawed at his mind like the insects gnawed at every pain sensor in his flesh. He'd known this man in a past life.

Suddenly, the insects stopped their feasting. They scuttled back to rest on the metal board Corpus was strapped to. Their master was returning. Fear spiked through Corpus. The slowly moving dot on the code map slid a tiny bit closer to its destination. Corpus forced himself to calm down.

To still his shaking body and quaking mind. He couldn't let this monster find him before the police. Surely they were on the case by now. They had to be. He just had to hold on for that, and everything would work out.

The Spider raged into the room. He walked straight up to Corpus and punched him in the face. Again. Again. Again. Corpus felt a tooth come loose. It slid down his throat along with the blood from his gums.

'Liar!' the Spider said with each vicious strike. 'Liar. Liar. Liar. Liar.'

He finally stopped, watching Corpus bleed as he mastered his temper. Corpus rasped on his bench, barely conscious.

I am a liar, Corpus thought, *but not in the way you think.*

The Spider clicked his fingers. His little insects went to work. Instead of biting, they healed. A fire ant scuttled down Corpus's throat and retrieved his broken tooth, then put it back in place. Others cleared away the blood and patched his skin. Corpus's foggy mind came out of the mist again.

'It wasn't there,' the Spider growled finally. 'The file. There were police waiting. You knew. You tried to trap me.'

'I didn't...' Corpus said.

But hope flared in his chest. The police *were* on the trail. They'd put the pieces together. They'd find Rama's file. Break everything wide open. If they could open the encryption. But of course they couldn't. They'd need him for that.

'Liar!' the Spider roared again.

Corpus braced himself for another attack. It didn't come. The Spider was pacing. Talking almost to himself.

'I went back after I lit up that cop's avatar, but the file wasn't where you'd said it was. Maybe the police got it. That one in the Sabi avatar. He was strong. Did he find it? Not the other one. She was weak. Stupid. They can't have it, or I'd know. Where is it?!'

He was looking at Corpus now, his multiple arachnid eyes blazing.

'Where is it?!'

'I told you,' Corpus said. 'I told you where it was. I promise.'

Corpus hated how his voice whined when he said that. It was the threat of pain. It consumed everything. Corpus was so weak. Weaker than he wished he was. He should have been able to hold out for longer. Keep the existence of the file secret. Still, The Spider hadn't gotten it. The police must have. He hoped they had. It would be more motivation to get him out. He just had to hold out for events to unfold. Cause and effect. If this, then that. A programmer's solace.

'I won't let them oppress this place,' the Spider said, pushing his face right up to Corpus's. 'It's the only place I'm whole. Where I can be myself. A mighty Spider.'

Something clicked in Corpus's mind. Those words. That manic desire and fear. He couldn't help himself. He had to push back.

'You're not a spider,' he taunted. 'You're just an ugly troll.'

The Spider's twisted mouth turned into a grin.

'Finally figured it out have you?' he said. 'But you don't know the half of it.'

Before Corpus could say anything else, the Spider snapped his fingers again. Insects rushed inside Corpus's open mouth. Down his throat. The only noise he could make was a muffled scream. The things feasted on his insides. His digital heart and lungs and liver. The pain was indescribable.

'Even if they do have the file, they can't hack it,' the Spider said. 'But I can hack you, hacker. And when I find you, I'll be one step closer to keeping my home free of tyranny. They'll never be able to read it without your help.'

As Corpus writhed in pain, the dot on the code map crept closer to where he was jacked in. Closer to where he made his home in the real world.

29

Mendez cleared me with the doctors and checked me out of the hospital. The only clothes I had at the place were jeans and a t-shirt, so I scrambled into them. All four of us rushed through the halls. I was still shaken, my mind spinning. Switch. The seven-legged spider. How did it link up? I'd missed something. I must have. I was an idiot. A failure. At least my body felt refreshed, invigorated by the rest and new information.

Rommel and Mendez were in business mode, fully focused.

'I'll pull some favors to get another interview with Jazlin Switch right away,' said Rommel. 'We can have things ready to go in a few hours.'

'Min Joon,' Mendez added. 'Can you go directly to the digital confinement jack-in and speak with the military's techs? I want you make sure you're familiar with all the procedures.'

He nodded. 'I have a self-drive that can take me there.'

'Ada,' the Sheriff continued, making me snap my head toward her. 'What do you need to prepare? Do you need any files? Anything extra?'

I couldn't think. It was all too much. I couldn't show it though. I had to say something. I looked down at my jeans and t-shirt. 'Can I go and get some real clothes?' I asked. 'What I need most, is to feel comfortable. Professional.'

Mendez smiled, like it was the right thing to say. Then her smile dropped. 'I need to get back to the station. We need to run that image of our killer through the databases for an ID. I want to supervise it myself. No fuck ups this time, especially with conspiracy theories flying around. Cline needs to give me some answers on how he missed this footage scrubbing. Do you have a police transport, Ada, or should I buzz one?'

I was about to say I needed one, when Rommel cleared her throat.

'I'll take her,' she said. 'As long as it's not too far out of the way?'

'I'm in Boulder Junction,' I said sheepishly. 'It's fine, I can -'

'No problem,' the senator said. 'The National Guard's office is right near there. I need to speak with them about ongoing support with this refugee situation if we're going to keep this footage out of the public eye.'

'They're not refugees, they're Nevada citizens,' Joon said.

Rommel nodded but her smile was tight. 'Regardless, I need to talk about restoring peace. I'd rather do it in person. Nothing like a handshake and face-to-face, I find.' She looked at me and her smile turned genuine again. 'It will be good to have some face-to-face with our hero here too. You can bring me up to speed on anything else you need. I'll help where I can. It's in all of our interests that this thing is solved quickly.'

We split up at the doors, Joon and Mendez going left, Rommel leading me right. There was a black car waiting with the door open. It was compact but clean. She indicated for me to get in. I shuffled across and looked around. I'd expected something more luxurious for a senator, but it was standard government issue: seats for 4, a small bench in the middle for work if needed. Rommel was proving to be salt of the earth. She got in and clicked a button on her wrist-comm, then pressed a finger lightly to her ear. She was calm under fire. Her life had been personally threatened and all she seemed concerned about right now was the public. The car started moving just as Rommel started talking.

'This is Senator Sheila Rommel, I'm looking for immediate clearance on behalf of the Las Vegas Police department to interview Jazlin Switch. No, I will not hold.'

I tried to filter out the conversation, not wanting to be an eavesdropper. Instead, I watched the hospital building get smaller in our rear-view as we circled around an on-ramp and sped up for the highway. It was the smartest route, going right around the back of the Strip, avoiding any unrest on the streets. We settled into busy traffic that flowed perfectly as only fully automated transport could. Rommel was confident on the phone, but not rude. No shouting. My mind wandered back to Switch again. To her spider tattoos and the one that man had. Surely they weren't the same person? That was impossible. But how were they connected? I'd never seen or heard anything about the significance of those tattoos anywhere. My bustling mind then swung toward Corpus and the file. Were we following the wrong lead seeing Switch again? Corpus's life was in danger and he potentially held the key to stop all of this in its tracks. There was a connection with Switch there again too. It all came back to Jazlin Switch—the center of the spider's web.

The end of Rommel's conversation pulled me back to the present.

'Yes,' she said, quiet but firm, 'a matter of state security. This needs to be low drag. Tell the general I'd see it as a personal favor.' She waited a moment. 'Good. I appreciate it. You too.'

Rommel clicked off her call and looked at me. 'We'll be good to go in an hour.'

'Thank you,' I said quietly, feeling my blood pressure rise at the thought that I'd have to face Switch yet again.

Senator Rommel sat back and blew out a breath. 'I tell you, give me military efficiency any day of the week. In politics you need eighteen committee meetings and sign-offs in triplicate before you can change a light bulb in your office. Just give me the damn thing and I'll screw it in myself.'

'Amen to that,' I agreed. I'm not sure why. It's something my mother would have said. But Rommel's steady manner helped put my edgy nerves at ease.

'Now,' Rommel said, turning to me. 'What about you? Are you feeling up to task after that incident in the Holos? I've been in battle too and I know it's no picnic, virtual or not. The aftermath can be the hardest part.'

I closed my eyes for a moment. That ghost in the lift. The blast. Then Switch's face. Dad's. It all blurred together. I opened my eyes again. Clasped my hands together to stop them from shaking. 'I'm okay,' I lied.

Rommel put her own hands over mine. She looked me in the eye. 'If you're not, there's no shame there. I'm here to talk.'

Her touch helped me steel my nerves again. She had faith in me. Mendez had faith in me. I wouldn't let them down.

'I'm good,' I said more firmly. 'Really.'

Rommel let go and nodded. 'Good girl. You'll go a long way with an attitude like that.'

I ran my hands through my hair, considering how we might approach Switch. Could we seek a trade? Surely she'd use the chance to manipulate us. The silence in the car felt thick, so I looked back to Rommel.

'We'll catch this guy, Senator.' I said. 'There has to be a connection with Switch. I just don't know what it is. I don't like not knowing.'

'None of us do,' Rommel said. 'But do you really think Switch might help lead you to this new killer?'

'She'll know something. It's a matter of getting it out of her.'

'That man in the footage looks dangerous,' she said. 'You need to be careful.'

I opened my mouth to say it was my job, but she held up her hand.

'Yes, I know. You're police. Still, caution is warranted here. You have to remember I'm ex military. The Joe in that footage has the look of a trained killer—something I can't put my finger on.'

I didn't know what to say to that, so kept silent. Rommel looked out the window at all the Immersion Apartments stacked up to the left. Here in traffic you almost wouldn't know what was happening on the other side of them on The Strip.

'Do you trust Agent Joon?' Rommel asked, surprising me.

'I do,' I said, without pause. I meant it too.

'Good,' she said. 'I've looked into him and he seems clean. He only has a short file on record though, which is always a flag. If you ever have doubts there, or want extra support, just say the word and I'll make some calls.'

I nodded. The tone of her voice reminded me of a worried parent. That same tone of voice my mother used when I finally left home. It was the only real time I'd heard it from her since dad died. Leaving hadn't been a pleasant day, so I pushed the memory away.

'It's not Agent Joon I'm concerned about,' I said. 'It's Switch. It's this new face and not knowing what their connection is. It's finding Corpus alive. Time is getting shorter and shorter. I don't want someone else to die on my watch. But Switch is a box without any edges. I don't know how to open her up.'

Rommel considered thoughtfully, toying with one of her gold stud earrings while she did. 'You know what Switch's weakness is?' she said, finally looking up.

I leaned forward, itching to find out.

'She's a genius.' Rommel said, deadpan.

'Some weakness,' I shook my head.

'No, really,' Rommel continued. 'My daddy was just an average farmer, but he built one of the biggest ranches in Utah from the dirt up. He got up early every day. He did the work. And, he knew people. He once told me that the problem with geniuses is they think they're always the smartest person in the room. Most of them have egos the size of the state too. That makes them easy to predict. They always do what's best for them. If you want them to help you, get to know who they are. What they want. Know more about the situation than them, but make them feel like they're the only one who can solve things. Make them think it's all about them. Then they'll work hard for you. They'll trip themselves up trying to prove they're as smart as they think they are. Add your own hard work on top of that and everyone else will respect you for the effort you put in. That's what makes a leader, not a clever mind. I'm not the sharpest tool on the property, but I work harder than the others do. I get to know people. I let smarter folks do the tricky thinking for me and I reward them for it, but I always have the control. You just make Switch think she has all the information when she doesn't. Make her think you need her to help. She'll start working for you then and not even know it.'

I shook my head, not believing it could be so easy.

'Just try it,' Rommel said. 'You'll see. I asked Mendez about you. You already work harder than most. You're smart too.'

'I don't know about that,' I said, thinking to the fact I couldn't click this case together.

'You are,' Rommel said. 'Learn to take a compliment. That's part of the problem. You're not good with people yet.'

She didn't know the half of it.

'Don't worry,' she continued, reacting to my frown. 'Being good with people is a skill you can learn just like everything else. Apply yourself, work hard, and doors will open up for you, especially after this case is solved. I promise.'

The look she gave me made me beam inside. I had a career ahead of me. A future. Of course, I second guessed it right away. 'I don't need you to open doors for me,' I said. 'I don't need any special favors. Any credit I get needs to be because of my work, not because of who I know. I don't want you bending any rules for me.'

Rommel looked momentarily shocked, then smiled a big, genuine grin. 'They're not favors if you deserve it, dear,' she said. 'But I will back you up. Anything you need, just ask. And remember, I don't break the rules. I help make them in the first place.'

Her light tone made me laugh. I liked Rommel. She'd made me forget about my worries. She'd also given me advice I could use. A very rare thing on both counts.

30

I grabbed my immersion helmet off Ferret Head the technician and got ready to enter Digital Confinement. No stupid suit this time, no gloves, just the helmet and my suit and tie.

All I could think about now was that tattoo. That man's face. It bore no resemblance to Switch's avatar aside from the ink. I didn't want to believe they could be the same person. It didn't make sense. Mendez's ID search through the police's national databases showed up nothing either. She'd filed it to Interpol and asked the FBI to help as well. Again nothing. That guy was a ghost. A spook. A specter. That fact had me seriously on edge.

'Are you sure you want me to come in too?' Joon asked me for the eighth time.

He was nervous. It was the most anxious I'd seen him. Good. He should be.

'We're partners aren't we?' I said.

Part of me wanted him to share the fear I felt seeing Switch face-to-face. Part of me thought maybe he'd ask something I missed and help spark a lead. Two heads are better than one. Plus, the odds I'd be a target for Switch were split in two now. Thanks, statistics.

The pair of us jacked in and went through the firewalls. Each step felt like I was diving deeper and deeper into an ocean trench. The pressure built until I equalized, then built again before feeling almost normal. We came into Switch's den together. She sat in the center of the room as always, meditating. Passive yet alert. We stayed at the entry, silent. Joon peered around at the stark space and the Bosch painting. I only had eyes for Switch. She inhaled deeply, as if smelling us. Then her eyes snapped open. When she saw Joon, she raised an eyebrow.

'Two ugly stock avatars this time?'

'They wouldn't let me come in using my real self,' Joon replied casually. 'They seem to think it's more secure this way.'

'Oh a user? One of the pure?' Switch said.

'Someone who thinks the Holos is more real than real.'

'Hyperreal,' Switch said thoughtfully. 'So you've read my manifesto?'

Joon nodded. Of course he had. The squirt was smart and committed, I'd give him that. With that skull cap he could digest the manifesto in a few moments. I didn't like that he'd read it though. It might give him some bad ideas.

'I like your thoughts about freedom bringing order,' Joon said smoothly.

Was he trying to ingratiate himself through false flattery? Either way, I wasn't going to have Switch pandered to.

'Freedom bringing order?' I said. 'Ridiculous. They're opposing goods.'

Switch's mouth twitched.

'Order doesn't come from more oppression', she said, 'it springs from more space.'

I snorted. What rot. Switch went on unruffled.

'What do we say when something is chaotic? It's crammed in. There's too much mess. It needs space to breathe. That is the way more freedom brings order. If there is no order, there is simply not enough freedom.'

Joon clasped his hands in front of himself. His silence sounded like he agreed. Maybe that manifesto really had given him some bad ideas. I wasn't about to entertain the debate any further. That wasn't what we were there for.

'But we're getting side-tracked,' Switch said, echoing my thoughts. She clasped her hands together in her lap, still sitting. 'More dead bodies. Yes?'

I nodded. We had to play this smart like Rommel suggested. Get control back. Let Switch think she was boss and had everything under her own command. We had the advantage—information.

'And missing seven days in the Holos before found?' Switch asked.

'The first person was,' I confirmed. 'The other one less time.'

'Oh, this is getting interesting,' she said. 'Do you have extra evidence to showcase?'

We'd come prepared for this. I'd had Cline arrange a limited file on the murders of both Lilith and Rama, with background information on each victim. I'd left any trace of myself out, just in case she remembered my real face and saw I had motivations to pin her to the wall if I could. Like Joon had once said, the more you know about someone, the more you can control them. There was nothing on Corpus or Yu Ying in the files. Nothing on Rommel's new Holos Crime bill. Certainly nothing on our suspect. We included everything the scan team had noted—images of the rooms, the blood. Switch would like that. It might be enough to appease her. I'd then ask her about her tattoos off-handedly. Pretend I liked them. Appeal to her vanity. That would get us to the real information behind any other intelligence she might give us.

I made a show that I was going to click my wrist for a file exchange. No sudden movements. Switch smiled. She stood up and walked to her bookshelf on the wall, pulling out one edition with a blank spine. As she came back, she opened it toward me.

'Share it across to this,' she said. 'Books were the original form of virtual reality after all. I like to pay tribute to that perfection and peruse like a philosopher.'

I hit the file and sent it without any snark about her being a poser. It took a lot of effort to keep my mouth shut with that one. Maybe I was getting more mature. Switch pored over the document, her eyes moving at an impossible speed through the material. She then walked a small circuit around the room, musing. Joon and I kept our backs to the wall, silent. All part of the plan. Put the pressure on Switch to come up with solutions, rather than have us feed her information. Switch came to the center of the room again and sat cross-legged—an enlightened Buddha entertaining her student's questions.

'It's abundantly obvious your killer operates physically,' she said. 'I acknowledge your notes about the helmet scratches being too uniform. You're right.'

I nodded curtly at the compliment. Inside I wanted to snap my fist into her face. I hated this creature with all my being. It was a real physical effort to restrain myself. Switch clearly wasn't finished yet though, so I waited for her to continue. Joon did too.

'Further, both exhibits eyes exploded,' she said. 'The right eye each time. The probability of that is tiny. Your killer is likely left handed. I'd infer he injected them with some covert chemical through their cornea. That's what caused cell rupture. It would simulate how I killed, but isn't the same.'

I remembered our suspect had a syringe in his hand when he entered the room. My heart beat harder against my ribcage.

'What about Lilith going missing in the Holos only a few days before she died, instead of a full week?' I asked.

Switch looked at me disapprovingly. 'She gave up her location. She gave into the torture.'

'But she was used to pain,' Joon cut in.

'Physical pain, yes,' Switch said, 'maybe psychological too. But everyone has their pressure points. According to her file, Lilith didn't covet close friends or contacts. The killer would have known that. He would have also read that she supports victims of abuse. It's her main motivator. All you'd need to do is parade an innocent victim in front of her. Torture *them* instead. She was too much of a bleeding heart to let others bleed for her.'

Switch's words floored me. It was all clicking in now. I recalled the unrecorded show in the Holos where fans said Lilith was with a young girl on stage. And… a human spider. I'd overlooked it at the time because there was so much else happening. Overlooked it because a search on the girl's likeness had only turned up matches to AI-powered avatars. It hadn't been a real girl, but Lilith wouldn't have known that. Then there was the spider. The tattoo. It had been our killer on that stage. Now we knew what his avatar looked like. One of them at least.

'Fucktrumpets,' I swore under my breath.

Switch tilted her head. 'You know,' she said. 'You used the same class of immature curse last time I upset you.'

I froze. Was she assessing me for weak spots? For pressure points?

'You probably think it's endearing,' Switch continued. 'Think it's a quirk others might smile at. A titillating way to untwist the tension you're feeling. You might even resort to child-like jokes with an adult twist sometimes too.'

Knock, knock. Don't come in. Ada's not here. She can't breathe.

'I think deep down it's a response to take you back to immature times,' Switch continued. 'You yearn to recreate the feelings of safety you had around puberty when you were dealt the darkness of the real world. I'm sure most people find your efforts annoying instead of endearing. You're an adult, not a teenager. Still, you can't help yourself, can you?'

The axis of the world shifted. The floor felt unsteady. I wanted to scream. I wanted to claw her eyes out. I wanted to shove her psychoanalysis up her pucker hole.

'Why don't you walk east 'til your hat floats?' I snapped.

I squeezed my eyes shut. As broken as I was, I wouldn't let her see the cracks.

'Oh, how provincial of you,' she said. 'I didn't pick you were from the Mid West until now. Chicago?'

I refused to answer. Instead, I tilted my head to mimic her posture and smiled sweetly.

'You're incredibly astute,' I said, faking a pause. 'You know, I love those tattoos too, but why do the spiders only have seven legs? Is it to represent that part of your soul is missing?'

Switch blinked, shocked for a second. Then a light went on behind her eyes. A smile spread across her lips. She looked delighted. 'My tattoos?' she said. 'Now why would you want to know more about them? Has Filton been implicated somehow? The little worm.'

'Senator Fukami?' I asked, puzzled. That wasn't even close to the answer I expected and it threw me for a trip again. We hadn't included mention of him in our files.

'Senator?' Switch raised an eyebrow.

Shit. Another slip up. I was supposed to be the one controlling the information. Fukami had only been elected to office years after Switch was caught. When Switch turned serial murderer, the first people she killed were the developers that had worked on the project. Only Corpus and Fukami were spared. Fukami had been hounded by the press on why Switch had left him alone. They all knew she wanted Corpus dead but on the subject of Fukami she'd remained tight lipped. Were they lovers? Did he know how'd she'd done it? After years of denial, the controversy settled down. He'd used his trillions of dollars to do good in both worlds and rebuild his good name. Then he'd run for office. With Nevada now the most powerful state in the union, he was only a step or two away from running for president. Sheila Rommel was of course putting a spanner in those plans, promoting laws to govern Holosian citizens like the rest of the world. I couldn't fill Switch in on what Rommel was doing. It would trigger the psycho even more. If Switch wasn't already involved in these murders somehow, she might find a way to manipulate us into letting Rommel die—her bill along with her. Switch would despise laws in her world. Like she'd already said, for her, only freedom bought order.

I watched Switch closely, on guard.

'Of course Fukami is a senator,' she continued. 'He always took the opportunity to crawl up the chain of command.'

'And you think he has something to do with these murders because of your tattoos?' I pressed.

'You don't obviously,' she said, reading me like a trashy blog. 'You surely realize he has the same tattoo though?'

I turned to Joon, questioning. He shook his head slightly. He obviously hadn't known either and he was the Fukami fan. I'd assumed he would have said something earlier if he did know anyway. It now seemed we had to speak with Senator Fukami regardless of the political fall out. This was solid linking evidence to the killer.

'What do the tattoos mean then?' I pushed on, not wanting to give anything to Switch. The more information we gave her, the more she knew, the more she could manipulate us for her own means.

'So if not Fukami, why the suspicions about my spiders?' she said, ignoring my question.

I stayed firm, silent, not wanting to give anything away. Joon was a rock as well. Switch tapped her chin, thinking.

'Surely Corpus isn't implicated?' she probed further.

'Corpus?' Joon asked, suddenly looking as rattled as I felt. 'How do you know that? What have you done with him?'

'What have *I* done?' Switch asked, her eyebrows knitting.

Joon and I shared a look. He shouldn't have said anything.

Switch shot to her feet. 'Corpus is missing! For how long?'

I kept my mouth shut.

'Three days and counting,' Joon confirmed, the little shitbag.

Switch's calm features were now a rage of anger. Pure animal. 'Why didn't you tell me?' she growled.

Joon and I instinctively backed up. I'd never seen her agitated like this. Not in the hundreds of hours of interview footage of her. Not in any of her addresses. Not when she was sentenced to life of solitary confinement. She was normally ice. Liquid nitrogen in deep freeze meditation. Now her muscles twitched everywhere, her hands, her face, even her chest. It made the 7-legged spiders resting on her collar bones seem alive, like they were poised and ready to strike.

'Fukami wouldn't dare. He wouldn't.' Switch muttered.

'Wouldn't dare kill Corpus?' Joon asked tentatively. 'Why?'

'Because he knows that if he did he'd have to deal with me.'

'But you're on record saying you want Corpus dead,' Joon said.

Switch watched Joon, then me. I stayed silent, shifting uncomfortably. I'd had a feeling this wasn't as straightforward as I first thought. Switch picked it up instantly. My heart plummeted out of my body. Her saying she wanted to kill Corpus had been another manipulation.

'You know I never wanted Corpus harmed, don't you?' Switch said to me. 'You know more than you let on.'

It was Joon's turn to look at me as well. His avatar's face was a picture of confusion. I felt the same inside, working to fit all the pieces into place.

'When you threatened Corpus,' I started slowly, 'you said if anyone robbed you of the pleasure of killing him, you'd find a way out of custody to kill them too. So, you didn't really want him dead. You were warning people off him.'

Switch's look was all the confirmation I needed. But that begged another question.

'Why would you want to protect Corpus?' I asked.

Switch looked at me with hate in her eyes. 'Because I'm his big sister,' she said.

The words were like a punch in my throat. I actually took a step back. That couldn't be right. Switch continued on in a rush before I had time to process anything.

'I need to help him,' Switch said. 'I can take you to where he's jacked in. All you need to do is let me out of here,' she looked to the roof and calmed herself. 'Three days already. He's been tortured for three days. We're running out of time.'

I stood stock still. There it was, the manipulation. The lies. Instead of answering, I simply grabbed Joon's arm and pulled him back from the room as fast as I could.

31

'There's no way we're letting that animal out of its cage,' I said, pacing the briefing room back at the station.

I straightened my tie, redid the buttons on my jacket. Then I did it all again. I wanted to scream immature obscenities, but Switch had ruined that for me too.

The feed to Switch's virtual cell was on screen in front of us. She'd now returned to her calm state, in control. Liquid nitrogen. She repeated the same thing over and over again, knowing we were probably listening.

'I'll help. If Corpus gets killed, it's on your heads. Let me help. My true capture for his life. No tricks. I'll lead you to his jack-in spot in person. Unlock the DNA activated security. I'm his sister. Search for proof. I'll help…'

I knew she was lying. Everything Switch said was rooted in falsehoods. I knew it in my bones. She'd said to me during her first slaughter that only the darkest people would die there that day. My dad was as light as they came. A believer in the good of humanity. Now he was dead, seven years rotting in the ground because of Switch's rotten soul. I couldn't take a single thing she said as fact. Nothing. It was all designed to feed her own agenda. Her own ego.

Gibson, Cline, the Sheriff and Joon all watched with me.

'We're not fucking doing it,' I said again, anxiety rising. 'She's lying.'

'Calm down, Agent Byron,' Joon said flicking off the feed. 'We're not saying we will do it, just floating the possibility and looking at all the angles.'

'She's manipulating us,' I said. 'Telling us convenient lies we can't disprove so she can escape. Switch and Corpus were both part of the Great Reboot. No public information on who they are in the real world exists. She's taking us for a ride. Just think about it. Switch is five steps ahead of us and we haven't even given her information beyond the bare basics. Imagine what she'll be like if she has all the facts, even if she's in jail. She'll warp you all to her way of thinking.'

Everyone in the room shifted uncomfortably.

'Look,' I continued. 'We now have further reason to suspect Fukami is part of this somehow.'

'Careful,' Mendez warned. 'What if that's a lie too? You can't believe some of what she says and ignore the rest. We need proof before making any allegations.'

'Agreed,' Joon echoed.

I shot him a glance designed to shrivel his mollusk-cock back into its hole. It worked. He broke eye contact.

'We also have the lead that Gibson and Cline pulled up on this Bleesh character,' I continued.

'He'll be at LoveDeath Nightclub from 9pm tomorrow all night if his past habits are anything to go by,' Cline confirmed.

'I know the place,' Joon said. 'It's no picnic.'

'There's also this,' Cline said, clicking his wrist-comm to pull up the main screen in the briefing room.

An image of a tall woman flickered onto screen. Her figure looked like it had been lifted from some teenage boy's fantasy. Long legs, perfect butt and oversized tits that seemed bolted on with gravity-defying precision. She had pointed ears like an elf with doe eyes to match. The look on her face was pure hatred though. Puffed lips pulled back in a sneer and nose screwed up in distaste.

'This is Bleesh's key associate and Holos bodyguard. Avatar name, Poison.'

'Real identity unknown obviously,' I said, rubbing my temples, trying to push Switch and her filth from my mind.

Cline bobbed his head in apology and pressed on. 'From reports we've seen, she has ghosting capabilities and a spitting venom attack that eats avatars away. Hence the name Poison.'

'That description matches the person that ambushed us in Corpus's office,' Joon said.

It didn't match the spider avatar from Lilith's last sighting though. Did that mean anything? This guy could have a hundred avatars. He could be Bleesh *and* Poison *and* this Spider. The uncertainty of identity in the Holos was a major clusterfuck for any investigation.

'Did your attacker in the Holos manifest to look like this at any time?' Cline asked Joon and I hopefully.

'No. She was ghosted the whole time,' Joon said. 'Does it say if Poison can ghost without the blue silhouette anyone else would have?'

Cline shook his head.

Gibson cut in, all action. He wasn't waiting for certainties. 'Right, so you'll go in undercover. See if you can get an admission that Bleesh really was involved beyond mere boasting. Find out more about this Poison character too, see if either of them can reveal extra details on the murders not widely available. If we can get a hint at who they are in the real world that would be key. We can't apprehend them in there, but we can sure as shit get them to talk.'

We all sat in silence for a few moments, contemplating the objectives. I looked down at the cuffs of my shirt. They were twisted. I took a second to straighten them again. This Bleesh intel was progress but I didn't want to forget our other avenues.

'And what about Fukami?' I asked. 'He has more motive than anyone to crush the chances of Rommel's bill being passed. Switch has implicated him now too. That's an awfully big coincidence. We need to know more about this tattoo and if there's a link.'

'Fukami is scheduled to front a political rally in the Holos tomorrow afternoon,' Cline said, clicking on his wrist-comm for information. 'You could go in prior to the Bleesh intel mission and ask a few pointed questions while you're in there.'

Good old Cline, always with the different angles. He was definitely smarter than Joon gave him credit for.

'Is that wise?' Joon asked on cue.

'Is it wise to ask a suspect some questions?' I asked, turning up my dick-shrinker glare to eleven.

Joon visibly took a deep breath to steady himself.

'Okay, so we go in tomorrow and front Fukami off the record?' I said.

'I think that's a good idea,' said Mendez stepping in. 'Tell him we're concerned for all politicians' welfare at this point and are merely asking his thoughts on the case. Right?'

It wasn't the line of questioning I would have gone with, but I nodded.

'The rally will be a busy one,' Joon said. 'Let's plug in a couple of hours early to get a good spot and see if we can catch any chatter in the crowd.'

'I don't want to be in that pit of a world any longer than I need to,' I said.

The Holos still put me on edge. I'd experienced nothing but death and violence in the virtual world. Why anyone would want to go there of their own freewill was beyond me.

'Trust me, we need to.' Joon said. He looked at me pointedly.

'Right,' I said. 'We'll go in early.'

'Jack into the same port room as before,' he said. 'Go up the same elevator and get to the Politisphere at 2 p.m.'

'Right, so we're agreed,' I said. 'Switch stays where she is. We get in and tackle this case our own way. Anything else?'

Cline made a swiping up motion with his hand and the big hologram screen in the briefing room flicked to a new image. It was a picture of Senator Rommel looking important, with a long scrawl of legalese underneath.

'At Agent Min-Joon's request, I've compiled a report on both the Holos Crime bill and the two currencies mentioned in it.'

'SureCoin and Mercury?' I asked.

'It's more about money than power,' Joon said. 'The more we understand about the possible motivations behind these murders, the better chance we have of searching out extra clues and ideas.'

I nodded. This was going to be about as entertaining as a pap smear. But, like with most police work and medical procedures, the boring and uncomfortable work is what yielded results. Cracking cases required being thorough and I was a bonafide thoroughbred.

'Alright,' I said, rubbing my hands in mock excitement. 'What's clause 1.1 say?'

32

Joon came out of the briefing room feeling like he'd just wasted two hours of his life. Using his neural interface, he'd absorbed all the briefing facts about Rommel's bill in a matter of moments. Since he'd requested the briefing, he felt like he needed to sit through the rest though, to help the others understand the nuance. Gibson had asked blockhead questions. Cline was reasonable. Ada was okay too, for a technophobe. In short, Mercury was a crypto token that was traceable like old-style finance. Even more so. There were serial numbers and transaction records linked to a real world, verified identity. If you weren't properly verified, you couldn't access an account. SureCoin was the opposite. Pure, anonymous crypto. Safe if you had your access codes, no way to get to it otherwise. And no way to trace it. That key aspect had made it the preferred token of early Holos users, so SureCoin became *the* online currency by natural selection. One other thing had stood out to Joon: if Rommel's bill somehow succeeded in pushing forward Mercury as the mandated currency of the Holos, then the value of SureCoin would tank. Anyone holding that currency would lose a lot—and that was basically anyone who used the Holos now, Joon included. Senator Fukami might lose trillions. The cost of Mercury had already surged at the possibility of it taking over. It had been like a gold rush. And yet people were still hanging onto SureCoin, hedging their bets. Some thought there was no way you could stop them from using a decentralized currency like that anyway. Cline had phoned Mercury on the spot and asked them to provide a list of their biggest coin holders. They'd asked for a warrant. So much for 'easily traceable to real people'. It grated Joon's nerves how manipulative their marketing was. If they weren't going to be transparent, then they shouldn't say they were. How companies still got away with that was ridiculous. The list wouldn't arrive until after Corpus was either dead or the case was solved, so they were back to Bleesh and Fukami tomorrow. It had been a long day.

Joon rubbed his eyes. The fluorescent lights of the station felt extra bright after the darkness of the briefing room. Ada was just behind him.

'That was mind-numbing,' she said. 'I need to go and stretch my legs or something.'

Joon nodded.

'This whole thing has been a whirlwind. I wouldn't mind blowing off some steam either. Got any ideas?'

Ada considered Joon with an odd look in her eyes.

'I'm not asking you on a date, nanna,' he said.

The detective seemed to enjoy some light-hearted verbal sparring. It was when she got into political debates that she truly fired up—or shut down if losing an argument. Joon wanted to stay away from that for now. He needed to get to know her better. See if she could truly be on his side or not.

'How about a run?' Ada asked.

'I don't run unless I'm chasing someone. Or being chased.'

'Again with the innuendo,' Ada said. 'You sure you're not into older women?'

'I read your file,' Joon said. 'We're the same age.'

'That's right,' Ada said. 'It's easy to forget when you're shorter than me and have such a baby face.'

Joon felt his cheeks flush behind his facemask. He didn't like being treated like a child, even if Ada was just teasing. He had to keep his cool though. She wouldn't win this round.

'So what do the elderly do around here then?' he jabbed. 'Go to museums and look at ancient print photos?'

A smile spread across Ada's face. 'Actually, that gives me a great idea.'

Ada refused to say anything more as they left the station. She just sequestered a self-drive that navigated silently through the streets. She'd even plugged in the destination manually instead of using voice commands. Ada liked keeping secrets then. That wasn't necessarily a good sign, but fairly standard in their line of work. After all, Joon had secrets too.

Their route took some twists and turns, skirting the constant 24/7 protest that was now camped on the Strip. It was such a weird scene there, with no cohesive voice to the protests. On one side, freedom advocates were being riled up from a wide array of influences—from Fukami at the most sensible, to Bleesh at the most extreme. Then there were Rommel's supporters, some of who also aligned with the Justice for Lilith camp. Those last folks were being spurred on by Chance Bradley and other right-wing law and order wackos. In the middle was the general jack-in population, who were simply too scared to remain in the Holos until everything was sorted out. The National Guard was there, keeping watch. Senator Rommel had her influence everywhere. That presence kept any major violence at bay. For now.

The car pulled down a back alley and crept silently into a concrete lot surrounded by razor wire fencing. Some kind of compound. A sign above the entrance said 'Vegas Battlezone.'

Joon looked to Ada in questioning.

'I take it you haven't been here then?' She beamed. 'It's a real Vegas institution. Like a museum… of sorts.'

The buildings were low and squat, made of concrete, like imitation army bunkers with roller doors. Five antique army tanks sat parked in a row. The self-drive slowed to a stop. A military museum maybe? Ada got out without further explanation. Joon followed, nervous but curious.

They went through the front doors. Instantly, there was the thud of gunfire. Joon ducked, grabbing Ada's arm and pulling her down too. His head swiveled side to side, looking for attackers.

'Relax, spankblanket,' Ada said. 'It's a shooting range. We're going to blow off steam with some real guns.'

Joon straightened, embarrassed at his reaction. He checked his steriglass mask was in place as they headed to the counter against the far wall. There was a tall, clean-cut man there, dark-skinned, shaved head, dressed in a khaki jumpsuit. He had the air of an ex-soldier about him— perhaps a veteran of the Unification Wars. The only badging on his uniform was the Vegas Battlezone logo though.

'Ms. Byron, good to see you again, ma'am,' the man said as they approached.

'You too, Jackson,' she said. 'I've got a friend today, but we'll do the usual if you've got a pair of my black beauties. I left mine at home.'

'Yes ma'am, two Colt 1911s coming right up.'

Jackson turned and went to a rack neatly stacked to the roof with traditional weaponry. He returned with two metal handguns, two sets of noise-cancelling headphones, and two large boxes of .45 ammo. The guns were old but well oiled and in good condition. Ada picked them both up.

'Grab the bullets and earmuffs, can you?' she asked and moved away with a polite nod at Jackson.

Without much choice, Joon took the ammunition and ear protection in his hands then followed Detective Byron. She obviously knew her way around the place. It was relatively empty of people. The bark of gunfire sounded from time to time through the halls. There was war memorabilia all over the walls, including propaganda posters from the World Wars, Vietnam, The Gulf War, and The Russian Collapse. Thankfully, there was nothing from the Unification Wars. Joon wouldn't have been able to stomach having all that emotion glossed over in a well-designed call to action.

Ada cocked her head at one of the posters but kept walking. 'You know, something's been bugging me,' she said.

'Other than your inability to work any technology less than a decade old?' Joon said.

'Very funny. No. You said that military software was used to scrub the footage of our killer.'

'Yeah, so?'

'So a torture trace is military tech as well. There's also the fact that our murderer must have had some kind of stealth training to avoid any eyewitnesses who could have seen him enter and exit our kill sites. Maybe he's ex-military.'

'Or current military,' Joon said, picking up the idea. 'It would fit with our conspiracy theory that this goes beyond the killer himself. Perhaps he used some kind of toxin developed by the military as well in the syringe he was holding. A way to rupture cells without leaving a chemical signature—like Switch suggested.'

Ada considered. Nodded. 'It would also explain why he's not in any databases we have access to,' she said. 'Perhaps we can run his profile through a military one. Senator Rommel could help.'

'I think we might be better hacking in,' Joon said cautiously. 'The fewer people we involve the better. We don't know who's a part of this. Rommel was military once. *She* could be involved.'

'The senator?' Ada scoffed. 'She's losing more out of this than anyone! She's had her life threatened, her bill thrown into doubt. She has no motivation for these murders. None.'

'Maybe,' Joon said slowly. 'I've had an FBI contact placed on her security detail.'

'You're having the senator watched?!' Ada turned to Joon, shocked.

'I'm making sure she's secure,' he corrected.

'Yeah, right. So noble. And did your spy see anything suspicious so far?'

'So far, nothing at all to implicate her,' Joon said truthfully.

To his disappointment, Rommel appeared to be squeaky clean. He couldn't get transcripts of all her communications, but none of her calls were with unusual contacts. When his mole had been able to catch snippets of conversations it was one-hundred percent Holos Crime bill, one-hundred percent of the time.

'Good,' Ada said. 'I'll ask her to get a search cleared then. Also…'

'Hang on, aren't we here to blow off steam?' Joon interrupted. 'Don't you ever switch off?'

Ada's face turned dark. Had that been the wrong choice of words? Switch. Joon had indeed read Ada's file. He knew about her history, her father. Joon hadn't wanted to bring it up directly yet. They weren't friends. She'd teased him already about sharing personal details about his family too. The conversation died and they kept walking. Joon kicked himself for cutting her off.

They rounded a corner and came out to a private shooting range. Ada's expression shifted as Joon stopped dead. It was like he'd stepped back in time. This wasn't the shooting he was used to in the Holos. That virtual option was *more* real if anything. The targets there felt lifelike, even if they were fantasy zombies or other monsters. This place was full of gel mannequins in a sparse room. It was quaint. So outdated it was laughable. His face beneath his mask must have shown only shock, because Ada seemed to think he looked impressed.

'Cool, huh?' she said.

'Mmm, hmm,' he said, not showing his disappointment.

Ada set down the two Colts on a flat bench that formed the divide at the front of the range. She then grabbed the bullets from Joon. With swift precision, Ada clicked out the magazine, loaded eight bullets, reinserted the magazine, checked the safety, and extended the gun to Joon.

'Have you shot a real piece before?' she asked.

'Of course I have,' Joon said.

'No, I mean a real gun,' she said. 'None of that Glock polymer or taze crap you test at the academy.'

Joon just shook his head. He'd fired bazookas before in the Holos for god's sake, and she was questioning his weaponry skills?

Ada handed him the gun. It was indeed heavy. Solid. The weight of it surprised him. The grip was cold in his hand.

'Now,' she said, 'be careful. The grip safety will disengage as you hold it properly. There's also a thumb safety on the side that flicks down like this. It's cocked and locked right now. When the grip safety comes off, it'll be ready to go with a good trigger pull. Misfire here and there's no jacking into a new avatar, right?'

'I wouldn't want my avatar there hurt either,' Joon reminded her. 'That's why I gave you the flowers in hospital remember? For saving me.'

'Yeah, for 'saving' you. Right.' Ada said sarcastically. 'You were just trying to woo me and you know it.'

Joon shook his head. He'd show her. He walked up to the shooting line, clicked off his safety and took aim.

'Wait…' Ada said.

He fired. The noise was insane. The blast ripped through his ears and reverberated off the walls. The gun kicked so hard Joon almost dropped it. Vibrations shook through his arm, into his shoulder, and across his chest. It rattled his teeth. The physical sensation was intense, especially without any distraction of actual battle or game around him like he'd have in the Holos. His shot had hit nothing but the wall at the far back. He looked down at the weapon in his hands and set it on the bench like it had bitten him. His ears were ringing.

Ada laughed. She'd managed to get her earmuffs on and now stood there with her hands on her hips.

'Like I said, a real gun. They don't make them like they used to.'

She picked her Colt up, moved into position with a wide stance, and steadied her hips. Joon grasped for the earmuffs and got them over his head before she squeezed the trigger with finesse. Bang. Bang. Bang.

The bullets tore through one of the nearby mannequins. Its gel torso splattered away, leaving a gaping cavity in the middle. The third shot hit the head, eviscerating half the face. The devastation was incredible, especially in the stark light of the shooting range. No blood. No gore. Just gut-churning destruction.

Ada looked at Joon with a satisfied smirk.

'Want to have another shot?'

Joon wasn't sure if he did. He looked at the mannequin. A mistake would mean true death for sure. An ugly death. The reality of that couldn't be escaped. His hands trembled at the thought of something going wrong. Still, he couldn't lose face in front of Ada. He wouldn't. Joon gingerly took up the gun.

He walked up and stood, raising the weapon toward another untouched mannequin. His arm quaked, but he worked to hold it firm. Ada moved in behind him. She put her foot on the inside of his and shunted his stance wider. Her thigh brushed into his and she grabbed one of his hands. She made him clasp it over the other one holding the gun.

'Don't be arrogant,' she said, loudly enough to hear through Joon's earmuffs. 'A gun with this much power needs both hands until you're used to it.'

Ada clicked the safety off for him and stood back again. Joon clasped the gun, trying to concentrate and get a bead on the target. He was having a hard time.

'Be in the moment,' she said. 'It's all muscle memory. You've fired guns before in the Holos. Synced it should be no different. Just respect the weight of the gun. Squeeze the trigger, don't jerk it. Lean into the shot.'

Joon listened. He calmed himself, bringing his mind into the here and now, like he would if he were in the Holos. He rooted his feet and shifted forward as he aimed. Then on his exhale, Joon squeezed. The roar of it still took him by surprise. The slide mechanism hammered back and the barrel lifted again, but it didn't catch him off guard like last time. The target mannequin burst open in a spray of ballistics gel. Joon shot again. Missed. He paused, aimed once more and fired. Another hit, this time the shoulder. He stopped, stood up straighter. The acrid smell of gunpowder hung in the air. The thrill of hitting the target tingled all over his skin.

Ada clapped him on the shoulder.

'There you go, spankblanket,' she said. 'A real weapon. Maybe we should ask Jackson to let us try the AK47s next?'

33

The lights of the Holos hurt my eyes. I thought I'd blasted enough targets apart last night to relax and sleep. Instead, I'd had nightmares. The violent end to our last mission played over and over again in my head. Switch's avatar took the place of the ghost that had really been there. The dream then cycled back to the day dad died. Back and forth, back and forth. I'd jerk awake, realize it was a dream and fall asleep again, only to have the nightmare pick up where it left off.

I rubbed my eyes again, before realizing that I was rubbing my virtual avatar's face. In the real world I'd be rubbing the front of my helmet goggles. If only they'd injected coffee into my veins before I plugged in, instead of attaching cables to me, I might be able to function. This clunky avatar didn't help either. I was stumbling around in a cruddy code puppet.

Despite my foggy head, our mission was clear: seek out Fukami, probe him for information, then stake out Bleesh. We had to find something that would lead us to Corpus, to save his life and get to the truth. Get to this mysterious file he'd apparently hidden somewhere. Rommel had agreed to help have the military databases searched for an ID on our killer. It'd turned up nothing so far but she was seeking classified clearances too. The whole thing was so frustrating. I'd only be able to get some rest once this was solved. Until then, all I'd do was keep turning it over in my head. Keep mentally running full speed ahead until I stumbled over the finish line. Protestors would keep clashing. The markets would stay volatile. Vegas would be a mess. I would be a mess. I had to push forward. I had to figure this out.

Joon stood next to me in the lift as it ticked up floors toward the Politisphere. He was relaxed, confident, at home in his fully synced body. I drew off his sense of calm to settle myself too. I wore the beautifully crafted slip Sabi had given me last time. Joon had recovered it from Corpus's office and insisted I wear it over my crappy stock avatar. Despite the slip's elegant code, it did nothing for my coordination. I felt foolish, parading high-style and low function on a serial killer investigation. But in the Holos, it seemed the best way to blend in was to stand out.

Joon drummed his fingers on his thighs as the lift moved, stopping and starting at each floor.

'Thanks again for last night,' he said. 'I really enjoyed it.'

'You're welcome,' I said.

He'd already mentioned it like eight times already.

'You're a real surprise, you know?' he continued. 'When I was told you were a Ph.D. I'd expected more of an intellectual.'

'Is that a compliment or an insult?' I laughed.

'It's an observation,' he said thoughtfully. 'You're obviously smart, you dress the part, but you don't talk like a Ph.D. You certainly don't act like one.'

I fell silent, thinking back to when I studied criminology. It was all home study, with lectures online. I didn't jack into the virtual classes, I simply plugged into them via video link. There was no physical college for me either. I hadn't wanted to leave mother on her own. I felt a strange sense of duty to her—to look after her since dad died. I guess I partly felt at fault for his death and wanted to make it up to her. I studied early mornings, late nights, and worked at a Starbucks during the day to help with money. There were always files and books stacked around the dining table, with more information in my laptop. One night while studying, I thought I'd had an epiphany about Switch. Mother was there, so I told her.

'I think Switch has a god complex,' I said. 'She has delusions of grandeur. Maybe her real motive was forcing her will on the world. Shaping it into her own image to gain a sense of control in her life. It's easier to justify evil actions if you believe you have a divine mandate to do it for the greater good.'

Mother had put the kitchen knife on the bench and stared hard at me.

'Listen to yourself,' she said. 'God Complex, delusions of grandeur, divine mandate. You know what she is? A killer. Don't dress it up in language that makes you sound smart.'

I opened my mouth to reply but she barreled on.

'You want a fancy word? Try psychopath. That's it. She killed Dylan. People used to call him an artisan when they wanted him to sound fancy, but he was a mechanic. A husband. And now he's dead because he pandered to the whims of his daughter. I won't do it anymore. You need to drop this nonsense and work at something real. Something helpful. I'd rather you were a waitress full time for god's sake. You want to feel a sense of control again, take a self-defense class. I'll take you to the shooting range myself. But don't be a cop, oh sorry, 'criminologist'. It's not safe. Now pack up that junk and get it out of our house.'

I studied in my room after that and kept my revelations to myself.

'This is us,' Joon said, bringing me back into the moment.

We stepped from the lift and looked around. This wasn't The Politisphere—it was Mall and Media. Maybe Joon wanted to go to Feed HQ and ask them some more questions about Yu Ying. We continued down the street, but not toward The Feed.

'Why are we going to see Sabi again?' I asked Joon, now realizing where this detour was taking us. 'We already had her sort that footage. We don't need her anymore.'

'I think we do,' he said, pushing towards her studio at double pace. 'You'll see.'

He didn't say another word after that and I wouldn't give him the satisfaction of asking. We were ushered through like VIPs again, no waiting, all fawning. Sabi sat in her studio, lounging in a high-backed chair peeling a tangerine. She looked up as we entered. Smiled. No disgust like last time, thanks to the slip I wore. She simply nodded in appreciation. The current avatar she was working on sat in the middle of the room, covered in a black sheet, like a masterpiece too precious for the real world to see.

'The beautiful have arrived,' she said. 'Come darlings, sit, I've been waiting.'

We sat on two other chairs that hologrammed to life and solidified in the corner. Sabi finished peeling her tangerine. Breaking it apart, she languidly slid one slice into her mouth, savoring the taste.

'Perfectly coded,' she said, indicating the citrus in her hand. 'Taste is such a magnificent sparker of memory. This brings me images of my grandmother painting with her simple brushes while I peeled fruit for her. It hurt her old and delicate fingers to do it on her own. She preferred to use all her strength to create art. I was only too happy to help. I loved her creations. She only ever used three colors. Black. White. Red. When something was just perfect, she marked it callously so it was not. Told me it symbolized true humanity. That all children start perfect and are marred by life. She only hoped my imperfections became lovely ones.'

I stopped myself from rolling my eyes. What was it with these jack-ins telling sob stories about their grandparents?

'Speaking of imperfections,' Joon said, not wasting time, 'what more can you tell us about the security footage of our killer?'

Sabi's face darkened. She pushed a button on the arm of her chair and a shimmering green filter came down over the walls. I was not quite sure what it was. The look reminded me of the firewalls I'd seen in digital confinement. Liquid but solid. A digital grid to block something out.

'We'll not be interrupted or eavesdropped on now,' she said, looking at me.

'Good,' Joon said. 'Tell us.'

Sabi paused, considering her words carefully, even though it was just us in the room.

'The police should have known the footage was scrubbed,' she started. 'Any analyst who missed it was either inept or covered it up.'

The meaning of what Sabi was saying hit me in the chest. Covered it up? She thought Cline was a mole. My rationality railed against the idea. Old shaggy was harmless. So did that mean he was crap at his job? I didn't want to believe that either. He'd helped me so many times.

'But you wrote in your message it was manipulated with advanced military AI,' I said.

'It was,' Sabi nodded. 'But the police should be able to pick that up if they have any sense to look at the right things. Joon tells me you suspected something was wrong. They should have double-checked but didn't. Why?'

At the time I'd assumed it was because Cline had confidence in his abilities. I hadn't questioned it because I was the tech Luddite. Now, I realized I should have pushed. If I had, and Cline had refused, we'd have a stronger sense of any possible involvement. As it stood, this was a hint at corruption but hardly a smoking gun. I really didn't need this right now.

'So apart from looking at catching a killer, we have to be looking over our shoulders as well?' I said with frustration. 'If there is some kind of conspiracy, then whatever is in that Corpus file is more important than ever. We need to know what's going on. We need to find it.'

There was instant silence in the room. Sabi and Joon shared a meaningful look. Sabi cleared her throat. She furrowed her delicate brow, causing a crease to run across her forehead that intersected with the vertical divide down her face. Joon turned my way. He waited, as if trying to decide something, then slowly and deliberately spoke.

'Ada,' he said. 'I found the file.'

His words didn't compute for a second. I blinked.

'It's a stunning piece of work,' Sabi said to Joon, suddenly animated again now the secret was in the air. 'I still can't hack it. If Corpus wasn't the one tasked to break it open, I'd have thought he'd built it. It's so intricate.'

I sat there dumbly, listening to Sabi gush about the file. Heat rose in my cheeks.

'Any brute-force attempt would shatter the contents of the file completely,' she continued. 'Any attempt to copy it would just send a Trojan into the systems of the hacker and wipe every single one of their cloud drives. No. I won't risk losing my work over that.'

'You found the finger licking file?' I said, standing up. 'When?!'

Joon rubbed his hands together nervously but didn't look away.

'When I went back to search Corpus's office,' he admitted, 'I already suspected police corruption by that stage so kept it quiet. The contents are too important to fall into the wrong hands and be deleted. That's why I said we should come into the Holos early but didn't mention Sabi. I didn't want to stake out the rally for longer. We needed to come here to see if she'd made progress on getting it open.'

I felt my cheeks flush white hot. The implication was clear. I couldn't be trusted either. And, we were just about to leap into a stakeout mission together. I started to launch into a tirade of the filthiest swears my already sailor vocab could manage.

Sabi stood. 'Now could be a good time to give the officer her gift, Joon,' she interrupted.

I narrowed my eyes at Sabi. A gift? What in bonkerballs was she talking about?

In answer, Sabi made a flourish with her hands. The black sheet over the avatar in the middle of the room dissolved.

No.

I gasped. This couldn't be. It was... me. The real me. Perfectly rendered. Naked.

A mix of wonder and embarrassment and rage flooded through me. How had she done this? My mouth worked for words but nothing came out.

'Exactly the reaction I was hoping for,' Sabi said, clapping her hands. 'I knew you'd be one of the few who takes her earthly form in the Holos. Such a rare trait. No self-actualizing or body jumping for you. You're a most incredible subject. I can only thank Joon for getting the right images and body rhythms.'

'You what?!' I asked, whirling on Joon.

'I...' he stammered, seeing my reaction, '...I wanted to say thank you for saving my avatar by giving you your own.'

I looked at the avatar again, then Joon. This was not a gift I wanted. How dare he presume? How dare he suspect me of corruption?

'I took some hi-res images of your face for detail while you were sleeping in the hospital,' he said. 'I lifted your body rhythms from your hospital scans at the same time.'

'And my body?' I said, looking at it.

'I went through the police jack-in room footage when you changed into my suit and used that too.'

I stayed silent, a volcano of anger building inside me.

'Your body is wonderful,' Sabi said, helping Joon. 'Not the flabby mess most real-worlders let themselves fall into or the emaciated ones jack-ins hollow out to be. You've made yours a weapon. Honed and true. Now you have that same strength here in the Holos.'

I looked closer. Even the moles on my stomach were right. She'd captured every inch. The only difference was that a Sabi authentication mark was tattooed around my right thumb where my dad's ring would normally be. It was disgusting. Unnerving. A clone of myself, lifeless in front of me. Eyes devoid of light.

'You took photos of me while I was unconscious,' I said feeling quietly violated.

I crossed my arms over my chest.

'It was all for a good cause,' Joon replied.

'You invaded my privacy!' I snapped.

'You told me privacy is overrated,' he shot back, now annoyed. 'Especially if you have nothing to hide. Do you have something to hide?'

His words stopped me in my tracks. I had said that, but I hadn't meant it that way.

Joon pressed on. 'You need a non-stock avatar to change into for the mission. You need to be able to keep up in a fight if it comes to it again.'

'But...'

'If there is a conspiracy that involves the police,' Joon cut in 'the last thing we want is for someone to be able to track exactly where your avatar is at all times. You know full well, stock police avatars are tracked with code. This new body has a disrupter built in like most normal avatars. They'll know you're in the Holos, but not exactly where. They can't eavesdrop on conversations like they could with a police-sanctioned and coded avatar either. We need to do this.'

'I'm going undercover in my own body?' I said incredulously. 'I've been all over the news with this case. That's worse than having this slip.' I indicated my current form.

In answer, Sabi walked up to the inert avatar and pressed two fingers into its left palm. At her touch, the avatar's face changed. The skin tone changed. Suddenly I was an African. Unrecognizable. Sabi pressed the palm again. I was tall and blonde. Slavic. Again she pressed it. I was a bearded man with metallic tattoos all over his face.

'I call it the avi of a thousand faces,' Sabi said proudly. 'But the body rhythms stay the same no matter what form you take. You'll feel totally synced. Joon's avi has the same tech, not that he ever uses it.'

'I do if I need to,' Joon said defensively but still smiling at Sabi. 'I just like the main face you built for me.'

'Wait. Synced?!' I said, my shock growing further still. 'I'm not going synced. No way.'

Sabi's face fell. This obviously wasn't the reaction she was expecting. She looked to Joon like he'd brought in an escapee from a mental asylum.

'It's absolutely safe,' he soothed. 'We're jacked in at a police station under constant public surveillance. The whole force can't be corrupt. They can't get to us while our real-world bodies are on live feed—not without major repercussions. You know the Stockholm Effects, have experienced them. That's the worst that can happen, even synced.'

'The worst that...' I trailed off. He'd never understand.

'You'll be stronger, faster, have perfect reaction time,' Joon continued. 'You can't get into LoveDeath in a stock avatar either. Any remotely-enabled recording and tracking functions like in police avatars are blocked by coded security. You'll get barred at the door.'

'Why didn't Cline put that in his research?'

Joon simply arched an eyebrow in response. Had Cline known and not said anything to sabotage the mission, or was it just more incompetence?

'There's also this,' Sabi added. She curled the index finger of the left hand in a beckoning motion, once, twice, three times. The right hand started to glow brightly. Sabi pointed it at the wall. A thick jet of silver light blasted from the hand. The beam lanced past us into the green firewall around the room. Everything sparkled and shimmered. A hole ripped in the firewall, code being eaten up. Sabi cut off the beam and the liquid started to repair itself again.

'If that was a troll, they'd be back to ones and zeros,' Joon said. 'Scattered back into the chaos. A real weapon. Your own built-in Colt 1911.'

I stared. The raw power of it was stunning. And that power would be in my hands, literally.

Sabi must have seen the awed look on my face so continued. 'You'll never have to fear anything in this,' she said. 'You'll be unstoppable.'

I considered the avatar again. My own face mirrored back. My true self but stronger. Hyperreal. I didn't feel like myself in this current stock avatar. There was always that sense of wrongness. But then, I didn't feel at home in my own head either. Would this be any different? I looked at the body again. Sabi had said it was beautiful. I didn't see that. She assumed I was comfortable in myself. I wasn't comfortable. It was simply all I had ever known.

But had that ever helped me?

Maybe this was a chance to face my fears. Go through them. I knew I was a liability in a virtual fight as it was. If we had to escalate things with Bleesh, or if his bodyguard Poison did turn out to be the ghost we'd faced before, I'd need to be armed and ready. I looked at the hand where the silver blast had cannoned from. The skin was smooth. Clean. Temptation worked its way into my psyche. It crumbled the last of my resistance. We were at the police station, being monitored on live feed for safety.

Surely I could give that weapon a try, just this once, for the mission.

34

The Fukami rally was buzzing. The heat and smell of humanity was all crammed into one space, bodies pressed against bodies—I'd never felt anything like it. Crowds of more than fifty were discouraged in the real world because of pandemic protocols. Here though, you could experience the atmosphere and sensory overload of concerts or conventions without fear. Everything requiring large groups to converge was moved to the Holos—apart from illegal protests of course. Unlike those protests on the street in Vegas, which terrified me, this was oddly exhilarating. I could feel the electric energy of the gathered people wash over me. Could sense every breath on my neck. Maybe it was that I felt stronger in this new avatar, knowing I had a secret weapon in my fingers that could blast a clear zone around me if I wanted. Maybe it was that this crowd's energy was wholly positive. Excited. It was infectious when synced up with the reality of it. I had felt separated in my code puppet from all the experiences before this. Now, my body, my intuition, told me it was fully real. Everything flowed. Memories of my first time here bumped up toward the surface but I pushed them back. Now wasn't the time for a meltdown. This time was different. I was in control. I had power. I was with another agent who had his own solid abilities. It would be okay. *I* would be okay.

I forced myself to focus on the mission, following Joon as he wove through the crowd. We didn't even bother looking for people tailing us. Joon had left my other body in a digital dumpster in Mall and Media. If anyone decided to check in on the code-tracked avatar, they'd think I was in an alley beside a Babylonian design shop called The Black Sun. The fact my avatar could no longer be monitored gave me a sense of freedom. We were now disguised too. I'd had taken on the face of a strong Japanese man with similar features to a young Filton Fukami. Joon had shifted his avatar to be a petite woman that could pass as my sister. I felt an odd sense of release in being anonymous. No one knew who I was. I could get the information we needed without following the book. The professional in me resisted, but the raw cop seeking justice said *let's do this!*

We made it to a spot on the high side of the square, perched on a balcony with a good view of the stage. The crowd was enormous—tens of thousands of people from all walks of virtual life. It was like The Arterial but with an added sense of anticipation. Rather than personalities all mixed in together, I could see patterns and groups gathering in certain spots. There were the cyberpunks—transhumans who had outfits or add-ons that went beyond flesh and blood. They had guns embedded into limbs, or guns that *were* limbs. They had eyes like Terminators or hair as fluorescent as their tattoos. There were the sex fetishists, leather-clad and studded. There were the fantasy freaks—warriors and maidens and wizards and goblins. There were the space junkies with light sabers and blasters and swathes of silver on their clothes. There were the fashionistas. There were the religious nuts. There were the gamers and the ravers. There was the military: Navy. Air Force. Army. All in uniforms, together but separate.

The fact that Joon had kept me in the dark about Corpus's file still rankled. He'd had it all along and kept quiet. *The key to the case.* If we were to do this, solve this, we needed allies not conspiracies. Police work wasn't done in a vacuum, whatever some movies and immersive adventures would have you believe. Maybe one of our own police contractors could have hacked it. Still, Sabi had gotten on top of that footage when Cline hadn't. If she couldn't get into the file, then it must be next to impossible. That left us back to square one. No. We *had* made progress. Joon was starting to share things. That meant he trusted me. Considering he could have kept this under the table still, I now trusted him fully too, even if he was a shithead.

A roar went up from the crowd. If I thought there was electricity in the air before, then this was a pure lightning storm. Stomping thundered around the square as Filton Fukami walked onto stage. Lights flashed. Letters scrolled in the air with his message of Anonymity. Freedom. Fulfillment. I flinched as cannon blasts shot confetti into the air. I hadn't realized how on edge I was. There was no stampede though. No Jazlin Switch slaughter. Just the sounds of adoring fans going berserk with affection. On stage below, Fukami held his arms wide, accepting the attention. He reminded me of Jesus on the cross, except Fukami's arms were nailed up with narcissism. Finally, Fukami lifted his hands higher, indicating silence. Attention swept through the crowd.

'Welcome to the FREE!' he said.

Another burst of applause erupted.

'I have incredible news,' Fukami boomed on. 'Your push to keep our home away from the influence of oppression is helping. We have seen the price of the Holosian Crime bill blow out beyond what it initially floated at.'

More cheers. More adoration.

'And!' Fukami continued, 'Senator Rommel is getting desperate. I've just heard word that she has further altered the bill in your favor.'

Silence. No one wanted to miss a word. Even I edged forward. Rommel hadn't told us anything about this.

'Her lawyers have made amendments to confirm that it will remain totally legal for Holos residents to manipulate NPCs in any way! NPCs will retain their fantasy designation, so all activities with them will be protected by freedom of speech!'

The noise was insane. My mind spun. I had no idea what he'd just said, but these guys were going nuts. The military section on the ground let loose with a volley of celebratory fire into the air. Fukami held his hands up again and the noise dropped enough for me to yell at Joon.

'What's an NPC?'

'Non-player character,' he said. 'Characters that are just computer generated, not actual humans in avatars. Fukami just confirmed that you will still be able to do anything you want to an NPC in the Holos without breaking any law.'

That did seem positive. Still, it meant people could rape, torture, and murder avatars that appeared to be absolutely real in every sense. Even ones that looked like children. It wasn't right.

'We are winning the fight!' Fukami continued. 'Keep pushing. Keep vigilant. Our freedom is at stake. Our fulfillment! Make your money talk, your voices shout, and your actions scream we will not be chained!'

Vibrant neon letters streaked overhead. WE WILL NOT BE CHAINED. More cannon confetti. Music ramped up around the square and Fukami left the stage, replaced by a DJ. The rally was shifting into a concert. I looked to Joon. He clapped wildly, swept up in the moment. I slapped him on the stomach to snap him out of it. His hands dropped and his face went stoic, perhaps to hide his embarrassment. I'd seen enough.

'How do we get to Fukami?' I asked.

'Leave that to me,' Joon said, 'I have an idea where he's going.'

35

We pushed through a current of people as they streamed the other way. Joon ducked and weaved in his female avatar, its smaller form more suited to finding gaps than creating them. I followed close behind. We finally reached the stage and went around back. There was a roped-off area set up there. VIPs mingled as Fukami shook hands with people, saying a few words before moving on. As we got to the gate, Fukami spoke with two men who had guns strapped to every appendage. One's skin was all military camo. The other's left eye was a short gun barrel. Before the guards at the entry could stop us from walking through, Joon called out in a loud voice.

'Senator Fukami, we'd like a private word please.'

The guard, who was built like a redwood, stepped in front of us. Fukami turned and considered us. Joon looked totally non-threatening in his avatar. I'd chosen my 'Young Fukami' look on purpose too. Even in this age of uber identities, people tended to open up to those who looked like them. Fukami excused himself from his present company and walked to the entry.

'I'm sorry, have we met?' he asked.

'We're fans,' Joon said. 'We'd like to ask a couple of questions.'

Fukami's calm facade dropped to one of annoyance.

'I'm so sorry, I'm quite busy right now,' he said, 'You'll have to get in touch with my PR team. They'll be able to answer anything you need.'

He then turned his back and started to walk away.

'Will they be able to tell us about the disappearance of Corpus?' I said loudly.

Fukami stopped dead in his tracks. He leveled a dark gaze back at me, then nodded to his guard. The behemoth took a step towards us. I held my ground.

'Jazlin sends her regards,' I added toward Fukami. 'She said if you're involved, she'll be paying you a visit.'

Fukami's mouth dropped open. He looked around to see if anyone was taking notice. Everyone was, especially the two military characters he'd been speaking with. The guard at the gate was just about to grab me when Fukami cleared his throat.

'Take them to my car, Blane,' Fukami said to the guard, then looked at me. 'This had better not be some kind of joke.'

We were ushered to a black limo parked nearby. Inside was absolutely nothing like I expected. Instead of leather seats and champagne buckets, it was a full-sized office. A mahogany desk sat in the middle with chairs around it. Clocks lined the walls, showing the time zone in every major city, virtual and real. Multiple doors led from the room. Each had a label above it: Politisphere, Feed HQ, Arterial, and so on.

Joon took in a sharp breath at the sight. 'This is a mobile portal,' he said in awe. 'It can take Fukami anywhere he wants to go in the Holos.'

'I didn't think something like this was possible,' I said, looking around.

'Nothing is impossible when you invented the place,' a voice said from behind me. Fukami was there, alone. No guards. He appraised both Joon and me, looking each of us up and down.

'I assume you're police,' he said. 'You should have said so. I'd be willing to help with your investigation.'

This kind of logical leap from a small amount of information reminded me of Switch. It was unnerving to have someone form a correct conclusion so quickly. Or did someone else warn him already?

'We *are* police, Senator Fukami,' I said, wanting him to feel on firm ground before making it unsteady again. 'Vegas PD.'

Joon extended an adoring hand in Fukami's direction. 'I'm with the FBI. It's a real pleasure to meet you,' he said, a big grin on his female face.

Fukami shook Joon's hand and I cleared my throat.

'We interviewed Switch, Senator,' I cut in. 'She suggested you might be involved with the disappearance of Corpus.'

Fukami clasped his hands in front of himself. 'I didn't realize Corpus was missing until now.'

He looked from me to Joon and back, trying to get some further insight from us. I held firm; Joon still had that stupid smile on his face.

'Switch is trying to mislead you,' Fukami continued. 'Playing games to discredit me. I admire Corpus. We worked together a long time ago. He is a gentleman. Intelligent. He has a positive vision for this world, unlike Switch. I truly hope you find him.'

'You all worked together though, didn't you?' Joon asked.

Fukami nodded.

'So you know that Switch is Corpus's sister?' I said without further preamble.

I expected Filton to be shocked again. Wanted him to be. He might slip something if he was off balance. He wasn't.

'Yes, I know,' he said without missing a beat.

Shit. That wasn't the answer I wanted. That meant Switch really did have motivation to help us find Corpus. Perhaps. I scrambled in my mind for another question. Something that would lead away from us asking for Switch's help in this.

'Did Switch like Corpus?' I asked. 'Did they get along?'

Fukami seemed a little off-put by the direction this was taking. He unclasped his hands and indicated the chairs at the big desk.

'Should we sit?' he asked.

Joon took a chair obediently, all his attention on the senator. I sat at the same time as Fukami. He regarded me for a few moments. I waited for him to speak, letting silence put pressure on him. Thankfully, Joon had the sense to do the same.

'Corpus was very dear to Switch,' Fukami said slowly. 'If harm came to him, she'd do everything in her considerable power to take revenge. The feeling wasn't mutual though. Corpus knew his sister was crazy. He didn't hate her, just pitied her. It was that weakness which allowed Switch to thrive, flying under everyone's radar.'

I opened my mouth to ask another question but Fukami continued.

'I'm wise enough to know that if she truly set her mind to it, Switch could escape digital confinement. I would not risk a horrible death at her hands, no matter how slim the odds. I had nothing to do with Corpus's disappearance.'

'Even though you're politically motivated to do so?'

Now Fukami laughed. The light of it didn't touch his eyes, although he was certainly amused. 'Not at all,' he said. 'Corpus is more for freedom than oppression.'

'And yet he's proposed laws before,' I pushed. 'And you're against any rules whatsoever.'

Again Fukami laughed. 'No rules? I'm a programmer. Rules are what make this universe possible. Cause and effect. If this then that. Rules are everywhere. Rules are necessary. It's being controlled I'm against. Corpus helped support laws against avatar kidnapping and torture before Rommel or I floated anything. Of course, his desire to do that may have been sparked by guilt that his sister was being tortured to find her whereabouts, even if Switch did manage to resist it. Corpus wanted to ensure no one else could be subjected to an eternal hell like his sister. He had a point too, but I think he didn't go far enough. All grievous harm to people against their will is what we want to stop. That's just good business. And that's what Senator Rommel just put forward in her altered policy. I'm very happy with those changes—letting people use AI avatars for their fantasies, but protecting real people who don't want to partake.'

'So you're saying that your public stance doesn't fit your actual opinion?' I pushed.

This time when he laughed, the light of it did sparkle in his eyes. The effect was unnerving, seeing the emotional side of this man. It made it harder for me to imagine him as a possible killer.

'No politician believes everything they say,' Fukami smiled. 'You have to match extreme opinions with extreme to wind up support. The point of our future-led democracy is you meet in that sane middle. We're almost there—if Rommel would agree to keep SureCoin as the currency instead of Mercury.'

Nothing about balancing extreme opinions on the left with extreme opinions on the right sounded sane to me. You should do what you said. Believe what you said. Fukami's answers were putting me off balance instead of my questions doing that to him. I looked to Joon for help; he straightened.

'And what about the file?' Joon asked innocently.

My mouth went dry. Surely he wasn't going to bring that up. Tell the conspirator we know about his conspiracy?

Fukami and Joon stared off for a moment. Each seemingly comfortable in the silence.

'Which file?' Fukami finally asked, his face a mask.

Perhaps he really didn't know what we were talking about. Without breaking eye contact, Joon clicked his wrist-comm. A hologram of a face sprung to life in front of him. The assassin. Bald head. Goatee. Spider Tattoo. Fukami sat up straighter.

'Do you know this man?' Joon asked.

Fukami shook his head, eyes only on the image. There was a darkness in his eyes as he saw the face. Fukami looked angry. 'I've never seen him,' Fukami said, 'but I can tell you about his tattoo.'

I glanced at the seven-legged spider adorning our assassin's scalp. Fukami was staring hard at it.

'I used to have one just like it, before I had it removed,' he said. 'Jazlin and Corpus still have them, I believe.'

Fukami clicked a button on his desk. A screen shimmered to life between us. Another click and a seven-legged spider spun into view on the screen. As I looked, a web spiraled out of its abdomen, forming strands around it, seven main ones all interconnected at certain sections. Each strand then branched into seven more strands, mirroring into a 3D lattice that started to funnel away from the spider.

'Holy shit,' Joon said under his breath. 'That's the way the Holos is laid out.'

'Exactly,' Fukami said, impressed. 'Most people don't see it. They simply get lost in the lights and grandiosity of The Arterial and think it's just a basic grid. I'm glad to see you're so perceptive.'

Joon actually blushed at the compliment. He watched the screen, enrapt. The spider continued to spew out layers of eternal connections, each more intricate than the last. It would build on as two by two by two to make eight, then one layer would melt away. More would add on again in the same pattern.

'And I suppose you're this spider in real life then?' I asked, folding my arms across my chest. 'The all-powerful creator.'

'Me? No.' Fukami said, staring at the screen with an odd look in his eyes. 'The design of the Holos might have been my idea, but you need a team to bring anything of this scope to life. The first founders included me, Corpus, Switch, and others. There were seven of us in all. Seven developers, seven layers of the Holos, seven sub-layers, seven sub sub-layers, seven sins, seven virtues, seven legs to the spider. We thought it was symbolic, calling ourselves The Guardians of the Web. We said we'd work to keep our invention pure. Free. Make it like real life but without the same ugly constraints put on it.'

'So what happened?' Joon asked sincerely.

'Switch happened,' Fukami said. 'She infected the place. Slowly at first, then more overtly. Oh, she was brilliant, the mad often are. She contributed more to the world than any of us. Her synced avatar idea made embodiment so real that we couldn't tell the difference from true life anymore. Then she wanted to include death so there really was no difference. She wanted to include what she called the ultimate consequence. Make the game more thrilling. She thought by doing that she'd keep people free but stop their dark desires from going pitch black. I thought she was joking. I realized that most Holosians prize their avatars like real bodies. That the consequences of avatar death were already high enough to keep things exciting. She disagreed. Said it was a false economy. True death was the only real truth humans know. I argued there was no way someone could be killed for real via VR anyway. I'll never forget what she said: 'if we can give someone a major epileptic fit by shining some flashing lights in their eyes, think what we could do when hijacking their entire sensory system'. You, well, know the rest.'

'She succeeded,' I said.

'Success is a loaded word,' Fukami said. 'I prefer to think that *we* failed. One of the guardians became an attacker. It wasn't right.'

Silence hung in the air. Fukami clicked a button again and the screen disappeared, lifting us all from our contemplation. The movement snapped me back to the task at hand. The knowledge opened up new avenues for us to go down.

'Did you know all seven of your original team members in real life?' I asked. 'Could our killer be one of them?'

Fukami shook his head. 'No and no. I only ever met Corpus and Switch in virtual, so I don't know who they are or what they look like in the real. We all respected that anonymity. We didn't need to know each other in the flesh anyway. We had our virtual space. It's where we built everything from the inside out.'

'What about the others?' I pressed.

'Two of the other developers were good friends of mine,' Fukami said. 'Two others were based in Taiwan where all the best haptic hardware is manufactured. I often met with all of them in both real and virtual.'

'Could any of them be our suspect?' Joon asked, picking up my thread of thought.

'No,' Fukami said flatly.

'Why?' I asked.

'Because Switch killed them. They were the first victims of her slaughter. I only escaped because I was working on something else that day. Corpus was spared for obvious reasons and he has now, as you say, been kidnapped. It has to be someone else.'

'And you're sure the others are all dead?' I asked.

Fukami nodded, his gaze cast down.

'After they died, I erased all data on The Guardians of the Web. Any reference in the Holos and other digital spaces is gone. I had my tattoo removed. Corpus said he was keeping his to remember our friends. That was his prerogative. We've barely spoken since it happened, except when I need programming work done that no one else can do.'

Joon and I shifted in our seats. This definitely wasn't what I'd expected from this interview. Our biggest lead seemed to be hitting a dead end.

'So how could our killer have this design as a tattoo?' I wondered out loud. 'Who else knows about it?'

Fukami stared into space, lost in his memories. Then his eyes flickered.

'There was someone,' he said slowly. 'Someone who wanted to join. Talented, but totally unhinged. We were introduced as part of a military program I was running.'

My pulse started racing. Military. It fit my theory, even if Rommel's search hadn't turned up any hits yet.

'Military? What program?' I asked.

'We ran several at the time,' Fukami said. 'They were a big funder of our research. Still are. There was simulation training where we helped lower the fear response in soldiers going into battle by acclimating them to worse in virtual. The person I'm thinking of was part of a rehabilitation program for PTSD. He became attached to the idea of living forever online. The first jack-in. He'd lost a limb in battle and wanted to be whole again in virtual. I showed him our image of the seven-legged spider to explain how not everything needs to be complete to be whole. I didn't know then what kind of person he was.'

'What kind of person was he?' Joon asked, fully alert.

'A despicable one. He mirrored the worst in human nature. Even Switch despised him, and she was tolerant of most desires. I couldn't understand how the military could tolerate him, let alone continue to help him be part of the program.'

'Can you remember his name?' I asked.

Filton shook his head.

'They just had subject numbers. But he wanted us to call him the Spider after he saw our symbol. Switch and Corpus had another name for him. The Troll.'

Tingles went up my spine. Joon tapped his wrist-comm and a shot of Bleesh burst to life in front of him.

'Could this be one of his current avatars?' he said quickly.

'I can't know for sure,' Fukami shook his head, eying the hologram. 'That's the problem with the virtual world. Everyone could be anyone. But I know this vermin. Bleesh.' He spat out the last word like it tasted rotten.

'How?' I asked.

'He takes everything I say about freedom and makes it ugly,' said Fukami. 'He puts it online like he's a supporter of mine. Whips the worst of my base into a frenzy. Claims the right to freedom of speech to say the most vile things and bring out the most vile ideas. He's a stain on the Holos.'

'But he *is* part of your supporter base,' I said, pushing Fukami, 'An advocate for zero laws. He's doing this to stop Senator Rommel's bill from passing. This is the kind of hatred you get from appealing to the extremes.'

Fukami stood up straighter. Looked me in the eye.

'I can't be responsible for the way the political system works. It's just how human nature operates.'

'And yet you've used it to create evil like this,' I said, indicating the image of Bleesh. 'People like you should know better. You should come out and condemn him, but that would be less votes, wouldn't it?'

'Be fair, Detective Byron,' Joon cut in. 'I'm sure the senator does what he thinks is right.'

'If this troll is that same soldier,' Fukami said over Joon. 'He was twisted before I had anything to do with him. I didn't create him.'

'And *is* he that soldier?' Joon asked.

'Perhaps,' Fukami said, nodding a little. He clicked his screen again, sifted through some files before finding what he wanted. 'The troll was finally cut out of our PTSD program at military directive four years ago on October 31st if that helps.'

Joon did his own digital digging, his avatar's eyes flickering with file light behind them.

'Cline's work says Bleesh became active in December four years ago. The dates line up. It could be a match.'

Fukami was nodding more now like we had him convinced. He steepled his fingers and looked at me.

'What can I do to help?' Fukami leaned forward. 'This murderer is a threat to the Holos. It's my legacy. I would protect that any way I can.'

Joon shot me a furtive look. Could we trust this man? Or had we just alerted him to our biggest leads, so he could spin us off the right path? Surely Fukami wasn't this good of an actor. He seemed totally sincere, but wasn't that the mark of a good politician? Didn't he seem sincere on stage too?

'We're hoping to track Bleesh down tonight,' Joon said slowly. 'Do you have any questions we could ask to confirm whether he's this soldier you mentioned? Any insight into how we might find him in the real world?'

Fukami thought for a moment. 'I might have something even better than questions.'

He clicked open a panel on his desk and punched in a handful of numbers. There was a hissing noise in one of his drawers. Pulling it open, Fukami put his hand inside and lifted out... nothing. I frowned.

'Look closer,' he said, holding out his index finger.

Right on the tip was a tiny prick of color.

'What is it?' I asked.

'A trace dot,' Fukami said, smiling.

'There's no such thing,' Joon said.

'Not for synced avatars, no,' Fukami said. 'It's impossible to track one unless you resort to very ugly means. But most trolls are cowards and go unsynced in case their hate catches up with them. If Bleesh is that kind of coward, which I'm sure he is, this will be the answer. The tech is a patch based on what the police use to track their stock, unsynced avatars in the Holos, but reversed out so we'll know where he is in the real world.'

'I'd know about this tech if it were possible,' said Joon again.

Fukami arched an eyebrow. 'I haven't let the technology become available because I value people's privacy too much,' he said. 'But this is a special case. I'm hoping I can rely on your discretion?'

He extended his hand toward Joon. They pressed their index fingers together and the dot transferred at the touch. Joon narrowed his eyes, apparently studying it in code sight.

'How does it work?' he asked.

'It becomes a part of an unsynced avatar's code,' Fukami explained. 'The malware latches on to the signals and follows them back to the jack-in point. All you need to do is get Bleesh to swallow it and hope he's not wearing synced.'

'Swallow it?' I asked, incredulous. 'How do you expect us to do that?'

'I didn't say it would be easy,' Fukami said. 'I'm sure you'll think of something.'

I considered the dot on Joon's finger, plans already racing through my head. It was time to go to LoveDeath.

36

The thud of bass coursed through my body as we entered LoveDeath. Melodies of classical music wove in with electronic glitch snarls. I went through the front scanners with my arms wide. The green code-light at the door checked our avatars for active recording or tracing. We were let through without fuss. I thanked Joon inwardly for convincing me to change into this new and improved body.

Swirling lights flickered in different colors around the club, illuminating a scene from some kind of twisted cinematic fantasy. People oozing punk sex appeal danced in the crush. Half were naked, others half-clothed. All had knives on thighs, guns on arms, swords crossed over backs. A transgender angel with a skull head, perfect breasts, and bladed wings danced on a podium while a bald man knelt in front of her, sucking her cock. The angel had a dagger in her hands, cutting her lover's bald head to the beat so blood oozed down his face and body. Similar scenes dotted around the place—a mix of lust, sex, and death. A pack of cute, Japanese schoolgirls sat in a corner, sipping from pink teacups, watching it all, giggling. Joon walked beside me in his avatar, which was altered yet again from his normal one. He was now a tall, athletic Caucasian, covered from hip to neck in an intricate tattoo—a hellish motif from Dante's Inferno. He feigned boredom like he'd seen this scene at LoveDeath all before. Maybe he had. I did my best not to scream at the top of my lungs 'grow some morals, you sick pack of jagoffs!' Instead, I casually walked to the bar, resplendent in my current avatar that was something like a goth version of Cleopatra. Joon had talked me into taking the façade, and he was right: anything else would've stood out like chilly nipples. Some especially erect examples did indeed walk past just then, attached to a woman who looked entirely made of mirror ball.

Bringing my attention back to the bar, I signaled for someone to serve us a drink. Joon leaned his elbows on the bar top, scanning the crowd. He looked perfectly in place.

'What do you want?' I asked.

'A glass of milk,' he said.

'Milk?' I shot him a surprised look.

'Anything else is coded to make you feel drunk or high,' he said. 'Take my advice and stay away from the Cocaine Cowboys,' he indicated a list of cocktails that shone above bottles of every conceivable liquid.

The barman came over and lifted his chin to ask for my order.

'One whiskey. One milk!' I shouted over the noise.

The barman poured our orders directly from spigot-tipped fingers and slid them toward me.

'A hundred,' he yelled.

Joon waved his arm casually and a golden SureCoin exchange lit across into the central register. Satisfied, the barman went on to his next customer.

'See anything?' I asked Joon, handing him his milk.

'Not yet,' Joon shook his head, eyes still roaming the place.

His gaze rose to an upper mezzanine reserved for VIPs. Booths hung back in the shadows while groups of people drank near the balcony railing. I sipped my whiskey. The heat of it glided down my throat and warmed my belly. The light rush of alcohol filtered up to my brain. I flexed the fingers in my free hand. This body, this avatar, was incredible. Every sound, taste, and physical sensation radiated through it. It was a struggle to separate myself from the illusion. To realize that I was really plugged in at police HQ, helmet and haptics on, walking and climbing steps on a run disk. If anything, I felt stronger here. Freer. More alive. The fact sparked fear in me that this could easily become addictive. I saw now why millions lived their lives jacked in instead of staying in the real world. In a way, this was a real world, with consequences and relationships and hopes and dreams. Just different ones. Still, my instincts railed against the idea that the Holos was as legitimate as the world I grew up in. Fake. Constructed. A beautiful lie. Not as worthy. I leaned back onto the bar. Had the run disk in our simulation room just raised a bench to form behind me at the same height? It felt solid. Real. I sipped my whiskey again and brought my focus back to the club. Getting lost in philosophizing wasn't going to help us catch this killer.

My attention was drawn to movement on the dance floor. People parted to make way for someone. Then I spotted her. A dark, elven beauty moved through the crowd: Poison. Bleesh's bodyguard. I went to make a move when Joon stopped me.

'Just watch and wait,' he said, leaning in, a big smile on his face like he was telling me a joke. 'She'll lead us to Bleesh.'

Forcing myself to calm, I downed the rest of my drink and signaled for another. Poison continued to move through the dance floor. Most people shuffled out of the way as soon as they spotted her. Some whispered and pointed. She was famous here—or infamous.

A giant lump of a man, dancing with reckless abandon, blocked Poison's clear path on the floor. He twirled and raved in manic moves, lost in the thrall of the club's beat like some kind of techno Viking. Without breaking stride, Poison shoved him out of the way. He tumbled and crashed into another group of dancers. I glanced over to the security guards at the door. They simply stood, stoic and unmoving. The man who had been pushed was another story. He sprung off the ground and turned towards Poison, looking to see who pushed him. Anger flashed over his face.

'Slut!' he shouted, loud enough to be heard clearly over the music.

Instantly people started backing out of Poison's vicinity. She smiled darkly. The big man held his ground. He flexed his impressive pectorals and pointed. *You. Me. Let's go.* At the signal, people started cheering. The music shifted to a darker tone and a voice came over the PA.

'Challenge made. Bets close in one minute.'

There was a flurry of activity. People formed a wide circle around Poison and the man. Two hologram screens shot up from the dance floor next to each of the combatants. Stats glowed to life on the screens. Betting odds sat beneath. Poison had hundreds of wins next to her name. No losses. The man, apparently called Odin3, was twelve wins, no losses. People tapped their wrists and the gold of SureCoin zapped toward the screens. Betting odds scrolled. Totals were summed—Poison a clear favorite. It reminded me a bit of the policy markets. Gambling with high stakes. The more you knew about a contender, the better placed you were to bet. That's why the Futarchy system had been put in place. Betting markets were better at flushing out relevant information. Cutting through the noise. Unless there was a killer running loose, throwing things off.

While punters continued placing bets, Poison and Odin3 paced at far ends of the circle, eying each other. The music still played, but I could hear the Viking slinging insults at his opponent.

'I'm going to slice you up. Rip your arms off and jerk off with them. Pop your tits like piñatas.'

Poison remained silent. Her eyes didn't waver from Odin3. Her hand went to a sword hilt that jutted from behind her left shoulder. She pulled it free, not from a scabbard, but from her actual back. The blade dripped with her blood as it came out of her skin. There was no hint of pain on her features, just a look of hatred in her eyes. If I knew how to bet, I would have placed a week's wage on her right then. That emotion was information.

I looked to Joon for cues on how to react naturally and keep our cover. He simply watched and sipped his milk.

'Is this a thing here?' I asked, indicating the fight circle on the dance floor.

He nodded. 'The winner gets ten percent of total bets,' he said. 'It's cheap entertainment for the house. It also stops most people picking fights.'

'I thought it would encourage them,' I said.

'You have to fight to avatar death,' Joon explained. 'And if you try to back out once it starts, security kill you. No one in here has cheap avatars. Most are emotionally tied to them more than their real bodies.'

My jaw dropped. I looked over to the guards dotted around the room. They each had hands on hip guns, ready to draw. All other eyes were on Poison and the Viking. A countdown had started on the screens. Ten seconds until bets closed.

The crowd started to cheer louder, working into a frenzy. Odin3 beat his chest and pulled two evil-looking knives seemingly from nowhere. Poison held her sword loosely at her side.

'Five!' The crowd chimed together as the countdown flicked on the screens. 'Four. Three.'

Odin3 held his knives up and screamed a battle cry.

The crowd kept counting. 'Two!'

The Viking began to charge toward Poison, who crouched into a fighting stance.

'One!'

Everyone in the club roared. Music thundered to life. Odin3 leapt in the air, blades bared.

Then, Poison disappeared in a blur.

I blinked through the laser lights of the club. Before I could pin anything down, blood sprayed. The top half of the Viking tumbled into the crowd in a gory mess. His bottom half dropped to the ground like a sack of wet meat. In barely a second, Poison glittered back into sight on the far edge of the circle. The crowd was a riot of activity. Some were already cheering the win. The ones who had been hit with Odin3's severed torso were scrambling off the ground. Others just stood in shock. A pinging of gold shimmered everywhere from a new betting screen in the middle of the dance floor. A thick ray of golden light shot into Poison, who glowed like a god. Her payoff. Other SureCoin sparks flew into people who had laid bets, paying their stake. Dancing had already resumed in some spots. The music thrummed on. Guards came out and dragged the Viking's remains from the dance floor.

My attention came back to Poison, who stood with her head raised toward the VIP balcony. There, a figure emerged from the shadows of the booths against the wall. He stood, clapping. A horrid smile sat on his troll-like face.

Bleesh.

37

Poison stalked up the VIP stairs towards Bleesh. No one got in her way this time. The rest of the club was back to dancing or fucking or sucking or whatever they'd been doing before the fight. Bleesh welcomed Poison with a smack on the ass and a round of drinks.

'Did you notice a silhouette when she ghosted?' I asked Joon, turning my gaze to him so we weren't so obviously watching above.

'No,' he said, 'but the lights in here make it hard to tell. One thing's for sure, though, Poison is synced. You can't move that fluidly otherwise. There'll be no tracking her. We'll have to watch her but focus on Bleesh.'

I snuck a glance toward the pair again. They were talking, Bleesh holding court as other lackeys hung on around them.

'Let's hope Fukami's theory that most trolls go unsynced is right,' I said. 'How do we get up there?'

Joon peered around, took in the security guards standing at the bottom of the mezzanine stairs. They formed a solid avatar wall that bristled with blades.

'No idea,' he said. 'Look around at everyone here. Tell me what you see.'

Unsure where this was going, I looked anyway. All around, people were caught up in their own fantasies, doing what they wanted.

'It's like a performance,' I said slowly. 'Everyone's the star of their own show.'

Joon tipped his head in agreement. 'And every star is attractive in their own way.'

I looked again. He was right. As grotesque as I thought some of the ideas and outfits were, all were geared to draw the eye and illicit temptation. Muscles, cleavage, jawlines, cheekbones. The clothing and makeup all accentuated those curves. It was like a Halloween frat party. They were all dressed to be sexy. Nobody wanted to be a real monster. Except Bleesh. He stood out as being truly horrid among a cast of pretty things.

'He doesn't want to be attractive,' Joon said, mirroring my thoughts. 'He wants to be feared. How do we use that to our advantage?'

I stood at a loss. The music and lights and flesh on display were clouding my thoughts. It was hard to shut it out and calculate logically what to do. I thought of my psychology research from my PhD on the Specter Slaughters. What does evil want? To feel powerful. To feel like it matters. To feel like it has control of the world. I watched Bleesh as he talked with Poison, imagining the bodies of Christos Rama and Lilith and Yu Ying. I paused on the fact that Corpus was still being tortured somewhere. It was more about money than power, Rama had said. Was it really? Did this crude troll just want something so crude as cash?

Then a bolt from the blue struck me. A thought so clear it had to be right. 'He just wants attention,' I said to Joon. 'He wants what everyone else here wants. He just gets it a different way.'

Joon looked to Bleesh again, then away. Pursed his lips in thought. Nodded. 'I think you're onto something. But what does that mean for us?'

'Just follow my lead,' I said, an idea forming in my head.

I stepped away from the bar into full view of the mezzanine floor. I started pointing and waving and jumping up and down like a star-struck fan. Joon stood by, looking at me like I'd gone crazy.

'Oh my god, it's Bleesh!' I yelled to Joon, pointing up again. 'It's Bleesh. Bleesh!' I waved my arms to get the troll's attention.

The movement caught his interest and he glanced my way. I jumped up and down, clapping my hands with excitement then waved furiously.

'Bleesh! Bleesh!' I blew him kisses, fanned myself like I might faint, every over-the-top gesture I could think of.

Joon came over and grabbed my arm, trying to stop me.

'What are you doing?' he hissed under his breath. 'This isn't undercover protocol.'

'But it's Bleesh!' I said loudly.

By now all of the troll's crew were looking down at me with barely concealed disgust. Except Bleesh himself. He had a smug smile on his face. He raised an eyebrow at Poison, like *see, I'm the man.*

I held up my index figure to signal he wait and skipped to the bar, yelling to the avatar who'd served us before.

'You! I need two drinks. Whatever he's having!' I pointed again up to Bleesh who sipped some strange, bubbling concoction.

In a moment, the barman had two cocktails queued up on a tray. I nudged Joon to pay. He shook his head in resignation.

'I hope you know what you're doing,' he said and zapped SureCoin into the register.

I held up the drink tray as an offering to Bleesh above, kneeling down as if giving thanks to a deity. When I raised my head to look, Bleesh beckoned magnanimously for us to come upstairs. He signaled to the security guards, who were looking our way by now as well, to let us through. I nudged Joon excitedly, continuing my act but winking at the same time.

'You have that tracking dot, right?' I murmured, smiling. 'Give it to me.'

Joon fell into step behind me, stealthily transferring the dot to a fingertip on my free hand. The mission was now firmly with me. We slid through the security guards and up the stairs. Every few seconds I glanced over to where Bleesh stood, pretending to be breathless, checking he was there. My natural anxiety in the moment actually worked in my favor. All part of the act. As we made it to Bleesh, I bowed again. Poison moved slightly in front of her charge, in case I got too close. I fawned at her.

'You were amazing back there!' I said. 'I wish I could slice men in two like that! You turned Odin3 into Odin1.5,' I mimicked a cutting motion in the air and giggled. 'Poison, isn't it?'

She nodded without a word.

'You didn't use your legendary venom attack during the fight?' I said. 'I would've love to have seen that.'

'I only use it against worthy opponents,' she sneered.

'Well, no venom or poison in these drinks either!' I laughed, swirling one with my finger. I sucked the liquid off to show it was safe, letting my tongue linger as I looked Bleesh in the eye, then winked.

He barked a horrid laugh in return and I held the tray out to him.

'Oh, these are delicious!' I said at the taste of the vanilla-flavored drink. 'What is it?'

'You've never had a Cocaine Cowboy?' he croaked in delight. 'I have dozens a night.'

My mouth started to tingle with an odd sensation, half numb, half alight with taste. My smile faltered for just a moment. It was the drink Joon warned me about earlier.

'Oh, well, I'll have to try them one day,' I said, 'This one is for your friend.'

I offered the tray toward Poison.

'No, no, no,' Bleesh said, plucking it off the tray and handing it to me. 'I want to share a drink with a fan. You recognized me, yes?'

I took the drink. Joon stood at my shoulder, clearing his throat just loud enough for me to catch it. He was watching Bleesh. The troll moved oddly. Not slow exactly, but not perfectly either. Jerky in his movements. He must be unsynced. We couldn't blow this.

'Of course I recognized you,' I chirped in my most sycophantic voice. 'You're the provocateur prince! The troll of trolls. Bad boy Bleeshy! I can't get enough of you!'

Bleesh looked around at his crew to make sure everyone was taking note. He waved his drink under his nose, inhaling the scent deeply. I watched his lips, waiting for him to take a sip. He didn't.

'Tell me,' he said instead. 'What's your favorite moment of mine? Something that got you slick between those long legs of yours?'

He looked me up and down lecherously. I almost vomited in my mouth. To cover it, I inhaled the smell of the cocktail in my hands. Just the fumes made my mind swirl. Confidence sparkled through my brain. Exactly the jolt I needed.

'Lilith!' I blurted. 'You showed her what a dirty bitch she was. Is it true that you bathed in her real blood after you killed her?'

Bleesh nodded the whole time, loving every moment.

'I coded the taste of it if you'd like to go vampire and drink it with me later,' he said. 'After these, of course.'

He clinked glasses with me and waited for me to sip. With no choice, I did. Liquid heaven poured into my mouth. Every tastebud and molecule in my body sang with it. The room lifted to three shades brighter. My pupils must have just dilated to triple their normal size. Electricity sparked through my body. Bass and melodies thundered through my pores like liquid. Music was now a part of me. The sensation almost swept me away. After the initial rush, my mind zapped into laser focus. I was one with the Holos. The whole thing. Not just the music. I knew every part of it. Everyone and everything.

'Good?' Bleesh smiled.

I nodded, unable to speak.

'Have some more then,' he sneered, and threw his own drink right in my face.

I gasped at the shock of it, standing there dripping. Bleesh's dark laughter felt like razors cutting into me. Shame bubbled deep inside me but was pushed back. Aggression surged forward. I rushed to punch Bleesh full in the face. Poison blocked it easily. Joon stepped in quickly, pulling me back by the arms.

'You smear of a human!' I yelled, struggling to hit Bleesh. 'You incel insect! I'll rip your head off and spit down your throat!'

Joon wrestled with my squirming arms, finally wrapping a lock on them. I could feel his heat shudder into me from behind. It was like he was going to melt into me. The whole club swayed in my vision before sharpening again. Bleesh looked to his posse and grinned.

'Oh you pretty ones,' Bleesh crooned. 'Can't handle your narco. You're all beauty and no bite.'

He lunged forward and grabbed my dress, kissing me hard. His thick, slug-like tongue slithered in my mouth. I gagged on it. Joon let my arms go and I shoved Bleesh back. Joon jumped in front of me with insane speed, ready to strike. A dagger flicked into his hand from his wrist. He brought the tip up just inches from Bleesh's black eyes. Poison whipped her blade to rest on Joon's throat at the same time. Joon's dagger stopped mid-swing. He was fully in control, unlike me. I wiped my mouth furiously in disgust. I snarled, about to leap in again when Joon's trailing hand came up to stop me.

Bleesh watched, amused.

'Go on then, faggot,' he jeered at Joon. 'Try it. Fight for the honor of your little pussy bitch here. The slut came onto me. Wanted it. Didn't you see her begging before? She loves it.'

He flicked his tongue at me lewdly. The drugs of the cocaine cowboy still swirled through my system. My teeth clenched so hard it felt like they would shatter. It took every inch of my self-control not to just attack in a blind fury.

Bleesh stood his ground, watching Joon. The troll took a step forward, his eye flush with the tip of Joon's dagger.

'Go on,' he said. 'Do it. I have plenty of copies of this avi sitting in the cloud. Not like your Sabi there.'

Bleesh grinned, indicating the check mark on Joon's bicep, clear as day with his arm stretched out, holding the knife like he was.

'One wrong move and you're scrambled,' Bleesh said. 'Poison will see to that.'

Joon's eyes flicked to Bleesh's bodyguard, who smiled with sharp teeth.

'I tell you what,' Bleesh said, stepping back again and rubbing his hands. He looked totally relaxed. In control. 'I'm feeling generous tonight. I'll give you a fighting chance.'

Bleesh looked at Joon then me.

'Fag boy here fights Poison. If he wins, you guys walk out like nothing happened. If he loses, I get to rape your pretty cunt and put the footage up on the Feed.'

That foul mouth of his just never stopped.

'No deal,' I snapped.

Bleesh raised his eyebrows. 'You'd rather I just slaughter your friend here and now?' he asked.

'No,' I said, battling the urge to spit in the troll's face. 'He's not fighting Poison. I am.'

38

Anger boiled through my body. Nothing else mattered at that moment. The mission. The victims. Corpus. Our safety. All I wanted to do was wipe the smile from Bleesh's face and lop the head from Poison's shoulders. A tiny voice deep down screamed to run and jack out. To continue with the case. That voice was a whisper in a storm, silenced by the winds of rage.

'What are you doing?' Joon asked in my ear as we were ushered downstairs to the fighting floor. 'What's your plan?'

The whole club had already formed a circle for the battle. Bets were madly being placed and we hadn't even taken positions. I had no stats. My name was listed as Unknown Contender. No one put money on me. No one.

'I plan to win,' I said, grinding my teeth and licking my lips.

That cocktail had been amazing. I wondered if I could get another one before the fight. We made our way into the circle. Security guards stood in the inner ring, guns at the ready in case I fled. Poison stalked on the other side. Bleesh still watched up on the mezzanine. A coward's retreat to safety.

'You're out of your depth,' Joon said. 'Be smart. We should make a run for it.'

'I fight,' I glared.

'That's the drugs talking,' he said. 'Stop. Think. There's more at stake.'

'Oh, I'm clear,' I said, my jaw tweaking from side to side, breath coming in deep heaves. 'Now stand back.'

I went to push him back, but he grabbed my wrist. He pulled out a dagger and flipped it up hilt first, handing it to me.

'At least take this.'

'I don't need it,' I pushed the blade away. 'You might be too scared to use your claws in here and give yourself away, but Sabi made my body a weapon too, remember?'

Joon's eyes went wide. He looked at Poison again.

'You can't!' he hissed. 'You scramble her, you torch a key suspect. We'll never track her down.'

'We have Bleesh,' I said, eyes back on Poison. 'He's the key anyway.'

'We have nothing,' Joon said. 'Just fucking stop and think about it. We need his location or he's a ghost.'

'No time for thinking,' I snarled, pushing him back.

The DJ started his final bets countdown. SureCoin clattered toward Poison's bet screen. Mine was silent. Angry, I looked to Joon.

'Bet on me,' I said, my loathing rising still.

'What?!' he said. 'You're fucking crazy.'

'Bet!' I said.

He shook his head in disgust but flicked his hand toward the screen. Gold rushed toward it. He hadn't gone light either. A smile flicked to my lips. This was going to be fun.

'Five!' The crowd chorused to launch time. 'Four!'

'You can't do this,' Joon tried one last time.

'Three,'

I could and I would.

'Two,'

I turned to face Poison.

'One,'

I beckoned her to come toward me with the index finger of my left hand. Once, twice, three times.

'FIGHT!'

I held out my right palm and blasted.

A thick beam of silver arched across the circle. Poison had nowhere to run, no time to react. It hit her full in the chest before she even had a chance to disappear. She tore apart like an exploding supernova. People behind were caught in the crossfire too, all obliterated. The blast tore a gaping hole in the club wall, out into the night.

Then the beam cut off.

Total silence hung in the air. The carnage was incredible. Bodies and half-bodies lay everywhere. Poison was completely gone. I looked at my hand, expecting smoke to be pouring from it. It looked utterly normal. No fire. No current. Just the flesh of death incarnate.

The sound of SureCoin transactions pulled me out of my trance. Ten percent of all bets clinked into my avatar's digital wallet. Joon was getting a crazy amount as well, enjoying thousand-to-one odds on his outlay.

I looked around. Everyone just gaped at me in shock. I stared up to the mezzanine. Bleesh stood there, rocked. His expression made me so happy I could've burst into song. I blew a kiss in his direction and smiled. It was like I'd punched him full in the face. He staggered back. After a moment, he regained his balance and rushed back to the rail.

'Kill them!' he screamed. 'Kill those fuckers!'

The command snapped everyone back to attention. Every guard, every dancer, every Japanese schoolgirl with a pink teacup in her hand turned to us with murder in their eyes.

'This is more like HateDeath now, amiright?' I nudged Joon.

'Run!' he said.

Dropping into fighting stance, I held my palm out again toward the first guards who pulled guns on us. They dove back, expecting another attack. My hand did nothing. I looked at it dumbly. Did it have to recharge? Joon wasn't so stupid. He barreled past me, grabbing my arm as he went, dragging me along. I started to run too. Shots rang out behind us. Bullets ripped through furniture to the side as we dodged through some tables. One shot hit a guard full in the chest. Blood sprayed. I laughed at the sight, perception warped by the cocktail in my system. Still, I ran. Joon grabbed a pistol from the dead guard's hand in one smooth swoop and started blasting a clear path to the door. Partiers dove away. I thought we might make it, when the huge trans angel from the dance podium blocked our path. Its skull face opened in a scream. Without breaking pace, Joon launched a kick into its solar plexus and sent it flying backward. The thing smashed through the club doors, opening the way for us. We sprinted over its body and wings out into the main street.

The strip was packed. Friday night. People were gathered around the hole my blast had ripped in the wall on the far side of the club. The distraction was a blessing as we bolted into traffic. Horns blared. We sprinted away. Joon kept glancing back over his shoulder. I looked back too in time to see a group of goons running from LoveDeath and jumping into a row of cyber-trucks. Lights shone and tires squealed. Joon searched frantically for a way to escape. A way to get to ground level and jack out properly. The closest lift was not far off. He pointed. We might make it. I streaked forward while Joon looked back. Right at that moment, a harpoon speared from the side of one of the trucks. It spiked through Joon's shoulder. The point came out of his chest and pulled back again, ugly barbs ripping into his flesh. Joon screamed. The end of the harpoon was attached to a cable. It buzzed. Joon was pulled off his feet, reeled backward like a giant fish.

'No!' I shouted.

I turned around, scrambling back. Joon struggled to free himself from the harpoon. He sliced the end off with his claws and the thing ripped free. By now the cyber-trucks had circled around him. He struggled to his feet as five of the giant security guards jumped from their cars. The angel of death from before also emerged, tall and menacing. I sprinted forward ready to dive into the fray again.

'Go!' Joon waved with his good arm, trying to get me to leave.

He spun to fight. He was too late. The angel raised a bladed wing and sliced down, cleaving Joon in two from skull to scrotum. His body dropped apart to the ground, mouth open in shock, eyes wide.

I growled. A sense of rage built from deep within at the sight. This wasn't right. This wasn't justice. My growl turned to a primal scream.

I held out my hand, curled my left finger back three times as the trigger, and blasted them all into their next life.

39

I jacked out to see Joon's body shuddering on the ground. Alarms rang everywhere. My head spun. The noise collided with the effects of the digital drugs in my system. Even untethered from the virtual world, everything pulsed and swirled. My confused state was nothing to Joon's distress though. He managed to wrench his connection free. He saw me and howled like a dying animal. It was pure despair. The door slammed open. Gibson. He assessed the situation and went straight to Joon's side. I did too. I pulled all of the cables away from his body.

'Agent Joon,' Gibson said, holding him by the shoulders. 'You're in the real world. You're okay. It was just virtual.'

'You're with us, Joon,' I said.

'Medic!' Gibson yelled into his wrist-comm.

Joon thrashed away from Gibson. He stumbled to his feet and crashed into the wall. He held himself up, his legs shaking.

'I need to go back in,' he said. 'I need to get my body. We can save it. Sabi can save it.'

He struggled toward the Holos stack, reaching for the connecting cables he normally jacked into his skull cap. Gibson held him back, holding him upright in the process.

'You're in shock,' Gibson said firmly. 'Sit down. Sit down.' He tried to lower Joon to the ground but Joon wouldn't go.

'No,' he said. 'My body.'

'Joon,' I touched his arm. 'There's no body to save. It's gone. It's...'

I trailed off. I didn't want to say I'd blown it apart beyond any chance of repair. Not even a string of code would be left.

Joon did slump down then. He hit the ground like a marionette with its strings cut. A medic arrived. It was the same man who'd helped me last time. He dropped a bag of equipment on the floor and rifled for the right options. Joon leaned to the side and vomited. The liquid slid across the floor.

'It was all for nothing,' he moaned, sick still dripping from his mouth.

The medic had found what he was looking for and jabbed Joon's arm with a needle. As the plunger went in, Joon heaved a breath.

'It wasn't for nothing,' I said, trying to soothe him. 'We got him. We got Bleesh.'

'No,' Joon shook his head. He lay down on the ground, putting his hand over his face. 'We got nothing. You fucked it up.'

My warm sympathy flared to hot anger, the last of my digital drug high crashing fast and hard, making me erratic.

'I did nothing of the sort,' I snapped. 'I got Bleesh.'

Joon coughed and retched again. He sat up and leveled a hate-filled gaze at me. My statement had snapped his mind momentarily to attention.

'He splashed his drink all over you,' Joon said. 'The trace dot was in it. Not even our conversation was recorded because of the privacy coding of the club. Or are you too high to remember?'

The statement obviously drained him. He rested his elbows on his knees, his head hanging. He panted. The medic checked his vitals.

'I'm clearer than you think,' I said. 'The trace dot wasn't in the drink.'

Joon stopped, confusion lining his features as he looked up again. He blinked. His eyes went in and out of focus.

'What?' he said.

I held up an imaginary glass toward him to help explain. I swirled it with my finger like I had Bleesh's, then made a show of licking the fingertip.

'I knew that filthy troll would force himself on me at some point,' I said. 'I wanted his kiss. We got him, Joon. The dot was on my tongue and he sucked it down hook, line, and sinker. We've got our killer right where we want him.'

Joon vomited once more, this time all over the front of me. His eyes rolled back in his head. He was out. But I wasn't. I had the target right in my sights.

40

Our team sat in the briefing room for an emergency meeting. Gibson. Cline. The Sheriff. Me.

Joon had been sent to hospital for monitoring. His vitals were stable, but the avatar death had rocked him, even when he'd had serious Stockholm Effect training. Still, we had to press on. This new development wouldn't wait.

Footage from outside LoveDeath played on the Feed screen. News stations and vloggers and Feeders had picked up the story, spouting all sorts of conspiracy theories. The blast was from a Neo Specter Slaughter group. It was a secret ploy by Senator Rommel to cause chaos in the Holos and whip up support for her bill. It was a kid hacker just playing around with a new toy. The novelty was why the story was getting so much attention. Hundreds—if not thousands—of avatars were scrambled nightly in the Holos, just not in this spectacular way, so they never made for good news. Thankfully, for us, the recording ban inside LoveDeath meant all that came out of the mess were people's highly exaggerated and distorted versions of events. The result was a shitshow of he said, she said, they said, we did.

'You have a lot to answer for,' Sheriff Mendez seethed.

I sat there nursing my temples. An atomic-level migraine was trying to pulverize my brain to mush. The high from the cocaine cowboy in my system fully collapsed between the jack-in room and here. True reality came rushing in. My sense of accomplishment at what we'd done hadn't disappeared, but how we'd done it had my moral compass spinning. Joon had lost his avatar. I'd obliterated many more. But we hadn't really killed anyone. Had we? They were just digital people. Their true selves were alive and well. Weren't they? I hoped Joon was coping, physically and mentally. I wanted to tell him I was sorry. I wanted to explain it was worth it. Guilt mixed with the endless anxiety that seemed a permanent fixture in my life now. My skin prickled with heat. Pretty soon I'd start sweating rivers and begin to shake. I needed to hold it together. I swallowed and pushed it all down. *Don't feel, just do,* I thought. *Get up. Move forward.* But feelings kept rushing in.

The sheriff was furious. I'd gone against protocol by using a non-stock avatar to go undercover. But how else could you do it? I shouldn't have been so stupid to use Sabi's weapon so recklessly at any rate. Everything felt so twisted right now. So unreal. I looked at my hands. They were mine, weren't they? I wasn't still in the Holos. Or was I? It had felt the same there in my synced avatar that looked and felt just like me. How could I tell the difference between here and there? Switch's words echoed through me. *When you come out, you're changed. You can't go back from that. When you try, you realize that you were just in a simulation. But it felt so real. So, what do you feel now? Is the solid world real, or just another simulation?* I touched the silver ring on my thumb. My dad's ring. My anchor. No, this was real. If it wasn't, nothing was. We were in the true world, not that shadow place.

'How did you do all that damage?' Mendez pressed. 'Was it Agent Joon? Trust him to have access to firepower like that in virtual.'

I didn't say anything. I wasn't about to admit it was my own special avatar function. The evaporating of Bleesh's henchman hadn't been captured on film either. Still, Joon shouldn't have to wear the jacket for my stuff up. I wanted to say it was me, but didn't. Maybe if I kept quiet, they'd just move on about it.

'We didn't break any laws,' I murmured instead. 'We were in the Holos.'

'There's a difference between breaking laws and acting with integrity,' snapped Mendez. 'You're on a fine line here. I should take you off the case.'

I held my breath. Bit my lip. The goal of catching this killer was all that was holding me together right now. My last tether to sanity. If that was cut away, where would I be then?

'You're lucky there's been no mention of police involvement in these reports, despite how crazy they are,' Mendez continued. 'How you got away undetected *and* managed to get a trace on Bleesh is beyond me. I suppose it was worth the sacrifice.'

'What sacrifice?' Gibson said. 'A bit of a virtual knocking around?'

'Have some god-damned respect,' I found myself saying with much more force than necessary. 'Joon's body was destroyed.'

'So what?' Gibson said. 'He can get another avatar. He'll be fine in a day or two.'

'Could you get another one of your stupid thumb heads if I ripped it off?' I growled.

Who even was I? Defending a virtual lifestyle?

'Enough!' the Sheriff slapped her hand on the table. 'Detective Byron, I'm willing to cut you a little slack because of your results today, but one more word out of line, and you're done. Entendida?'

I locked my jaw tighter than a pit bull and nodded.

'Now,' Mendez said, 'How do we activate this tracing dot?'

'Senator Fukami gave us an access link,' I said slowly. 'I believe we follow that. Joon had all the technical details.'

'I'll be able to figure it out if there's a link,' Cline said. 'If we need to ask Agent Joon, we will.'

I eyed Cline warily. There was too much pointing toward him being a mole. I didn't want to hand him the link. Mendez caught my reluctance.

'It's okay, Ada,' she said. 'Cline explained how he missed the footage scrub. We've done a full sweep of his communications and he's clear. He's also on notice, aren't you, güey?'

Cline looked down, then up at me in apology. 'I won't make excuses,' he said. 'I'm sorry. It was an error. One I won't repeat. If this trace fails, I'm done. I want to catch this guy as much as anyone.'

'He's made up for his mistake too with some solid thinking,' Mendez said.

I looked to Cline for an explanation and he smiled tentatively.

'How?' I asked.

Cline swiped his wrist-comm to find what he was looking for. 'I had a thought that these murders are mostly about manipulating information,' he said. 'Physical murders veiled as Specter Slaughters. Different claims of responsibility. Why? They're putting false signals out there to throw Rommel's policy pricing into chaos. It's been working too. So, how do you combat misinformation? You put better information out there. I realized we could release the footage of the killer if we blurred out his identity using the latest military-grade AI and authentication stamping. No spider tattoo. No link to Switch. No panic. But you have proof they're physical killings showing all of those jack-ins that the Holos is safe. It should stop the refugee crisis overnight. Senator Rommel approved everything and made it possible while you were in the Holos.'

He hit the right key on his wrist and the briefing room screen flicked to life again. On it was Feed footage of the first crime scene. You couldn't see our killer's face or tattoo, but he was clearly entering and leaving Rama's apartment at the time of the murder, needle in hand. Info scrolled below. News headlines proclaimed NEO SPECTRE SLAUGHTERS NOT REAL.

I should have been happy but wasn't.

'But you've just given our killer the heads up!' I said. 'We've traced him without him knowing and you're jeopardizing that! Couldn't we have just waited twenty-four hours? He could be smoke in the wind by the time we catch up with him.'

Cline's smile didn't fade. It only got wider. Senator Rommel's face cut into frame behind him on the news feed. She stood in front of a press gallery, giving a statement.

'This latest good work by police to find this footage shows just how important our bill is,' she said. 'If Mercury was the only currency in the Holos, we would be able to match this killer's photo with his active avatars and know exactly where he is right now in both worlds. As it stands, we have no other solid lead on this killer. He remains active and totally unknown.'

'See,' Cline said, cutting off the screen. 'The killer thinks he's safe for now. Some refugees are starting to plug back in. The Strip is still a mess, but it's a start. More importantly, Rommel's policy has narrowed down near to a dollar again. The public are reacting to being threatened by this killer by sinking everything into the bill to get it passed. Bleesh will be furious. He'll be working harder than ever to get to Corpus and swing things in his favor again. To sew doubt about this footage being doctored somehow. He'll be as distracted as possible and we're just about to rain fire on him. This thing is over. We've won.'

I sat back, trying to process everything. We were on the edge of breaking things wide open. We just needed to use the tracing dot and hope Bleesh hadn't cut and run.

41

The Spider smiled as Corpus screamed.

Corpus gritted his teeth. Tried to still his mind and dissociate from the pain. It was impossible. There was no escaping the reality of agony. His tormenter's blades scoured his skin. Burned into his flesh at every nerve cluster and sensitive muscle. He howled his impotence to get away. Just a few words would end this suffering. A location. An admission. He shouldn't. Wouldn't. He could do this. It was only a matter of time before he was free. He had to believe it or go mad. The police would find him soon.

'Not long now,' the Spider said, wiping Corpus's blood off his knife.

His incisors and hairy face looked ghastly in the stark, fluorescent light of the room. Weren't torturers supposed to work in the shadows?

'Not long until I have you,' he repeated.

The Spider turned his many eyes toward the screen on the wall. A counter had begun in the corner. Less than 48-hours until Corpus was found, it said. Either way, this would all end then. Corpus had already held out this long. He could see it through. He could make that counter pause for a while if he set his mind to it. Buy himself some extra time. Keep his anxiety at bay. His fear. His doubt. His terror. When the Spider left, Corpus had been able to hold out against his captor's automaton insects. It was their programming that made it possible. The swarm caused pain in patterns. Because Corpus knew what was coming, he could better steel himself against it. There was less anxiety and more knowing. A game almost. He'd had most of last night without the Spider and his unpredictable nature. But then, the killer himself had come back renewed and enraged. Had set to work with his knives again. No pattern. No rhythm. Just erratic torture from an erratic mind.

Suddenly, a beep made the Spider pause. He stood up straighter, letting his knife fall to his side. The creature lifted two fingers to his throat as if checking his pulse. What was there? The trigger for a comms device? The

Spider stared into space, growling at whatever he saw with those eyes that no longer looked at Corpus. He then started laughing, deep and menacing and cruel. The Spider snapped back to attention, taking in his prey. He clicked his throat again and the map in the corner flickered to something else. The Feed. There was a news clip, showing a blurred figure leaving a crime scene. Senator Sheila Rommel came on next, saying that even though the authorities had the face of the killer, they didn't know his identity. He could be anywhere.

'They know what I look like, but not who I am, where I am,' The Spider chuckled. 'Anonymity really does have its own power, doesn't it? No one will find me. Not even The Master knows my true location.'

That made Corpus jolt. The Master? So this beast was admitting he was being controlled in other ways. The reference made him think The Spider might be slipping.

'They're onto you,' Corpus said, hopeful he could delay his torture some more. 'They'll be breaking down the door any moment. Some database somewhere has your face on it.'

The Spider really laughed now.

'Oh no, no, no, no,' he said. 'That's the thing about the military not many people realize. They keep secrets better than anyone. They even keep secrets from each other. The higher up it goes, the darker the black box gets. And I'm the darkest of them all. The one that got away. They won't let that spider out for anything. If they owned up to me, they'd have to own up to breeding monsters.'

The Spider held up his knife, studying it. With a swift movement, he buried it into Corpus's side. The agony and surprise jolted through his body as one. The Spider twisted the blade further.

'Do you know how the United States Army tried to eliminate the growing problem of PTSD during the last war? How they tried to avoid payouts for breaking men and women? They realized that it wasn't just the things you saw in war that tore you apart. It was the things you *did*. How could a country boy come to terms with his clean self-image if he'd killed a child in crossfire? What if the prom queen had to torture a prisoner for information that might save her platoon? What if you fell prey to bloodlust and raped the enemy as part of the spoils of war? But, but, but... what if you'd done it all already in simulations? Got used to it as part of a pilot program to desensitize you to those horrors. To make you immune to fear. To show you what you could do if the moment demanded it and come to terms with it *beforehand*? They taught us to claim it as the inevitable price of war. The inevitable price of victory. They taught us to bundle virtual and wartime experiences together and separate them apart from your life at home. Log into the game. Win. Log out and come back the same as when you left. They spun out the jack-in process so we never really knew if we were on a mission or if we were in a training exercise. But they never asked what if we grew to enjoy the game? To crave it, so you could feel like you were alive. What then? And what if you were injured in battle, thinking you might be able to log out and be whole again, only to realize your leg was gone for real? What then? What then?'

The Spider wrenched his knife further upward into Corpus's body, waiting for an answer. All Corpus could do was cry out in pain. The Spider's disgusting face was pressed right up against Corpus. His spittle landed on the hacker's skin and sizzled like acid.

'I'm not in any of their databases because they're ashamed of me,' The Spider said. 'But The Master isn't. He knows how powerful I am, even if I am incomplete. He knows I will complete my mission. I will find you and kill you and keep my playground free. The Master has granted me new life and all I have to do is take that gift from a few others. It will be your turn very, very soon.'

The map on the wall shuddered into life. The counter narrowed once more. Corpus's whole body shook with the effort to stop it from moving faster. He fought with his entire will to hold back the words he knew would end it here and now. A location. An admission. He knew who this fiend's Master was. The file would reveal the entire plan.

Corpus just needed the police to do their job and everything would work out. It had to. It had to.

42

A noise pulled Joon out of his drug haze. Where was he? The hospital? He opened his eyes. Everything was blurry.

A figure stood before Joon in the dim light. There was something in the person's hands. Joon worked to focus. Then everything snapped into clarity. A gun!

Joon shuffled back, suddenly in fight or flight. He scrambled to rip his monitor lines off to escape.

'Whoa whoa! Calm down, spankblanket,' Ada Byron said, with a worried frown as she stepped into the light. 'It's just me!'

Joon paused, his heart still thundering. He glanced at the gun Ada was holding.

'I thought you might like a present,' she said.

Ada held out the gun, grip first, smiling weakly. Joon just stared at it. Ada bit her lip and placed the weapon on the table next to Joon. She patted it tenderly.

'I didn't think flowers would cut it,' Ada said softly. 'Figured a Colt 1911 of your own might help. I talked the guys in at Vegas Battlezone into selling me one. It'll give you something to make you feel safer out here, you know?'

Joon didn't know. His breath was still ragged. He'd thought she was there to kill him. He remembered his actual death in a blink. Another blink and he remembered the jack-out room after. Ada had said his avatar was gone. She also said they'd hooked Bleesh.

He forced himself to stop the flood of emotions and sensations. He had to remember his Stockholm Effect training. The mind had control of the body. He was present and here. He wasn't tethered to the virtual. *That's because my lifeline was severed.* The thought rose up unbidden. He wrestled with it. The whole of existence was scrambled.

'My body,' was all he said.

Ada sighed. She took a seat on the foot of Joon's bed.

'It's gone,' she said. 'I'm…' Ada visibly struggled to speak before starting again. 'I'm sorry. I didn't realize it could be fixed. I used Sabi's weapon on the people who attacked you. The avatar was collateral damage.'

Collateral damage.

Such a cold phrase. Butchered. Obliterated. Slaughtered. All would have suited better. The full memories of their mission sunk in. How Ada had lost control in LoveDeath. Or had she? She'd had enough presence of mind to get the tracing dot in the troll.

'Bleesh?' Joon croaked. 'Do we have him?'

'Soon,' Ada said. 'They're tracing him now. We're pulling a strike team together for first thing tomorrow. The best of the best. All on a need-to-know basis. Not even Rommel has been given any details. I thought that might keep you happy.'

'Happy?'

The word felt like dirt in Joon's mouth. How could you be happy when your life was ashes? Less than dust. A piece of him had been torn out and scattered to the wind.

Ada must have sensed his thoughts. She gripped his leg gently through the sheets, an uncommonly warm gesture for her.

'You survived, Joon. Will survive. I know it's a shock, but you once said to me that people shouldn't be defined by their race, or gender, or anything physical. I think I'm starting to believe you. What counts is the person you are at the core. Who you *choose* to be. You don't need an avatar to reflect that. It's more than flesh and blood or strings of code. It's the soul of you. That's your identity. Nothing could destroy that. Well, except maybe a Colt 1911.'

Silence hung between them. Joon didn't want to hear any of this, especially from someone who'd carelessly evaporated part of his being. It was all her fault. If she'd just told him her plan, or that she'd hooked Bleesh already, he would have gotten them out before things went so wrong. She wasn't a team player. It was all about herself and her obsession to be the queen of the case. Joon closed his eyes. He couldn't even look at her. He willed her to go away.

Ada's hand didn't leave Joon's leg though. She just sat there in silence. After a long time, she sighed.

'When I was little, I had this big race,' Ada said. 'It was an inter-school championship. Everyone was there to watch, my parents, my friends. I was so nervous. I wanted to win so badly. The gun went off and I started sprinting. I ran so goddamn hard that I tripped over myself half way. It was horrific. I tumbled and ripped a hole in my knee. The other ankle was sprained. I lay there crying, just shattered. Everyone ran past me and I was left out there on the track. A loser. It was just a race, but it was my whole world. I looked into the stands and saw dad watching. He was motioning for me to get up and keep going. I couldn't understand why. The race was over. I'd lost.'

Ada paused and swallowed. Joon kept his eyes shut. He didn't want to listen.

'But I got up,' Ada went on. 'I limped as best I could over that finish line. Dad was whistling and cheering in the crowd. Others joined in too. There was a standing ovation when I made it to the end. I couldn't figure out why. Later, Dad sat me down and said he was more proud of me than if I'd won. He explained that winning is great, but what people truly respect is someone who gets up and keeps going after they've been beaten down. I try to live up to that lesson whenever I can, Joon. No matter how fucked things get, I suck it up and keep limping. You've been beaten down worse than any foot race. But you're not dead. I hope you get up. I'll certainly respect you a hell of a lot more if you do.'

Ada patted Joon's leg and stood up.

'For now though, get some rest. You really look like shit, you know?'

Ada left without another word. Joon squeezed his eyes shut. He didn't want to get up. He wanted this useless flesh prison of his to die as well and join his real body in darkness.

43

The SWAT team was ready to go. Vests on, helmets on, taze guns charged. I sat with them in the van as it weaved through Vegas streets toward our destination. I kept touching the ring on my thumb. My anchor to reality. This wasn't some game. Some simulation or training program. This was deadly serious. God I wished I was allowed to pack my Colt.

The end location was in a well-to-do part of town that housed the best coders and digital designers in the city. I wished Joon was there too. I'd heard nothing from him since last night. The hospital said he wouldn't be allowed out until lunchtime at best. We couldn't wait for that. Gibson was with us instead. He'd managed to wedge his fat head on the action by pulling rank as my direct report. He wanted to be there as support, he'd said. He wanted to take credit more like it. No info had come through from the military databases on Bleesh yet. We hadn't pushed Rommel though. We didn't want any alerts going off if this guy was military. Someone might warn him we were close and he'd be smoke. We didn't have the luxury to wait. This needed to happen now. We had to proceed like this killer was as dangerous as we feared he was. That's why we'd gotten SWAT to jump in.

'Right. Listen up,' I said to the team. 'Intel suggests this place belongs to a developer by the name of Brian Radcliffe and his artist wife Aleesha. Both are respected people and we're not sure how they are involved. However, we believe this man will also be present,' I flicked up an image of our killer from the security footage. 'He may be holding the family hostage. These people have two teenage children, so let's be aware of them in this too. If you see any laptops, PCs, tablets, phones, wrist-comms, immersion rigs, Holos stacks, or any other technical equipment, bag it as evidence. If you see our key suspect here, arrest with extreme force.'

The van slowed. Our SWAT Team leader, a tank of a human called Lieutenant Raimes, stood.

'I'll run point with Detective Byron,' Raimes said in a bass tone. 'We'll hit the front door with Wells and Orson as back up. Agent Gibson will cover any other exits with the rest of the squad. Fan out. Stay on comms. Be on alert. Set taze guns to flatten. We wrap this up clean and professional.'

Everyone present gave a single nod. The van stopped. We filed from the back quietly into the early morning light. Pristine, white-picket-fenced houses lined the street—the picture of American Dreams past. The banality of it didn't match the scope of this crime, but in my experience evil often wore a beige turtleneck. The house in front of us was the same as every other one on the street. A carbon copy. The only thing that marked it as different was the number out the front.

At a signal from SWAT Leader Raimes, the team took their positions. Gibson kept low, scuttling around the back of the house with four other agents. The other four of us moved toward the door. Wells and Orson carried pneumatic battering rams, at the ready. Raimes went just behind them, me in the rear. The idea was that Raimes would clear the room of danger, I would sweep in to cuff the suspect and make the arrest. But you can have all the plans in the world until you get shot in the face.

'All ready?' Raimes said quietly into his comm piece.

'Red team all ready,' a voice said in my ear.

My heart was battering in my chest. I was afraid it would break through my rib cage like we were about to bust through the door. My hands shook. My breath came in short, sharp bursts. I didn't have much time to dwell on it. Raimes began his whispered countdown.

'Three, two, one…'

On the unspoken zero, Wells and Orson shattered the front door to splinters. Raimes charged in like a rhino on ramproids. I stuck close, hot on his heels as we entered a timber-floored house. All the walls were a bland, off-white. We rushed through the foyer.

A man stepped into the hall. He was tall, green-eyed, wearing a turtleneck. Briefing photos told me it was the owner of the house, Brian Radcliffe.

'What is this?' he asked in surprise.

Raimes stuck a taze gun in Radcliffe's face who put his hands up straight away. I looked back to Orson who was right behind me.

'Cuff him,' I said.

The officer did as he was told.

'What are you doing?' the man gasped, then yelled. 'Aleesha!'

Raimes and I thundered past Radcliffe into the kitchen. Sitting at a table were two teenagers halfway through eating breakfast. They'd stopped at the noise and were looking directly our way. Their mother stood behind them. As soon as she saw us, she put her hands in the air holding toast and a butter knife. A teenage girl at the table was frozen stiff. The boy, older, ran. He flung open the back door of the kitchen and was gathered up by Gibson. The boy struggled and another SWAT member latched on too.

'Where's Bleesh?' I yelled at the mother. 'Where is he?'

Her mouth moved but no sound came out. A stream of piss ran down her leg.

'Check the basement,' Raimes barked at Wells who had swept into the room as well. 'Orson, check upstairs.'

Raimes pulled out some cuffs and moved to truss up Aleesha.

'No!' the teenage boy said as he struggled in Gibson's arms. 'Let her go, you fucks. I was just playing!'

His words made me stop. I swung toward the boy. He scowled at me with his preppy face. There was a glint of silver under his hair. He had a neural mat skullcap installed like Joon's. A way to get info logged into your brain at the hit of a button.

'That's right, slut,' he said. 'I'm Bleesh. Let my mom go. She doesn't know anything, you pig.'

44

I stalked outside the interrogation room. Chip Radcliffe sat in there. Bleesh. Our sweep of the house had turned up laptops and Holos equipment, but no killer. No one that matched our footage of Rama's murderer. An initial scouring of Chip's digital equipment had turned up nothing yet. He'd been careful. Everything was encrypted with serious security. There was a chance only he'd be able to unlock things. If he refused, it could take weeks to get in. Weeks we didn't have. Corpus could turn up dead any day. Chip's parents were in other interrogation cells too. All separated. We needed to get to the bottom of this thing without them corroborating their stories. They hadn't asked for a lawyer yet. They thought they could settle things and it was all a misunderstanding. Their precious Chip hadn't done anything wrong, surely? I wanted to rush in there and start firing questions at the little shithead, but Gibson had asked me to wait for him. He was taking his sweet time though. Where was he? Still talking to the parents?

I paced. I needed to get my strategy right in my head. Chip hadn't said anything since the house. He had admitted he was our troll, so he had to know something about the murders. Maybe our killer from the footage chose a female avatar in the Holos and was Bleesh's bodyguard, Poison. Chip—Bleesh—had to have some information, or this was all for nothing and we were behind the eight-ball yet again.

Then I spotted Joon. He strode with purpose down the halls right for me. He looked recovered, if pale. I mustered a smile. Maybe my pep talk at the hospital had gotten through to him after all. Joon didn't smile back.

'I got word you caught Bleesh,' he said. 'I also heard you don't have anything on him and he's not our killer from the footage.'

'Hello to you too. He's in there,' I indicated toward the door. 'He's basically a kid, but he's eighteen, so we don't need his parents there to question him.'

'I don't care how old he is,' Joon replied. 'He killed me. We're pinning something on him and making him pay.'

I paused. This didn't seem like Joon, but then, the need for revenge did strange things to people. If anyone knew that, it was me. It seemed like my pep talk didn't have the desired effect after all. Hatred and anger had done all the work to get him out of bed. At least it was something. It's what had gotten me out of bed when dad had died.

'I'm waiting for Gibson,' I said. 'He wants to be here.'

'No time,' Joon said, putting his hand on the door.

'What do you mean, no time?' I said, grabbing him by the arm.

He jerked back, looking at my hand like it was made from flesh-eating bacteria.

'I mean,' he said, 'the reason I know you caught Bleesh is because my security detail on Senator Rommel caught a conversation she had with the Sheriff not long ago. Rommel wants to do a deal with Switch immediately now that this guy doesn't look like our Specter. My contact said she was adamant. Rommel is hell-bent on catching this killer before he gets to Corpus. She wants that bill to pass and this is the key. They could come in any minute and derail any questioning of this pathetic excuse for a human in there.'

'She wants to do a deal with Switch? But this could still get us a lead.'

'A waste of time according to Rommel. She wants this killer ASAP. She also said it will be a coup to catch Switch in person. She doesn't want to risk any more delays. My guy said it sounded like the Sheriff agreed with her. Rommel is fast-tracking everything with her influence. If we don't do something now, Bleesh will be cut away and get off with no charges.'

My gut churned with indecision. I still didn't trust Switch would hold up her end of the bargain, but maybe it really was the quickest way to get the killer and save Corpus. Maybe Bleesh *was* just a sidetrack. Joon only wanted to question him for personal reasons. His motivation had nothing to do with the case. And yet, there had to be something there. There were too many coincidences. And Bleesh was a grade-A scumbag either way. He couldn't get off without repercussions.

'Okay,' I nodded, 'Let's do it.'

We entered the room. Chip looked up. He actually smiled at us, but kept his mouth shut. I walked up and stood across the table from Chip. I wasn't going to take a seat. I liked the height advantage, looking down on him. I considered the camera in the corner that was recording everything we said. Then I eyed our suspect again.

'Chip Radcliffe, I'm Detective Byron and this is my associate Agent Min Joon of the FBI. We want to talk to you about the claims you made online as the troll Bleesh regarding the murders of Christos Rama and Lilith Lace.'

Nothing. Chip just folded his arms.

Joon didn't say anything either. He stood next to me, surveying the room. His eyes went to the Holos Stack on the wall. We kept stacks in interrogation rooms to virtually recreate crime scenes with suspects. Reliving it in a way that felt real and present often tipped them over the edge into confessions.

'We know you didn't murder Christos Rama,' I said.

Chip's eyes narrowed. 'Then why am I here?'

I punched my wrist-comm screen and pulled up an image of the actual killer from our security footage.

'Do you know this man?'

I didn't need Chip to answer to know he didn't. He looked confused when seeing the picture, like it was something he didn't expect at all. Did that mean he expected someone else?

'No,' he confirmed, then turned his eyes back to me. 'I've never seen that man before.'

Was he telling the truth? Lie-detector software plugged into the camera system would help confirm whether his micro-expressions or tone caught anything I didn't but, for now, I believed him.

Joon stepped closer around the table so he stood right over Chip, looking at the top of his head. 'You have a neural cap,' Joon said, running his hand over his own short-cropped hair that showed off his.

Chip nodded silently, looking a little nervous at Joon's proximity, but trying not to show it.

'I thought you went into the Holos unsynced' Joon said. 'Why would you have a neural cap if not to enhance your online experience to the fullest?'

Chip chewed his lip as if wanting to speak. Joon waited, taking a step back to give him some space.

'It's not just about experience,' Bleesh said. 'It's about influence. That extra interface speed helps me learn faster. Manipulate people to my way of thinking easier. It helps me keep my playground free. As for staying unsynced? It means I never lose sight of the true reality of things like most sheeple do.'

I frowned. 'How do you influence the world by claiming responsibility for murders you didn't commit?' I said.

'If you know I didn't commit them, then why am I here?' he asked again.

I ground my teeth, thinking of Lilith's dead body in her house. 'Because you claimed responsibility and named Lilith Lace as a target as the next victim *before* she turned up dead.'

'I had nothing to do with that,' he said. 'It was a lucky guess.'

'A lucky guess?' I asked, not liking his choice of words.

'She was a slut,' he said matter-of-factly. 'She wanted to make new laws and impinge on our freedoms. She deserved it more than most.'

I wanted nothing more than to hammer kick his smug face right there, but I kept my legs in check. Joon shuffled his feet. Was he thinking the same thing as me?

'You know,' Joon said, splaying his hands in a gesture of offering. 'If you like, we can show you her crime scene, fully re-created in True-Res. Would you like that?'

Chip licked his lips. Actually licked them. The action reminded me of the ugly troll he was inside.

'Why would you do that?' he said.

Joon shrugged. 'A sign of goodwill. Maybe you'll tell me something I want to know afterward. An exchange of knowledge.'

Chip's dark eyes glistened. The eyes of a traitor if ever I saw them. He wasn't going to tell us anything useful, even if we paraded him around the station on our shoulders hailing him as a hero.

'Sure,' he said slyly. 'I might tell you something—if you show me first.'

'Great,' Joon said, 'we have a deal then.'

A deal? What was this bullshit? As far as I knew, we didn't even have a fully rendered re-creation of Lilith's murder scene cued up in the system. Joon was up to something. He went straight to the wall and picked up an immersion helmet.

'Detective Byron will need this,' he said. 'You and I can just jack in through our neural links, right?'

Chip nodded slowly. Joon went to the Holos stack and typed a flurry of commands on the main screen with expert hands. A chime sounded in the air.

'Accept the Wi-Fi link prompt and you'll go in,' Joon said.

Chip's hand went to his temple and he double tapped it. Another chime sounded and Chip's eyes rolled back to show the full whites of his eyes. The effect was eerie. I'd never seen Joon jacked in from the outside. Is that what he looked like too?

Joon hit another button.

'Okay, he can't hear us right now. He's in a holding room with music on.'

'What are you doing?' I asked. 'You're not showing him that crime scene.'

'No, I'm not,' Joon said. 'I'm going to interrogate him in there.'

'Just do it here,' I said exasperated.

'You don't get it,' Joon said. 'I didn't plug him into a police controlled zone. I plugged him into the actual Holos. Anything I do to him there is perfectly legal.'

'What?' I said, not liking where this was headed.

Even if Chip was a psychopath in the making we couldn't break protocol during interrogations.

Joon looked at the camera on the wall pointedly. 'We're not breaking any laws,' he said.

I didn't know if he was telling the truth or not. I might have been a police officer, but this was way out of normal procedure. Surely I'd know if there were loopholes for this. After Switch, torture was definitely ruled illegal for military and police, but only in digital confinement that was state-controlled infrastructure. Who knew what was really the case here. And yet, Joon was willing to do it on camera? He must know something I didn't. It wouldn't show exactly what we did in there, but there'd be an indication. Our movements and voices would be captured either way.

'There's something else,' Joon said. 'I need to borrow your avatar. The one Sabi coded for your undercover mission.'

'What? Why?'

'I just do,' he said. 'You owe me that much.'

'Owe you?' I said.

'Yes,' he pushed the helmet into my chest.

'Because of you, I no longer have a proper digital body. I refuse to go into the real Holos in something unsynced.'

I shook my head. This was ridiculous. *He* was ridiculous. I still felt a sense of guilt from torching his avatar though. But let him use mine? One that looked and felt like me. It felt icky. I'd literally be letting Joon inside me. Forget the sexual undertones that might have. He'd know every inch of my skin. How I moved and reacted to certain things. It felt like a violation of self.

'But isn't my avatar synced to my body rhythms?' I asked, trying to scratch for a logical reason for saying no. 'It won't be a perfect match to you.'

'It will be close enough,' he said, his eyes hard. After a pause, he added more softly. 'Please. We need to do this now. The clock is ticking.'

I grudgingly took the helmet he held out to me and strapped it on. *This had better work*, I thought. Joon moved quickly and the clear visor in front of me went black. A moment later, I emerged on the other side. I was in a room, standing in a stock avatar like I used in my meetings with Switch. Across from me was a stock male avatar.

'Chip Radcliffe?' I said.

'Took long enough,' he answered.

A shuffle behind me caught my attention. It was... me. The sight made me stop. I looked into my own eyes, like a full 3D mirror. There was life behind those eyes now, not like when the avatar was unoccupied in Sabi's studio. They blazed with green vibrancy. Joon smiled at me with my own lips and nodded. Creepy.

'You both chose women avatars?' Chip snorted. 'Is that Chink cop a faggot too?'

I turned on him, itching to throat punch him. Could I do that here? Joon stepped between us though.

'Does this make you more comfortable?' he said.

Joon twitched his fingers and his form changed. It went through multiple options, before resting on the disguise I'd chosen for LoveDeath —the gothed-up Cleopatra.

Chip's eyes went wide. 'You?!' he said. 'So that's how you got me?! But, but...' His eyes darted from Joon to me, trying to make sense of everything.

'This is going to hurt,' Joon sneered.

Chip backed up, his hand going to his temple like he was about to log out. Joon knocked Chip back quickly, stopping him. Before I could even react, Joon did something I didn't even think was possible. He jammed his index fingers deep into Chip's temples. They punctured right into the skin, digging directly into his brain. Joon's thumbs gouged into Chip's eyes at the same time too.

A gurgling cry went up from Chip. He started shaking. Joon's body shook violently all over too. I was frozen in shock. What was this? What was happening?

Then the pair both screamed as one. Their tremors synced, vibrating together in a howl of noise. Abruptly, they both fell deathly silent. Chip's nose started pouring with blood and Joon began to laugh.

45

Images strobed through Joon's mind. LoveDeath. Him and Ada from Bleesh's view. Bleesh throwing his drink over Ada. At the sight, a deep sense of pleasure welled through Joon, who was now connected directly into Bleesh's emotions. He began to laugh with malevolent amusement. His skin prickled with the thrill of control.

Joon pushed deeper into Bleesh's mind. Back.

There was a woman being raped by Bleesh. Joon felt it all from the first person. Every thrust. Every slap. Bleesh didn't radiate lust though, he just felt bored.

A spiral of more horrific images created a dark tunnel into a pitch-black psyche.

A man was decapitated by Poison while Bleesh watched. Poison whispered a few indistinct words. The bodyguard's face morphed into a fat teenager eating chocolate. Riots—the real world on Feed vision. A sense of accomplishment. The face of Holosian right-winger, Chance Bradley. Everything fuzzy and distorted. There were numbers. A series of them. Joon tried to burn them into his memory. The thought was replaced by a dark figure in a back alley. A spider. He laughed. Joon concentrated, holding as hard as he could to the memory. The spider spoke.

'They'll never find me. I'm safe in my sweet bunker,' he said. 'I'll make you famous.'

The figure ghosted away no matter what Joon did. The scene went blank. Black. It exploded in a burst of scrambled pixels.

Joon gasped up. He was on the floor of an interrogation room. The series of visions shadowed across his eyes again for a moment. It was like the real and the virtual collided in his vision. The pixels made it feel like the real world was glitching. Or maybe Joon was simply seeing through the master code. Then he saw Ada. She stood at the Holos stack, panting.

184

Joon's arm ached. Had she hit him, or was that from Bleesh?

Then Joon saw Chip Radcliffe. He was slumped in his chair, eyes open, crying, shaking, his nose bleeding. Joon blinked again, clearing his vision. Ada turned and moved toward Chip. The boy shrank away.

Sound rushed back in.

'Don't hurt me,' Chip said, scrambling backward again. 'Not like that. I'll tell you what you want.'

Ada turned to face Joon.

'What did you do?' she asked.

Joon pushed himself up.

'I looked at his memories,' Joon said raggedly. 'I synced our neural links through your avatar. I saw directly into his mind. He's not our killer but he did have some kind of role.'

'No,' Chip said. 'I didn't kill anyone.'

'You're Chance Bradley as well as Bleesh,' Joon said, the meaning of his visions crystallizing momentarily in his mind. 'You incited real-world riots. That's illegal no matter where you posted from.'

Ada's face went white.

'What?'

Joon wasn't done yet. The sense of satisfaction inside him grew. He had this troll. 'You know who did the killing as well. You spoke with him.'

Chip's eyes went wide. 'What? I don't. I didn't.'

'The Spider,' Joon said. 'You spoke with him in some dark-web backwater. He told you to take responsibility for the murders.'

Chip stared into space. His skin was chalky, sweaty. He realized. 'That spook? B-but... I... He told me if I took responsibility I'd be famous. Said I should coordinate an announcement with other trolls to help keep the Holos free. He's not the real killer. He's just another media manipulator like me. Someone who wanted the Holos bill gone.'

'You know he's the real killer deep down,' Joon said coldly, panting. 'You saw his avatar's capabilities. You used them as inspiration to code your friend Poison's avatar who's just another idiot gamer like you from down the street. But the Spider told you where his hideout is. A sweet bunker? What else do you know?'

The connections in Joon's mind were coming apart now, fading like dreams. He tried hard to hold onto them. Because Chip wasn't synced to the stock avatar he'd inhabited, things weren't perfect. Ada's body had been close enough to synced that it had helped though. He had enough.

'What?' Chip was confused, tears streaming down his face. 'What hideout?'

'You know,' Joon said getting up. 'I know you do.'

'I don't,' Chip said, backing up further, sinking to the ground against the wall, curling up into a ball.

Joon stood over him. 'Confess,' he said. 'Tell us and you might still get out of this without going to prison for life.'

'But I don't know anything,' Chip cried. 'I just did what he said. I just wanted to be famous. To influence the world. I don't know anything.'

At that point, the door to the interrogation room slammed open. Gibson stood in the doorway, his face red. He glared at Ada, then Joon, and down at Chip Radcliffe.

'You two!' he said. 'What do you think you're doing?'

Ada's mouth worked like a fish that had somehow flopped out of its bowl and had found itself on the floor. No words came.

'We're interrogating a suspect,' Joon said, straightening.

'Don't let her hurt me again,' Chip blubbered from his ball on the floor. 'She attacked me. She attacked me.'

Gibson looked from Chip to Joon, then fixed his gaze on Ada.

'You're in so much shit, Byron, I don't even know where to start.'

46

Gibson left Chip where he was, locked the door, and marched us into a separate room. I'd never seen the giant thumb so angry.

'Sit down,' he said, before shoving his head back out into the hall. 'Cline. Get in here. Now!'

After a few moments, Cline's shaggy face came into view. He furrowed his brow when he saw me and Joon.

'Pull up footage from interrogation room three,' Gibson ordered.

Cline stepped into the room, still silent and Gibson swung the door shut behind him. Cline swiped up a hologram screen. Gibson whirled on us.

'We got valuable information -' Joon started.

'Shut it,' Gibson barked. 'I don't want your spin. The footage will show us what happened.'

'But...' I tried, wanting to explain it all happened in virtual.

'If you hit that kid, you're finished,' Gibson said. 'No questions asked. I don't care what you got. You were supposed to wait. You're not running this investigation. I am.'

'Running it in the wrong direction,' Joon said.

Gibson rushed up and pointed a finger right in Joon's face.

'One more word and I'll kick your face in, boy. None of this virtual pansy Stockholm shit. There's no cameras in *this* room.'

I scanned the room and saw he was right. Joon didn't budge or back down though. He just locked stares with Gibson, looking like an angry Chihuahua next to a thick-necked hyena. Both bared their teeth.

Mercifully, light flickered on the hologram screen Cline had pulled up. It drew Gibson's attention. Chip sat there on-screen in his chair, picking his nails. Cline swiped forward to where Joon and I entered. Our first conversation ran through. Gibson crossed his arms, watching carefully. I held my breath as Joon explained to me on screen that we'd interrogate Chip in the Holos. That it was legal.

'Idiots,' Gibson said under his breath. 'Any lawyer will pull that apart.'

We jacked in. It was surreal to watch. Joon logged his connection and his eyes rolled back in his head like Chip's. And yet he walked and spoke, looking like some kind of ghoul. I simply stood there with my helmet on. You couldn't see my facial reactions. Suddenly, Chip backed up against the wall. His all-white eyes looked somehow shocked, terrified.

'This is going to hurt,' Joon growled.

He plunged his fingers and thumbs into clean air, nowhere near Chip in the real room. Joon speared his index fingers deeper into an imaginary skull. He and Chip both started shaking. Chip screamed. Joon started laughing that horrid laugh. I rushed forward, bringing my arm down again and again, barely a foot away from Chip. I didn't hit him physically, but it looked like I was thrashing him in virtual. Really, I'd been trying desperately to knock Joon's arms free. The program had thrown our spatial awareness out, making sure we didn't connect with each other in the real room. The whole scene was bizarre, like some kind of mummers play. Then I stopped on-screen and ripped my helmet off. I'd had the sense to engage log off. I rushed to the Holos stack. My fingers scrambled over the buttons. I hadn't known what I was doing. Somehow though, I'd managed to disconnect things. Joon and Chip both fell backward onto the ground. I looked to Joon and he opened his eyes, shaking his head. Then I rushed toward Chip to check he was alive. The kid scrambled back.

'Don't hurt me again, not like that.'

That's when I realized he'd thought I was the one who had invaded his mind. Joon had been in *my* avatar in there. Fuck. Chip would be telling anyone who listened that Detective Ada Byron was the one who attacked him.

'I've seen enough,' Gibson snarled. 'Cline, cut it.'

Cline shut off the screen.

'No,' Joon said. 'Keep watching. We got him.'

'Bullshit!' Gibson said. 'Did you record what happened in virtual?'

Joon slowly shook his head.

'No, but I saw -'

'What you got is footage of you beating a suspect. Who cares if it's in virtual? We're supposed to uphold justice. How do you think this would play out in court? Do you think you'll look like a hero? And you,' he turned to me. 'What do you think Mendez will say when she sees this? She told you to act with integrity after your last virtual stunt. It's not just about the law. It's about being a fucking professional.'

'We didn't...' I said.

'Clean out your locker, Byron, you're done. Get out.'

Fear flared inside me. This couldn't be how it finished. I hadn't done anything wrong. Had I?

'No, I…'

'Out!' Gibson roared, taking a step toward me.

I fell silent. He was serious. Deadly serious. All heat left my body. I felt suddenly cold.

Joon shuffled to the side of me. He tapped his wrist-comm. He'd totally screwed me and now he was sending text messages? I clenched my jaw wanting to say something. Gibson gave me a shove toward the door.

'Now, Byron,' he said. 'I never want to see you again.'

He turned on Joon then. 'As for you. I can't wait to show the FBI this.'

'Neither can I,' Joon snapped. 'They'll actually watch the whole thing.'

I didn't wait for the rest of the conversation. Numb, I left. I took one last look at Cline who watched me with sad eyes. Gibson turned and grabbed the door, slamming it in my face. I was finished. My life as a cop was over. Everything I thought I was—gone.

47

I left the station in a daze. The whole world seemed surreal. I drifted through the streets, walking without direction. Nothing seemed tangible —like a waking dream. Next thing I knew I was sitting in my apartment alone with my head in my hands. I wasn't even sure how I got there. I looked around at my place. Tidy furniture. Organized benchtops. The picture of Dad and me. Clean windows looked out onto our building's garden. I used to feel safe here. Centered. Now I couldn't even think of it as real. It was just something I'd manufactured over the years. A cubicle to live in that meant nothing. The last weeks had pulled the entire fabric of reality out from under me. Could I still be in the Holos somehow and have everything twisted? Was I really in my apartment, or was I somewhere else jacked in? No. My fingers went to my thumb where dad's wedding ring sat. Cold metal like his cold body. Like my cold soul. I spun it on my thumb and stared at the deep scratch in the side of it. How had I gotten to this point? I'd been so excited when getting assigned a murder case. I thought that I'd start making a real difference as a detective. Then it had turned to Switch. Always Switch. She poisoned everything in my world. But then, hadn't I made my whole world about her? About trying to understand her? About bringing sense to what she'd done? About stopping anyone like her from tearing other family's lives apart? And where had that gotten me? My own life in ruins, confused about the nature of things, totally unable to grab onto anything. My wrist-comm buzzed, scaring me. Joon was calling. I ripped the thing off and threw it against the wall where it kept buzzing. I held my breath, waiting for the noise to stop. Finally, it fell silent but my mind didn't. A jumble of self-loathing and regret flooded through me, tearing me further from the banks of sanity and order.

I slapped myself in the face, hard, just to feel something real. It stung. I slapped again. Again. Again. The physical sensation was something to cling to.

Or was it?

Wasn't that pathetic pain just something else you could make up in the Holos? The Stockholm Effect writ large?

I was sweating, my hands clammy. My cheeks burned. My hair was wild. The wrist-comm buzzed for a while again, then stilled. I went to the drawer where I kept my Colt and unlocked it. Drew the gun out. The chill of its metal kiss felt solid against my palm. Now this was real, wasn't it? A vintage. A classic. An original. I turned the gun over in my hands, studying the barrel. Just another creation of the human mind. A creation that could also destroy, though. The ability to turn ones into zeros. I sat down again, staring at the weapon. Was this the ultimate reality in front of me? A way to log out of everything and truly see what was on the other side. A way to escape thought. A way to escape the Holos. A way to escape life. A way to escape Switch. Was darkness the only true reality? Or was there something else there on the other side?

Something wet dripped down onto the gun. I realized I was crying. My throat clenched in pain. I sobbed, gripping the Colt and flicking off the safety.

My breath shuddered.

I tried to fixate on a thought that might stop me. Any thought.

So many things clambered inside me, it was all just a blur of fear and anxiety and despair and uncertainty. Was there a purpose to all of this? Why was I even alive? *Was* I alive? Should I just finish it and be sure for once?

Then Switch's face intruded like it always did. That shark's look. Her words: '*Is the solid world real, or just another simulation? The only way to find out, to jack out of the master simulation, is to die and burst up from the darkness.*'

I raised the gun, aimed, and squeezed the trigger.

A bullet ripped out of it and slammed into the window of my apartment. The glass shattered. Desert heat flooded inside the climate-controlled space—nature invading the fake.

Fuck Switch. I wouldn't do it. I'd never kill myself. I wouldn't let her get to me.

That thought sparked another. My chest constricted. She'd said those exact words to every one of her last interviewers. *The only way to find out, to jack out of the master simulation, is to die and burst up from the darkness.*

I'd watched those clips again and again. I thought it was repetitive. Was that because Switch had an agenda there? Is that why they'd done it? Killed themselves? Was being in her presence while she said it an extra trigger that made the words sink in even more. Suddenly, I was sure of it. I'd experienced that will of presence when she'd grabbed me. She'd held my arm firmly, despite me knowing I should be able to break free. The combination of her persuasive words and her dominating aura would be a death sentence. Here I was thinking about ending it and I'd only seen the videos.

I clicked the safety of my Colt back on and let it fall to the ground. I wouldn't let her control me. Not anymore. I needed to be free of her. As long as she sat in that simulated cage, she was still a threat. We needed to catch her for real. Pull her out of the digital world where she held the power. Expose her into the harsh light of day and show everyone she was just flesh and blood like the rest of us. Not a god. Not a devil. Just a sick person. I needed to put her into the past. Embrace the reality of the case I had to solve now. It was so much bigger than my shit. So much bigger than a specter who was now simply haunting my world.

And I had a way to do that. Rommel wanted to let Switch lead us to save her brother, Corpus. I'd been wrong to resist it. I needed to embrace that fear. Cautiously, but clearly.

Yet I'd blown that chance. The thought made the tentacles of despair work to pull me down again. The police would be able to do it without me. Shouldn't I be happy with that at least? But did I trust them to do it right? I couldn't just sit by.

My wrist-comm buzzed again. I ignored it, shaking my head clear. How could I convince Gibson and Mendez to keep me on the team? No one was going to do that for me. I had no friends in this. I thought I'd had Joon but he'd turned selfish as soon as his own want for vengeance took over.

A banging on the door made me jump. 'Ada, you in there?' Joon's voice. 'Ada?!' Another loud knock.

I stood up to go to the door when a bigger thud sounded. Another. Was he trying to kick the thing in? With his skinny legs?

I strode forward and jerked the door open just as Joon kicked. He stumbled forward as he hit air and fell face-first into my arms. I grabbed him, steadied him. He held my biceps and heaved himself up.

'Oh, thank God,' he said.

Then he realized he was hugging me, holding my arms. We both took an awkward step backward to create space between us.

'I heard the gunshot when I was on the street,' he said. 'I thought…'

I turned to the shattered window, glass everywhere. 'I just needed some space to breathe.'

'No time,' he said. 'Didn't you see my calls? My messages?'

I thought about the buzzing wrist-comm and shook my head.

'Rommel has organized to clear a deal with Switch, but she's insisting you're on the team.'

'What?' I said. 'But what about Gibson? What about Bleesh and Mendez?'

Joon shook his head, smiling.

'You left in too much of a rush. That idiot Gibson had no idea what he was talking about. I did have something. I memorized Chip's master password. I saw the numbers when I was in his head. It unlocked his security software and let Cline log into all Bleesh's accounts. I refused to leave before they looked. It was the jackpot. It proves he's both Bleesh *and* Chance Bradley. He's been calling for riots in the real world as both personalities. He's played a big role in what's been happening on the Vegas Strip, telling people to jack out and seek justice on one hand and spewing full-freedom rhetoric on the other. They're charging him for inciting violence and for hate speech.'

'What?' I could barely believe it.

'The announcement is going to go out tonight to pull attention away from the fact we're closing in on the killer. As long as you help us get terms with Switch.'

'But the interrogation footage,' I said. 'Didn't Mendez see it?'

Now Joon really smiled. 'Cline "accidentally" deleted it,' he said. 'You know, he's not really such a bad guy. We didn't need that footage with the data from Chip's equipment. Now it's just his shitty word against ours.'

I was floored. Maybe people did have my back after all. Rommel did certainly. She'd insisted I be part of the team. Cline had saved my skin. Joon had rushed to my place and tried to kick the door down when he thought I was in danger. The thought of it made me well up with sudden emotion. I had friends. Partners. People who took me seriously as a cop. I still didn't feel proud of what I'd done with Chip, but it did get results. Was that justice? I'd need to make up for it and prove I could do better. That I could solve this thing once and for all. I knew I could.

'When do we talk to Switch?' I asked.

'Rommel is meeting us first thing in the morning at the digital confinement facility,' he said. 'She needs us to be ready for a full briefing first. Get as much rest as you can. We'll need to be as sharp as possible if we're going to pull this off.'

48

Senator Rommel stormed into the digital confinement facility carrying a folder. Joon and I were already waiting with the Sheriff. We stood to attention as Rommel entered. With her were the Chief Justice and the District Attorney of Nevada. Wrinkles from a lifetime of making hard decisions were etched into both their faces. Rommel nodded toward the public surveillance camera in the corner for a moment. I looked up and the red light blinked out, before coming on yellow. I'd never seen that before.

'Now we can talk,' Rommel started. 'Your killer's name is Entown Stephenson. That doesn't leave this room.'

The directness of her approach took me off guard. She obviously felt like there wasn't enough time for pleasantries. Rommel stared hard at both of us to reinforce the importance of what she'd just said. Nothing left this room. But the name meant nothing to me.

'In government terms,' Rommel continued, 'Stephenson is probably the most dangerous man alive.'

She let the words sink in for a moment. The Chief Justice and District Attorney both shifted their feet.

'So who is he?' Joon asked.

'He's the assassin who brought down the Kim regime in Korea.'

'The Savior of Seoul?' Joon gasped. 'What? But he's a hero!' Joon's confusion deepened as he thought. 'He died killing Kim Yo-jong, didn't he?'

'No such luck,' Rommel handed me the paper file she was holding. 'None of this is saved in any drive or database. I had to pull an ungodly number of strings to get the classified clearances. I didn't even know his identity during the war—and I was a senior officer. This is what we have on him now.'

The folder felt like there was nothing in it. When I opened the thing, there were only two pieces of paper inside.

'I'll burn those after reading,' she said. 'Don't say anything more aloud, in case there are extra bugs in here.'

Joon shuffled close and started reading over my shoulder. On the page was a military record of our killer. It was stamped 'Honorably Discharged', followed by a list of specialties: Bomb expert. Munitions expert. Poisons expert. Mixed martial arts expert. Master of hostile infiltration. Master of disguise. Adept at enhanced interrogation. Court Martialed for war crimes—murder of civilians, rape and torture to gain intelligence. Pardoned because of extreme, complex PTSD resulting from his successful missions during the Peninsula Unification Wars. Left leg amputated from the hip. Severe body dysmorphia. Possible psychopathy. Put into a virtual rehabilitation program because of the danger he posed to himself and others. Acted out violent fantasies constantly in virtual reality. Attempted same in physical world. After unsuccessful rehabilitation, was imprisoned at a maximum security facility in solitary confinement but allowed to roam in the Holos for services rendered to his country. Became attached to the idea of absolute freedom in both worlds. Escaped confinement but injured during. Last known whereabouts, Las Vegas outer limits. Thought to have perished in the desert. No body recovered.

All of this info fit with what Fukami had told us. That there was a soldier in one of his programs who wanted to join the Guardians of the Web. That he was a genius, but twisted. Fukami had said he didn't know his name. He was just a number. Not any more. Our killer had an identity. But was this guy working alone? Or did he have help from somewhere? The uncertainty weighed me down. I didn't want to rush headlong into this. Normally, full-sprint ahead was my only setting. Perhaps that had to change.

'So as far as the world knows, he died a hero in Pyongyang?' I asked.

Rommel simply nodded.

'And you say you didn't know him personally?' Joon asked carefully.

'No,' Rommel said blankly. 'He was part of special forces, not under my command of ground troops. But I had heard about him. He's a real piece of work. A pit bull that was let off his leash instead of being put down. He's a stain on our international reputation when it comes to my war. We need to shut him down, immediately.'

Her war? This was personal.

'We're willing to negotiate with Switch if it means she can lead us to Corpus,' Rommel continued. 'We'll then set a military-led sting and take Stephenson down when he arrives at Corpus's location.'

'Military sting?' I asked. I wanted to be the one who caught him.

'That's part of the deal. No way around it. He's too dangerous. You know Switch better than anyone, so you can arrest her with your police SWAT team. You'll get full credit for arresting Switch and also get a commendation for saving Corpus. But *we* lay the trap for Stephenson. We'll kill him on sight. There will be no risking him getting away. If it makes you feel better, I'll let you be there as a witness. Make sure he's dead as well for your own satisfaction. I owe you that much.'

'But what about a trial?' Joon said. 'What about an explanation for the public?'

'No trial,' Rommel said. 'We know he's guilty. We have the footage of him at the scene with the murder weapon in his hand. If you're lucky, you'll have Corpus crack this file you think he has. That will be explanation enough. Stephenson's identity will be redacted from all records though. We don't want him being linked to the government in any way.'

I closed the folder and handed it to Joon. 'I still don't like it,' I said. 'What if Switch tries to pull something? What if we're too late to find Corpus?'

'We're never releasing Switch from prison after this,' Rommel replied. 'It's an extra win that we'll have physically caught her after all these years. A silver lining in this whole dirty business. You'll be one of the most well-regarded detectives in the world for locking her up.'

Still, the idea unsettled me. There was something wrong with this. Perhaps Switch was better off in digital confinement. Even with all her boasting about being able to break out, she hadn't been able to actually do it in seven long years. The transfer would be a big risk. Did Rommel only want this case wrapped up because her policy was on the brink of being accepted? The motivation wasn't pure. But did motivations matter if the result was right? I wanted time to run through the case again properly. Tease out all the tangled strands. The file. Fukami. Bleesh. Corpus. Switch. This Spider—Stephenson. It felt like it could all still click without doing this deal. We didn't have time though. Didn't I want this anyway? It would mean I'd finally be free of Switch. Finally be able to rest at night knowing I'd done my part. My career would be cemented. I just had to push through my fears to get there.

'I've asked my colleagues here to sign off on any terms Switch might want,' Rommel interrupted my thoughts, indicating the District Attorney and Chief Justice. 'You're plugging in now.'

Joon was already preparing to jack in. He had a specially designed confinement helmet in hand and was pushing the dials. The fact that he wanted to go in gave me much-needed confidence. This had to be our best chance to save Corpus. Joon had the file and no one else knew it. If we got to Corpus and he could hack it, everything would unravel.

Joon handed me my confinement helmet.

'Right,' I said to Rommel. 'We'll be back shortly.'

Switch leapt up as soon as we entered. It was unlike all the other times. Rather than feigned indifference, she was fully engaged.

'Did you find Corpus?' she asked right away.

'Not yet,' I said. 'But we have more information.'

Switch waited for it impatiently.

'A man called Entown Stephenson is behind this,' Joon said.

Switch hissed. 'The fucking troll!'

The bottom dropped out of my stomach. How could she know who Entown Stephenson was?

'So Fukami is involved then?' she continued.

'What?' I snapped. I was still grappling with the fact Switch knew this spook's identity. Switch obviously realized my confusion, so explained.

'Fukami became friends with that despicable creature as part of a soldier rehabilitation program we ran. He wanted to let him become a Guardian of the Web. Like I would ever allow that.'

I grasped to make sense of what I was hearing. Fukami *knew*. He had become friendly with Stephenson. Had he played us? He must have known Bleesh would be a dead end. A bone to throw us without being the whole carcass. Did that mean Fukami was also involved on a deeper level? The puppet master to all of this, keeping freedom through fear? Or were these more of Switch's lies? Surely not. It fit too well with there being a conspiracy to the highest levels. It didn't get any higher than Fukami.

Joon pushed on, apparently conscious of time. Fukami and his involvement would have to be sorted once we had this part of the puzzle. It would be in the file that Corpus could crack.

'We estimate we have half a day left at most to get to your brother', Joon said to Switch. 'After that...' he left the thought hanging.

Switch kept her hands straight at her sides.

'And I assume you're ready for me to assist?'

'Yes,' I said slowly, deciding to make a play. 'But you tell us how to get to his jack-in point from here. We're not letting you out.'

'No,' she said flatly. 'That won't work.'

I crossed my arms over my chest.

'Why?'

'Were you not listening?' she said. 'He's defended by DNA locks. It'll take days to drill through the doors otherwise. Time we don't have.'

'And you'll open the DNA lock because you're his sister and there's enough of a match? How convenient. If that's the case, then this Entown Stephenson won't be able to get in either,' I persisted.

'A fiend like that finds ways,' she said. 'And you want to catch him, don't you?'

'Of course we do,' Joon said.

'Then you'll need to fly there first, or you'll be in the Spider's Web instead.'

I clenched my fists, not willing to give in, but knowing we needed to roll the dice on this. There was too much pressure from Rommel not to. Thankfully, Switch was feeling the pressure too. She wanted to save her brother as much as anyone.

'Look,' she reasoned. 'I can lead you verbally from here to my physical venue. You'll be able to verify it's me, chain my body, and wheel me out. There is no risk for you. After that, I escort you straight to Corpus. Cross my cardio musculus.'

She made a cross over her heart. It made me shudder. Every hair on my body must've stood on end in the real world. 'How will we know it's you?' I asked.

'Because I look like my avatar without tattoos,' she said. 'Although, I imagine I'm eminently older by now.'

'Okay,' Joon said before I could cut in. 'After we secure Corpus, you'll be held at a maximum-security prison for life, no plea bargains.'

God bless the little spankblanket. We were singing from the same hymn sheet there.

Switch considered Joon for a long while. Then nodded.

'As long as I get visitations from Corpus and a computer to read on.'

'No computer,' I said. 'You can have books. Read like a philosopher.'

Switch narrowed her eyes at my jab, but didn't say anything.

'Fine,' she said, opening her palms toward me. 'We have an understanding. Do you want me to tell you my address, or should I manifest a map?'

50

Enclave Court was in an exclusive part of Vegas. Golf course surrounds. Swimming pools in every yard. Security guards at every gate.

Except one.

If Switch was to be believed, this was her address—a three-story mansion that stood seemingly empty. The lawn was trimmed but the house itself was worn. Paint flaked on the edges. The pool was swimming with frogs. Still, it was an ostentatious address for someone who lived her entire life in the Holos before this. She obviously had money. Lots of it. Was it from before or from what she'd earned in helping shape the virtual world? That was something I'd have to find out later. For now, Joon and I were on the hunt. We were backed up by SWAT leader Raimes and his key offsiders, Wells and Orson—muscle to combat Switch's cunning. Gibson's voice crackled in my ear. We'd run by the terms with Rommel and all had been agreed to. Sheriff Mendez tasked Gibson with personally escorting Switch out of digital confinement. We had the more dangerous part: actually cuffing her in the flesh. Evening was starting to fall already, with its dusty pink and desert orange hues.

We came to the front door. It was locked tight with a ten-digit keypad; old tech for someone who should be a technophile. I looked around. A window was broken on the second floor—another sign of the disrepair this place had fallen into. There were no easily accessible points on the ground level though.

'I'll do a sweep 'round back,' Orson said. Raimes nodded.

I hit my wrist-comm. 'Gibson. Ask Switch what the code is to get in.'

Some murmuring and Gibson came back online. 'She said you should have been able to guess it. It's her birth date.'

I dredged my memory bank for the number, then punched in 06061992. It was one tiny scrap of real information we had about her identity. Since The Great Reboot wiped all records from online, it had done nothing to help us find out who she was in the real world though.

Plenty of people were born on that day.

A grinding behind the pad unclicked the lock. The door cracked open. Inside was oddly clean. No heaps of dust and cobwebs like I expected. Maybe she had a contractor that cleaned the house and mowed the lawn occasionally. I turned on the hallway light but nothing happened. No globe.

'Head down the left-hand staircase at the end of the foyer,' Gibson relayed. 'You'll get to the bottom and find a locked door to the basement.'

Raimes held his earpiece and spoke. 'Orson, how's that sweep going?'

'All clear,' his gruff voice said on the other end. 'There's a back entrance here that's locked tight too.'

'Good,' Raimes said. 'You stand guard there in case Switch somehow breaks free of us and tries to get out that way. Wells, you guard this door. I'll cover the top of the stairs when these guys go down.'

All confirmed, Joon, Raimes, and I crept cautiously through the house. There was just enough natural light from the windows to see. Shadows filled the place and my imagination put a stalking killer inside each one. I noticed a reprint of Bosch's Garden of Earthly Delights on the hallway wall. There were other classical works as well, all showing other worlds, neatly arranged but unlit. An old Apple Mac sat on a desk in a glass casing. One of the first-ever models, I guessed. There was a creaking upstairs. Both Raimes and I swung our taze guns toward it. It was nothing. Just the sounds of an old house. We moved on through the place and came to the basement stairs Switch mentioned. It was a descent straight down into the dark. Joon clicked on the torch at the front of his taze gun. I did the same. Raimes waited silently at the top of the stairs as we went down. At the bottom was another 10-key pad.

'Right, we're here,' I said to Gibson. 'Same code?'

'No,' he answered. 'This one is the date she was reborn, Switch says.'

I thought about it for a second. The date of the Specter Slaughter? Surely not, that would be too obvious. Instead, I tried 01012025. The date of The Great Reboot. It was a chance for everyone to leave behind an old life if they wanted to.

The door clicked open. The moment of truth. Time to enter the Specter's cave.

51

Entown Stephenson stalked through the upstairs hallway of Corpus's home. He'd done it, finally. Mission objective was almost signed off. The hacker had held out, not cracking until the computer trace program cracked for him. Entown had left his bots to continue torturing the pathetic programmer too. He was now in an endless cycle of physical anguish to keep the mapping signal strong. This assassination would feel extra sweet. Corpus and his sister had blocked him from joining The Guardians of the Web. Corpus had turned truly soft afterward too. He'd said law in the Holos could be a positive thing and that Switch had gone too far in her murders. Entown knew now she hadn't gone far enough! If she'd wiped out all of the pretenders in the virtual paradise, it would still be a pure Eden of deliciously dark delights.

Entown checked the syringe in his pocket. Inside it was the nerve agent he'd used for the other killings. The Master had given him the chemical and mapped out everything. Had given him purpose again after he'd lacked it for so long. Entown had laid low in his bunker like a coward for years, only lurking in the most shadowed parts of the Holos lest he be discovered and dragged back into his military prison. He needed to be free in both worlds. If you were imprisoned in one, the other felt tainted somehow. The Master had reinstated the glory he deserved. He was a goddamned war hero. He should be celebrated, not shunned! Now, he could move between both worlds again. Creeping in one, yes, hobbling on his mechanical leg, but still, it felt powerful. It felt... right. In the Holos, he had a new avatar built using a symphony of coding to morph to his desires and ghost to nothing. It was a weapon worthy of his spirit. All thanks to The Master. Entown would be able to repay him soon. This was the final piece of the puzzle. It would shut the gate to opening the file, killing the last opposition to full virtual freedom. He would alert the media to Corpus's body and pass it off as another Specter slaying. It would make that Holos Crime bill crumble to dust, keeping things as they were—a brave world for brave souls. And he would be free to move amongst them again. His payment for loyal service. Repaid in full.

Entown reached the top of the stairs when a noise from outside caught his attention. Someone was at the door. He melted back into the shadows, hiding behind a pillar. Beeps from outside heralded a newcomer. But who?

The door opened and three people stepped inside. A short Korean man, a tall redheaded woman, and a cop the size of a line-backer. Entown nearly hissed. The police. He'd seen the woman on The Feed. These were the agents he'd crashed into in Corpus's office. They'd somehow gotten here too. Never mind. This was a chance to kill more of those who might bring oppression to the Holos. The syringe would only kill one person, but he had his knives.

The floorboards creaked beneath Entown's feet. He held his breath and moved fully behind a column. He waited, listened, and heard the police walking through the house again. They were going down some stairs. There might be more officers outside. Very good. They'd all save him some time searching for Corpus's jack-in room and breaking in. They'd trap themselves with nowhere to go and he'd come at them from behind.

Entown pulled a blade from his boot. Silent kills weren't as satisfying, but they'd have to do.

He made his way to the window he'd come in through and climbed back out, as quiet as a spider on its dragline.

52

Switch's jack-in room smelled like a cheese maker's underarms. You'd think she'd have put in proper ventilation in a house like that. But where she'd skimped on airflow, she'd spent big on digital equipment. Tubes ran from the wall into her body, which lay tilted back at 45 degrees against a thin, run-disk platform emerging from the floor. Some of the tubes were for food. Some were for waste, inserted in areas that could also be stimulated by the very same pipes for sexual pleasure. Some people really had no shame, as long as they were getting rubbed the right way. Screens scrolled with inputs and outputs. Switch's eyes were covered with a streamlined visor display. State of the art, even for now. I studied the facial features I could see. They were indeed very similar to her avatar. Strong cheekbones, diamond-cutter chin, thin lips. The whole thing set me on edge. It felt like someone was watching us. I couldn't shake the sense of wrongness.

'You in?' Gibson said in my ear.

'Yeah, we're in,' Joon replied. He had the same comm link in his ear too. He checked the display units for god-knew-what and nodded. 'There's a serious amount of input coming in through the system, consistent with deep-brain stimulation. It's definitely her.'

'You want me to start taking her through the firewalls?' Gibson asked.

'Wait a moment,' I said.

I pulled out a set of police-issue, magnet-powered manacles and snapped them over Switch's wrists. Then I pulled out some of my own manual lock cuffs I'd bought at an antique store. I put those around her ankles. Finally, I leveled my taze gun at her evil face. 'Okay,' I said. 'Clear.'

There was a long pause on the other end, before it crackled to life again. 'Right. Exiting first firewall,' Gibson replied.

Sounds of movement filtered through my earpiece. I kept a sharp eye on Switch's real body, while Joon watched the display panels. Her face grimaced in pain. Good. I hoped coming up from that prison hurt her as much as it hurt me going in the first time.

'We're through the first firewall,' Gibson confirmed.

'No significant change on display input here,' Joon said. 'We can't jack her out yet. Go through the next one.'

Again noises on the other end suggested they were moving. Switch's real face grimaced again. My gut churned more. Something really wasn't right here, but I couldn't put my finger on it. Then *her* finger twitched.

'Wait a moment,' I said to Joon slowly. 'If she's walking in digital confinement, shouldn't her run disk be moving too?'

Joon turned. Switch still lay back at a 45-degree angle on her run disk's plank.

'Maybe it's broken after all these years,' Joon said. 'This must have been one of the first prototypes of this design I'm guessing.'

'Okay, we're through to the next section,' Gibson interrupted. 'One more to go. Tell me when to proceed.'

Again Switch's mouth sneered. Her nose crinkled in pain. Her fists clenched and whole body tensed.

'Stop,' I said. 'Shouldn't her feet be moving if she's walking? Something? I'm not sure this is Switch.'

Joon looked at me like I was crazy. 'What do you mean it's not Switch?' he asked. 'Look at her face.'

I did and she groaned, gritting her teeth.

'Gibson? Status?' I asked.

'All fine here. Switch under control, getting ready to move to the next firewall.'

'No. Stop.' I said. I studied the body in front of me. If she'd been here for years, totally unkempt, her nails should be longer. Her hair too. This wasn't right.

'What's wrong?' Gibson asked.

The body in front of me moaned loudly. Thrashed for a moment, then went still again, panting. Panic crept into me.

'Gibson, take her back into confinement, now!'

'What are you doing?' Gibson said.

'Byron's got the jitters,' Joon said.

'Stand up!' Gibson barked. 'Get off the ground.'

Static buzzed on the connection

'What?' I asked, pressing my finger to my ear.

'Not you,' Gibson replied. 'Switch. She just sat down and closed her eyes. Stand up!'

I looked at the body in front of us, my hunch becoming a howl. We'd been had. This was all a trick!

'Gibson! Drag her back through the firewall now!' I yelled. 'Raimes, you up there?'

'All clear still,' Raimes confirmed. 'Wells? Orson? Status.'

Silence.

'Hey!' Gibson's voice rang out. 'Shit,' he said. 'Her avatar's gone slack. I think she's dead.'

Joon looked to the screen frantically.

'Vitals are the same as before here,' he reported.

'You idiots,' I said, looking at the body plugged in before me. 'This isn't Switch. It's Corpus. Switch isn't here!'

'Wells, Orson, report,' Raimes voice crackled on the link. 'Hey, you...'

A trio of zaps from a taze gun sung out from above.

'Secure Corpus!' I snapped at Joon.

Things were happening too fast. My gut was twisting in fear. We'd let Switch trick us. Was she somewhere else already and got to Raimes?

I rushed out into the stairwell. Just as I got out the door, Raimes's body crashed into me. His neck was cut from ear to ear. His weight pushed me against the wall. I struggled to get out from beneath him. Behind Raimes's shoulder, I could make out someone stalking down the stairs, knife in one hand and syringe in the other. No. It wasn't Switch. It was Entown Stephenson. He'd found Corpus ahead of us.

'Joon!' I managed, getting an arm loose.

He turned to see me in trouble, moved to help.

The Spider took his time. One slow step after the next.

'No, Joon,' I called. 'Secure Corpus. Stephenson is here!'

With my free hand, I slammed the door to the jack-in room closed. Corpus was too important. The digital lock of the room snapped shut. Heaving Raimes' body off me, I raised my taze gun. Too late. Stephenson's foot speared at me from out of nowhere. My gun crunched out of my hands. I swung a punch to crack Stephenson but hit nothing but air. His arm wrapped around my throat. Squeezed. I grasped at it helplessly. Tried to kick back or gain some leverage. My feet slipped on Raimes's blood.

'Help,' I managed between breaths. 'Joon.'

Stephenson was too strong. Had caught me off guard. I tried to pry my fingers between his arm and my throat. No air. Stars flashed at the edges of my vision. Black was closing in.

'Orson! Gibson! Anyone!' I heard Joon's voice in my ear. 'Send back up, now. Byron? Talk to me!'

I couldn't talk though. My windpipe was being crushed. It didn't matter how quickly they'd get here. It would be too late for me. The stars in my vision turned to black holes. The darkness grew bigger until all I could see was defeat. It was over.

There was no getting up again from this.

53

Joon hammered at the locked door of the jack-in room. He could hear struggling in his headset but nothing from behind the sealed steel barrier. He looked back at Corpus. She wasn't going anywhere. *He?* Fuck. What was going on? Joon tried the handle. No luck.

'Byron!' he yelled, both at the door and through the headset. 'What's the code? I can't open it.'

No response.

'What's happening there?!' It was Gibson.

'Send back up now!' Joon repeated. 'Stephenson's here! Raimes is dead. No response from Wells or Orson.' He slapped the door again. 'Byron?'

Still nothing.

'He's got Byron!' Joon repeated.

'I'll be there as soon as I can,' Gibson yelled, then… 'Any units close to Enclave Court in West Vegas get there now! Number 13.'

Joon tried the door once more. He searched for the code in his memory. Had Ada said what it was, or just punched it in? He should have been paying more attention. Gibson said it was the date Switch was reborn. What date was that? Ada was the Slaughter expert, not him. He blinked through files, searching for the date of her first killings. He entered the date in the door. The light flashed red. Shit. His hand scrambled for his Taser. Maybe he could fry the circuits, but that would lock him in for good. He remembered the Colt pistol Ada had given him. The weapon hung in its holster under his hoodie at his side. He wasn't supposed to carry it, but the thought of having it there while backing up Ada felt right. It was useless too though. Useless like him. He couldn't shoot through a 2-foot thick steel door.

'Byron!' Joon slapped the door impotently.

Total silence on the other end. He turned back to look at Corpus. Switch's sister, not her brother. They must have been identical twins. Joon didn't know what to believe right now. He just hoped Corpus had some answers. She'd be able to crack the file if it really was Corpus. But would Ada be dead already?

Joon looked at his feet. Blood pooled through the bottom of the door. Too much for anyone to be alive on the other side.

54

Joon waited in Corpus's vault for back up to arrive. He checked her again and saw she was fully synced. He thought about trying to shut down the equipment and powering off to jack her out, but he didn't know any of the passcodes and there might be complications. He'd have to wait for a crew to perform an anesthetic jack-out when they arrived to unplug her safely. Had she really masked herself as a man in virtual? It certainly wasn't uncommon for people to choose a different gender for their digital self. It rocked Joon to think the greatest hacker of all time was in front of him and still helpless. It looked like she was still being tortured. Grimaces and groans escaped her lips at regular intervals. A nightmare he couldn't wake her from. That torture had been all the input Joon had seen on the screen, not the deep-brain stimulation of digital confinement. How could they have been so stupid? Ada had warned them not to trust Switch. But then, she *had* led them to Corpus. Not a complete monster then.

After what felt like an eternity, Joon heard faint sirens. Mere minutes after that, there were rushing footsteps.

'Gibson,' he said into his comms. 'You're here?'

'Yes,' his voice came on the other end. 'Orson is on the doorstep dead. One of his eyes is popped like the other murders. Wells had his throat cut at the back door.'

'That was Stephenson, our killer,' Joon confirmed. 'And Raimes? Ada?' he asked.

'Raimes is at the bottom of the stairwell,' Gibson said stoically. 'That's the blood you reported. No sign of Ada.'

Maybe she was still alive. But if Stephenson had her, maybe she was better off dead.

'Can you open the door?' Joon asked.

After a moment, the door handle rattled on the other side. It stayed closed though.

'What's the code?' Gibson asked.

'If I knew, I'd be out already,' Joon snapped.

'I'll pull Cline in to see if he can hack it,' Gibson said. 'It'll be quicker and safer than trying to cut through this thing.'

Another hour and Joon felt the rush of cool air as the door swung open. Raimes's body had been taken, the pool of blood outside cleaned up. Cline's shaggy face looked triumphant at unlocking the door, but settled into a frown befitting the situation.

Gibson swept the house and found nothing else. It was confirmed that Orson had been killed the same way as the other murders. At Joon's request the scan team did an AI reconfiguration of Orson's ruptured eye. The simulation indicated a strong probability that a syringe had been punched right in the middle. That's how Stephenson had done all the other murders then for sure. He'd stabbed a needle into his victim's eye with whatever cocktail was in there to set up a chain reaction of cell rupture. Because the eye exploded, regular scan procedures hadn't picked up the original entry point. This knowledge didn't give Joon any sense of satisfaction. It was just a grim footnote to this whole business.

A team came in with anesthetic and put Corpus into a deep sleep before bringing her out again. As her brain stilled, the output display on the wall went dark. Safely untethered from the virtual world, the team brought her awake.

Corpus sobbed when she opened her own eyes and saw the police.

'It's over,' she gasped. 'Is it over?'

'Not yet,' Joon said softly. 'He's still loose and has one of ours. We need your help.'

55

Corpus shrugged off extra medical attention when she heard the Spider had Ada. She knew the detective must have been integral in freeing her from torture. Corpus said she'd do anything she could to help. The only thing she said she needed was a long, hot shower. The team waited for her to clean up and dress. Before too long, she was ready, even if she did look pale and weak, dressed in a too-big shirt and pants.

Corpus unfolded her weeklong ordeal at the hands of her captor, confirming her identity as the famous hacker and the fact that she was Switch's identical twin sister. She also told about how she was snatched from her office by the Spider and taken to some kind of digital dungeon she couldn't escape from, no matter how hard she tried. Corpus broke down when Joon told her it was Entown Stephenson who'd been her captor—the Troll she and her sister had kept out of the Guardians of the Web. She knew exactly how dangerous he was. How sick and twisted he'd become. All of that fire and fury would now be unleashed on Ada. Corpus said nothing about the file, so Joon kept quiet too.

'How did you get to me before The Spider did?' Corpus asked instead.

Joon paused. Gibson cleared his throat but said nothing.

'We had your sister direct us here,' Joon finally admitted, 'but she was using the information as a diversion to get out of digital confinement. She escaped.'

'You let Jazlin out?!' Corpus's face went whiter than it already was. 'Oh god, why?'

'To save you,' Joon said.

'But so many more will die,' Corpus put her face in her hands. 'You should have let Entown have me. What were you thinking?'

'That she was your sister and wanted to help you,' Joon said. 'We thought it was safe. We thought we had it under control.'

'Nothing to do with Jazlin is safe,' she sighed. 'She's never helped anyone but herself. Digital confinement was the best place for her. This can't have happened.'

'Do you know where she was jacked in?' Gibson grilled Corpus.

'No,' she said. 'If I knew, I would've alerted police anonymously years ago. She belongs in a cage. You have to understand why I kept our connection quiet. I would never have heard the end of it. I would've had to start all over again. I *will* have to start all over again.'

'I understand,' Joon said, putting a comforting hand on her arm.

He knew more than anyone how an avatar felt like the true you. He'd have to start all over again in the Holos soon himself. The thought was gutting. He'd been putting that reality off, concentrating on the case in this world instead.

'The courts might not understand though,' Gibson said from behind her. 'Unless you help us find Switch.'

'Anything,' Corpus said. 'I'll do anything.'

'First things first,' Joon cut in. 'We need to find Ada. If she's alive, she's in serious trouble. And she knows more about Switch than anyone—she could help lead that manhunt.' He turned back to Corpus. 'Do you have any idea where Stephenson might be?'

She shook her head. A single, helpless tear ran down her cheek.

'Let's regroup at the station,' Gibson said. 'We have to get Corpus checked at a hospital first.'

'No, I can help now,' she insisted, wiping her face clear. 'I will hold up. If Entown has her, every moment we delay will be hell for your detective.'

Corpus's resemblance to Switch's avatar was uncanny. Instead of that cold visage though, she was utterly fierce, utterly human, even in this state.

Not even bothering to argue about it, Gibson clicked his wrist comm.

'Cline, is the ambulance ready to go out there?' he said.

'Sure is,' Cline's voice came over the link.

'Good,' Gibson said, leveling a gaze at Corpus. 'Cline and I will ride with you to hospital. You can brief us more on the way if you want to help that badly.'

'I'll come too,' Joon said quickly, not wanting to let Corpus out of his sight.

First chance he got alone with her, he had to ask her about the file.

Gibson opened his mouth to protest, but Joon held up a hand. 'I insist,' he said. 'I think you'll be interested in something else I have to bring to light.'

Gibson cocked an eyebrow but didn't ask any more questions. Instead, he turned and walked out of the house.

Joon took Corpus gently by the arm to guide her out. She'd been through so much, but would have to go through a lot more before all this was done.

56

I awoke with a gasp. Tried to sit up. Realized I was pinned. I couldn't even move my head. It was strapped tight. I flicked my eyes around the room to see where I was. Morning light flickered through vertical blinds. The rest of the room was bare. Memory flooded back in. Switch. Corpus. Raimes. Stephenson. Darkness. I was fucked. Completely and utterly.

There was no sign of Stephenson. Then I saw the knives—the kind a serial killer might buy from an all-night infomercial. 'But wait! There's more! You also get this serrated blade to cut through aluminum cans *and* vertebrae!' The full set was laid neatly in a row on the table beside me. I struggled again to get free. No use.

Footsteps.

He was here.

I tried to force myself to settle, but my whole body twitched with dread. *What did he want? Why wasn't I dead already?* Then a more calming thought: *If he wanted something from me, maybe I could use it.*

Stephenson's bald head came into view. Those icy eyes. The monochrome goatee. He leered with perfect white teeth.

'Hello, Detective Byron,' he said. 'Glad you're awake. Now we can start.'

'Start dancing?' I asked. 'You might have to untie my feet or you'll be disappointed.'

'I won't be disappointed,' he said, tilting his head.

The sound of metal scraping on metal made me flick my eyes to the side. He'd chosen the smallest knife from his table of torture.

'Sorry,' I said, forcing myself to feel brave. 'I don't go for anything under nine inches.'

He pursed his lips together. Lifted the knife into the center of my vision. 'Some foreplay first then,' he said.

As quick as a whip, he sliced a cut down my forearm. I grunted in pain but didn't cry out. A small victory. I could feel the warmth of blood running down my arm, along my skin.

Stephenson watched it. Licked his lips. He then pulled a cloth out of his pocket along with a little tube of something. Bending down he wiped my arm and squeezed the contents of the tube on the cut. It stung like hell. I bit my lip, determined not to scream. Stephenson pinched the cut together. It stuck firm.

'Superglue,' he said, standing up straight again. 'First used in the Vietnam War as a way to close wounds on the field. Still just as effective today.'

Without preamble he cut me again on the other arm. Sharp and fast. I sucked in air, panting.

'We get to do this all day and you won't bleed out,' Stephenson grinned. 'A conscious victim is an entertaining one,' he said.

'Go chew on a light bulb,' I said. 'We'll catch you.'

'Will you?' he said.

Another slice, this time along my collar bone. The knife tip caught on bone as it ripped. *Farrrk*! My breath was ragged now. I was hot. Sweating.

'I find the psychological torment of this is so much sweeter than the physical,' he said as he carefully patched the wound again with his glue.

Tube spent, he pulled another from his pocket. He held up his knife again, red with my blood. His eyes were wide, pupils dilated, looking like effluent pipes to his soul.

'Where will I cut next?' he asked.

'Cut your cock off,' I managed between gritted teeth.

'Too hard to stick it back on,' he replied quickly. 'Didn't work with this either.'

He used his knife to tap his leg. A metal ting showed it was a prosthetic.

'Good technology,' he said, 'but not as good as the real thing. That's why I prefer the Holos. I feel properly whole. It's why you're in this mess. You wanted to take my playground away.'

'I didn't,' I said.

'YOU DID!' he roared in my face, before backing up, calm again. 'You, Christos, Lilith, Corpus. You can't chain us. The bill will fail and I'll be free again—like The Master promised.'

'The bill will pass no matter what you do,' I panted. 'Our country won't be held to ransom by a terrorist like you.'

He stabbed hard next to my head. The knife tip clanged onto the metal bench. I flinched but I still couldn't move at all, I was bound so tight. Tears escaped my traitorous eyes.

Stephenson smiled at that.

I searched for a way to stall things. To get out. What had he said? The Master? There it was. This wasn't *his* plan. It was someone else's. Conspiracy.

'You're just a puppet,' I said.

He didn't take the bait, just sliced another cut on my cheek. I couldn't turn away even if I wanted to. I looked into his eyes, hard. 'Fukami doesn't care about you,' I said through gritted teeth.

'Fukami?' he said, furrowing his brow. 'Oh no. Not him. He's the master's puppet too. I don't answer to him.'

My mind raced. Another player? A conspiracy to the top levels. I needed to keep this going.

'We have the file,' I said. 'We know Fukami's behind it. Know who all of you are.'

Stephenson grabbed my face, his fingertips pressing into the wound on my cheek. It was agony. I couldn't scream this time though. Stephenson held my mouth shut. He dribbled super glue over my lips. The toxic taste and smell made me gag. Still, he held me firm.

'Sssh,' he said. 'Sssh. Speak no lies. So many lies.'

He held my jaw together for a while. Stood straighter once my mouth was stuck.

'It doesn't matter if you have the file,' he said. 'Do you think now that Corpus is free, he'll hack it for you?'

I tried to open my mouth but couldn't. The stench of super glue rushed up my nose with each breath.

'The thing is,' Stephenson said, tapping the knife on the table. Ting. Ting. Ting. 'You have no idea how far The Master's fangs reach. I'm not the only one that's been guarding the web. Your friend for example. Agent Min Joon. He's one of us.'

I screamed against my fixed lips. Tried to strain upward. Impotent rage filled me. He was lying. Lying. Just like Switch lied about my dad. *Wasn't he?*

'Ah, there it is,' Stephenson said looking into my eyes. 'Psychological pain. Let's have some more of that.'

He dripped superglue into one of my nostrils, sealing it. I now had only one hole to breath through.

This was not the way I'd planned on celebrating solving this case.

57

The ambulance cruised through the Vegas streets on autodrive. No rush, no apparent emergency. Joon was a bundle of nervous energy. Ada was out there somewhere, at the mercy of Entown Stephenson—if she wasn't already dead. Joon needed to be doing, not sitting.

The paramedic on hand monitored Corpus's vitals. He was tall and lanky, like a stick insect in uniform. Corpus had every kind of cord and pad attached to her. Gibson and Cline sat by, watching her. They weren't even asking any questions.

'What happened with Switch?' Joon asked Gibson, breaking the silence.

'She got away,' Gibson said.

'How?'

Cline shifted in his seat.

'I went through the data the military had in the firewalls,' he said. 'It looked like she stilled her brain patterns somehow, getting them to a level low enough to jack out without damage. We think. For all we know, she could have died.'

'I don't think we're that lucky,' Corpus said, looking out a small side window at the streets passing by. 'My sister has a knack for surviving bad situations.' Her eyes went dark, like she was reliving a traumatic childhood memory.

Joon thought about the first interview between Switch and Ada. He'd read the transcript, committing the footage to memory as well. Switch had said she could almost touch silence if she tried hard enough. That there was screaming deep down. Everyone had thought it referred to the screams of her victims or some old abuse she had suffered. But what if she was talking about the deep-brain stimulation? That stimulation that abated little by little with each firewall you went through. Perhaps she'd used meditation to still her mind enough to escape. When the screams of the digital confinement algorithm were dull enough, she could cut them

215

loose altogether.

'I heard you order her to get up,' Joon said, looking at Gibson. 'What did she do?'

Gibson screwed up his nose in disgust. 'She fucking sat down and crossed her legs. Went into some kind of trance. She was impossibly heavy. I couldn't drag her.'

Joon thought some more. It was plausible. She'd spent years meditating in there becoming an expert at slowing, even stilling her mind. He'd have to assume Switch was out there somewhere. Joon watched Gibson again, who was staring at Corpus with a strange look in his eyes. He kept flicking his gaze to Joon.

'What happened with Ada?' Cline asked, wringing his hands.

'Like I told you earlier,' Joon said, not taking his eyes off Gibson. 'Ada tried to take Stephenson on alone. She sacrificed herself to secure Corpus.'

Cline nodded in admiration.

'Pity it was a waste,' Joon said.

'What?' Cline asked, confused. He and Gibson shared a look.

'Well,' Joon said calmly, watching them. 'We have this one now. The great Corpus, so helpless.'

Gibson and Cline went totally silent. Corpus looked to Joon with fear in her eyes. The paramedic paused too.

'Didn't they tell you?' Joon continued, pulling out his taze gun. 'I have the file. Now we have Corpus and Entown has Ada. With them both dead, it's checkmate. All we need to do is get rid of the complications.'

Gibson turned to Joon, his hand going toward his own taze gun.

'What complications?' he asked.

Joon nodded at Corpus, then the paramedic.

'Oh, I'm in on it too,' the attendant said coolly. 'We can easily make this look like an accident.'

Corpus tried to back up but the paramedic held her. Gibson clamped down on Corpus's wrists so she couldn't strike out. He pulled out some handcuffs.

'Stop!' Corpus yelled, 'I'm -'

The paramedic clamped his hand over her mouth.

'Shut up!' he said. 'This won't hurt much.'

Gibson moved to cuff Corpus.

'Hold on a moment,' Joon said to Gibson, raising a hand.

Gibson paused. The cuffs ready to snap on. The paramedic held Corpus firm.

'What?' Gibson said.

'I just want to know one thing. Did Cline help us cover up the footage? Or did Stephenson do that all on his own?'

Cline shuffled. He'd been edging away from the confrontation like it made him uneasy. 'Of course I helped,' he said.

'Just wanted to make sure,' Joon said.

Before anyone else could move, Joon raised his taze gun and blasted Cline full in the chest. 50,000 volts speared into the analyst who collapsed, convulsing on the floor.

All hell broke loose.

The attendant who had held Corpus rushed at Joon with a yell. Joon blasted his taze gun again and sent the stick insect sprawling. The ambulance cabin shook as the paramedic glanced off a wall and tumbled into Gibson. Gibson brushed off the blow with barely a grunt. He snapped his cuffs on Corpus and in one swift movement charged low at Joon. Joon tried to shoot again, but the stocky cop was raging-bull fast. He thundered into the FBI agent. Air heaved from Joon's lungs and his weapon went flying. He slammed down onto his back with Gibson on top. The cop lashed out again and again, his fists hitting the floor, barely missing Joon, who twisted his head from side to side to avoid being pummeled.

Joon heaved up his own punch and cracked the side of Gibson's temple. The blow did nothing but enrage the man. Gibson grabbed Joon's throat with meaty palms and squeezed, lifting him up before slamming his head into the floor. Supernovas burst in Joon's vision. All sense left him. He grasped at the fists around his neck, scratching and flailing for dear life. Gibson throttled Joon, rattling him like he wanted to snap his neck in two. Joon was a rag doll in an attack dog's grip. He tried to break free but couldn't. Consciousness started to slip away. No full life flashed before his eyes, just a single image—the desperate look on Ada's face as she swung the door closed to protect Corpus. Ada, who he'd failed. Joon struggled, trying to hold onto that image. Then he remembered. The Colt Ada had given him. It was still under his hoodie. With vision fluttering, he fumbled awkwardly to get to it. Gibson slammed him back to the floor again. Joon somehow got his hand inside his zipper and barely brushed the cold metal of the gun inside. He couldn't pull it free. Pain burned in his lungs, across his chest, and up his throat. Joon desperately lunged for the gun again. This time he found the grip. The Colt slid out. He whipped it up and pulled the trigger. Nothing. The safety was on.

Gibson growled as he realized what Joon had done. He took one hand off the agent's throat to grab that Colt.

Joon's thumb slipped along the grip's side and caught the safety. He snapped the trigger back at the same time.

The noise was earth-shattering. It thundered off the walls of the ambulance.

Gibson's body bucked upward, then dropped hard, straight back down onto Joon. Blood flowed, covering Joon's front as he struggled to get out from underneath the dead cop. Joon had somehow survived but now he was being crushed. He dropped the Colt and heaved as hard as he could, wriggling. With a wet sucking noise, he slid free. Joon lay there heaving in air. He took a second to gather himself, closing his eyes. When he opened them again, the barrel of the Colt 1911 was shoved right into his face. Corpus had it.

'Start talking or I'll blow your head off,' she said unsteadily. The barrel trembled in her grip.

Joon raised his hands slowly, not making any sudden movement. He swallowed, then heaved in more air before he could speak. It took him a few moments.

'You're safe,' Joon finally managed. 'They've been in on the conspiracy. I had to flush them out. I'm here to help you.'

Corpus glanced sideways at the dead body of Gibson. Cline and the paramedic were motionless but alive. She turned the gun away from Joon towards them.

'No,' Joon said desperately.

Corpus glared at him.

'Why not?'

'Because if you do, you're no better than them.'

'I don't care,' she said. 'You don't know what I went through.'

'I don't,' Joon soothed, hands still raised. 'But they'll get their justice, believe me. All we need to do is crack this file.'

'You have it?' Corpus asked.

Joon nodded.

'If we can find somewhere safe to jack in, I'll show you.'

Corpus paused, the gun still pointed at Cline.

'Please,' Joon said. 'Ada's out there somewhere. The file could tell us where the Spider has her.'

Corpus lowered the weapon, letting it hang at her side. Joon dragged himself into a sitting position.

'Ambulance,' he said, 'slow to a stop.'

The autodrive responded. Joon waited until everything was still, before he felt steady enough to stand. Blood was splattered around the cabin, gore dripping from the roof. He eyed Cline and the paramedic who were still out cold. They'd be like that for another half hour maybe.

'We need to get out of here,' Joon said. 'Do you have somewhere anonymous we can go?'

Corpus shook her head, looking at the mess. Her face was pale, shock setting in.

'Okay,' Joon said, holding out his hand to steady Corpus. 'I might have somewhere. I just hope she recognizes me.'

58

I frantically sucked oxygen through one nostril like air was my addiction. The hundredth cut for the day sliced along my thigh. Entown had stripped me down, physically and mentally. I wanted to die. Endless darkness would be better than this endless torment. Still, my body wouldn't let me succumb. My lungs heaved for life. My blood burned for oxygen. I felt weak all over. Drained. Exhausted. Broken but alive.

A beeping sounded. Entown stopped. He touched a small lump on his neck.

'Yes?' He carefully put down his latest knife and walked from the room. 'Is it done?' he asked, before shutting the door behind him.

I could hear a muffled conversation but didn't know what was being said. I didn't care. Instead, I looked down at my body, littered with cuts that had been glued together again. Those little gashes were never too deep. Entown was careful of that. A professional. Surgical.

I searched around the room for any way I could get out. I'd even take a knife to slit my wrists and bleed out on the table if there wasn't any other option. Then I saw my right wrist strap. It was loose, just barely. All my straining against the pain must have pulled it out. My forearm and hands were covered in congealed blood. Maybe it would be slippery enough to help me slide out. I heaved, every muscle in me going taught. I grunted against my sealed lips with the effort, collapsing back, sucking for air again. I was tired. So tired.

I looked at the strap. It was looser still. If I could just slip my arm through or wriggle a finger under the bonds…

The conversation outside got louder. Entown was arguing with someone.

I moved a finger up, just brushing the strap. Almost there. I strained hard again, trying to rip free. Movement. The strap loosened further. I was able to get a finger underneath. I would have laughed if my lips weren't shut tight.

Then Entown came back in the room. The look on his face was terrifying. Pure hatred and disappointment mixed in one. His eyes went to the loose strap on my arm. He stepped forward, brushed my finger back and cinched things tight again.

No!

My body gave up then. My muscles went to water. I truly wanted to die.

Entown took out his largest blade. Raised it to my face. I didn't care.

Just do it, I thought.

But he gently sliced between my lips, cutting the seal that bound them. My mouth tore open. Skin ripped away at the edges where Entown hadn't cut yet. The air that came in felt like heaven—until I remembered my situation. I simply lay there, breathing deeply, looking up at my tormenter like a pitiful, caged animal at its master.

'Seems you're more than just a plaything,' Entown sneered at me. 'Corpus got away with your friend Min Joon.'

A tiny spark of hope flared deep inside me. Small, but there. Entown *had* been lying then. Joon was with me, the blessed little spankblanket. And he had the key to unraveling the conspiracy. Perhaps this pain wasn't for nothing then.

'Let's hope for you they're willing to swap your life for the file,' Entown shattered my thoughts. 'Or you'll be rotting in the ground before too long and I'll have to go after them the hard way.'

59

It was a long trek on foot to where Joon wanted to go. He and Corpus moved from shadow to shadow, taking pains not to be seen. Both were flecked with blood. Joon's hoodie was caked in it. If anyone reported them, the wrong people could come to "help".

Joon ignored the constant beeping of his wrist-comm. He would have torn it off already if he didn't need it for later. He'd installed no-track software on it. They wouldn't find him that way. The comm vibrated again. Another message from Cline. The traitor had recovered and been in touch with his superiors. Each message was the same as the last. We have Ada. We are torturing her. Give up Corpus and the file. Save Ada's life. End her suffering.

Sometimes there were photos.

The cuts on her body weren't the worst of it. The look on Ada's face was. Joon now wished he'd let Corpus kill Cline. The thought of sending the analyst to prison to rot was little comfort after what he was letting happen to Ada. Joon clenched his jaw and pushed everything to the back of his mind. Ada was tough. She could hold out. He'd save her if it was the last thing he did. She'd saved *him* already, twice. Preserved his avatar against The Spider. Gotten him out of that hospital bed with her speech about getting up. It had hit a nerve deep inside. Hearing that Bleesh had been caught had been the final push, but hers had been the true spark of light beneath all that ugliness. Joon had to play this whole mess just right or all their work was for nothing. He wouldn't lose her like this. He had to pull himself up, bloody and broken, and trudge toward that finish line for her.

Corpus trailed Joon silently. She must have known instinctively that this wasn't the time for talking. They wove through the streets, all stealth. Eventually, they came to an innocuous apartment block, one Joon knew but had never actually been to in person. He hoped this was the right place or they were screwed. Joon went down the drive and came to a door. He knocked exactly seven times. Waited. Knocked again seven times.

There was a shuffling inside the apartment. Locks clicked in the door. It cracked open. A tall Japanese woman was silhouetted in the gap, rail-thin and elegant. She paused, squinting, unsure, then her face relaxed into softer concern opening the door wider.

'Joon, baby, it *is* you,' she said. 'What have you done? You're all over the Feed.'

Sabi then looked to Corpus. 'But you're not Ada?' she said as a question.

'She's not Ada,' Joon said quietly. 'Can we explain inside?'

Sabi ushered them into the small but comfortable unit. Japanese calligraphy hung on the walls. Jade-colored cushions were scattered in the living area for sitting. Coffee was brewing in the kitchenette. Sabi went and silently poured some, showing uncanny patience and trust in her friend. She handed Corpus and Joon each a cup, then sat on a cushion and waited.

'This,' Joon said, 'is Corpus.'

Sabi's eyes widened but she didn't comment.

'There's definitely a conspiracy to manipulate the Holos,' Joon continued in a rush. 'Some of the police are involved. I just don't know how deep it goes. I can't trust anyone.'

Sabi nodded once and sipped, waiting for more.

'What does it say on the Feed?' Joon asked.

With a wave of her hand, a screen appeared on Sabi's wall. Images flickered of Joon attacking Gibson and Cline in the ambulance. It was only a few seconds of footage. They didn't show the before and after. The comments and commentary below filled in the gaps for Joon. *A rogue FBI agent, thought to be corrupt, attacked police and kidnapped a key witness in the Faux Specter Murders. He is now assumed to be behind the killings. Police are hunting Agent Min Joon for questioning now. If you see him, report it immediately. Do not approach. He is armed and extremely dangerous.*

Sabi raised an eyebrow at Joon. He touched his wrist-comm and swiped the latest messages from Cline onto Sabi's screen. Sabi gasped when she saw the image of Ada being tortured. She read the accompanying text of demands quickly and put her coffee down.

'So you need the file?' she asked.

'Do you still have it safe?' Joon asked. He wasn't taking anything for granted. 'If we can get Corpus to hack it, we can find out where they're keeping Ada and save her.'

'Of course I have it,' Sabi said. 'But we'll have to view it in the Holos. Its coding can't even be read on real-world screens. It's virtual script only. You know that.'

Corpus nodded like she already knew too. The three considered each other. They were all more at home in virtual anyway.

'We'll have to borrow avatars,' Joon said. 'Corpus can't risk logging into hers in case the police have a trace on it now. And mine…'

Joon trailed off. He didn't want to tell Sabi that the masterpiece she'd created for him was now just blips in the void.

'That's not a problem,' Sabi said, wisely filling the space. 'I have plenty of shells.' She then looked to Corpus. 'Do you think you can hack it? The file?'

Corpus considered. 'I was getting close before Christos disappeared,' she said. 'But I'll need some time.'

Joon let out a long breath. Ada didn't have time. He considered the situation. An idea hit him. Quickly, he typed out a message to Cline on the burner chat room the analyst was using, angling his screen so the others could see what he was writing.

Will trade the file for Ada. Give me 24 hours to secure a swap location. Until then, send me a live feed of her so I know she's safe and not being harmed. Otherwise, we go straight to the media.

The trio sat and watched his wrist comm. Nothing. One minute. Two. The anxiety in Joon's chest was suffocating. Would they buy it? More importantly, if they did, could he manage to solve everything? Ada knew so much more than him. He needed her. Needed her to be okay. Still, he had Corpus and Sabi helping. That was something. Something significant.

Finally, an ellipsis appeared on his message screen, showing someone was typing on the other end.

12 hours, the message said. *Tick, tock.* After that was a link. Joon clicked. A room came into view. Ada was strapped to a steel table with someone hunched over her. The man turned slowly and looked up at the camera. Stephenson. He had a knife in his hand.

Joon wanted to dive through and throttle the monster.

Stephenson narrowed his icy eyes for a moment. Then he smiled. He held up the knife and put it down on a small bench next to Ada's torture table. Stephenson made a show that his hands were empty. Tapped his wrist. *Tick, tock.* Then he strode from the room.

Joon looked at his friend. Ada had no clue what was happening. Her head was held firm so she couldn't move it. Her eyes flicked the way Stephenson went. Then they flicked up to the camera. Ada watched for a long time, before slumping back. She looked close to death.

They had half a day.

'We need to jack in right now,' Joon said. 'We're on the clock.'

60

Dread. It was the worst kind of fear, waiting for Stephenson to come back. The Spider. The Troll. Whatever he was. I loathed the heavy feeling in the pit of my stomach. The one that rose like slow bile into my chest and throat before infecting my mind. Dread. It was dirty and dark. At least you can lose yourself in terror. The moment of sheer panic when you let everything go and your whole world is pain. It's pure and blinding. Release from the mind to the physical—not that mess of anxiety and imagining the next round of torture. Lying on that stainless-steel table in that unforgiving room, my torment solidified something for me. The Holos needed real laws to protect people against torture like this. Against all kinds of mind violence. I could die in this real-world prison and it would be a blessing. In the virtual world, someone could be subjected to this kind of pain for a lifetime without the risk of dying. That psychological agony was so much worse. Maybe that's why Stephenson seemed to revel in it even more than bodily torture. There was no release from it for the victim.

Release. I'd thought the Holos was evil, but now reality was worse. There was no escaping the darkness of man whatever world you were in. That darkness simply took different forms.

I kept looking at the camera in the corner. Was he watching me now? The Spider. I could see the strap on my arm was loose again but dared not try to escape. He'd left me for now. Every noise and creak in the place made me think he was coming back. The thought made me sick. Yet part of me wanted him to come back so I could swap dread for terror. To release my mind into pain. Part of me, but not all. I was fractured. A broken thing. I wasn't even making sense to myself. I was frozen, looking at that camera blinking. Why had he stopped? Was he now hunting my friends? Not knowing amplified my suffering.

Another noise. A door closing. Was he coming or going? I held my breath. Silence.

The light through the blinds was dying. It must be twilight. The death of another day. How long had I been there? It felt like it could be weeks. It might only be hours.

I looked at my bonds again. Maybe he wouldn't see me in the dark if I was trying to get out. Maybe he wasn't watching anyway. Maybe he was. So what if he was? So what if he came back? This was all pain. It was just a different kind.

I steadied my breathing. I had to find stillness somehow. It made me think of Switch meditating in her cell. Where was she now? Was she already killing again? Causing pain to others? I had to get out to stop her. Keep running that race. I had to. I had to. I just had to get up and get past another monster first. Stephenson. A lower-level enemy before the final boss.

I flexed my arm. Movement again. The strap was definitely loose. I strained. Struggled. Wriggled my fingers on my right hand. Got them under the strap again. I watched the door as I did. No sound still. My fingers worked the strap, pulling it bit by bit. Darkness fell.

After hours of trying in the cover of night, I finally made the strap click loose. The end stuck out of the buckle like a party popper ribbon ready to be pulled. I gritted my teeth to stop from crying out. Only one more clasp to go and it would give way completely. It wasn't celebration time yet. My head was still held tight, so I couldn't bend down and use my teeth to help. Twisting my wrist around instead, I managed to pinch the end of the strap between two fingers. If I could just jiggle it looser.

My whole being concentrated on that strap. Every ounce of will tugging it to and fro. My fingers slipped off it again and again. Each failure felt like Stephenson's knives slicing me. I clenched my jaw in determination. Kept trying. Failed. Tried again. Fraction by fraction, the strap started to give. The final clasp looked set to slip free with a heave on my end. Would it be enough? I wrenched my wrist back. It didn't work. I tried again. It slid a little. Yes. A bit further. Further.

A noise. My eyes snapped toward the door. I could just make out a thin line of light beneath the frame. I waited. The door stayed closed. No shadows passed on the other side.

I wrenched again. The clasp popped free. My hand came free. Oh, god, yes. Instantly, I grasped for my head, eyes wide like a frenzied beast. I needed to get my head out.

The door stayed closed.

I fumbled then found my head restraint. Shaking fingers tugged it loose. I sat bolt upright, thinking I was done but my other arm tugged me back. Shit.

The door stayed closed.

I worked that arm free, then my feet. I swung off the bench. Stumbled. Steadied. I looked around trying to figure out what to do. Should I try the window? The door? The camera blinked. I should try the window.

I moved to step forward and an arm slid casually around my neck.

I would have screamed but the arm choked me in the darkness, pulling me back into a warm body.

'Sssh,' the voice said. 'Quiet. It's okay.'

It was a familiar voice. One I hadn't heard in seven long years. My heart ground to a halt.

Dad?

My heart thumped double time. I grasped at his arm and it loosened. I turned.

It was him! My father. Alive. *Impossible.* But there he was in the flesh, exactly like I remembered, strong and vibrant. I thought for a moment that maybe I'd died and gone to heaven. Dad smiled.

I wanted to ask a thousand things. To untangle the possibility of it all. To tell him I was sorry. To tell him I was glad that he hadn't really died. That the technicians had lied to me. That they said they didn't save him when they did. To tell him who I was now. To weep about my torture. To ask him where he'd gone. But all that came out was:

'Dad?'

'Sssh,' he said, pulling me into a hug again.

His body was warm around me. Safe. Loving. He held me for a long time in that embrace. I felt like a little girl again… like before the hate of the world tainted me. I felt right. I felt like everything would be okay.

Then I remembered. Stephenson.

'Dad, we have to go,' I said quickly. 'He'll be back soon. That monster. Stephens-'

'Sssh,' he said, holding me tighter, stopping me from moving. 'You're not going anywhere. You haven't suffered enough yet.'

I didn't understand. I pulled my head back to look at him again. That gorgeous, comforting smile on his face. It turned into a horrid grin. His teeth were pointed. His breath stunk like rotten meat.

'You're not going anywhere,' he repeated, gripping my arms tight. His fingers dug into the cuts on my skin. 'Your friends haven't given me the file yet. It's time to play some more.'

61

Corpus worked in Sabi's studio. They'd come directly through a jack-in point Sabi had designed for stealthy entry. She was a savant herself when it came to code, and more than a little paranoid. Joon's kind of person. Corpus's too it seemed. They had hit it off right away talking about their favorite coding languages and offshoot dialects. They'd both agreed excitedly that advances in recent DWIM architecture made it easier to program quickly, but nothing replaced raw languages when it came to creating something elegant from first principles.

Sabi watched over Corpus's shoulder as Joon paced. Every few moments he checked the livestream Cline had sent him. Ada was there on that table in the dark, occasionally shifting but going nowhere. At least it was proof she was alive. Proof she was being left alone.

Corpus's fingers danced over a virtual keyboard. He'd chosen a male avatar again. Straightforward without adornment. He looked comfortable in the shell. Not like in the real where she'd been a shell of a person. Where *he'd* been a shell of a person, Joon corrected in his mind. This was Corpus's true self right here. It was impossible to miss. Him. The way he sat contented. In flow. Corpus turned the file around and around, teasing at strands of code one at a time, working to pry the knot loose. At the same time, he multitasked in other windows. He checked policy markets. He scrolled the Feed. He dove into the dark web and pulled out encryption keys. The pace at which Corpus maximized and minimized screens made Joon's head spin. He couldn't keep track. Yet Corpus barely broke a sweat. Finally, the hacker stabbed the keyboard in front of him three times with a single finger and everything coalesced. A golden image of the file shone above him and Sabi.

'Wonderful,' Sabi said. 'Whoever put this together is a genius. A master.'

Corpus was perversely enjoying this too. A smile played on his lips the whole time. Sabi pointed to the 3D display.

'See how that's wrapped around the no-copy code?' she marveled. 'It's like they're one and the same.'

'I see it,' Corpus said. 'The no-copy part can't be separated. But if we crack the lock here we might be able to hold everything else together.'

He hit another button on his keyboard and the display blazed with light. The whole thing solidified into a physical representation of a virtual puzzle. Corpus stood up and touched the strand Sabi had pointed out. It was real in his hand now.

'Perfect,' Sabi said.

'Nothing's perfect,' Corpus said. 'You know that. We're all broken, just some more beautifully than others.'

With that, he pulled a strand outward. It came loose and the file shattered into fragments.

'No!' Joon said, thinking it had been corrupted.

But Sabi and Corpus were still smiling.

When the light of the shell had dissipated, it revealed a tiny galaxy of dots. They were sub-files, all strung together by a web of barely visible strands. Corpus touched one of the subfiles. It zapped into view, enlarging.

It was a picture of Fukami. Numbers tallied underneath. SureCoin. Mercury. The profits were staggering.

Joon stood there dumbstruck. This was it. Fukami. He was involved after all. He'd been investing in Mercury heavily for a long time, and would stand to make trillions when the law bill passed.

'More about money than power,' Joon said.

Corpus looked over his shoulder and nodded.

'Can we copy this?' Joon asked.

Corpus shook his head. 'No. The uncopiable part is still woven in.'

'Screen snap? Film?'

'No.' Sabi touched another dot. It too blew up to visible size. Gibson. Another dot. Cline. Another. Entown. The soldier's personal history was all on display. Much more detailed than the file Senator Rommel had provided.

Joon stepped forward. He put his hand on the screen and took all of Entown's info inside him. In a second, he knew it was hopeless.

'No,' he said softly.

'What?' Sabi asked.

'I thought it would tell us where Entown's bunker is. It must be where he's keeping Ada.'

'Bunker?' Corpus asked, eyes still on the files.

He shifted them around, seemingly reading and sorting them without having to make them larger.

'We had a suspect called Bleesh who knew Entown had a bunker somewhere. 'A sweet bunker' were the exact words. Entown thought it was some great joke.'

Corpus continued to shuffle files, but Sabi sat down, thinking.

Joon looked at the live feed on his wrist again. The light was dying in Ada's cell. Things were shifting into shadows. Darkness. Light. Joon realized how stupid he'd been. The light in there had been coming from a curtained window on the far wall. Bunkers didn't have windows, did they? Bleesh was lying—or mistaken. This was hopeless. The sense of elation he'd felt at seeing the file open splintered to dust. They had proof of corruption, but they couldn't get to Ada. He couldn't sacrifice her for this, no matter what. He couldn't. She was too good of a person.

Sabi moved to Joon's shoulder and looked at the livestream. Her head shifted. 'Sweet bunker?' she murmured to herself.

Corpus zapped through more files like a focused laser. He stabbed one with his finger and it all came up, drawing Joon's attention.

The whole plan was mapped out. Reasoning. Work flows. Payments. Every person involved. It was the master file. Joon gaped. This couldn't be right. But there it was in True-Res. His heart sank. There were more people involved than he wanted to believe. This wouldn't just change the Holos forever; it would change America, the whole world, if these people were left unchecked by justice. Joon had an impossible decision to make.

'We have to turn this file over,' he said quietly. 'We have to show the media. This is bigger than Ada.'

Joon's eyes roamed quickly, searching for something. Any last-minute thing he could use. Sabi turned away, pulling up her own screen and scrolling. Joon tallied all the people on the list. Saw something important, or rather didn't see it.

'Sheriff Mendez,' he said. 'She's not on here. That must mean she's clean. We can get her to help arrest everyone. Use this list to build a team that can do it. Use deduction to get clean cops and FBI agents to help. We have to work fast though. We might be out of time. What's Rommel's policy paying on the markets?'

Corpus clicked a few buttons on the type pad in front of him.

'$1.10,' he confirmed. 'We're not too late, but it could hit the threshold any time and go into law. We have to stop it. Stop all these fuckers from benefitting. They weren't trying to stop that bill from happening. They just wanted to profit from it.'

Joon looked at his wrist-comm and paused. Ada was up and off the bed. She was struggling with someone? It looked like she was choking. Then Joon saw something that defied reality. Something that explained how a bunker could have windows. Ada's father. He was supposed to be dead. Was dead. That could only mean one thing…

Right then, Sabi clapped her hands. She swiped her screen into Joon's eyesight.

'A sweet bunker,' she said.

There was a picture of a military-style bunker in the desert, concrete jutting from the rocks and sand. A rusted chain link fence sat around it.

'Sugar Bunker,' Sabi explained. 'Just outside of Vegas. It's an old nuclear bomb test facility. Abandoned by the military and locked tight.'

Joon could have kissed Sabi. She was a genius. A sweet bunker. Entown's hideout.

Then a scream from Joon's wrist-comm rang out. Ada.

They had to get to her, now.

62

My scream felt like it would rip my vocal cords right out of my throat. My dad, my protector, had forced me back onto the bench. He'd bound me again. Held tight. Too strong against my weak body. Reality collapsed around me. My mind couldn't cope. The room was a black hole. Dad was a pinpoint of light in the middle, bright and terrifying. He sharpened Entown's knives. The implements of torture that had already torn me apart. Maybe I was hallucinating. Maybe the torture finally snapped me. Maybe this was my new reality. I cried, looking at my father as he worked the edge of the blade to a razor's edge.

'You shouldn't have left me to die, naughty girl,' he said. 'You failed me. You gave up on me.'

'No,' my scream was now a silent whisper. The mere mouthing of words. '*No.*'

'But I didn't die,' he continued. 'I became a disciple of Switch instead. Her power was beyond anything I ever thought possible. You'd have to feel it inside you to understand. That power.'

I writhed on my bench, trying to get away from the words. Trying to get away from the truth of them. Dad stepped forward again. I'd left him when I shouldn't have and this was my punishment. After all these years, I was getting what I deserved.

'I studied Switch just like you did,' Dad stepped close enough to rest a cold blade on my foot, not cutting, just waiting. 'But I didn't loath her like you. I understood her. The Holos shouldn't be caged. Only freedom can bring true, lasting order. So I came up with a master plan. I recruited protectors for that glorious place. Built a web of people dedicated to its freedom. People like Entown Stephenson and Filton Fukami and your new police friends. Everyone. I brought the threat of death back into the virtual world just like Switch wanted. She was right. It's the ultimate consequence. A thrill-bringer like no other. The prospect of dying makes you feel more alive. I should know. I got closer than most. But I couldn't

231

replicate her secret of murder, so I used Entown to simulate it. To make perception a reality until I could free Switch from her own cage. Unleash her on the world again. Thank you for doing that too. Your police friends told me she broke free. Just another failure of yours.'

Dad slowly dragged the edge of the knife along the sole of my foot. I couldn't move it away. Yet the pain was nothing against my father's words slicing into me.

'I didn't want you in my plan,' he said, 'because I knew you were weak. That you'd fail when it mattered and give up when things got tough, like you gave up on me. You're useless. Dumb.'

He sounded like mother.

'You're a waste of my sperm. Nothing but a dumpster for the seed of others. Well, I'll show you what you're good for.'

He crawled up on the bench then, unzipping his pants. I struggled to slide backward but was held in place by the straps. All I could do was weep. Useless like he said. I couldn't even shake my head to rattle away the despair that closed in on all sides. Stupidly, I tried to rub the ring on my thumb. Dad's ring. It wasn't there. Had he taken it back too? I looked. Nothing on his hands. Nothing in them but the knife. I looked down at my own hands, pinned as they were. Those hands were caked in blood. My blood. There was a smear on the thumb where I'd rubbed. And there was something beneath. A ring, but not a metal one. A tattoo with a check mark. I struggled to make sense of it. It didn't compute. I just stared as my father climbed over me, his face sneering into mine. I looked back at him. That ugly face.

I knew then it wasn't him. He'd never looked like that in his life. Was never filled with hate, even when angry. The truth of it rushed up inside me. It bubbled out of me in a manic laugh. I must have sounded and looked insane. The face of my father. The heart of a spider. This was Entown. And this wasn't reality. It was his virtual playground.

'What's funny?' he growled in my father's voice.

He must have simulated the perfect tone of that voice from old recordings as Rose had done. Now all he'd need. My fears. My breaking points.

'You're not my father,' I whispered, no longer straining to get away. 'You're a monster. A troll.'

Entown's smile faltered on dad's face then. But then he grinned again.

'Very smart,' he said. 'But no matter. I'll rape you with this face on and you'll never be able to get it out of your head. You'll know your friends betrayed you. Joon hasn't contacted us to give up the file for you. He's left you to die. That analyst of yours, Cline, let me use your avatar for this. He gave me your personal history so I could torture you better. He abandoned you like the reject you are. You're alone in this world and you'll die that way.'

That should have hurt. It didn't. Because I wouldn't die today. I'd never told Cline about what my avatar could do. Had kept that to myself. And this cretin had no idea either.

I started laughing harder.

I laughed as I twisted my right hand in its bonds to face my tormentor. Laughed as his grin turned to impotent rage. Laughed as he moved to pull down his pants and get his revenge.

I welcomed the effort. Beckoned it with the index finger on my left hand, curling it back. Once. Twice.

'Set the body free and the spirit will soar,' I said. The Spider's look turned to confusion. He had no idea what was about to happen.

One final curl of the finger.

A blast of light shuddered out of my avatar. The bolt of destruction ripped Entown to oblivion. It melted the strap off my wrist as it seared through its code too. A chunk of my thigh rent off as well. I didn't care. Didn't feel it. All I felt was dark satisfaction of seeing my father's imposter split to dust. Dad could rest now, forever. I'd never let Entown ever bring him up from the grave again. Dad could rest because I would never give up. Not until this was finished.

As quickly as it started, the beam cut off. I was left alone. Blessedly alone, on the table with my right hand free. I lay there panting for a moment until I realized this wasn't really over. I wasn't out of this yet.

I ripped my left wrist loose, unclasped my head, my feet, and swung off the table. My avatar had been cut to shreds and stuck back together again. My leg was a smoking ruin, but I didn't care. Somehow, knowing my true body was intact gave me the strength to press forward.

I limped toward the torture chamber door. It swung open easily. The next room beyond was a simple space. A jack-out port there all ready to go. Entown's portal to real-world murder. My portal to bring real justice to all worlds.

63

My eyes snapped open. My visor flipped upward. Cords swam around me, sticking out from the concrete walls and roof. I had a drip in my arm. Digital displays lit the room in a green and red glow. The room reeked of body odor and mildew. Of wonderful, boring reality.

Entown convulsed on the floor, still plugged in. His body was in full Stockholm Effect from his avatar being shattered. Blood oozed from his nostrils.

Suck a fat one, I thought.

I was tethered to the wall. A great harness was locked around my body, with tether straps on the roof as well—a way to fly or fall in virtual to stunning effect. This creep had taken precautions to keep my virtual prison real and my real prison secure. I turned and rattled the tethers. They were long enough for me to walk around a few feet in either direction if I wanted, but no further. Long enough to get to the end of my run disk. The end of my virtual prison. Frantically, I searched around for something to use as leverage. Something to snap the bolt around my harness. Nothing within reach.

Then Entown stopped shaking. He gasped. Groaned. Growled.

I struggled to slip out of my harness. It was too tight.

Entown heaved himself upright. He took his display helmet off. Shook his head clear. Looked my way. His real blue eyes bored a hole in my soul. Pure hate and loathing.

I backed up as far as I could. The tether on the roof forced me onto my tiptoes before I could get back right into the wall.

Slowly, Entown stood. He unhooked his cords, trembling. Drew a real knife from his belt. A real blade there would be no coming back from.

I backed up further.

'You'll pay for that, bitch,' he sneered and rushed in.

I yelled with rage. Instead of backing up again, I sprinted forward to meet him.

The advance took Entown by surprise. I swung on the harness, up in a sweeping arc above the swipe of his blade. He staggered as his blow met air.

I kicked downward, sending his knife clattering to the ground. Spinning around mid-flight, I then lashed out at his face. He expertly ducked underneath and I hit only air. My swing hit the top of its arc and I sailed back toward him. He wobbled to the side but my lead thigh caught him on the shoulder. Sensing an advantage, I scissored both of my legs into a pincer grip around his neck. I locked my knees together tight. He struggled. Punched my thighs. Tried to get an arm through to break the lock. No chance. I'd never let that happen. He tore his fingers into my skin and ripped down. After the cutting of his blades in the Holos it felt like nothing. I wasn't letting go for all the donuts in cop heaven. I gripped onto the roof harness to keep me up. Pulled his weight off the ground so he couldn't get a purchase on the ground.

Entown had fed my body fluids through that drip while I was out. Kept me healthy for trading. For torturing. Now that I was free of the Stockholm Effect, my body surged with strength. I heaved him fully off the ground, his feet kicking free air.

Entown's punches and scratches grew weaker. My grip grew tighter. I wrenched my thighs around his throat, squeezing off his grunts of effort. His hits became slaps. The slaps became grasping fingers. I roared with the effort it took to hold him up. Finally, he went slack beneath me. Still, I held on, making sure he was out cold. I squeezed tighter still until my legs shook.

Finally, I couldn't hold on any longer and let him go. He splatted on the floor like the sack of shit he was. I followed him down, letting go of my harness straps and finding my feet. I searched Entown for weapons, pulling every blade from his pockets and tossing them away. Except one. I picked up the knife he'd dropped after my kick. Big. Sharp. Serrated. I used it to cut my harness off. The relief as each cord fell away must be what a butterfly feels breaking free of its chrysalis.

Then a noise from outside the room made me turn. Someone was rushing down the stairs outside. Toward this room. I swung around and held my knife high, ready to behead whoever stuck their neck in the door.

It swung open and I froze. Switch. Her face unmistakable. The features of a predator. I screamed then. Thrust my knife right at her eyes.

A hand from behind Switch surged up to meet mine, grabbing my wrist. A familiar head came into view. Joon.

'Stop!' he panted. 'Ada. It's alright.'

I struggled, not quite believing it. Was this another trick? Was I still in the Holos? Had I been duped to think I had jacked out when I hadn't?

'We've come to rescue you,' Joon soothed. 'This is Corpus, not Switch. Remember?'

I looked at Corpus. She met my gaze. There was warmth in her eyes. Understanding. Not the megalodon stare of her sister. It was still hard to believe it with all the adrenaline coursing through my system. This wasn't Switch.

'Looks like Detective Byron rescued herself,' Corpus said, smiling at me and looking down at Entown's body. 'Maybe we'd better concentrate on locking up the others.'

Others? What others? My head spun.

Joon bent down to Entown, flipping him over. He wasted no time, tying the killer up with the harness straps I'd cut to the ground. Joon checked Entown's vitals, all precision and professionalism.

'Did I kill him?' I asked, hopeful.

'No,' Joon said. 'He's alive. Just. A good thing too. He'll make a good witness once he realizes how he's been manipulated.'

I didn't understand. Sense was slowly returning to me but anxiety continued its grip on my system. I was waiting for the rug to be pulled out and the veil to lift into torture once more.

Then I did understand. The file. Corpus. They'd cracked it. They knew who was involved. Had evidence to prove it. This thing was over. It was really over.

I'd done it. We'd done it. The Specter Conspiracy would come crashing down.

64

Turmoil gripped the station. Corrupt police filled the holding cells. Cline mumbled some weak apology as I walked him to lockup. I ignored his words for the pathetic excuses they were and shoved him into his cage. The door snapped shut and I walked away. He was dead to me now. I could have ranted and raved. Called him a traitor. Spat on him. No one would have looked sideways at me. I didn't need to though. There was no closure in stepping on a squirming rat. He was finished. I had bigger vermin to crush. There was no time to worry about the darkness and anxiety that still churned deep inside me. I had purpose to drive me forward. With shaking hands yet a driven mind, I continued on my way.

Mendez led a tight ship rounding everyone up. She felt responsible that this happened under her watch. She showed no mercy to anyone, even those who had minor roles. They'd done it for money. Broken their vows as law enforcers in order to expand their influence into the virtual world. I was still breathless at the scope of it.

The FBI had been infiltrated as well. Joon had spearheaded the skewering of that side. Had teamed up with a few he trusted to help. There was more he had to do there but, for now, he was here. We had some questions that needed answering. Gaps that needed filling. There were three people who had those gaps in their heads. The first two were in adjoining questioning rooms.

I strode into the first room. Senator Sheila Rommel sat there in cuffs. There was no fight in her, just resignation. She'd seen the news reports; knew it was a matter of time until we'd proven everything beyond doubt. Jail would be a blessing. If she was let loose to roam into the real world, Holos zealots would find her and kill her.

I settled into the seat across from the senator. Joon stood behind me. I steepled my fingers, ready for interrogation.

'Senator,' I said steadily, 'you know what charges have been leveled at you. You entered a conspiracy with Filton Fukami to manipulate

237

cryptocurrency markets for your gain. You told Fukami early on about the inclusion of Mercury into your bill so he could buy it at a low price and get rich as the popularity of the bill spread. He in turn agreed to say on record that the exemption of the virtual murder, rape, and torture of AI-powered avatars was progress. It was a way to have his supporters feel like they'd won at least something. Better business for everyone. More Mercury-tracked tax for the government. Laws passed for you. You killed Christos Rama when he uncovered the conspiracy and was set to blow it open. You killed Lilith when she told you that she would never back Mercury. That she would use all her influence to keep the Holos anonymous with SureCoin. You had Entown Stephenson generate fear around the Specter killings to initially blow out the odds on your policy before the public used the reality of those killings as fuel to get behind new laws. Stephenson thought he was keeping the Holos totally free, when really you used him to do the opposite. It was working too. I saw the polling numbers. After you released that blurred footage of him and made adjustments to your policy, the odds for the bill dropped like a stone. Your laws were much more attractive with the ability to track killers and other criminals through their Mercury accounts. Even the civil unrest caused by the trolls' threats worked in your favor. People don't respond well to threats. You knew that. They'd swing back to support law and order for safety once it was offered after the chaos of riots.'

Senator Rommel was silent, so I continued.

'You know the evidence against you has been supported by your master file. How it was all mapped out. Corpus cracked it open for us. You can now choose to make things easy, confess fully and get secure detention at a fortified facility for life, or risk the death penalty for being instrumental in the murders. Ironic you brought that back into Nevada law, isn't it?'

The Senator was still for quite a while. She then slowly nodded.

'Yes,' she said. 'I was part of this conspiracy. But I was not the mastermind.'

I glanced toward the mirror on the wall. I hoped the person on the other side was paying close attention.

'And who is the mastermind then?' I continued. 'You're at the top of the chain in the file.'

Senator Rommel shook her head. 'I don't know,' she said. 'He's high up in the military. That's why I agreed to go along. Our military complex is the only thing that can run this country properly. Bureaucracy is too inefficient. Democracy is dead. I trust a true chain of command more than I trust some parliament.'

'And why do you think he's military?' I asked, not wanting to get drawn into the political argument.

'Because he told me so,' she said blankly.

'And you just accepted that?' I scoffed. 'Couldn't he be lying if you never got a face or name?'

'No,' she said, gaining confidence. 'No one could pull the intel and planning together for this if they weren't military. No one had that kind of access or knowledge of Entown Stephenson.'

'Okay,' I said. 'Let's assume that's true for just a moment. Was it you or this 'mastermind' that approached Entown to be a part of the plan?'

'That was the mastermind's idea,' Senator Rommel said without pausing. 'I wasn't lying when I said Stephenson was a national threat. I supported using him only because I knew it would lure Entown out of hiding. He was a liability to the military. I thought if we could pin this on him, and have him caught once he'd done his job, it would kill two birds with one stone. The mastermind convinced me it would work and that he knew where Entown was hiding in the Holos.'

'So that's why you agreed to have Switch released?' I said. 'Because you really thought she'd lead us to Corpus, which would lead to catching Entown?'

Rommel nodded. 'I also thought bringing Switch to justice in the real world might lead to knowing how she carried out her executions. If we know how she killed virtually, there will be security applications for it.'

Rommel looked drained at the admission, like she couldn't quite believe it hadn't worked out exactly how she'd hoped.

'So by learning Switch's techniques you want more ways to kill America's enemies?' Joon said next to me. 'A way to have ultimate power over the Holos as well?'

'You have to know, I was thinking of the country when I did this,' Rommel insisted.

'Really?' Joon said flatly. 'You murdered and planned to get rich for the good of the country.'

'It's not murder if it's war,' she said, exasperated. 'The Holos needs laws. You know that as well as I do. It's chaos in there. Strict laws wouldn't pass but key ones needed to. The safety of people is paramount. The government needs tax to run. Mercury would allow the tracking of taxes *and* the tracking of criminals. It was the perfect solution. So what if I made some money in the process? It meant that Filton would get on board more easily. Everyone knows he's greedier than a fox and more cunning than one too.'

'You seem to have thought about it a lot,' I arched an eyebrow. 'But you didn't plan this? That's hard to believe.'

'I...'

I held up a hand to stop the senator's reply.

'I have to say,' I spoke over her. 'I'm disappointed in you, Sheila. I thought you had a vision. I thought you had the country's interests at heart. That you were looking out for me too. Now I know you're just a selfish bitch who only cares about herself and her ambitions. That you'll use people and say whatever they want to hear to get them on your side. You're like Switch. I've had enough of your lies.'

Rommel opened her mouth to reply but I nodded toward the mirror. 'I think he's had enough of them too.'

Joon clicked his wrist-comm. The glass of the mirror went clear. Behind it, cuffed to a chair, was Entown Stephenson. His monstrous eyes could have melted the glass between him and the room. He kicked out with his metal leg which thudded on the glass. His hands were bound by three separate manacles. His neck was cuffed to the high-backed chair he was in. The door had been triple bolted and an FBI and police guard stood outside.

The senator's face went white.

'Now you have a very dangerous enemy there,' I said. 'One who knows you betrayed him—by your own admission. We can play it back again if you like.'

The senator looked up at me in panic, then to the now clear mirror.

'But it wasn't *my* plan,' she stammered. 'The mastermind was the one who contacted him first. He knows that. I was just following orders.'

'Right,' Joon said sarcastically. 'It was the boogie man who did it. I had the FBI put you under surveillance as soon as you'd been threatened. Not because I thought you were in danger, but because I thought you could be behind it. This whole time you've never been in touch with some mastermind. You've been in touch with Fukami to talk about the bill— but I passed that off as politicking, not collusion. I should have had my team record all of your discussions with him. Now that we have the whole picture, we know better.'

Rommel looked frantic. She kept glancing at Stephenson, then us, grasping for something to say.

'But the master hasn't been in touch since the plan was deployed. He cut ties on purpose. He said he had to make sure the policy market process went smoothly from inside the Senate.'

The words died on her tongue as if she knew the excuse was a weak one.

'So it's another senator now, not military?' Joon asked. 'This is sounding familiar. You already accused Fukami at the start of the case when he was supposed to be your ally. Did you plan to double-cross him too?'

'If I'd done this, why would I have listed myself in that file as a player?' Rommel snapped. 'Why? I didn't even know what was in that file. I thought Christos had some of my transaction details as his proof. Truly.'

I couldn't believe what I was hearing. Even now, Rommel was lying through her teeth. Her comment about not listing herself in the file hit home though. After poring through the information dozens of times, I'd asked myself the same question. Why would you create something so incriminating? The scope of the conspiracy would have been hard to keep track of otherwise, so there was that. And the file was heavily encrypted. Still, it was a huge risk, unless you were the mastermind and didn't leave your name on it. That made sense. It also meant it could be anyone. Mendez even. But she didn't have the motive. Switch perhaps. But how, when she was in digital confinement? She was still at large but had been totally silent. I'd expected people to turn up dead but none had. We needed answers before some kind of bloodbath began on that front.'

I turned to the glass divider in the room.

'Is that true, Stephenson?' I asked, looking at him through his window. 'Did the mastermind contact you and bring you in under Rommel's command? Do you know who the mastermind is?'

He paused, looking darkly at Rommel.

'It was all her,' he said. 'Let her fry!'

He kicked the window again.

'It wasn't me!' Rommel said frantically to us. 'It wasn't. Ask Fukami. He'll tell you.'

I had nothing but contempt for this woman now. This liar. This manipulator. She'd told me to make everyone else think they're smarter than you so they'd do what you want. Well, I'd played into her game too neatly. The thought infuriated me. She'd treated me as a pawn as well. But I'd made it to the end of the chessboard and was now stronger. She was done manipulating me. I knew Fukami wouldn't help Rommel. He was too selfish for that. That second senator was next on our interrogation list. This was going to be an interesting discussion.

65

Fukami looked older in real life. Greyer. Less muscle tone. Still, he held a presidential bearing. His confidence under interrogation was surprising. I'd expected him to buckle, but he knew what we had on him. Not much. His lawyers knew it too. Six defense attorneys stood behind Fukami like a bunch of well-dressed sharks. Fukami did all the talking in that small, bare room that may as well have been his own office. Joon and I sat across from him like we had in the Holos, expecting information that might help us.

'There is zero proof that I was involved in the murders,' he said.

He was right of course. The master file showed clearly that he wasn't involved in that part. But conspiracy to manipulate money markets was a serious offence.

'Further,' Fukami interrupted my thoughts. 'I helped you when I thought your troll, Bleesh, was Stephenson. I gave you the means to catch him. I helped the police every step of the way.'

'And yet it wasn't Stephenson,' Joon said. 'It was just a kid.'

'A kid you're having indicted as an adult for inciting riots,' Fukami reminded us. 'A kid who I'm told gave evidence that led to you catching Stephenson.'

I must have looked shocked that he knew this—he gave an incredibly self-satisfied smirk.

'Switch told us you knew exactly who Entown Stephenson was,' Joon pressed on. 'She said that you'd actually befriended him and wanted him to join the Guardians of the Web.'

'Are you going to believe a convicted psychopath or me?' Fukami said. 'I hated Entown as much as Switch and Corpus. Sure I knew who he was, but I didn't want to incriminate myself anymore than I needed to. As soon as I realized he was involved and that these murders might be part of the conspiracy, I contacted Rommel to call it off. I really did think he might be Bleesh.'

'Bullshit,' I said.

'I can prove it,' Fukami insisted.

He clicked his fingers and a lawyer flicked on a screen. It was the recording of a video call. Fukami's face was largest, then Rommel's came online. Before Rommel could even say hello, Fukami launched into a tirade.

'You,' he said. 'If you're behind these Specter murders I'm out. This wasn't part of the deal.'

Rommel's reaction was calm.

'Relax,' she said. 'Everything's going to plan. The policy odds are bigger on the market now. I suggest you take advantage of that and invest further. They'll be narrower soon enough.'

'You don't understand,' Fukami said. 'I had the police come by my rally today. They had footage of a soldier called Entown Stephenson. You don't realize how dangerous he is.'

Rommel crossed her arms.

Fukami's jaw slackened. Realization hit him hard.

'You do understand! Are you crazy? This needs to stop. I've given them a way to catch him.'

'Good,' Rommel said. 'I'll be happy if he gets caught. They'll have their scapegoat then. I'll have my laws. You'll have your money. It all helps us. It's all part of the plan. Thank you for being a part of it.'

She cut off the call. The recording went dark. Fukami looked back to us, smug in his righteousness. I shared a look with Joon. His FBI informant had told us that Rommel and Fukami had had multiple conversations on his watch, but that he didn't have direct specifics of the calls since they were held behind closed doors and firewalls. We'd assumed it was just them negotiating the bill's provisions. If we'd known what they'd really been talking about, we might have been able to stop this sooner.

'Once I knew the scope of this, I sold all my Mercury currency,' Fukami continued. 'Dirty money I was glad to be rid of. You can check that too.'

'And made a handsome profit, I'm sure,' I said. 'The value of that crypto has crashed now that the conspiracy has hit the media. Rommel's policy is dead in the water too. No one's backing that turd now.'

'I donated the entire profits to charity,' Fukami said. 'Check that as well.'

'Sounds like an admission of guilt,' I countered. 'Why would you give it to charity if you didn't know you'd done the wrong thing?'

'Insider trading is illegal, but it's not murder,' Fukami said. 'I never wanted to be a part of that. I wanted to create reasonable laws that would stop things like that. Avatar kidnapping. Pain. This isn't what I wanted and a court will see that. I welcome standing trial if I need to, but am willing to help you prosecute Rommel and everyone else involved so I don't have to go to court.'

There it was.

'In exchange for what?' I said.

Fukami didn't dirty his hands with this negotiation. It was one of the six lawyers that stepped forward. A statuesque man in his fifties.

'Full immunity,' he said.

I almost laughed.

'But,' the man said. 'He will step down as a senator, immediately, without contest.'

'He'll be kicked out when found guilty for insider trading,' I said.

Of course, Fukami knew that. He was just protecting his ego or his reputation. There probably wasn't much difference between the two for someone like him.

'He'll have no charges laid against him,' the lawyer said. 'In exchange, my client offers full cooperation. He'll back up any information you have already with secondary testimony.'

'Can you give us the mastermind?' I asked right away, keeping a close eye on his reaction. 'The one who put this all together?'

Fukami paused then. Just for a second, but he paused.

'Rommel was the one who planned the whole thing, as far as I know,' he said.

'Then why would she list herself in our key file?' I said. 'If she was so clever, why risk incriminating herself like that? Why not just leave her own name out and track the rest?'

'I have no idea,' Fukami said. 'But the fact she's on the file at the top is the simplest solution. You're overthinking it. You have your white whale. I suggest you harpoon her.'

This whole thing stunk. It was getting more rancid by the minute. I glanced at Joon. By the look on his face he smelt the rot too. He didn't look at Fukami as a fanboy anymore. He looked at him with disgust.

'There is more help you need from me as well,' Fukami continued. 'Now that Switch is out, I need to be able to patch any code loops in the Holos that could allow her to kill again.'

My stomach clenched. 'She's been inside for seven years,' I seethed. 'You said you've already patched the code.'

'I believe I have,' Fukami countered. 'Which is why we haven't heard word of any Specter deaths yet. We've blocked her, but she's smart. If she's actually still alive, she'll find a workaround. We need to stay one step ahead of her.'

This wasn't good. He had leverage. If this hit the media, there'd be an outcry to let him use his resources to protect lives. He might even get a chance to stand for office again, backed by the support. I wasn't going to let things go that easily though.

'Corpus can help us with closing the loop on Switch,' I said. 'He wants to stop his sister as much as anyone.'

Corpus had been an incredible help already. Had proven an amazing resource in the few days between me getting Stephenson and all of the arrests going down. He'd teased out all the relevant files, compiled them, and backed them up with other evidence he was able to find in the Holos network. Corpus's name was already being put into play as a replacement senator now that Rommel and Fukami looked certain to be indicted. Well, Rommel at least. Fukami pursed his lips, thinking. He was obviously aware of what Corpus had done already. He didn't seem pleased, but wasn't displeased either.

'That's true,' he said. 'Corpus can help with Switch. But he'll need full access to my source code and all the support I can offer too. Something I will gladly give if we make this deal.'

'You think Corpus will work with you after you were part of a plan that included his own kidnapping and torture?' Joon replied.

'Like I said, I wasn't a part of that. I was only in it for the money.'

He went silent then, folding his hands over his lap. I watched the lawyers, then looked to see if Joon had any further questions. He shook his head. Before I made any bargains, we had to speak with Stephenson again. Perhaps his spite could be used to implicate Fukami if he'd been involved further. If there was a mastermind beyond what we knew, Entown would be the one to unearth it. He'd been played the whole time. A puppet. If there was anything I'd learned during this whole shit show, it was that brilliant people hated to be manipulated even more than the rest of us.

I pushed back from the table. 'Wait here,' I said. 'We'll be back.'

Joon took my cue and followed me from the room. Guards took station at the door as we locked Fukami in with his lawyers. They were comfortable enough. They could wait.

Joon and I navigated the corridors toward Entown's cell.

'What do you think?' I asked.

'I think he's hiding something,' Joon said. 'I used to think he was a visionary. Now I think he's a greedy businessman. A hypocrite.'

I didn't want to say that's what I thought the whole time. I truly didn't feel ahead of the game anymore. Even though this case was coming to a close, it still didn't quite feel like all the strands were coming together. Yes, we'd made arrests. Significant ones. But had we made *the* arrest? The fact remained, Switch was still out there somewhere too. Rommel could be the mastermind, lying to avoid the worst of her punishment. Or she could be telling the truth. Entown knew the answer.

We turned into the holding cell corridor. I stopped. The passage was empty.

'Where are the guards?' I asked.

Joon looked, surprise spreading across his face, then alarm. We started running at the same time. I made it to the door first, my heart pounding. Stephenson can't have escaped. He can't have. I tried the door. It was locked. Thank god. Pressing my thumb into the keypad, my clearance ran through and the green light appeared on the handle. We went inside.

Blood.

Gouts of it spread along the floor, flowing from Entown's face. His body was still. Cold. Dead. A syringe hung from his left eye.

He hadn't escaped, but he had.

Set the body free and the spirit will soar, I thought.

66

I watched the footage for what must have been the hundredth time. It was the same as a month ago when it was fresh. Entown kicking the glass of his interrogation cell, telling me that Rommel should fry. As I closed the door to Rommel's cell on the other side of the window, all went to static. There was no other footage of what happened. The guards who had been at his door couldn't be accounted for. Footage of the inside of the station had shown they were never there to begin with. Yet I'd seen them stationed there with my own eyes. Even after asking Sabi and Corpus to see if the footage was scrubbed, we'd had no luck. Whether it was the military or this 'mastermind' or someone else, I might never know. The result was the same regardless; Entown Stephenson was dead. As far as I was concerned, that was justice. I just wish I knew what he knew before justice was carried out.

I thought about Rommel's trial. With Fukami's backing evidence it had been short. He'd gotten his deal. Rommel had held her ground that she wasn't the master architect of the plan, positioning herself as a high-ranking soldier who'd merely carried out orders. She insisted in a rousing speech that all of it was for the good of the country. That we needed proper laws in the Holos if we didn't want to world to succumb to evil. The judge had sat back in his chair, banged his gavel for order, and told the jury to disregard her comments and look at the evidence. The jury took fifteen minutes to deem the senator guilty on all charges. It had been quicker than even Chip Radcliffe's trial where he was found guilty for inciting riots as both Bleesh and Chance Bradley. He was in prison. Rommel, though, was another story. When the jury pronounced her guilt, the judge had nodded grimly. Then he did something that surprised everyone.

'Given the nature of your crimes against society as a whole,' he said, 'I'm going to let the people decide your fate. One option is life in prison. The other is death by electrocution. I'll draw up the bill myself and put it on the open market today. I'm betting the public won't be merciful.'

The judge was right. The bill for execution was ratified within a day. She was dead less than a week later.

Now, I was left filing everything away for use when Switch became active again. She was still at large. Feed theories had her swanning on beaches in Australia, enjoying the freedom she had recently acquired, retired from digital life. People thought they were safe from her killing again. My gut told me different. It also told me that Fukami had somehow engineered all of this. That *he* was the mastermind. He'd left Las Vegas. Gone to an anonymous location because the public harassed him for being corrupt. They hadn't forgiven him like I thought they would. All over the Holos, there were forums and meet-ups talking about his evil, saying he should pay and that if anyone saw his avatar, to mob it. Of course, who knew what avatar he was wearing now. He could pick anything he wanted. Live anywhere he wanted. There was no justice for the ultra-rich. I wasn't so naive as to think it would play out any other way. At least he'd never be senator again. There was no way his power would reach beyond the digital world. How much he could achieve behind the scenes still bugged me like a mosquito in a dark room. I couldn't rest easy. I still had nightmares. I told myself I wouldn't give up until I'd somehow pinned him down and nailed Switch to a wall. This wasn't over for me. Not by a long shot. My next case would be finding that Specter... if it was the last thing I did. I'd only ever wanted to understand her crimes and stop others like her from emerging. Now that the real thing was back, my purpose in life was clear.

A knock sounded at the door. Joon.

'Hey,' he said. 'I've packed up my office here. Thought I'd come to say goodbye.'

I smiled. The little spankblanket had grown on me. Maybe some jack-ins weren't all that bad, even if they were perverts. They weren't hurting anyone. Most of them. Those that did, Joon and people like him stood up to. I saw that now. Admired him for it. He stood for justice, same as I. So what if it came from a different place or manifested in different ways, in different worlds? Both places had equal merit. Reality isn't just the things you can touch. It's everything you experience.

I stood up and moved to give Joon a hug. He shied back. That hadn't changed apparently. Then he swept in and wrapped his arms around me fiercely. Just for a moment. A brief, beautiful embrace. We stood apart. I smiled again.

'Are you going to go for the Sheriff's position now that Mendez is going to be Senator?' he asked.

I shook my head. 'I don't have the stomach for politics. 'She'll be great though. It's just a shame Corpus isn't running for the other seat.'

Joon shrugged. 'He'd be a hypocrite like Fukami if he did. You can't advocate freedom and anonymity and then run for government. Like Corpus said in his statement—the smaller our government is and the fewer laws we have controlling our lives, the better.'

'But he could help find a sensible medium,' I countered. 'There has to be a balance. You need *some* laws, right?'

'That I can agree with,' Joon said.

'Hey,' I said. 'Don't stop arguing with me now that we're all done.'

Joon smiled. We stood in silence for a while.

'So are you going back to the FBI?' I asked him eventually.

'I am,' he nodded. 'I've been put in charge of a task force to help find ways to encourage ethical cultural change in the Holos. Instead of heavy-handed laws, we'll work to establish new norms that promote safety, order, *and* freedom.'

'Good luck with that,' I scoffed.

He opened his mouth to start an argument, then smirked. He knew I was baiting him.

'If I can help somehow, let me know,' I said. I'd really grown fond of working with him. The yin to my yang.

'Same to you,' he said. 'If you ever get a sniff of where Switch might really be, I'll come running.'

I shook my head. Right now, that felt like it might never happen. But I would do my damned best as lead detective of the LVPD, that was for sure.

'You can at least help finish putting these case files in proper order,' I sighed. 'That brain cap lets you work quicker than my old analogue eyes and swipes.'

I indicated the screen in front of me. He stepped in, sifting through things on the left-hand side of the screen. I kept working on the right. I wasn't just going to stand there like a lump, even though I wasn't as fast. I minimized the footage of Stephenson and pushed it away. There was also the footage of Rommel pleading that she wasn't the mastermind. I pushed a few more files into folders. Joon stepped back, showing he'd done his lot. He was too polite to ask if I wanted to help with my end. I was almost done anyway. I was about to seal it in a zip folder when a message alert pinged on my screen.

I looked at it and laughed. 'Too little too late,' I said.

Mercury had finally released their currency data to us. The group had gone into free-fall once the conspiracy broke. It had been impossible to get records, even for the trial. It had been a mess of finger-pointing instead. Now, it looked like someone had finally grown a conscience and dragged it up. It was a token that didn't matter anyway. Curious, I still opened it, scanning the contents. Fukami was there. Rommel was there. The amounts were staggering. Rommel had lost it all. Fukami had sold at a good time but it had been verified he had indeed given it to charity. It didn't make me feel better. He was probably just doing it for his image.

'Holy shit,' Joon said, reading ahead of me.

A name I didn't recognize caught my eye. The amounts were as big as the Senators', yet I had no idea who it was. Robert Rezz. How could that be right? I checked the buy and sell dates. The amounts. More about money than power. This didn't make sense. I clicked the name and more info came up. After all, everyone had to have a verified identity to get a Mercury account. I found the birthdate and social security number.

'Can you check that social security number in your federal system?' I asked Joon.

'On it,' he said. His eyes flickered and a beep sounded. He swiped the info directly onto my screen. We both stood there dumbfounded. From out of the screen stared Switch—but not. Short hair. Glasses. Male affect. It was Corpus. The address wasn't hers but the date of birth was one that chilled me. I hadn't paid enough attention on the previous screen, but now it seemed ominous. The date my father died. The date of the first Specter Slaughters.

'When did Rommel say the mastermind last contacted her?' I asked slowly.

'April 5th,' Joon said.

'And what date was Corpus reported missing?'

He paused. Looked it up. 'Same date,' he said.

We both stood in silence for a while.

'Free the body and the spirit will soar,' I murmured.

'What?' Joon asked.

Finally, things clicked into place. Too little. Too late.

'Corpus. It means body in Latin,' I said absently, only just making the connection. 'Switch is the Specter. The spirit. Free the body and the spirit will soar. Free Corpus and Switch will soar.'

'Shit,' Joon said, letting it sink in. 'He had it planned from the start?'

'Do you think Corpus could have used Entown to send Switch a message by writing that phrase at the crime scenes?' I asked. 'Like he was signaling the plan? That if Switch helped the police free Corpus, she could break free herself?'

Joon just stared. We were both looking at the screen but really looking into space. I couldn't quite believe it. Corpus had been kidnapped, hadn't he? Tortured. Or was that part of his deception from the start to free his sister and avoid suspicion?

'We walked right into it,' I said.

'But why everything else?' Joon said. 'It seems pretty elaborate just to free his sister. If he was such a great hacker, why not do it earlier?'

'I don't know,' I said, my mind a whirl. 'But there's one way to find out.'

Joon turned to me. I grimaced. 'Are you game to jack in if it means you might die?' I asked. 'If Switch is waiting?'

To his credit, he didn't even think. 'I wouldn't leave my partner hanging now, would I?' he said.

We left the room, marching as fast as we could to the closest jack-in port.

67

Joon and I rushed through the marble streets of the Politisphere. Already, Mendez supporters were handing out leaflets pushing new legal reform. I knew it was propaganda. She hadn't even officially resigned her sheriff's post yet.

Keeping focused, Joon and I twisted down the alleys, bee-lining for Corpus's office. If we were lucky, he'd still be there. He'd been so careful with his plan to be tripped up by a tiny detail. Perhaps he was arrogant enough to resume life as normal, thinking he was in the clear. If we were right. But there couldn't be any other explanation, could there? He'd invested in Mercury. Bought and sold at exactly the right moment. He'd said he thought Switch was evil, but that could easily be a lie. What if they were planning this escape all along?

I forced myself to slow down as we neared his door. We could be walking into anything here. To Switch. To her way of killing. I had my Sabi avatar though. She'd patched the holes in my thigh. Left a golden scar there to remind me of my strength. My protection—the ability to scramble Switch's avatar at the curl of my finger—calmed me. If she was there, I'd fry her in a blink. No chances given.

Joon met my eye. Gave a single nod. Knocked.

No answer.

I was about to knock again when the door swung open. There was no one inside. Hairs prickled up my neck. I braced for an attack.

Joon cautiously stepped inside. He was in a new avatar that looked closer to his real-world body: just a bit taller and more androgynous. He had his claws up. Glowing. Ready.

The space inside Corpus's office was well lit, ordered. On the desk was a little ball, like a solid packet of green code. I saw immediately what it was—a replica of the file Corpus had hacked for us. It was just sitting there, like a lure. Bait.

I knew then that Corpus realized we were coming. Perhaps he'd left that final clue at Mercury for us to find, hoping to continue some kind of game.

Knowing I shouldn't, but doing it anyway, I picked up the code packet. My touch sparked a hologram keypad to life. Ten digits. I didn't even need to pause to know what it was.

'Don't,' Joon said, as I punched a zero into the first box. I didn't stop. I quickly put in the date of the Specter Slaughters. 07/07/2035.'

The file opened like a flower. A single streaming link sat inside. I clicked it. The screen enlarged to full height, looking like a portal to another room. It wasn't though. It was simply a virtual meeting link. A screen with True-Resolution graphics so it felt like you were face to face. Corpus's avatar stood there, waiting. He grinned, expectant.

'Hello my saviors,' he said, holding out his arms to welcome us.

Another dark figure stood behind him. She emerged from the shadows. Switch. It was her. No tricks. She wore her singlet, spider web tattoos shining bright. She didn't speak, just stepped aside to reveal someone with them as well. The figure was sitting. He was bound. Hands tied. Mouth gagged. Tears streamed down his senatorial face. Fukami.

I stood stock-still. My finger itched at my side. I wanted nothing more than to blast the whole scene, but that wouldn't achieve anything. This was just a window link into what was happening somewhere else in the Holos. A conference call. Corpus smiled again.

'I'm glad you made it,' Corpus said. 'You really are a smart one, aren't you?'

He paused. There was no warmth in his eyes like I was used to, just the unemotional calculation of someone who'd planned this all along.

'There are a few things my sister and I wanted to say to you. But first, I want to show you exactly what happens when you try to bring laws we don't want to our web,' he said, looking over his shoulder at Fukami. 'To ruin our experiment.'

'Your experiment?' I said, my mind racing for ideas on how I could stop this. 'What experiment?'

'To see if full freedom can work, of course,' Corpus said. 'I used to think that a few laws might be a good thing. That my sister had been wrong in wanting total freedom of choice. Now, I know that laws can never bring real order. Worms like this always want more power,' she looked at Fukami. 'You put in one law and they want one more, then one more, until it's *all* control. Be warned. Do not try to put laws in place yourself or you'll become corrupt as well. Balance by degrees is an illusion.'

'Total freedom can only be balanced with one total consequence,' Switch added.

'I see that now,' Corpus said, holding his sister's hand. 'I'm sorry it took so long.'

'You've paid your penance,' Switch soothed her brother. 'Seven days of torture. One day for each year I was inside. We both needed to know what true pain feels like if we are going to make others experience it.'

Switch then looked at me. 'And you.' She smiled.

My whole body recoiled. I wasn't afraid of her anymore. I just knew she'd start lying now. I wished I could jump through this link and strangle her with my bare hands. All I could do was watch. Listen for a way to find her while my whole body shook with rage.

'I recognize you now,' Switch smiled. 'I read up on your history. You're the innocent girl I let go on the day I brought the thrill of death to my world. You know, I remember your father too.'

I did bring up my arm then, hissing beneath my breath. I held my right hand out toward her in a stop signal. It trembled. The weapon in my palm could disintegrate this link with a twitch of my fingers. I couldn't stop her, but I could silence her. Joon placed a soft hand on my back, as if to stop me.

'I remember everyone I erase,' Switch said softly. 'All of their faces. I forget no one. It's all in my access memory.' She tapped her temple.

'Don't you dare,' I managed to get out in a whisper.

'I'd like you to know,' Switch continued, 'that of all the lives I took that day, he was the only one who ran toward me instead of away. He was trying to stop me. He was the only truly good soul I had to kill. That necessary evil still haunts me.'

A sob burst out of me. My left hand went to my mouth. My right hand was still held out as a shield. I wouldn't show weakness here. I wouldn't. But tears were already pooling in my eyes. I brushed them away. Was this another lie? I didn't think so. Didn't want it to be. I wanted to believe my father was a good person. To know it beyond all doubt.

'Unfortunately, sometimes even innocents have to die for the greater good,' Switch said calmly. 'It's why I did my time in peace. I deserved some punishment for killing him. But now I have to resume my work. My brother has seen to that. Now, you'll finally see how our experiment can be reality. How death keeps the thrill of dark deeds alive. How it will help freedom find balance with justice. We will only kill those who deserve it. Kidnappers. Thieves. Rapists. Pederasts. You have my vow that no more innocents will die like your father had to.'

Corpus stepped closer to us as Switch melted back to Fukami's side.

'The rest of the world acted as I predicted,' Corpus said. 'If this, then that. Cause and effect. A code script executed perfectly. This next phase will be the same. It's not so hard when you see the ones and zeros.' He counted off ones on his fingers, curling them back down again as he did to represent nothing. 'Rommel taken out for wanting laws. That troll Entown dead so he couldn't darken our playground further. The very idea of virtual laws corrupted by association with the market. You doing your job as officers to have the senators take the blame. Of course, there's always a few glitches. That reporter Yu Ying almost figured it out. Thankfully, Stephenson patched that bug. You, Ada, got close to being unique too, but ultimately you helped the code. Now, we just have this loose end.'

I had so many questions, but all I could do was stare hatred at Switch. She put her hand on Fukami's shoulder. He flinched. Started whimpering.

'You don't have to do this,' I said. 'If laws were in place there, it would be *more* like the real world, not less. We know the law works. We know it.'

'We can use cultural norms too,' Joon said. 'Nuance. Absolutes solve nothing.'

'Is the real world free of suffering then?' Corpus's eyes widened. 'Have we tamed our darker nature by putting each other in cages? By appealing to culture?'

Switch shook her head. 'We need to go through to the other side.'

'See this through to the end,' Corpus echoed.

'This time, we'll do it properly, together,' Switch continued. 'We'll only kill those who have hurt others, or those who try to stop us,' she locked eyes with me then. A warning. A challenge.

Before I could react, she tightened her grip on Fukami's shoulder.

'And we'll start with this tyrant,' she said.

Fukami whimpered loudly. Switch closed her eyes. But nothing happened. Fukami had said he'd patched the code allowing Switch to cross the reality of death into the Holos. Maybe he'd been right.

Then Fukami began to shudder.

'No!' Joon said. He clicked his wrist-comm. 'All agents, listen. If anyone knows where Filton Fukami is in real life, get to him now. He's in danger. I repeat. Jazlin Switch is active.'

There was a cracking in response. Voices barking back over the comm. But it was too late. Much too late. All we could do was stand there and bear witness.

Fukami's eyes started bleeding. A howl escaped through his gag. Vomit began to seep through. This wasn't the light show of an avatar melting. It was a real body dying.

This was no copycat. The master had returned. The Specter. Thanks to her twin, the ultimate mastermind.

Free the body and the spirit will soar.

ACKNOWLEDGMENTS

The first person I have to thank is you. If you made it this far and are now digging into the acknowledgments, that's serious commitment. Like, who normally reads this part? Without readers of similar commitment I could never pull this weird career off.

To those who helped make this book what it is, you're all responsible. Alexis Orosa for your insightful editorial feedback. Charlie Bewley for your continued humouring of my insanity. Scott Walker for your eagle-eye edits. Kalle Carranza for your colourful Spanish knowledge. Elvin Verlaat for your programmer's language. Stefan Koidl, Johan Aberg and Tom Jilesen for your epic cover art. Thank you, thank you, thank you.

To my Kickstarter backers. You guys put the zap in my electric boogaloo. Thrill Switch would never have gotten to print without your support so I'm eternally grateful. Keep backing independent art, it keeps the world much more interesting.

Finally to Tara and my boys. Thank you for your patience, love and support. You're my inspiration.

ABOUT THE AUTHOR

Tim Hawken is a literary hooligan from Western Australia who writes dark sci-fi and fantasy. He is a 2-times winner of the AHWA's Flash Fiction Competition, has been shortlisted for an Australian Shadows Award, and likes to add a twist of wicked humour to his work.

Tim posts a 100-word, art-inspired story most days on Instagram (@tim_hawken).

FOR MORE OF TIM
HAWKEN'S WORK VISIT

TIMHAWKEN.COM

MKD 2023

Printed in Great Britain
by Amazon

27486743R00148